A NEW FRIEND

Emmy's Story, Part 3

by
Kenneth Lee McGee

For Ty, Isabella, Benjamin, Noemi and Allison

Grandchildren are the greatest!

I would like to thank Denise and Stephanie for their support and for sharing their knowledge and opinions. Without their help, this book would not have been possible. I would also like to thank Liz and Sue for reading my books. I will forever be indebted to the people of WriteOn Joliet without whose knowledge I would have never learned the skills necessary to become the writer I am today. You can't imagine how clueless I was in the beginning.

I want to thank the people from my church who have graciously allowed me to include fragments of their lives as inspirations.

A special thanks to Sue Midlock for creating the cover. http://suesart.wixsite.com/rosewoodseries

I want to thank my wife Sheila for letting me bounce ideas off of her. She might think I'm nuts at times, and she might be right. I would like to thank her for her suggestions. Some of which I have used.

Prologue

"I had turned fifteen and was going to the old St. Raymond's church with my family. We sat in our pew, and I turned and looked over my shoulder. There was Peter Bertucci."

Mama Bertucci looked across her oval-shaped, wooden kitchen table at nineteen-year-old Emmy Colasanti. Emmy smiled as she sat with her feet tucked under her, her elbows on the table and her chin in her hands. Her bright blue eyes sparkled with excitement as Mama began her story.

"I sat next to my mother. My younger brother Vincent sat next to me. Carmen was away in the Navy. Papa sat on the aisle next to Momma."

"What about Karla?" Emmy asked.

"My mother held her on her lap. She was only a few months old," Mama answered.

"Sorry I interrupted you. Please continue."

"I looked over my shoulder at Peter sitting two rows behind us. He smiled, and I smiled back at him."

"Did you know him?" Emmy interrupted again.

"Not really." Mama shook her head. "My family belonged to that parish for a long time, but I later found out that the Bertucci family only recently started going to mass there. Anyway, I kept looking back at him. I didn't know his name or anything, but he kept smiling at me. Vincent looked back at him and started teasing me until our mother shushed us."

"Did you talk to him after mass?"

"I looked for him, but I didn't see him anywhere. I walked outside and saw him standing on the sidewalk waiting for me. He grinned and said, 'My name is Peter Bertucci. What's yours?' I told him my name... Maria Catarina Lombardi."

"Did he try to kiss you?" Emmy grinned.

"Good heavens! No!" Mama waved a hand obviously flustered. She paused, and then continued, "I was only fifteen, but I looked older than that."

"Like Diane. She's only two and a half years older than me, but she's always looked much older. I've always looked younger

1

than I am." Emmy put a hand to her mouth. "I'm sorry."

"It's all right, dear." Mama patted Emmy's arm. "I was already over five and a half feet tall. Just like now. But I had a much slimmer figure."

"I saw a picture of you when you were in high school. You were hot, Mama!"

"I was not!" Mama stammered and then ran a hand through her dark, gray-streaked hair. "After that, we would see each other at mass every Sunday." Mama paused and then she grinned. "When I turned sixteen, he kissed me. I still remember that kiss."

"Oooh, Mama. Did your mother or father know? Did you start going on dates?"

"No one else knew, and I wasn't allowed to go on dates. When I turned seventeen, Peter would come over to our house with his best friend, Daniel Keasling. One, or both of my parents, acted as a chaperone—usually my mother." Mama sighed. "She was very strict. When I reached eighteen, Papa gave me permission to see Peter alone. We were in love, and a month later he asked my father for permission to marry me."

"A month later!" Emmy sat up straight. "That is so romantic." Emmy tightened the purple ribbon holding her long curly hair in a ponytail. "What happened next?"

Mama waved a hand and shook her head. "Papa told him I was too young. He threatened to throw him out of the house until my mother reminded him how old she had been when they got married. Papa finally gave him permission, and we got married on June 2, 1963. Peter and Daniel had started their construction company, so I worked in their office."

"Did you know right away after you met Peter that you wanted to marry him?" Emmy asked.

"I knew I would marry him after our first kiss. After he kissed me, I never thought about any other boy. I knew he was the one for me."

Emmy sat silently for a moment. She bit her lip and confessed, "I've kissed more than one boy."

"Times are different now, Emmy."

"So how long were you and Peter married? Tony told me

his father passed away when he was three."

"We were together for over twenty wonderful years. Then his heart gave out, and he left us." Mama reminisced about the years she shared with Peter, and about raising her three children by herself.

Emmy looked at Mama and thought about how protective her own parents had been toward her. She realized something else. "So Mr. Keasling knew Karla from the time she was a baby, huh?"

"Yes, he would always tease her when she got a little older."

Emmy paused, and then asked, "Why did Mr. Keasling wait so long to get married?"

Mama looked at her. "I suppose it's all right to tell you. Daniel fell in love with a girl when he was twenty-three, and he asked her to marry him. She accepted his proposal. They planned to get married the week after Peter and I. But three weeks before the wedding, she broke it off and it broke his heart. He never allowed himself to get serious about any other girl after that. He dated other women, but he never allowed it to develop into a serious relationship."

"Did he still see Karla while she grew up?"

"Yes, he remained a close family friend, so he would see her once in a while and would always tease her. Anyway, when Karla got older, he didn't see her for a couple of years. Then she graduated from high school, and they saw each other at her graduation party. In spite of the difference in their ages, they started dating and fell in love. They kept it a secret as long as they could, but Papa found out and threw a fit."

"I can understand that," Emmy said. "I know how my father would have reacted. He would have bought a gun and shot the guy."

"Papa forbade Daniel from ever seeing Karla and threatened to send her to Italy to live with family, but once again Mother stepped in. Daniel and Karla were married on June 11th in '77. She was only nineteen."

"Just like me now," Emmy said. Then she closed her eyes as they filled with tears. She thought about Tony, who, only a few

3

minutes earlier, left to go back to college at the University of Notre Dame. Then her thoughts turned to Kenny Colwell. The lifelong friend she first met on the way to school when she was seven and had grown up with.

"Oh, Mama, what should I do? I love Kenny, but I think maybe I still love Tony, too. How will I ever choose between them? I know one of them will be hurt no matter who I pick."

Mama reached across the table. She put a hand on Emmy's cheek and wiped away a tear. "When the time is right your heart will tell you who to choose. You are still a young lady and don't need to be in a hurry to decide."

Emmy jumped up from the chair and ran around the table. Mama stood up and held out her arms. Emmy wrapped her arms around Mama who squeezed her tightly. "Oh, Mama, I love you so much."

Chapter One

"Mama, I want to do something special for Emmy on her birthday. Let's throw her a surprise party. I talked to Kristen, and she thought it would be a good idea. Emmy won't be a teenager anymore just like Kristen." Tony Bertucci talked on the phone to his mother from his dorm room in South Bend.

"Tell me again, when is her birthday?" Mama asked as she sat on her wooden rocker in the den.

"It's the eighth. It's on a Saturday this year, and I can be home."

"That sounds like a good idea, but have you talked to Kenny about it? He might not appreciate what you want to do," Mama cautioned.

"I emailed him, and he thought it would be fun, but he can't be there. The band will be in Montreal."

Kenny Colwell, the singer and lead guitar player for the rock band Fridays At Five, also happened to be Emmy's boyfriend.

"I'll help you with the plans if you need," Mama said.

"I want to invite the whole family and all Emmy's friends, and I'd like to have the party at our house."

"How do you plan to get Emmy to the house? Don't you think she will be suspicious since it's her birthday? Have you thought about that?" Mama asked.

"I did a little." He ran his hand through his straight black hair. "Why don't you invite her over for dinner? Tell her that you want to fatten her up like you always do."

"That won't work because I'm still giving her cooking lessons, and she will want to come over early to help me cook." Mama thought about an alternative plan. "We can ask Kristen to take her out for dinner that night. Then at the last minute they can stop by the house to pick up something she left here. That's probably what she will be doing anyway—going out to eat with Kristen, I mean."

"What did she leave at the house?"

"She left a sweater here, but it really doesn't matter. It's simply an excuse Kristen can use to get her here. Kristen can pull it

5

off. She's very good about getting people to do what she wants."

"Yeah, that's the truth." Tony remembered how his cousin Kristen convinced him to take her to the prom his sophomore year of high school.

With a lot of help from Mama and Kristen Keasling, Emmy's best friend, Tony planned Emmy's surprise party.

Finally, the day of Emmy's birthday arrived. She slept in and didn't get out of bed until nine. She wondered if anyone would remember her birthday. She remembered how last year in Colorado no one mentioned anything about her birthday until after dinner. She thought about the significance of this birthday; she would no longer a teenager.

As she drank a glass of orange juice in the kitchen, the phone rang. She checked the caller ID, jumped up on the kitchen counter and smiled as she answered.

"Hello, Kenny."

"Happy birthday, sweetheart! How does it feel not to be a teenager anymore?"

"I feel so much older and definitely more mature. I didn't even sleep with my teddy bear last night, and I put my favorite blankey in the drawer."

"That does sound like you are more mature. Did you sleep with the nightlight on or off?"

"I kept the light on. Maybe when I'm as old as you, I'll sleep with the lights off."

"Oh, Em," he said with a sigh. "I wish I could be there today."

"I know you do. I understand. You're kinda like one of those firefighters who travels all over the world fighting forest fires and oil fires and stuff."

She baffled Kenny with her comparison.

"Really? You care to elaborate about that?"

"I read about this fire in Colorado and how firefighters from all over the country are there trying to put it out."

"And that made you think of me somehow? I don't get the connection."

6

"I mean that those people have to be away from their families because of their job and so do you."

"Okay, I'm glad you thought of me, but those people put their life in danger doing their job. I don't do that."

"In a way you do. You are a celebrity, and there are stalkers out there who might try to hurt you."

Kenny laughed. "So far, thank God, I haven't been 'stalked' by anyone."

"Speaking of jobs," she said slowly.

"Did you get that position, Em?"

"I did! Can you believe it? I didn't think I had a chance. I'm giving my two week notice on Monday, and will start with Robertson Industries on the twenty-fourth."

"I'm so happy for you, Em."

"I'm a little nervous about the job, but I will think of it as a challenge," she said.

"What are you planning for today? Are you and Kristen going out?" He knew very well what would happen later, but couldn't let on, or he would spoil the surprise.

"She wants to take me to dinner tonight. Otherwise, it will be a normal Saturday. I have to do laundry, clean the apartment, buy some groceries—you know, all the fun stuff."

"That sure sounds like more fun than I'll be having. I have to entertain an auditorium of screaming female fans."

"You are such a funny guy, Kenny Colwell." Emmy wrinkled her nose even though he couldn't see her.

"I wish you were here with me. You could protect me from all those fans."

"Right. I will stand on stage and be your bodyguard. Seriously, what do you guys have lined up today?"

"A couple of radio interviews, the usual meet and greet. I want to get a run in sometime. When we do 'Sweet Girl' tonight, I'm going to tell everyone in the place that it's your birthday and see if they will sing 'Happy Birthday' to you."

"That will embarrass me even though I won't be there. Are you going to call me like you did last year?"

"I'll try. I won't do it to embarrass you. I'll do it because I

7

love you."

"Oh, thank you. I love you, too." Emmy heard some commotion over the phone.

"I'm sorry, but I need to go. Andy is rushing us out the door. I'll try to talk to you soon. Love you."

Thirty minutes later, the phone rang again. Emmy assumed it was Kristen.

"Happy birthday, Emmy. I hope I didn't wake you up."

"Thank you, Tony, and you didn't wake me up. I've been up for hours. You remembered my birthday. That's so sweet."

"If I remember correctly, you are no longer a teenager."

"You won't be one for much longer, either."

"You're right." He ran a hand over the heavy stubble on his face. "I sure wish I was there to see you today."

"Well, you called. That's so thoughtful of you."

"I should go. I've got a lot of stuff to get done. Have a good birthday, Em. I wish I could see you." He stifled a laugh.

"Thanks for calling. I'll talk to you again soon."

Tony, his sister Heather, and her friend Alex Khryzman, arrived back in South Hampshire from South Bend shortly after two in the afternoon. Since first having been settled in the 1850s on the north side of the Kinmundy River, SoHam, now a city of over 150,000 people, spread for miles on both sides of the winding river.

Kristen arrived at Emmy's apartment at five.

"Let me fix your hair, Emmy. I want to braid it for you just the way you like it. I want you to look extra special when we go out tonight." Kristen worked on Emmy's long, dark curly hair, which reached halfway down her back. "Is it all right if we go to La Cantina for dinner. I have a taste for Mexican."

"We can go there if you want. I never get tired of that place. Did I tell you that I talked to Kenny earlier?" Emmy asked as she sat to allow Kristen to braid her hair.

"Where are they today?" Kristen asked as she pulled on Emmy's hair.

"Ow! That hurt. The guys are in Montreal. They will be in Canada for a couple weeks. Oh, Tony called me, too."

"He did. How's he doing?"

"He seemed busy. We didn't talk too long. He wished me a happy birthday. He said he wished he was here so he could see us."

"See us, or only you?" Kristen flipped her salon-styled, wavy golden-blonde hair over her shoulder.

"Well, he would want to see you. You're his favorite cousin."

Kristen finished braiding Emmy's hair. Then they spent nearly an hour deciding what Emmy should wear. After Emmy finished getting dressed, Kristen mentioned, "I want you to wear your new sweater. You know the one I mean. It's light purple with a white trim. Please wear it. It's my favorite."

"I can't wear it. I left it at Mama's house last week. I won't need a sweater. It's too warm. I'll wear this top with my jeans. It's just as nice, and we won't have to make an extra trip."

Kristen pouted and put her hands on her hips. "I really want you to wear the other sweater. I like it a lot, and it fits you better. Please, can we stop and pick it up?"

"You are being selfish, Kristen." Emmy shook her head, but Kristen didn't give in.

"Pretty please!" Kristen pleaded with a look on her face that Emmy couldn't resist.

"Oh, all right. You win. Such a pampered princess. We can stop at Mama's and pick up your 'favorite' sweater. Now can we go. I'm hungry enough to eat a dozen tacos and a large burrito."

"That'll be the day when you can eat more than two of their tacos. You can never finish one of their large burritos." Kristen hugged her. *It will be worth it later, Em.*

"I guess it's all right. I need to take back some casserole dishes anyway. Mama made a bunch of food for me. I guess I won't starve to death on the way. You're being a big baby, but I love you anyway."

Kristen smiled. *I think we're going to pull this off. You still don't have a clue, do you, Em?*

The party was supposed to start at six thirty and guests began arriving at six. Tony arranged for them to park their cars on the block behind the house, so Emmy wouldn't see any of them.

9

Kristen assumed the responsibility of getting Emmy there, and she performed like an academy-award-winning actress.

"Oh, I like this song." Kristen turned up the radio while sitting at a traffic light.

"Yeah, whatever." Emmy looked out the window of Kristen's 1996 Acura CL as they headed to Mama's house. *I know this is my birthday, and I'm supposed to be all excited, but I feel kinda sad. I won't see Kenny, or even Tony, today. Diane didn't even call to wish me happy birthday. Neither did Mom nor Daddy, but I didn't expect them to bother.*

Kristen pressed the speed dial on her cell phone for Mama's house. That let Tony and Mama listen to them as they talked in the car. When they got close, Kristen let Tony know by using a code phrase. Tony instructed everyone of their imminent arrival.

"They are almost here. Kristen is about to park the car. Everyone should stay in the living room and maybe squat down or something. I'll turn out the lights."

Somehow all the guests fit into the living room. They couldn't hide but tried to be inconspicuous. Tony closed the heavy drapes and turned out the lights to make the room as dark as possible. Tony hid in the dining room in case Emmy came in the back door, which led into the kitchen. Kristen and Emmy arrived at Mama's house and parked out front. Emmy walked up to the front door and right in without knocking. Kristen followed behind her carrying the box of dishes. Emmy paused in the front entryway.

"Mama, where are you? I brought back your casserole dishes, and I need that sweater that I left here last week. Mama! Are you here? Why is it so dark?" Emmy stepped into the dark living room and turned on a light.

Everybody hollered, "Happy birthday, Emmy."

She jumped back, screamed, and then turned around to face Kristen. "Favorite sweater, huh? Did you know about this? Was this all your idea?"

Kristen smiled at Emmy and said, "Actually, Tony thought of it first, but Mama and I planned everything."

Kristen set the box of dishes on the floor, and Emmy gave her a big hug.

10

"You are in such big trouble, Kristen Lynn Keasling. You're gonna get it later."

"Did we really surprise you, Emmy?"

"Yes. I had no idea. You guys pulled it off." She held back her tears. *This is so much better than last year when I thought you guys forgot.*

Emmy didn't see Tony, who still hid in the dining room. She saw Heather and Alex and wondered why they came without Tony.

"Oh, Heather, thanks so much for coming. It's good to see you, at least. Too bad Tony couldn't come, but he did call me earlier today. Why couldn't he come with you?"

"He's been rather busy lately, Emmy," Heather answered.

Emmy didn't hear him as Tony tiptoed up behind her. Tony heard the sadness in her voice as she talked to Heather. He put his hands on her shoulders and turned her around. Her eyes instantly lit up as Tony lifted her up and hugged her tightly. She melted into his arms.

"You are such a liar. You told me you weren't going to see me today."

He shook his head. "I did not lie when I talked to you. I said I wished I could see you today, and now my wish has come true. Happy birthday, Em."

Emmy kissed him briefly to make him shut up. Mama came over to where they stood.

"Tony, put her down so I can give her a hug."

"Oh, Mama. I am so happy. Kristen told me that you knew about this and probably planned everything."

"I had help, Emmy."

Emmy looked around the living room. She noticed so many friends. Mr. and Mrs. Keasling stood in front of the fireplace with their son, Derrick. Barry and Linda Newton kissed in the corner. Emmy hadn't seen them since their wedding in May. She smiled as she saw Mr. and Mrs. Colwell standing behind the couch. Emmy looked around the room again. *Oh, my God! Mom and Dad are here.* She saw Diane and looked for Diane's boyfriend, Craig, but didn't see him.

11

Mama prepared way more food than necessary. Afterward, Emmy opened presents. Some of the gifts were funny and some embarrassed her. Like the gift Barry and Linda Newton gave her—a rather sheer nightgown.

"I think you need to try it on to make sure it fits right, Emmy," Barry teased.

Linda smacked him. "Are you ever going to grow up and behave? Emmy, don't listen to him. He's still a child."

Emmy held the nightgown up in front of her and swayed her hips seductively. "Barry, you wouldn't know what to do with me if I was wearing it."

Everybody laughed at her joke, especially Tony and Linda.

Mrs. Colwell handed her a gift and informed her, "This one is from Kenny. He had it sent to our house, and I wrapped it."

"So you know what it is. Is it something I can open in front of everyone, or should I open it in private?" Emmy asked.

"You can open it here. It's nothing that will embarrass you—too much, anyway."

Emmy opened the gift as everyone watched. She wondered what it could be. The heavy box could be just about anything. She ripped the paper off and looked at the box. Nothing on the outside indicated what might be inside. She shook it a little and something moved inside.

Emmy looked at Kristen and Tony, who sat on the couch with her. "I don't know what it is."

"I think you have to open the box, Em. I'm pretty sure that Kenny's gift is inside," Kristen said.

Emmy stuck her tongue out at Kristen. "It's taped."

"I'll get it." Tony used a box-cutter to cut the tape for her.

Emmy opened the box and carefully removed the gift. "It kinda feels like a book under this fabric."

"Why don't you remove the cloth?" Kristen grinned.

Emmy made a face at Kristen as she carefully unwrapped the black velvet fabric.

"It is a book." Emmy cautiously turned it over in her hands.

The book appeared to be very old with nothing on the hard cover to indicate the title or who the author might be. Emmy opened the book and turned a few pages. She looked at Mrs. Colwell, and then at Mama.

"I can't read it. I think it might be in Italian. Can you read it, Mama?" Emmy asked, as Kristen got up to let Mama sit next to Emmy. Emmy carefully handed the book to her. Mama looked at the title page.

"It says, 'Una Storia Dell'arte Di Fare Carillon da Pietro Jacovelli.' That means... let me think for a moment," Mama paused then continued, "'A story of the art of making music boxes,' I think, by Pietro Jacovelli."

Emmy turned her attention from Mama to her father.

"Daddy, do you know what this is? Who is Pietro Jacovelli?"

Her father sighed. "He was your great-great-grandfather. The man who built your music box, baby."

"How in the world would Kenny know..." She bit her lip and started to cry. Mama put an arm around her.

Dad continued, "He called and asked us what we knew about the man who made your music box. All I knew was a name that my mother had mentioned a few times."

Mrs. Colwell continued the story. "Kenny did some research on his computer and learned that Mr. Jacovelli had written a book. Kenny knows the man who owns Paul's Bookstore, and he found a copy in a bookstore in New York City. There should be a note in the book explaining everything."

Mama handed Emmy the handwritten note from inside the book. Emmy opened the note and read.

Emmy,

I know how much you treasure your music box, so I did some research about your great-great grandfather on your father's side, Pietro Jacovelli, the man who made it. He lived in Naples and enjoyed a reputation as a maker of music boxes and other finely crafted ornamental wooden boxes. You already know that he made your box for your Grandmother Mary. Anyway, he wrote this book, and I thought you might like to have a copy. It's never been translated into English. Maybe someone can read it to

13

you sometime, although I think it might be kinda boring. I thought the book might hold some sentimental value for you. Happy Birthday, Emmy. I love you and hope you have a good birthday.

        With all my love and affection,
        Kenny

Emmy looked at Mama, the Colwells, and then her parents. "I'm sorry for crying like a baby." She paused for a moment to regain her composure. "I guess I'll have to put this note in my secret compartment now, but the book won't fit. I'll have to find a safe place to keep it."

She opened the rest of her gifts; she received some clothes from people and a few gift cards as well. She opened all the presents, and then Tony brought her one more.

"This one is from the whole family."

Emmy opened the box. "Oh, Tony. This is the most beautiful necklace I've ever seen."

"They're just glass beads," Kristen whispered to Derrick.

Tony helped her put it on and Kristen stood up and yelled, "Kiss her, Tony, kiss her."

"Knock it off, Kristen," Derrick warned his sister as he pulled her back down. "She's Kenny's girlfriend, so stop being a matchmaker."

Emmy turned to face Tony.

He leaned down to hug her and whispered, "I know you would rather it was Kenny holding you like this, so I won't kiss you in front of all these people." Tony didn't kiss her, but he held her for a time.

Finally, Heather poked Tony in the ribs. "Will you two knock it off? There are other people here you know."

Tony released Emmy and kissed her cheek quickly.

"Is everyone ready for cake? I made Emmy's favorite—white cake with lemon frosting and filling," Mama announced as Derrick carried the cake into the living room a moment later.

Emmy looked at the cake. "Mama, that's not my favorite."

"I know, dear. I was teasing. I made chocolate cake with

chocolate frosting. I added some raspberry filling. I hope you like it."

"I'm sure it will be scrumptious."

As Derrick lit the candles, Mama asked Kristen, "Do you have your camera handy?"

"It's right here, Mama."

"I think you might need it soon."

Tony helped Emmy blow out the candles.

Emmy poked his arm. "I could have done that by myself. Now I don't know if my wish will come true."

"What did you wish for, Em?" Tony asked.

"I can't tell you. Don't you know anything? It won't come true for sure if I tell you."

Kristen snapped a couple of pictures. She was about to put her camera away when Tony started feeding birthday cake to Emmy. He smeared some frosting on her nose as Kristen continued to take snapshots.

"Remember how I put snow on your nose that day, Emmy?"

"I remember," Emmy replied sweetly.

"Remember how I smeared the snow all over your face?" Tony asked.

"Don't you dare!" Emmy screamed.

But to no avail. Tony and Derrick held her so she couldn't escape as he smeared birthday cake on her face. Kristen got the pictures.

After cleaning up, Emmy sat on the couch next to Kristen while they ate their cake. Emmy whispered to Kristen, "This has been my best birthday ever. I can only think of one thing that would make it even better."

"What would that be, Emmy?" Kristen asked. She looked at her and understood. "Oh, you're thinking about Kenny. I understand. You wish he could be here, too."

Emmy leaned close to Kristen and whispered in her ear, "I wish I could taste Kenny's kiss."

"That would be the perfect way to end your birthday. I'm sorry he's not here with you."

15

"I can still dream about it." She bit her lip and then turned and faced Tony. "Thank you for the necklace. Did Kristen pick it out?"

"Yeah, I wouldn't know what to get. She knows about all that stuff."

The party wound down around ten, and Emmy hugged Mr. and Mrs. Colwell as they headed home. "Thank you so much for coming."

"We wouldn't have missed it for anything, dear," Mrs. Colwell said.

"Make sure you tell Kenny how much I appreciate the book."

It had been raining lightly for about ten minutes when all of a sudden the wind picked up. A lightning bolt flashed and thunder boomed loud enough to shake the house. It started to pour.

"Kristen, it is storming too hard for you and Emmy to go home by yourself," Mama said.

"I don't like to drive when it's storming like this. Can we can stay here until it stops?" Kristen asked.

"Yes, maybe you should spend the night. Where are Tony and Emmy?"

"The last time I saw them they were on the front porch."

Mama turned on the front porch light, saw Emmy and Tony and opened the door. Mama heard hail hitting the ground, felt the wind on her face and saw the rain pouring down. She witnessed Emmy run out into the front yard and gather up some hailstones.

"Emmy! What are you doing?" Mama scolded. "You get back inside this instant. Have you lost your senses? It is pouring."

Emmy ran back under the cover of the porch and showed Mama the hailstones she held in her hands. "I wanted to grab some of these before they melted. Look how big they are. They're as big as golf balls."

"You come inside right now, young lady. You are soaking wet." Mama made Emmy go inside, and then looked at Tony. "Why didn't you stop her? Oh, never mind. She probably wouldn't have listened to you anyway." Mama went inside and hollered, "Kristen, will you bring me a towel right away? Emmy is soaked."

Kristen brought a towel from the downstairs bathroom and handed it to Mama.

"Thank you, dear."

Emmy began to shiver as she held the hailstones in her hands. Mama put the towel around Emmy's shoulders and began to dry her by rubbing her arms.

"I hope you don't catch your death of cold." Mama looked at Emmy and smiled. Emmy's hair was soaked, and she looked like a young girl of maybe fourteen years of age. Mama hugged Emmy and held her tight. "You can be such a tomboy at times, but I love you dearly." Mama instructed Tony. "Will you get her a sweatshirt or something, so she can take off this top? It's soaked."

Tony thought for a second before running upstairs. He knew exactly what to grab—an old sweatshirt that hadn't fit him for years, but he saved it because of the Notre Dame logo on the front. He ran back downstairs and handed it to Mama.

"This might fit."

Mama looked at it and smiled. She remembered when she bought it for him.

"Go in the bathroom and take off your top. Dry yourself and put this on."

Emmy nodded. "Yes, Mama. I'm sorry, but I couldn't resist those hailstones." She handed the remnants of the hailstones to Mama.

What am I supposed to do with these? Mama sighed. She opened the door and tossed them outside.

Mama wasn't sure where to put everyone if Kristen and Emmy spent the night. Alex would use Marco's room and Heather had her room. Mama thought about what to do. She decided to make an exception just this one time. "Kristen, if you and Emmy decide to spend the night here, you can sleep in Tony's room. I'll make sure there are clean sheets."

"Okay, Mama." Kristen didn't argue with Mama because nobody dared argue with Mama—and the storm still raged. She thought she might spend the night here and brought an overnight bag in the car. Emmy changed and came back out to the kitchen. The sweatshirt was a little big for her, but at least it was dry.

17

Mama found Emmy to tell her the plans. "Just this once you can spend the night in Tony's room."

"Mama, are you sure?" Emmy blushed. "I know your rule about where I have to sleep. I've never spent the night in his room."

Mama nodded her head and continued, "You can sleep in there with..." Mama intended to tell Emmy that she and Kristen had to sleep in Tony's room, but Emmy ran off before Mama could finish.

Emmy blew a kiss at Mama, "I love you, Mama." She ran off to find Tony, but saw Kristen first in the hallway. "Kristen, I can stay here tonight and don't need a ride home."

"I know, Emmy, Mama told me..." Kristen didn't get a chance to finish.

Emmy ran down the hall looking for Tony. "Tony, where are you? I didn't bring anything to sleep in, so can I borrow one of your football jerseys?" Emmy didn't see her parents and Diane in the living room until the words escaped her mouth.

Diane asked, "A football jersey, huh? Is that your last present, Emmy?"

Emmy's father laughed a little, but Mom didn't say a word. Mama followed Emmy and finally caught up to her.

"Emily Colasanti, you didn't let me finish. What I meant to say was that you can sleep in Tony's room with Kristen. She is spending the night here. Tony has to sleep on the couch downstairs."

Emmy looked surprised, "Mama, I know you would never let me sleep in the same room as Tony. Where is he anyway?"

"He went to get our car," Dad said.

Mama hugged Emmy and whispered in her ear, "I know you wished for Kenny to be here."

Emmy blushed because Mama was right as usual. She hugged Mama and asked, "How do you always know everything?"

"It's my gift from God." Mama winked at Emmy with a twinkle in her eye.

The storm had subsided, but a light rain still sprinkled down. Emmy hugged her parents and Diane as they prepared to leave. The only reason they were still here was because of Diane. They hadn't really talked to her since she moved out of the house. Tony brought their car to the driveway, so Emmy's parents didn't have to walk in the rain.

Mom faced her younger daughter but didn't try to hug Emmy. "Did you enjoy your birthday, honey?"

"Yes, I've never has a surprise birthday party before. Thanks for everything."

"We enjoyed it. You are starting to grow up into a young lady."

As her parents left, Emmy felt saddened by a couple of thoughts. *Mom still thinks of me as a child, and I feel closer to Mama Bertucci and Mrs. Colwell than my own mother.* Emmy felt a hand on her shoulder. She reached up to hold the hand with her own. Emmy recognized Mama's hand without even having to look.

"We have to get this house back in order." Mama assigned everyone a job. With everyone working together, the house, and especially the kitchen, eventually passed Mama's high standards. "I'm going to bed. I'm tired," Mama said after all the work was finished.

Heather and Alex headed for the stairs. "We're going upstairs, Mama. You worked too hard today. You need to get some rest."

Mama looked at Tony, Emmy and Kristen, "Don't stay up too late and make sure you... Ah. Never mind. You are good kids."

"Night, Mama," all three of them said.

Tony, Emmy and Kristen moved to the family room in the basement. Emmy and Kristen sat on the couch. Tony sat on the floor facing them.

"Do you really like the necklace, Em?"

"I think it's lovely, Tony. I might not ever take it off," Emmy answered with a dreamy expression on her face.

Kristen began to giggle.

"What is so funny?" Emmy asked.

"Just an image of you wearing only that necklace on your wedding night."

Emmy blushed. "You are so bad, Kristen Keasling."

19

They talked for a half hour until Tony yawned and struggled to keep his eyes open. "I need to get some sleep, and you guys are on my bed."

Kristen teased, "And your point is...?"

"Well, unless you are going to share the couch with me tonight, I suggest you scram."

Tony rose quickly, grabbed Kristen and held her around her waist. Emmy sat back and watched as Tony held Kristen as she tried to get away.

"Let me go before I yell and wake up Mama," Kristen said.

Tony released her, but she didn't move. After a moment, Kristen hugged Tony, "You are so sweet. This was the best birthday any girl could ever have." Kristen kissed his cheek and then got up. "Come on, Emmy. Let's let sleepyhead have the couch."

Emmy looked at Tony. "Thank you for everything. I'll give you back your sweatshirt tomorrow. Do you have a jersey I can wear for tonight? I can't ask Heather for something. I would feel weird."

"You're welcome." Tony smiled at her. "If you want to wear one of my jerseys again, they're in the bottom drawer. I hope you won't be mad at me for smearing cake on your face."

"I once heard a phrase about revenge. It goes like this 'revenge is a dish best served cold', I think. I'm not sure exactly what that means, but I have an idea." Emmy smiled with a devious thought in her mind. "See you in the morning, Tony."

Chapter Two

"Hello, Emmy, it's Frances Rawlings."

"Hi, Frances, how are you?" Emmy balanced the phone to her ear with her shoulder as she dried a plate.

"I'm doing all right. Just missing Jeff. Did I call at a bad time?"

"No, I just finished the dishes." She set the last plate on the counter. "I kinda know how you must feel. I miss Kenny, and we aren't even married," Emmy said and then paused. "I'm sorry that you lost the baby. That must be awful."

"Thanks, at least Jeff came home for a few days after it happened. Joe Trabinni, his guitar tech, and Paul Joseph filled in so they didn't have to cancel any of the June shows. The other guys wanted to cancel, but Jeff wouldn't hear of it. You know the old saying about the show going on no matter what." Frances paused and took a deep breath.

"Are you all right, Frances?"

"I'm okay. I was thinking about my miscarriage."

"I know you guys have been trying to start a family." Emmy didn't quite know how to console Frances, who just turned thirty.

"The reason I'm calling is that I remembered how much you said you liked this neighborhood," Frances said to break the silence and change the subject. "There is a house that just became available to rent not too far from ours. It's 217 Hickory Street, which is only two streets down from us and about three blocks east. It might be too much house for you by yourself, but I thought I'd tell you about it."

Emmy wasn't exactly looking for a new place to rent when she got the call on Monday evening just two days after her birthday.

"I appreciate it. I really like the area, but I just signed a six-month lease in May, and I'm not sure I can get out of it."

"Oh, too bad. I know the owner has done a lot of work to the house, and I heard that he's charging a reasonable rent—for the area. I don't know what you pay now, but I think this place will rent for about seven hundred, plus utilities. I know Kenny has mentioned that he might like living in this area if he ever moves out of his parents' house."

"Maybe I'll check it out," Emmy said politely. *I can't afford to pay that much.*

"It's worth looking at, Emmy. That's a really nice street. Take care, and I'll talk to you soon."

"Bye, Frances, thanks for calling."

Emmy drove past the house in the Timberline Heights neighborhood after work the next day. She stopped and took down the phone number to call even though she was perfectly content living in the O'Brien apartment. That night she emailed Kenny about the house, and he called back the next day.

"Hey, Em. I talked to Jeff about that house and the neighborhood in general," Kenny said.

"Frances said you might want to move there someday. You never told me."

He explained, "I mentioned it casually one day. I don't know if it will ever happen."

"I drove past it after work yesterday. It looks very pretty. It's a two-story red brick house with white trim and a porch across the entire front. It's pretty big but not as large as your parents' house. I saw some mature trees."

"That's to be expected. Timberline is one of the oldest neighborhoods in SoHam."

"How do you know that?" Emmy asked and then giggled. *It's because you're such a dork.*

"Dad told me. Sounds like a nice place. It's possible I've even seen it before."

"I thought I would call the number and maybe get some information about the rent and all. Down the street is a large park area with a baseball field, tennis and basketball courts and a swimming pool. There's a small lake and even a band shell for outdoor concerts."

"Sounds like you did a thorough recon job." He chuckled. "Did you turn in your resignation?"

"I told my boss yesterday, and he said he was happy for me. He told me I did a great job for the company, and he was sorry to see me leave. There's one other thing."

"What's that, Em?" Kenny asked.

"I know I just signed a new lease a couple months ago."

"Don't worry about that, Em. If you like the house on Hickory, you should look at it."

"I thought about asking Diane to go with me. She fought with Craig again and moved out. She's staying with a friend for the time being. If she likes the place, we could move in together and share the cost."

"Let me know what you think, Em. I'll talk to you later. Love you."

"I love you, too. I'll let you know if we look at the house."

Later that day, Emmy called Diane. "There's this house I want to take a look at in Timberline Heights. It's really big, and I kinda hoped we could rent it together. If we still like it after seeing it."

"A house, huh? Is it bigger than our old house? I don't want to share a room with you."

"It's a lot bigger. It's two stories."

Diane thought about it. "I'll take a look at it, but I'm not making any promises."

"That's all right," Emmy said. "I don't know what it's like on the inside, but the outside looks well-maintained."

"I'm only doing this because I can't stay with my friend for much longer. I'm not going back to Craig's place. I never want to see him again."

"If you want to talk about what happened, I'm here," Emmy offered.

Diane stared at the phone and then chuckled. "I'm not about to discuss it with you, little sister, but I appreciate the offer."

"I'm not a baby anymore," Emmy said. "I can understand the problems you and Craig are having."

"Ain't gonna happen, Em, but thanks for your concern." Diane hung up abruptly.

Emmy made an appointment to see the house after work the next day. She picked up Diane, and they met the real estate agent handling the property.

"Hello, I'm Oren Bold. You must be Emmy Colasanti, right?" He handed Diane a flyer since Emmy looked too young to be renting a house.

"I'm Diane Colasanti. That's Emmy." Diane pointed to her sister, shook her head and hollered. "Emily! Do not try to climb that tree."

Emmy released the branch, ran over to Diane and held out her hand. "May I have a flyer, please?"

Mr. Bold handed one to Emmy, and then addressed Diane. "The owners are also interested in selling the house, in case you know anyone who might be looking."

"Thanks, but we're only interested in renting it now." Diane smiled as she admired his expensive-looking suit.

Emmy read the flyer. "The lot is 200 by 70. There is a two-car garage behind the house and a very large fenced in backyard with two black walnut trees."

"How on earth do you know what kind of trees there are in the backyard?" Diane asked.

"It says so right here." Emmy held the paper up to Diane. "There is a large deck behind the house with a picnic table left behind from the previous renter. Let's go inside."

"Follow me, please." Mr. Bold smiled at Diane.

Emmy scurried from room to room while Diane flirted with the real estate agent.

"Come on, Diane. Let's go upstairs."

"Be patient, Emily," Diane scolded.

Emmy dashed up the stairs and looked at the bedrooms. "Oh, wow! These are huge." She ran from room to room.

Diane and Oren followed at a more leisurely pace.

Emmy grabbed her sister's arm. "Diane, look! There are three bedrooms with huge closets. You might have room for all of your clothes. There is a spare bedroom where you could put the rest of your stuff."

"Very funny, Em."

24

Emmy checked the flyer again. "There is a full bathroom up here, and I saw one downstairs and there is even a half-bath in the basement according to this. There are so many rooms. I love this place. I could live here forever." Emmy wrapped her arms around her chest and spun around in the wide hallway.

"Nothing lasts forever, Emmy."

Emmy bounded down the stairs and Diane and Oren followed at a sensible pace.

"You will have to forgive my little sister. She gets very excitable at times," Diane said.

"Understandable. Did I mention that all the furniture in the living and dining rooms stays?" Oren asked Diane. "And all the appliances stay, of course. Including the washer and dryer in the basement."

"Cool!" Emmy sat on the living room couch. *This is so comfortable and the fabric is like brand new.*

"We'll have to think about it," Diane informed Oren. "Do you have a card with your number?"

He smiled and handed Diane a card. "All right, but houses in this neighborhood go quickly. I wouldn't wait too long."

Emmy pulled Diane aside.

"Stop it, Emmy. I want to discuss some things with Oren," Diane said. She glanced over her shoulder at Oren. *He's not wearing a wedding band, and he is definitely flirting with me.*

"Isn't that dining room table gorgeous? How about it? If you help with some of the expenses for a while, Grandma Isabel told me she would cover the rent until I can swing it on my own. I talked to her last night. I'll be making more money at my new job, and this location is almost perfect."

"Grandma still spoils you." Diane frowned.

"I know." Emmy grinned. "Please! Tell me you love this place, too. Please! Please!" Emmy put her hands together and practically begged Diane.

"It would be a way to thumb my nose at Mom by living in a much nicer house," Diane said. She took another look at the stained woodwork and the built-in book cases. "All right. I will move in with you just to keep my baby sister happy. It won't be forever, Em. Make sure you understand that up front, okay?"

Emmy bounced on her toes. "It will be so great!"

"Calm down, Em." Diane shook her head. "When Kenny gets home, he will want to move in with you, and by then I should be able to find a place of my own. I'll let you guys have the biggest bedroom."

"Oh, thank you so much, Diane. We will have so much fun here. I want to get a swing for the front porch and a new chair for the living room. That one is simply too old..."

Emmy rattled off a dozen ideas for the new house.

"Some of the shrubs need to be trimmed. I might be able to talk Tony in to doing that for us."

"You're using him," Diane warned. "Kenny might not want him coming around to see you."

"He likes working in his yard," Emmy said as she smiled.

"Yeah, whatever." Diane walked over to the real estate agent. "We'll take it, Oren."

"Great! Maybe we could grab some coffee and go over all the paperwork. I will have to run a credit check."

"I'd like that, but Emmy needs to come with me."

Diane could see his bubble burst.

Emmy and Diane signed the lease, and then Emmy dropped Diane off at her friend's apartment. Emmy pulled into the driveway at the O'Briens. *Now I've got to tell Mrs. O'Brien. This won't be easy.*

Emmy saw a light in the kitchen, so she jumped out of the car and walked over to the back door. She bit her lip as she slowly climbed the concrete stairs and rang the bell.

Mrs. O'Brien saw Emmy and hollered, "Come on in, dear. Dinner is almost ready."

Emmy entered the kitchen and stepped over to the stove. "This smells wonderful. I love your Irish stew."

"I probably made too much. You can take the leftovers with you."

"Mrs. O'Brien, I need to talk to you." Emmy bit her lip until it hurt.

Mrs. O'Brien turned to look at her. "What is it, child? Is

26

there something a matter?"

Emmy fought back her tears as she described the house and explained everything. "I'll pay for the rest of my lease, but this house is too good to pass up."

"It sounds wonderful, and your grandmother is willing to cover the rent. That's so generous of her."

"Diane and I are her only grandkids, so she spoils us. Especially me." Emmy wiped her tears away and then laughed.

"We will be sorry to see you leave, dear. You've been more like a daughter than a tenant."

"Thank you, Mrs. O'Brien. I hate to leave because you've treated me so kindly. I can't remember how many times you've let me eat dinner with you guys."

"You're always welcome to join us. You know that."

Emmy paused for a moment as she thought about the wonderful mother-figures she knew. *I'm so lucky. Sometimes I feel like I have three mothers besides my real one.*

"The house feels so empty now with the boys gone. Mr. O'Brien and I have talked about selling it and finding someplace smaller without so many stairs." Mrs. O'Brien pulled Emmy close and hugged her. "You don't need to pay for the rest of the lease. I wouldn't feel right taking money from you... or your grandmother... if you weren't living here." Mrs. O'Brien let Emmy go, and then wiped the tears from both of their faces with her apron.

"Actually, Kenny offered to pay..."

"I'm not taking money from him, either." Mrs. O'Brien smiled as she waved her finger at Emmy. "Just because he's a famous rock star does not mean he doesn't have to be careful with his money."

"I'm really gonna miss you, Mrs. O'Brien."

"You better stop by to see us, or else I'll send a leprechaun after you."

Though they felt sad to see Emmy go, the O'Briens didn't hold her to the new lease. Emmy ran back up to her apartment and called Kenny.

"Diane liked the place, huh? I'm kinda surprised she agreed to move in together," Kenny said.

27

"I don't think she plans to be there for very long." Emmy didn't tell him Diane assumed Kenny would move in when he returned. "I think one of the reasons she agreed was to upstage Mom by living in a big house."

"Does Diane have any furniture or kitchen stuff to move?"

"No, all she's got is her clothes and shoes and that kind of stuff. Mrs. O'Brien said I could keep the furniture she let me borrow. I'll have to call a moving company. Diane has the keys to the house, and Mr. Bold said we could move in this weekend if we want."

Kenny paid for a moving company to help Emmy with the move—against her will, of course. Kenny informed her that he might try to buy the house if she really liked living there. So, in the middle of July, Emmy Colasanti moved into a large house in South Hampshire with her sister Diane.

Kenny called on Sunday afternoon and asked, "Are you all moved in? Did Diane take care of the utilities?"

"She took care of all that stuff. We still have to unpack some stuff, but all the furniture is here and in place. I made a list of stuff we will need. It helps that some of the rooms are furnished. There's not much in the basement, but that's all right for now. We probably won't use it that much."

"You'll have to give me a tour when I get home," he said.

"I could take pictures and email them to you. I'd have to ask Barry to help, but I have the computer set up. There are two small bedrooms on the main floor. We're going to use one as the TV room and the other will be like an office. That's where the computer is."

"What about the yard, Em? Did you talk to Tony about helping you?"

"Not yet, but I will. I guess we have to mow the yard."

Kenny chuckled. "Somehow I can't see Diane doing any landscaping or any kind of outdoor work."

"I used to help Daddy with the yard. This is a lot bigger, but I can handle it."

Chapter Three

As Diane walked home from the park one hot, humid July evening, she met two men. They introduced themselves as Ethan Hanks and Fernando Ramos and struck up a conversation.

"Nice to meet you. My name is Diane Colasanti. I recently moved into 217 Hickory with my little sister," Diane said as she stood on the sidewalk in front of the neighbor's house.

Ethan smiled and pointed across the street. "Diane, that makes us neighbors. I live at 218, and Fernando lives down at the other end of the street in that dilapidated, run-down shack that looks like a stiff breeze would knock it down. He was born there, so he doesn't want to move, and it's not worth fixing up."

"No! No! No!" Fernando waved his hands. "Diane, you should know that Ethan is bitter and jealous because my house is paid for and worth twice as much as his barn, or whatever it is. I never did understand why they built it like that. I wasn't really born in the house, either." Fernando corrected his friend.

The friendly bantering between the two friends amused Diane. She kept glancing back and forth between the taller, more slender Ethan and the much shorter, heavier Fernando. After listening to the guys for a few more minutes, she mentioned, "I'm heading home. Would you guys like to stop by for a drink? I could listen to more of your repartee."

"Sounds good to me, Diane. I can fill you in on this new neighbor of yours. I know all his dirty secrets." Fernando slapped Ethan on the back hard enough that Ethan stumbled.

They walked back to Diane and Emmy's house, sat on the deck and talked. Diane brought out a bottle of wine and three glasses. Diane listened to the two friends who appeared to know everything about each other.

"If you want to know anything about the history of SoHam, just ask Ethan," Fernando said as he grinned. "He's been living here for a hundred years."

"Hey, old-timer! You've been here just as long," Ethan replied.

"Have you guys known each other very long?" Diane asked

29

as she checked out the much darker-skinned Fernando. She wondered if he touched up his hair since it was jet-black while Ethan didn't bother to hide the fact that his thinning hair was mostly gray.

"Unfortunately, we have known each other since first grade," Fernando answered as he poured the wine.

"Yeah. We lived next door to each other all through school," Ethan said.

"Here in this neighborhood, or somewhere else?" Diane asked as she sipped her wine. *This is pretty good. I hope it wasn't the expensive bottle I bought for special occasions.*

"Here in the Timberline Heights neighborhood. We went to Roosevelt together." Fernando held up his glass of wine to examine it.

"We shared a room for four years at North Park College, and after we graduated I started working at Robertson Industries." Ethan swirled his glass and started drinking the wine.

"I have a real job. I work at SoHam First National Bank..."

"That's not a real job." Ethan shook his head.

"Yes, it is. Don't listen to him, Diane. I started right after college and worked my way up the ladder. Now I'm a senior vice-president, and I just purchased a brand new BMW 535i," Fernando bragged.

"Everyone at the bank is a vice-president of something or other," Ethan teased. "And I drive a silver four-year-old Honda Accord which is totally paid for and should last for another ten years. I don't waste money on a flashy car just to impress people, and I would never buy a black car. He has to wash his every day, or else it looks dirty."

"Tell me more about each other. I want to hear everything." Diane smiled as she wondered about the age of the guys.

Fernando smiled at Diane. "I'll go first, since I'm older."

"No you're not! I'm older, but you can go first. That way I can correct all your mistakes."

"Fine, you senile old man."

Diane laughed as Fernando continued, "We are both divorced. I have two kids, but thank God, he never had any..."

30

"I'm happy that I didn't. His kids are troublemakers."

"We both fell in love with the same girl in high school..."

Ethan's shoulders shook as he laughed. "Yeah, and now if we see her we wonder why. She's... uh... she hasn't held up well."

"How old are you guys?" Diane tried to catch them off-guard.

"Thirty-nine and holding. How old are you, Diane?" Fernando drained his glass and reached for the bottle.

"I'll never tell." Diane flipped her long hair and smiled.

How long they had claimed to be thirty-nine was anyone's guess. Both guys assumed Diane to be in her late twenties, or maybe even early thirties. A few lines around her eyes made her appear older.

Emmy, just getting home from work, pulled into the driveway, hit the button on the remote and parked Kenny's red 1993 Civic in the garage. She left the garage by the service door and walked up the sidewalk toward the back door. *Shoot! I need to mow the yard already.* She heard Diane laugh and then noticed the two men. *Who are these guys?* She dashed past the deck and into the house without glancing at the guys or saying hello.

Diane heard her in the kitchen a few minutes later. "Excuse me for a minute guys. I'll be right back." Diane stepped inside to talk to Emmy.

"Who are those old guys out there with you?" Emmy held a glass up to the window. *Clean enough.*

"If you come outside for a minute, I will introduce you to our neighbor and his friend. You could have at least said hello."

"Do I have to?" Emmy fixed a glass of ice water.

"You should. We are going to be neighbors."

Emmy reluctantly went outside with Diane.

Diane stood behind Emmy and held her shoulders. "This is Emmy, my little sister." Diane pushed Emmy toward the guys. "Speak!"

Emmy turned her head, frowned at Diane, and then faced the guys.

"Hi, Emmy, I'm Fernando." He held out his hand.

"I'm Ethan." He waved from across the picnic table. "I live

31

in that house across the street."

"Yeah, the one that looks like a barn, Emmy. Don't ever go in there. He has hay upstairs left over from when the cows lived there."

Emmy smiled and laughed at the two guys, who were obviously good friends. Ethan and Fernando thought she was much younger than Diane and asked, "How is school going? Do you attend Roosevelt High? We did."

"School's all right." Emmy bit her lip

Diane explained, "She takes night classes at Paul Frank Junior College and works full-time during the week at a health care place."

"Are you kidding?" Fernando nearly spilled his wine.

"You look like a high school kid," Ethan said. *A young high school kid.*

"Yeah, I get that a lot," Emmy answered shyly.

Fernando looked at Diane again. *You could be anywhere from ten to fifteen years older than Emmy. Definitely old enough to ask out on a date.* When Diane went in the house to bring out another bottle of wine, Fernando tried to be sneaky. "Hey, Emmy, Diane mentioned something about turning thirty, so we were wondering if she has turned thirty-one yet. Has she?"

Emmy may have looked young, but she wasn't that gullible. "Oh, no you don't." She shook her finger at them. "I'm not telling you anything about Diane's age. You guys will have to figure that out on your own." Emmy smiled at the guys.

"You're pretty sharp for a thirteen-year-old," Fernando teased.

Emmy grinned as she walked into the house. She changed clothes and called Kenny.

"How was your last day at work, Em?" he asked as he filled a plate with food.

Emmy sat on the edge of her bed. "Okay, they had a cake for me, but after that I had to keep working until five."

"Too bad your boss didn't let you go home early."

Emmy let herself fall onto her back. "He's a jerk. I hope my new boss will be nicer. Oh, I need to mow the yard, and when I got home there were these two old guys on the deck."

"What!?" Kenny exclaimed as he sat down with the rest of the guys in the band. "Are they still there?"

Emmy giggled and then said, "The old guys were talking to Diane and drinking wine. They're neighbors. I don't know how they ended up on our deck."

Kenny laughed. "You made it sound like they were strangers hanging around."

"I need to get the oil changed on your car. I'll get that done this weekend," she said. She got up from the bed and walked downstairs. She walked into the kitchen and could hear Diane and the two men talking, so she walked into the computer room and plopped down in her new office chair. "I've got so much to get done tomorrow, and I might try to go to church with your parents."

"They would like that, Em."

"When are you coming home? I miss you," she said.

Kenny looked across the table at Andy Walker. He whispered, "Em, you know I won't be home until October. We're busy in the studio when we have days off from the tour. I can't come home."

"I get lonely at times," she whispered. "And bored."

"You have friends, Em. You and Kristen should do things. Go out and have fun."

"Are you telling me to go out and meet guys?"

Kenny sighed and turned his chair around. "It doesn't hurt to meet people. I'm not saying you have to go on dates and start a serious relationship."

"You better not be," she said.

"I gotta run, Em. I need to get something in my stomach and then we have to meet some contest winners. I'll talk to you soon."

On Monday, Emmy started a new job working for Robertson Industries, a very successful and thriving company headquartered in Melrose Grove about ten miles north of South Hampshire. Emmy soon learned that Robertson Industries occupied several floors of the modern-looking, glass and steel fifteen-story tall building. She was understandably nervous on her first day of work as she met with Shelly Rogers.

"This will be your reception desk," Shelly said as she pointed to the area near the front of the office suite. "You have a phone and computer, of course. The filing cabinets against the wall will be your responsibility. They have to be locked overnight. That's my Pothos, but I'm leaving it here. Do what you want with it." Shelly pointed to a glass enclosed space. "That is Mr. Oliver's office. The rest of the guys have desks scattered around. They don't like cubicles."

Emmy could hear the hum from the computers and the fluorescent lights overhead.

"The team is in that conference room right now," Shelly said as she pointed toward a room at the back of the suite. "There's a couch and some recliners back there. The team uses that area if they're brainstorming ideas and stuff."

Emmy noticed the floor-to-ceiling windows which formed the wall of the building.

"This area is the lounge." Shelly used air quotes to describe a counter against the wall with a wooden table and four chairs. "There's a fridge, a microwave and the coffee maker. The guys will try to get you to make their coffee for them, but you don't have to. I don't."

"I won't mind making coffee," Emmy said softly.

They turned around because they heard the team leaving the conference room.

"Are you ready to meet them?" Shelly asked.

Emmy nodded and then bit her lip.

Shelly introduced Emmy to the guys in the office as Ms. Colasanti and said, "I'll be training Ms. Colasanti for the next two weeks, and I've already told her not to take any crap from you guys." Shelly laughed and turned to face Emmy. "They are all sweethearts. You won't have any trouble with them."

Ethan Hanks acted just as surprised as Emmy when they met in the office on her first day.

"Hello! I'm Ethan Hanks. We met last Friday," he said as he shook Emmy's hand. "Are you our new administrative aide? Mr.

34

Oliver mentioned our new assistant might be starting today." *I wish I could remember your name.*

Shelly came to the rescue. "Ethan, this is Emily Colasanti, but she likes to be called Emmy."

Ethan nodded and smiled.

"Hello, Mr. Hanks. This is a surprise. I didn't know you worked here."

"I have been working for the company since I graduated from North Park College. Please let me know if I can assist you in any way. Have you met Mr. Oliver our department head?"

"Yes, I met him and Mr. Hawkins from personnel at my interview. Thank you, Mr. Hanks. It does feel good to see a familiar face."

Emmy was surprised that she actually got the job over the numerous other applicants. She told Diane about her first day of work at dinner that evening.

"You'll never guess who works in the office," Emmy said and then took a bite of the cheese-filled ravioli.

"Is it Bill Gates?" Diane asked facetiously as she poured herself a glass of wine.

"No. Mr. Hanks from across the street," Emmy said and then giggled.

"Really?"

"He looked so surprised to see me, and I don't think he remembered my name at first."

Diane took a sip of wine. "Tell me more, Emmy."

"Diane, it's a miracle that I got the job. It's like I had a guardian angel looking out for me."

"Who knows, Emmy? Maybe you did."

"Okay, Shelly... that's the lady training me. She's leaving soon." Emmy waved her fork around with a piece of ravioli on it. "She introduced me to the guys. There are five of them. They are researchers. Kinda like scientists except they use computers. Three are married with kids. Some of the kids are older than me. Two are divorced..."

"Tell me about the divorced guys," Diane said.

"I don't remember which ones they were. All these guys are

35

in their forties or older. They're too old for you, Diane."

"What did you do all day?"

"I followed Shelly around. She showed me where the office supplies are kept and how to use the phone system. Stuff like that. Mr. Hanks had me file some stuff away." Emmy ate the ravioli on her fork and then said, "The files are always locked up. The company apparently does work for the government, and some of the stuff might even be classified."

Diane rolled her eyes. "I'm sure they wouldn't let a twenty-year-old kid see classified documents, Em."

"Well, one of the guys said they keep top-secret files there."

"I'm sure he was teasing you."

"Oh, Ethan offered to let me ride to work with him. The guys on the team don't have set hours, but from what I gathered, they each have a routine. Ethan likes to work at the same time I'm scheduled. Oh, one of the guys is from Australia. You'd love his accent, but he is rather old and completely bald."

"Sounds like the perfect man for me," Diane said and then laughed.

Shelly is going to train me for two weeks, but I don't think it will take that long to learn my responsibilities and the guys' routines."

"Don't let them take advantage of you, Em," Diane said.

"They wouldn't do that," Emmy replied.

Fernando Ramos walked at least a mile a day around the neighborhood. He would mix in a run at times. He would see Emmy on occasion and would wave at her. On Saturday morning he saw her in the front yard and paused for a moment.

"Where is your mother, little girl? She shouldn't leave you outside by yourself." Fernando put his hands on his knees to catch his breath.

"Oh, hi, Grandpa." Emmy yanked on a stubborn weed. She lost her grip on it and fell back onto her bottom.

Fernando laughed but then offered a hand to help her up. "Shouldn't you be taking a nap? Where is your grown-up sister? I

36

would like to talk to her."

"She's at work. Shouldn't you be inside? It's too hot for someone in your condition."

"What condition might that be?" he asked, even though he was setting himself up for a smart aleck remark from Emmy.

"Senior citizens should stay indoors when the temperature gets above ninety. You could suffer a heatstroke."

"I'll be okay." He coughed three times.

"Are you all right, Fernando? It's rather warm to be running. Especially at your age."

"I'm fine, little girl." He wiped his brow. "Are you sure you're old enough to be in high school? I think you're still in junior high."

"That just proves that when you get to be eighty your eyesight is not what it used to be," Emmy said and then giggled.

"Maybe in a few years you will be old enough to go on dates and have a boyfriend," Fernando teased.

Emmy answered back, "I'll have you know that I am in love with Kenny Colwell of the band Fridays At Five, and I used to date Tony Bertucci, and he plays football at Notre Dame."

"Are you going to introduce us to your imaginary boyfriends someday?"

"Maybe I will, and maybe I won't." She grinned.

"I once saw a movie about a man who had an invisible rabbit for a friend. Is your boyfriend invisible?"

"Just because you haven't met him, doesn't mean he doesn't exist."

Fernando laughed and pulled on Emmy's ponytail like she was a child. Emmy cured Fernando of that by messing up his immaculately styled hair.

"Diane was asking me what I thought about you and Ethan the other day. I told her I thought you guys were both very handsome for someone on social security. I know you guys have been bugging her for a date. I think she might have been considering going out with one of you guys, but I told her you were both old enough to our grandfather."

"I might be old enough to be your father, but not Diane's.

And I certainly don't have any paternal feelings toward her."

"Maybe you shouldn't have told me that. I'll have to warn Diane about your intentions."

"I think she is old enough to understand my intentions, little girl," Fernando smirked.

"She said both you guys asked her out to dinner. Did you?"

"Of course. She is an attractive lady," Fernando said.

Emmy grinned. "I told her you guys are way too old, but maybe if she gets really desperate, who knows, anything could happen."

"Thanks for the vote of confidence." Fernando shook his head and waved a hand at Emmy as he jogged away.

Over the next couple of weeks, Diane flirted with both Fernando and Ethan, which encouraged both of them to keep asking her out on a date. Emmy and Fernando teased each other constantly, but she acted more serious around Ethan since she worked with him. Diane was more licentious with them which worried Emmy. Fernando finally convinced Diane to go on a dinner date, much to Ethan's chagrin. After dinner at Ciao Bella, a fancy Italian restaurant in the Hill neighborhood of SoHam, Diane discovered, in a most pleasurable way, Fernando's skill and experience as a kisser.

Chapter Four

The summer of 2000 broke heat records almost daily—especially in August. Emmy spent much of her free time either on her deck working on her tan, working in the yard, or at the pool down the street. One Sunday afternoon she had just finished mowing the yard and putting the mower back in the garage when Fernando and Ethan stopped by to see Diane.

Diane walked up to Emmy while Fernando and Ethan waited on the deck. "I'm going down to the pool with the guys. Wanna join us?"

"Yeah, sure. Is it open swim, or is it just for adults?"

"It's only for adults, but we will sneak you in somehow," Diane teased.

"Oh, Mommy. That would be so much fun to finally get to swim with the adults." Emmy made the word adults sound like a swear word. "Are you leaving right away?"

"In a few minutes. I gave the guys a glass of wine to try so they are talking about wines right now—like they are professional wine tasters or something."

"Give me a minute to change, and I'll be ready to go."

Ten minutes later, as the four of them walked to the pool, Ethan and Fernando still discussed the wine. Diane and Emmy rolled their eyes in disgust.

"I still think it was too sweet," Fernando insisted.

"What do you know?" Ethan laughed. "You never spend more than ten dollars on a bottle of wine. The crap you drink should be used for jet fuel."

Emmy and Diane laughed at Ethan and Fernando as they bickered about the wine. Emmy wore a t-shirt and shorts over her bikini. Kenny didn't like it when Emmy wore her bikini around other guys and she usually didn't.

They got to the pool, and Emmy told Diane, "Thanks for sneaking me in, Mommy. I like it when I can swim with the adults and not the little kids."

One of the pool workers overheard Emmy's conversation and looked at her trying to decide if she was serious or not. Emmy looked at the worker and smiled. She slipped off the t-shirt and shorts in front of Diane and the guys and dove into the pool. Ethan and Fernando didn't pay any attention to Emmy because they were admiring and gawking at Diane. Diane had no qualms about being seen in her bikini.

"Are you guys gonna swim, or are you just going to stare at Diane?" Emmy asked while balancing herself halfway out of the pool.

Ethan and Fernando stopped looking at Diane and turned their attention toward Emmy.

"We'll get in the pool in a minute." Fernando took off his t-shirt to expose his hairy chest.

"Are you afraid to get your hair wet, old man?" Emmy teased.

Ethan laughed because he knew Fernando hated to mess up his hair.

Diane noticed them staring at Emmy and got after them. "Will you old geezers quit looking at my little sister like that? You are both old enough to be her grandfather."

Fernando flashed his pearly white teeth as he grinned. "Does that mean I can't look at you either since I must be your grandfather, too?"

Diane smiled. "You can look at me all you want, Fernando. I know my grandfather would never kiss me the way you did."

"Gross! I don't want to hear about you kissing anyone, Fernando," Emmy said before she flipped back into the water.

After spending some time at the deep end of the pool, Emmy wanted to work on her tan so she climbed out. By this time, Diane, Fernando and Ethan were walking around in the shallow end. Emmy lay on her back on a chaise lounge chair and soaked in the sun—daydreaming about Kenny. A short time later she turned over on her stomach. Later, Fernando sat down beside her and looked at her.

"What?" Emmy turned her head to stare at him.

"Are you looking forward to being in high school this year, Emmy?" Fernando asked.

"Yes I am, Grandpa. Did you really go to school with Abe

40

Lincoln?"

"Abe was a couple of years behind me in school. In fact, I actually convinced him to run for president."

"That didn't turn out so well now, did it?" Emmy said.

They both laughed.

"Are you going to go in the deep end? I want to see if you can swim."

"I can swim just as good as Ethan. We learned to swim in that lake by the park."

Emmy watched as Fernando dove in and swam to the other end. She thought, *I like both of you guys, but I wish you didn't tease me so much. I'm not a child.*

Fernando thought about Diane and Emmy as he swam. *Emmy is so sweet. I almost feel like her father, but Diane is another story. I can tell she is more experienced.*

A few minutes later Ethan and Diane stood next to Emmy, dripping water everywhere. Diane wrapped a towel around her waist.

Ethan pointed at Fernando. "Emmy, don't let that old geezer bother you."

"Who are you calling an old geezer?" Fernando asked as he got out of the pool.

"You, old man. Remember you are older than me. Or is your memory failing like the rest of your old body?"

"Emmy, don't listen to him. He's five days older than me, but he can't remember it. Senile, you know." Fernando put a finger to his head.

She laughed at her old friends and stood up to put on her shorts and t-shirt while they were bantering back and forth. "I'm going home. I still have yard work to finish. I'll see you old-timers later. Don't forget where you live."

Diane stayed at the pool with Ethan and Fernando and didn't get home until much later. Two hours after the pool closed for the night, in fact. Emmy was in the kitchen when she heard the back door open.

"Where have you been, Diane?" Emmy asked sternly.

"At Fernando's. Ethan and I shared a bottle of his expensive

41

wine and ate cheese and crackers."

Emmy stood with her hands on her hips. "Good thing you took your swimdress with you."

"Good night, Emmy." Diane rushed upstairs to her bedroom. *I don't have to account to you for my actions.*

Emmy called Tony at school the next day and talked to him about football and his summer classes.

"I spent some time at the pool with Diane and the old guys yesterday."

"Emmy, you make them sound like they're a hundred years old. You told me Ethan works in your office with you, so how could he be so old?"

"He's not ancient, but he's twice as old as me, I think."

"Emmy, you're only twenty, so even if he's twice as old, he would only be forty."

"That's old."

"Someday you'll think forty is very young, Em. You may not think so now, but you will."

"Did I tell you I picked up *Hero For Hire*? That's the new Fridays At Five CD It's got this cute picture of a baby boy wearing a huge fireman's hat on the cover. I think the liner notes said he's Jeff's nephew."

"I thought you already had a copy?"

"Yeah, I have an advance copy that the guys signed, but I won't ever play that one. I bought two at the store last week, and I've been playing it nonstop. I'll keep one in the car and one in the house. I'm so glad Kenny convinced me to put that CD player in his car."

"Do you even have any CDs by anyone else?"

"I've got a few, but I hardly ever play them."

"Where are those guys now, anyway? I know they're in Europe somewhere."

"Last night they did a show in Thorpe, Surrey, according to the website. That's somewhere in England. They played a stadium by a college called TASIS or something like that."

"I've heard of England before, Em," Tony said.

"Can you tell I'm sticking out my tongue at you?" She shouted into the phone. "Kenny sent me an email. He told me they recorded their concerts for a live CD and DVD to release later. They played there for two nights in front of thirty or forty thousand people."

"Sounds pretty awesome."

"He said he stayed at a place called Sheila Cottage and wants to buy it, but it costs like half a million pounds or something."

"Sounds expensive to me," he said and then yawned. *I've got two hours of reading to finish, Em. I can't be talking on the phone all night.*

"He probably has enough money considering their last CD sold like twenty million copies. I gotta go. Talk to you later."

"Thanks for calling, Em. Good night."

That evening after six o'clock Emmy received a call from overseas. "Hi, Kenny, where are you?"

"In London. Just made it back to the hotel. We played the Royal Albert Hall. What a fantastic place. You've got to see it sometime."

"You did take some pictures, right?"

"Of course. Dad will have them if you want to see them before I get home."

"How did the concerts in Thorpe turn out?" Emmy lay on her back on the couch in the TV room.

"I think they went okay. I haven't seen any footage, or heard any of the mixes or anything, though." Kenny sat on the couch in his hotel suite.

"The college where you guys played was an American school, right?"

"Kinda. I think it started in Switzerland or something. I met this couple from Baltimore, Robert and Kerry Kennedy, who are part of the administration. We ate dinner with them at their house on the campus. It's this really big estate. They're really super nice people. Intellectual types."

"I picked up two of the new CDs to play. I won't play the copy you gave me. The CD player in your car works great. It sounds a whole lot better than the cassette player. Thanks for paying for it."

"No problem, Em," Kenny said. "Did I tell you about the release party in Los Angeles last Tuesday?"

"No, tell me about it."

"The PR company made us do it. We couldn't just release this CD and have it appear in the stores, the media made a big deal about it. We had to do this party thing on Tuesday, and then fly to London overnight. I'm still screwed up as far as sleep goes."

"What time is it there now?"

"It's six hours ahead of home, so it's shortly after midnight here."

"Did you meet any interesting people at the party?"

Kenny hesitated before answering, "I did meet someone, Em." He stood up and began pacing back and forth.

"That doesn't sound too good. What's her name?"

"Becky Morrison. She works in the Steward Music Group office in LA." He looked out the window of his fifth floor room. "I actually met her on Monday, and we had coffee together. We talked for a while, and I took her to the release party on Tuesday."

"Did you ask her to go with you, or did she have to be there for work?"

"I sorta asked if she would like to go. We grabbed a quick bite to eat and then went to the party."

"I see." Emmy flipped over onto her stomach. "Is she pretty?"

"Very pretty." Kenny told her before adding, "She is very pretty because she reminds me of you. An older version though."

Nice recovery. Emmy lifted her feet and moved them back and forth. "How much older?"

"I think she said she was born in 1977."

"So, she's the same age as you, huh?"

"I think so. I'll tell you more about her sometime if I see her again."

"Do you want to see her again?" Emmy asked not sure if she wanted to hear his answer.

"Maybe, we did get along really well."

44

"Did you kiss her?"

"No!"

"Did you want to?"

"Em!"

Several seconds passed without either of them speaking.

"She's not like all the women who hang out at the shows." Kenny broke the silence. "She's intelligent, and she's a Christian. She grew up going to church. I wouldn't have been so interested otherwise."

Again, neither of them spoke for a time.

"Talk to me, Em, please," he whispered.

"Will you promise to tell me if you see her again? Even if you know it will hurt me."

"I will never lie to you or keep any secrets that would hurt you, Em. You know that, right?"

"I know, but I have a bad feeling about this girl. Are you gonna be home at all before the holidays?"

"I'll be home for a few days once this European tour is over in October. It will be good to see you again."

"Do you still love me?"

"You know I do. I miss you, and I love getting your emails. It helps me make it through the day. Have you been to church lately?"

"No, I've been lazy. My weekends are so hectic that I've been sleeping in. I know I should go. Has your mother asked about me?"

"Yes, they miss seeing your face."

"I'll try to see them this week and try to make it to church again. I do kinda miss it."

Kenny heard a knock at the door. "I gotta go, Em. Jeff is here. We're going to some club where The Rolling Stones used to play. I'll talk to you soon."

Chapter Five

"Kristen and I are going to South Bend tomorrow to watch the game. We'll be back late on Sunday. I wanted to let you know in case you were looking for me." Emmy talked on the phone to her mother.

Mom sat in the kitchen drinking a cup of coffee. "Emmy, do you ever worry about Tony getting hurt and never playing football again? What would he do if that happened? How would he make a living?"

"I guess I've never thought much about that since I'm more worried about Kenny. Tony is so strong and nearly invincible. He's never gotten hurt really bad. Of course he gets banged up and bruised, but that's part of the game."

"Maybe you should think about going out with other boys. Maybe someone closer to home. Maybe someone who is home more than Kenny or even Tony."

Emmy rolled her eyes. "And I suppose you have someone in mind, huh?"

"As a matter of fact, I do. Mrs. Sanders down the block has a nice looking son who graduated from junior college. He has a good job working for a travel agency now. I told Mrs. Sanders that you were still single with a good job, too."

"Mom! First of all, Kenny and Tony aren't boys. They're grown men, and I'm not a little girl anymore. I can make my own decisions. Secondly, I'm not interested in Wayne Sanders, or any other man you might try to set me up with. I saw Wayne at Grady and Maris' wedding, remember?"

"You had a good time with him if I remember correctly."

"I had a good time at the wedding. It wasn't necessarily because of Wayne Sanders. I love Kenny and that's that. And a travel agency. Really, Mom? I don't think that's such a good job. Everybody books their travel online now."

"What do you mean by online? Is that on the computer? I still don't trust those, and even if I knew how to use one, I wouldn't."

"It's not that complicated, Mom."

46

"Are you still going to college?" Mom finished her coffee and set the cup in the sink.

"Yes, Mom, I'm still taking classes at night, and I love my new job."

"Are you ever going to invite your father and I over to see the house? Maybe we could have dinner together." *I want to see the inside of this place. I know it's in a better neighborhood than Raynor Park, but it might be a dump on the inside.*

"We will, Mom, but right now we are both so busy with work," Emmy said. *I'd have to run that past Diane. She really doesn't want you over here.*

"Did you buy any new furniture? I'm sure the house is bigger than your apartment."

"We found some used furniture, Mom. We bought a bedroom set for the spare room, and a couch for the basement," Emmy said.

"Are you and Diane getting along? You aren't fighting all the time, are you?"

"No, we are getting along better than ever. I think we've become closer as sisters because we are living together as adults." Emmy's sarcasm was lost on her mother.

"Is she seeing other men? I know she and Craig had a fight. I could never understand what she saw in him, and I know she lied to us about his age. I guess that doesn't matter anymore, but I never would have let her date a man five years older than her when she was sixteen."

"You'll have to talk to Diane if you want to know about her private life. You did talk to her at my birthday party."

"Yes, but not about anything important and nothing personal," Mom said. "Is Isabel still giving you money for rent?"

"Right now she is, but I think I will be able to pay the rent on my own soon, and one of these days I will start paying her back."

"You could always move..."

Emmy interrupted. "I'm not moving back home."

"I was going to say you could move in with Kenny..."

"Mom! We aren't living together."

47

"You might as well be..."

Emmy and her mom argued again. She became so exasperated with her mom and slammed the phone down.

She immediately called Kristen to complain. "My mother is going to treat me like a kid until I'm fifty. She's always going to try to make my decisions for me."

"Emmy, lighten up and chill. Your Mom loves you in her way. Just cut her some slack."

"You don't understand," Emmy said. "Your parents treat you like an adult."

Tony Bertucci walked around the campus of Notre Dame with more confidence since this was second year. Football practice had started, and Tony didn't have enough hours in the day for everything he needed to accomplish. Classes, practice and studying took twenty hours a day. He still shared a room in Dillon Hall with John Randolph, now in his third year on campus. This year John earned the starting tight end position, and he planned to make the most of his opportunity. Like Tony, he hoped to play in the NFL after graduating from Notre Dame. Tony claimed the starting middle linebacker position again for the Fighting Irish. He had already been mentioned as a possible All-American candidate.

In the early morning hours of September second, Emmy and Kristen drove to South Bend to watch the season opening football game against the Ohio State Buckeyes.

"Don't you dare start whining about your parents," Kristen cautioned Emmy as soon as they got on I-80. "I'm not about to listen to that all the way to Indiana."

"Fine. What else can I not *whine* about?" Emmy passed a slow moving semi.

"Don't whine about Kenny, either."

Emmy stuck out her lip in a pout. "Then I will just keep my mouth shut until we arrive."

"Fat chance of that happening," Kristen said. "I'm going to sleep. Don't get lost or crash the car."

"You can't go to sleep. You have to talk to me."

48

"You mean I have to listen to you complaining."

Emmy reached out and smacked Kristen's side. "Some friend you are. I should find someone else to be my best friend."

"Fine! Let's get it over with. What's on your mind?"

"Kenny told me about a girl he met," Emmy said but then paused.

"And?" Kristen waved a hand. "He meets girls all the time. No big deal you always say."

"This one is different. Her name is Becky." Emmy made the name sound almost obscene.

"Why? Tell me about her." Kristen turned down the radio.

"No, I don't want to talk about her," Emmy said.

"Then why did you even mention her?"

"Because." Emmy turned the radio up louder.

Kristen shook her head. "Why do I put up with you?"

Notre Dame won the game against Ohio State easily, as they usually did, and later that night Tony met Emmy and Kristen at Heather's place. He sank into Heather's old couch with Kristen and Emmy on either side.

"Could I have a massage, please?" Tony asked as he twisted his head back and forth.

"Why?" Emmy asked.

"Because I feel more banged up than normal."

"I suppose. Where does it hurt?"

Emmy and Kristen massaged his back and the spots where he told them it hurt.

Heather groaned. "This is pathetic. You girls are spoiling him. He's not hurt, so quit pampering him."

"It hurts here, too." Tony pointed to his shoulder.

Emmy and Kristen massaged him all over his arms and chest and neck. Emmy asked, "Is there any other place you want to be massaged?"

He smiled mischievously at her, and put a finger to his mouth.

Emmy grinned at Tony, and then looked at Heather and Kristen. "I can't do that! And certainly not with them in the room."

49

Tony turned red. "I want you to massage my lips. I want you to kiss me on the mouth."

Heather laughed. "Kristen and I can always wait in the hallway outside."

Emmy stood up and grabbed Heather's arm. "You don't have to go because I'm not going to kiss him because he is in such terrible pain."

"I'm feeling much better now. You can kiss me all you want, Emmy. I can take the pain."

Emmy turned around to face Tony and kicked his shin. "Oh, so it causes you pain to kiss me, huh? In that case I don't think I want to cause you any more pain, so I won't ever kiss you again. How about that, Mr.-Big-Time-Football-Hero?"

He rubbed his leg. "I didn't mean it like that."

Emmy sat on the couch beside Tony again and she and Kristen talked about him.

"Kristen, do you think I made the right choice when we broke up? This one is so weak and such a wimp. He is always getting hurt and complaining all the time."

"I think you made the right choice, Em."

"I'm right here. I can hear you guys," Tony said.

"Why is that?" Emmy played the *straight man*.

"It's because if this one complains so much now, what will he be like when he gets older? He's such a whiner," Kristen said.

Quick as a flash Tony grabbed both of them around the waist and pulled them onto his lap. His strong arms allowed him to hang onto them with ease. He tickled both of them as they squirmed and tried to get away. Kristen stopped fighting to get away before Emmy did. Emmy kept squirming and her heart raced. Kristen relaxed on Tony's lap and sat there—amazed at how strong, but yet gentle, he could be. He let go of them, and Emmy jumped off his lap. Kristen stayed on the couch next to him and Emmy sat in the large recliner across from the couch.

"You need to be careful where you are touching me. I know you were just playing, but..."

"I'm sorry, Emmy. I didn't realize where I had my hand. I didn't do it intentionally."

50

"Don't tickle me again." Emmy hugged her knees to her chest.

"Okay, sorry." Tony shrugged. "It was an accident."

"What's the big deal?" Kristen asked. "You always let him tickle you. He's about as harmless as a teddy bear."

"Not like that. He almost had his hand... never mind."

Kristen sat contentedly next to him on the couch. Only eight months apart in age, and the two youngest cousins in the Lombardi family, Tony and Kristen had always been closer than his other cousins.

Heather checked the time. "Will you girls quit bothering him so he can get up. He needs to go home."

"I can get up anytime I want. They don't weigh a hundred pounds put together." To prove his point he stood up and threw Kristen over his shoulder like a sack of potatoes and carried her around.

"Are you going to set her down?" Heather asked.

"I just wanted to prove I could lift her."

"I think you made your point." Heather pointed to the couch and Tony set Kristen down. He grinned and then sat on top of her.

"Get off of me, you big horse!" Kristen squealed.

"Heather, I think you might need a new couch. This one has some lumps."

"If you don't get off of me this instant, I'm gonna... gonna..."

Even Emmy giggled as Tony pretended to sit on Kristen. She saw that he held his weight above her. Kristen pushed Tony up, and he turned around to look at her. "I'm sorry. I didn't realize you were there."

Kristen shook her head. "You're such a dork, but at least you're family."

"Maybe I should sit in this chair." He looked at Emmy.

She held up her hand to keep him away. "Oh, no, you don't. You can tease Kristen, but you better leave me alone. I'm still mad at you."

Tony was tired from the game, but didn't want to miss his

51

chance to spend time with both of them. Emmy watched Tony and Kristen carrying on, but for the rest of the night she sat in the recliner and not with him and Kristen on the couch.

Okay, so maybe I'm mad at Kenny and taking it out on you. Emmy bit her lip as Tony told Kristen a story about his roommate John.

Tony looked at the time. "I guess I should go."

Heather stuck her head out of the kitchen. "Oh, so soon," she said sarcastically.

"All right. I know I've overstayed my welcome." He stood up.

Kristen jumped to her feet and hugged him. "I hope you're not too sore in the morning because we won't be here to give you another massage." Kristen looked at Emmy.

"Hmmmph!" Emmy snorted. "He's never getting another 'massage' from me."

Tony released Kristen and faced Emmy. "Are you still angry with me?"

Emmy tried to look angry, but slowly a smile made its way onto her face. She stood up and reached out for him. "Oh, I guess it was just an accident. I'm not mad at you anymore, but you still can't tickle me."

Tony placed his arms around her, but didn't hold her too close.

Chapter Six

"I want to see the new house. You haven't invited me over to see it yet. Don't you like me anymore?" Kristen complained to Emmy over the phone.

"Of course, I still like you. You're my best friend. Come over Friday after work and plan on staying overnight, and the whole weekend if you want. I don't have to work this Saturday at all. We can have a girls night out even if we don't go anywhere."

"Works for me. I can't wait."

Friday evening Kristen came over, and Emmy showed her all around the house and the yard.

"Emmy, this place is so nice. I love the way you've decorated it with your little touches here and there." Kristen picked up a football from a recliner and handed it to Emmy. "You are so much better at that than me. How do you know how to do that? You've always been a tomboy."

Emmy held the football as she frowned at Kristen. "It wasn't hard to do. I get a lot of ideas from magazines. If you ever get a place of your own, I'll help you decorate."

"No, thanks. I don't want my place to look like Sports Illustrated or some rock magazine." Kristen looked at a couple of pictures on the wall of Emmy and Kenny.

"I'm sorry my place isn't decorated all prissy and feminine like your room."

"I'm just teasing you. Don't get all riled up." Kristen picked up a copy of *Billboard* magazine and glanced through it. "Can you show me around the neighborhood?"

"Let's go for a walk. It's nice out, then we can grab something to eat. There's a new Mexican place, the Taco Casa, not too far away. I want to try it out."

Emmy took Kristen for a walk around the neighborhood and down to the park area before going out for dinner.

"I hope the food is good because this place is so convenient." Emmy ate another tortilla chip. "Try this salsa. It's really good."

"Oh, are you gonna share the chips? I thought you were going to eat them all."

"You snooze, you lose." Emmy snatched another chip.

Emmy filled up on the chips and salsa and couldn't finish her chicken tacos.

Kristen teased, "If you wouldn't eat so many of those cheap chips, you would have more room to finish the good stuff."

For some reason Kristen saying cheap chips struck Emmy as being hilarious. For the next twenty minutes Emmy kept repeating cheap chips until it drove Kristen nuts.

"Stop it! Stop it! I've had enough." Kristen waved her hands in front of her face.

"Enough of the cheap chips, Krissy?"

As they walked home, Kristen asked her, "What have you been drinking, and why aren't you sharing it with me."

Emmy looked at Kristen, muttered cheap chips and took off running. Kristen chased her, and they both ended up out of breath and laughing.

"I'm sorry I ate too many cheap chips, Kristen." Emmy giggled as they waited to cross Timberline Avenue. "Next time I'll let you eat all of them."

"You can be such a goof at times, Emmy. Though, I have to admit. Hanging out with you is never boring."

They got back to the house and watched TV for about an hour. After that, they sat on the couch and talked about her birthday party. Emmy laughed at how Kristen convinced her to go to Mama's house.

"You were so bad that day. Treating me so nice. Fixing my hair, and then pouting until you got your way about your favorite sweater." Emmy used air quotes. "But I still love you."

"It really is my favorite sweater of yours."

"Oh, please," Emmy replied sarcastically.

Kristen looked hurt for a second, but then she smiled. "Well, you don't have many decent looking sweaters. Anyway, I like the way it looks on you. It fits you better than some of your other ones, and the color is just perfect on you."

Emmy stared at Kristen. She thought about saying "cheap

chips" but didn't. "Were you disappointed that we stayed at Mama's house the night of my birthday instead of going back to my apartment?" Emmy asked instead.

"I thought we could spend the night by ourselves since we never get to do that much anymore, but I knew Mama would make us stay there when it started storming so bad. We can have fun tonight and stay up all night long."

"Remember how Tony smeared some birthday cake on my nose that night?" Emmy sat up on her knees.

"It was more than just your nose." Kristen touched the end of Emmy's nose. "You looked adorable with birthday cake smeared all over your face."

"Just wait. Your birthday will come around, and I will have my revenge."

"I'm never going to have another birthday party in my life."

"Yeah, right. Mom told me there's a picture of me at the house with birthday cake all over my face from my second birthday. Mom said it reminded her of that, and she almost cried."

"Since we're talking about Tony, are we gonna go to any more football games this year?"

"I might not be able to. I usually have to work Saturday mornings. I need the extra money to pay the bills. Diane doesn't make all that much."

"She sure has enough money to buy new clothes." Kristen knew about Diane's spending habit.

"I don't mind paying a larger share. If she and Craig get back together and she moves out, I'll have to pay everything."

"You could let Kenny pay a share," Kristen suggested.

"That ain't gonna happen."

"You're so stubborn." Kristen shook her head. "So how about going to a game?"

"After the way Tony treated me the last time, I'm not sure I would go anyway."

"Are you talking about when he tickled us?"

"Yes, I didn't like that."

"He's always tickled us."

"Exactly my point," Emmy replied.

Geez! No one ever died from being tickled. Kristen didn't see what the big deal was about tickling.

Diane returned home from work and saw them in the TV room.

"Hi, Kristen. How are you? What are you guys talking about? I heard you talking and acting like immature teenagers." Diane put a hand to her forehead. "Oh, wait. That's because Emmy is a young immature teenager."

"Am not!" Emmy stuck out her tongue. "I'm twenty."

"We were talking about Emmy's birthday party and the birthday cake," Kristen said.

"Yeah, Emmy looked hilarious with cake all over her face," Diane said as she shook her head. *I'd kill Craig if he ever tried that.* "I'm beat, and I'm going to bed. Don't stay up all night."

"Good night, Mom." Emmy blew Diane a kiss as she bounced on the couch.

"Knock it off, Em," Diane growled.

Emmy and Kristen went back to talking about boys and love for a few minutes.

"I think we should get ready for bed and watch a couple movies," Emmy said. "I've got a TV and DVD player in my bedroom now."

"Are you tired already?" Kristen looked at the clock.

"Not yet, but I want to put my pajamas on in case I fall asleep."

Emmy and Kristen headed upstairs to her bedroom after a few minutes and got ready for bed. Emmy looked at Kristen and got sentimental for a moment.

"You are so pretty, and I love having you for my best friend even if I'm mean to you at times."

Kristen stood with her hands on her hips. "Oh, so if I was ugly, I couldn't be your best friend. Is that what you are trying to say?"

"Absolutely!" Emmy teased.

"Stinker!"

"Do you think I'm pretty, Kristen?" Emmy looked at her reflection in the mirror on the back of the door.

Kristen put her hands on Emmy's arms and rested her chin on Emmy's shoulder. "Well, you are sorta pretty except for your hair... and your ears... and your eyes... and your nose."

"Do you really think I'm ugly and not at all pretty?"

"Sorry, Emmy honey, but you are rather plain looking. Nobody will ever want to marry you, or even have you for a girlfriend."

Emmy pretended to cry and Kristen giggled.

"Maybe, just maybe, someday, when you are very old and wrinkled like a prune, you might find a decrepit old blind man to be your boyfriend."

"Well, at least I have that to look forward to," Emmy answered sarcastically.

"Do you have any popcorn in the house?" Kristen asked.

"I think so."

They ran downstairs to check. They found some popcorn, crackers and other snacks. They brought plastic glasses and a cold, two liter of pop upstairs.

"That should hold us." Emmy pulled out a box containing her DVDs. "You can pick out the first one, Krissy."

Kristen looked through the dozen choices and picked out a romantic comedy called *Love and Other Problems*. "I've never seen this one. Is it new?"

"No, it's from the sixties. It's like prehistoric, but it's funny."

They laughed hysterically at the antics of the two main characters.

"Now I get to choose." Emmy grabbed one of her favorites *A Day In The Life Of Charger*—a family story about a young girl, her dog, Charger, and all the misadventures they shared. While hilariously funny at times, toward the end it became sad because Charger nearly died. Tears flowed uncontrollably during that part of the movie. They held onto each other until Charger recovered, and the movie reached the required happy ending.

Emmy picked up the remote and stopped the DVD. "I can't remember how many times I've watched that movie, and I always cry when it gets to that part where Charger almost dies."

57

"Yeah, I do, too," Kristen confessed. "We can't ever let Tony or Kenny know."

Emmy laughed. "I bet they cry, too."

In the morning Diane walked into the bedroom and saw Emmy and Kristen sleeping peacefully together. Diane noticed the empty bags of chips and popcorn, as well as broken chips, and kicked the empty two-liter of pop tossed on the floor. *I am not cleaning up this mess.* Diane thought. *You better not even ask, Emmy.*

Diane left to use the bathroom, and Kristen woke up and looked at Emmy sleeping so peacefully. Kristen softly brushed the hair off her face, and Emmy woke up slowly. Emmy turned over to face Kristen and smiled.

"Good morning, Kristen. Did I hear Diane just now?"

"She came in and saw us and the mess. I think she's kinda mad because I heard her kick the pop bottle."

"That's okay. I don't feel guilty about anything we did last night."

Kristen looked around and saw the mess in the bedroom. "I'm sure glad you have a maid to clean up this mess."

Emmy looked at Kristen. "Who are you talking about? What maid?"

"Isn't it Diane's responsibility to clean the bedrooms this month?" Kristen raised her eyebrows.

"Yes, indeed!" Emmy caught on. "It *is* Diane's month to clean the upstairs. I'm glad you thought of that."

They high-fived each other.

Diane walked out of the bathroom and back into Emmy's room. She sat on the edge of the bed. "Did you girls sleep okay last night?"

"I slept just fine," Emmy answered. "How about you, Diane?"

"I didn't get much sleep at all because you two kept me up all night with your laughing and crying and carrying on." Diane grabbed a pillow and hit Emmy over the head with it. Emmy and Kristen dove under the covers to escape. "And I heard what you said about it being my turn. I am not cleaning up this mess. No way, no how."

"But it's your turn." Emmy cried out as she stuck her head out from under the covers.

Diane shook her head. "Not gonna happen, baby sister. I'm not your mother or your maid. You guys made the mess. You clean it up."

"Fine! Be that way," Emmy said and then giggled.

"Are you hungry, Em?" Kristen asked.

"I'm starving," Emmy replied.

Diane pulled the covers off of them. "Then get up off your lazy butts and come downstairs." Diane went downstairs and started the coffee. Emmy and Kristen made it downstairs after a few minutes.

"Can you make pancakes for us, Diane?" Emmy turned to Kristen. "Are pancakes okay with you?"

"Pancakes are all right." Kristen poured herself a cup of coffee. "Do you have any blueberries or chocolate chips, maybe? Pancakes taste better that way."

Diane stared at Emmy and Kristen and asked sarcastically, "Anything else you want to order? I don't mind special orders. I've got nothing better to do. I'm here to serve your every desire."

"Someone is grumpy this morning." Emmy grinned at Kristen. "You should try to get more sleep at night, Diane." Emmy ducked as Diane tossed a wet dish rag at her. It missed her and struck Kristen on her shoulder.

"Hey! I didn't say anything," Kristen complained.

"It wasn't my fault I didn't get enough sleep."

"We didn't get much sleep, either, but we're not grumpy. I think it's because you miss Craig."

Diane glared at both of them.

Chapter Seven

Only four more days until you get home, Kenny. Emmy looked at the calendar and sighed as she saw the red circle around the day of October eighth. "I guess I'll keep busy at work and the time will fly by. Yeah, right! It's gonna seem like an eternity till you get home." Emmy jumped as Diane walked into the kitchen.

"Are you talking to yourself, Em?"

"I was just thinking about Kenny getting home."

"You're a goof. Why didn't you make any coffee?" Diane grabbed the empty Mr. Coffee pot and waved it at Emmy.

"Sorry, but I didn't want any, and I didn't know how long you would be in bed." Emmy opened a cabinet door and pulled out the coffee. "I gotta run. I'll see you tonight." Emmy headed to work.

For the next three and a half days, including her half-day on Saturday, Emmy stayed busy with work and her night classes. By the time one o'clock rolled around on Saturday, she was mentally worn out. She left the office and headed home. She wandered around the house and cleaned until satisfied it would pass inspection. She ate a light lunch and sat on the couch to watch football. Notre Dame played Stanford in South Bend. The Irish won, but the offense did not play well. Tony and the defense bent a bit, but stiffened when Stanford entered the red zone. The Irish won by six. Emmy emailed Tony after the game, but realized she didn't have much to say to him.

"Diane, are you gonna be here for dinner? Should I make something special?" Emmy asked when Diane got home from work.

"Don't make anything for me. Fernando called and he's taking me out." Diane rushed upstairs and a minute later Emmy heard the shower running.

She called Mrs. Colwell as she searched the fridge for something to eat.

"Emmy, are you excited? He will be home tomorrow afternoon."

"I can't wait. Is it all right if I join you for church in the morning?" Emmy pulled out a Tupperware container and opened it. *Yuck! What was this and how long has it been in there.*

"Of course, dear. You are always welcome. Pastor Ronnie asked about you last week."

"Is it all right if I hang around your house after church to wait for Kenny?"

"Do you even have to ask? You know you are always welcome at our home." Mrs. Colwell paused, but Emmy didn't say anything. "Emmy, is there something bothering you? Did you and Kenny have a little spat or something?"

Emmy found a pizza in the freezer. "No, but he told me about this girl he met named Becky. Do you know anything about her?"

"Not really. He did mention meeting her, but that's all."

"Maybe I'm being paranoid, but it seemed like he was interested in her."

"He really hasn't mentioned anything to us, dear. You will have to ask him about her tomorrow when you see him."

Emmy arrived at the Colwell home early enough for a quick breakfast before they had to leave for church.

"Good morning, Emmy. It's so good to see you." Mr. Colwell finished his last bite of pancakes. "Did Elly mention that today is the first Sunday with our new senior pastor?"

"No, isn't Pastor Ronnie still at the church?"

"Yes. Rev. Lyle retired, and Rev. Johnston replaced him. This is his first official day, but he's been here for two weeks."

"That's good. I really like Pastor Ronnie. He relates to the teens so well."

"I saved some blueberry pancakes just for you, dear." Mrs. Colwell set a plate in front of Emmy.

"Thanks! I love blueberry pancakes." Emmy grinned as she reached for the maple syrup.

After the morning service, Emmy talked to Ronnie Rojas, and he introduced her to the new pastor.

"Rev. Johnston, this is Emmy Colasanti. She is a friend of

the Colwell family."

"It's a pleasure to meet you, Emmy. I noticed you sitting with the Colwells. I assumed you were their daughter. It will take me a while to get to know everyone in the church."

"It's nice to meet you, sir." Emmy smiled as she thought about the differences between the new pastor and the one he replaced. *You've got a full head of white hair and a cheery smile. The other guy was bald and seemed kinda grumpy at times.*

Rev. Johnston stood just over six feet tall and was built like a football player. He had a firm, strong, but yet gentle, handshake.

Pastor Rojas explained, "The Colwells have a son, Kenny, and he is a member of Fridays At Five. Emmy and Kenny have been friends for many years."

"I believe I have heard of that band," Rev. Johnston said. "My daughter, Eleanor, listens to their music. She's nineteen and a student at Olivet Nazarene University. She's a music major."

Pastor Ronnie mentioned, "Emmy's a singer, too. She and Kenny often sing for the teens, and Emmy even writes songs."

"That's fantastic. My daughter will be here next Sunday. I'll introduce her to you."

"I'd like that," Emmy replied.

Emmy ate lunch with the Colwells and kept an eye on the clock.

"I know you're anxious for him to get here, dear, but pacing around isn't going to get him here any sooner. Why don't you read a book, or listen to some music?" Mrs. Colwell suggested.

"I couldn't concentrate enough to read." Emmy plopped down on the couch and hugged a small pillow to her chest. "I'm not even interested in the game... Yeah! Touchdown!"

Finally, a limo pulled into the driveway at 3:06. Emmy ran outside without her shoes as Kenny got out. He turned and braced himself as Emmy jumped into his arms.

"Do you still love me, or do you have a new girlfriend?" she blurted out.

"I still love you, Emmy, and I don't have a new girlfriend. Why would you think I did?" He held her tight.

"Because you met someone new."

"If you're talking about Becky, I haven't seen her since I left LA."

"Have you talked to her or emailed her?"

"Yes, but that doesn't mean she's my girlfriend." He set Emmy down.

She helped carry his gear out to the carriage house and up to his apartment. She kissed him and pulled him toward the futon.

"Em, I should say hi to my parents. They want to see me."

"Okay, but then we are coming back here."

They went into the house, and Kenny talked to his parents for thirty minutes. Then he and Emmy headed back to the carriage house. Once alone in his apartment, Emmy threw her arms around his neck and kissed him.

"Will you make love to me now?" Emmy asked.

Kenny's jaw dropped as he looked at her. He was surprised she would be so blunt—and willing. He didn't say anything.

"You don't want to, do you? It's because of that other girl, isn't it?"

"Emmy, we can't do that, and it's not because of Becky."

Emmy sat on the futon as Kenny stood in front of her.

"I knew that sooner or later you would meet someone you liked better than me. I can understand that."

Kenny sat next to her on the futon and put an arm around her shoulder. "I don't think of Becky as better than you."

"But you do like her?"

"Yes, I do like her, and she likes me. We haven't really had a chance to get to know each other, but we both want to."

"Did you kiss her in LA?"

"Yes, I did, but only once." Kenny looked at Emmy and sighed. "I know this is going to be hard for you to understand, but Becky is someone that I really want to get to know better. She comes from a good Christian family..."

"So, then her parents aren't screwed up like mine." She removed his arm from her shoulder and stood up.

Kenny jumped to his feet. "I haven't met her parents, but she talked about them when we were in LA and in her emails. This isn't because of your parents."

"It can't help matters that my parents are the way they are. I don't blame you for wanting to find someone else, Kenny. I'm glad you didn't try to hide it from me." Emmy stared at the floor and felt as though her heart was going to shatter.

Kenny put a finger under her chin and lifted her face. "I've always been totally honest with you, Em. I do love you, and I always will..."

"As a friend. You know I want more than that." Emmy turned her back to Kenny as tears filled her eyes.

"I know, but right now I can't offer you more than friendship." He gently placed his hands on her shoulders. "Neither one of us is ready to get married."

"Is Becky?" Emmy spat her name as she spun around.

"No, she's back at UCLA. She wants to finish her degree and be a teacher. She doesn't want to have a serious relationship until then."

"Does she date other guys?"

"I don't really know." He shrugged. "I never asked."

"So she's not really your girlfriend then, is she?"

"She's someone I want to get to know better. If that means she's a girlfriend, I don't know." He held out his hands.

Emmy pulled Kenny onto the couch. She sat on her feet and faced him. "What do you know about her? Is she pretty?"

"She's about five six with long dark hair. She grew up in California and went to Morning Star Christian Academy."

"What color are her eyes?"

"They're blue." Kenny realized he knew more about Becky than he had told Emmy. They were quiet for a moment, and then he brought up the subject of college. "Would you think about going to North Park after this year? I'll help you with your expenses."

"You know how I feel about that." Emmy jumped up and stood in front of Kenny.

"Let's take a look at your expenses. You pay $700 a month for rent. Utilities are another, let's say $300."

"They're not that much."

"Let's use that to make an even figure of a thousand a month. Do you know how much tuition is at North Park?"

64

"With room and board it's about $25,000 a year. Plus books and other living expenses."

"So, if you give up your house, you could save half of what it costs to go to North Park."

"Aren't you forgetting something?"

"What?" Kenny tilted his head.

"If I give up my house, I wont have anywhere to live."

"You'd be living at the dorm with Kristen."

"And if I'm going to school full-time, how will I have the money to pay for it?"

"From your... Oh, I get it."

"Duh! I just make enough to cover my expenses and school as it is. I can't afford North Park without a scholarship. I should have been a jock."

"You know you could always consider it a loan and pay me back in the future." Kenny stood up and faced Emmy.

"Yeah, and if you decide that you want to get serious about someone else?"

"Let's not even think about that." He put his hands on her shoulders.

"So, we're going to put our relationship on hold until I get out of school, huh?"

"I think we should."

She pushed him away and turned her back to him. "That's like blackmail."

"Why do you say that?" Kenny grabbed her shoulders and spun her around to face him.

"Either, I give up our relationship, for who knows how long, or else I go to North Park on your dime. Doesn't that sound like an ultimatum at least?" She frowned as she looked up at him.

"I can see your point, but I'm not going to force you to go to North Park merely so we can have a relationship."

"When I finish at Paul Frank, I will be taking classes at North Park."

"Maybe you could work part-time then and live in the carriage house. You could go to school full-time and..."

"Kenny."

"What?"

"Can we talk about this later?"

"I suppose. What should we do now?"

"If we are putting a serious relationship on hold for now, does that mean we can't make love?" Emmy asked as she grinned.

"You sure don't make it easy to say no."

"Then don't."

"Em," he said slowly.

"Can we at least kiss each other while we are in this non-serious relationship? Is that a real word?"

"I don't know, but I suppose we can still kiss each other once in a while."

"Good because we are going to start right now."

At church the next Sunday Emmy and Kenny met Eleanor Johnston, the pastor's daughter.

"It's a pleasure to meet you, Eleanor. I'm Kenny."

"Duh! I know. I've got all your CDs."

"Thanks. I appreciate our fans," Kenny said routinely.

Emmy poked him in the side. *That sounded so lame.*

"Hi, Emmy, my father told me that you like to sing and write songs. I'm studying music."

Emmy's eyes sparkled. "That's so cool."

"I hope to find a position in a school district."

"I'm taking night classes, but I'm not sure what my major will be." Emmy could see the family resemblance between Eleanor and her father. Eleanor had his cheery smile and green eyes. She was nearly as tall as her father, but quite slender. They talked about music, and she told Emmy more about Olivet Nazarene University.

"It sounds like it's just as expensive as North Park," Emmy said. *I can't afford either school. It's going to take me forever to earn my degree, but I swear I'll do it somehow.*

"You should check it out at least. A lot of the students get some form of financial aid. It's a great place to get a good Christian education."

Kenny nodded. "You should look into it, Em."

Emmy shrugged. "I'm not sure they would want me. I go to

church here, but I've been raised a Catholic."

"I'm pretty sure the college doesn't discriminate against any denomination. I think they look at the individual."

"Thanks, I'll think about it."

After lunch with his parents, Emmy pulled Kenny out to the carriage house.

"Em, are we going to repeat what we did yesterday?" Kenny asked as he grinned.

"No! We have to talk. No kissing until we get this mess straightened out."

"What mess?" Kenny followed her up the stairs.

"You know what I mean." Emmy slammed the door closed behind Kenny. "Becky!"

Kenny sighed.

"Sit down and listen to me," she ordered while pointing at the couch.

He plopped down on the old couch.

"College."

He tilted his head. "Yes?"

"You know how much it means to me. Maybe I can compromise my insistence about paying for everything myself."

"That would be all right with me."

"I'm not saying I will for sure."

"At least you're thinking about it. That's a start."

"Are you going to see Becky when you get back to LA?"

Kenny waited a few seconds before answering, "I would like to, Em."

"All right. Go ahead if that's what you want. I can't exactly stop you since I'll be here."

"You'll meet other guys. Maybe you'll meet someone you want to get to know better."

"You better not be talking in the biblical sense."

"No! I just meant... you know... biographically."

Emmy laughed. "You are such a dork, but I still love you."

67

Chapter Eight

One day in early November, Emmy returned home from work, changed clothes, heated up some leftover chicken and rice and sat at the kitchen table to go through two days accumulation of mail. *This could be interesting. It's definitely not a bill or junk mail.* She opened it and her mouth fell open as she read who was getting married. *Sean O'Brien. I haven't seen you since you left for the army.* She tilted her head. *But I seem to remember hearing that you received an early medical discharge. I wonder how you got my address.*

That mystery solved itself when she opened an email from Scott Simmons. He passed along her new address to Sean. She knew Kenny would be out of town and decided that this might be an opportunity to take him up on his insistence for her to date other guys. She could only think of one person she would like to date. She called Tony later that evening, and, after a few minutes of small talk, told him about the upcoming wedding.

"Tony, I got an invitation to Sean O'Brien's wedding. I don't think you ever met him."

"You've told me about him, Em. He's the son of the family who were your landlords, right?"

"He's the youngest son, and he's the one who used to tease me all the time. He received a medical discharge from the army. The wedding is December ninth, here in SoHam."

"Guess what, Emmy."

"I know you have finals again," Emmy answered with disappointment in her voice.

"Oh contrare, my pretty one. I don't have anything going on that weekend. They are official study days. Finals start on Monday."

"Really? You can go with me? Tony, I'm so happy."

""Hey! Hold on a minute. I didn't say anything about going with you," he teased. "Those are study days, and I'd much rather study for twelve hours a day rather than hang out with you."

"Really?"

"No, you goof. I'll go with you, but don't expect me to have

68

fun. I'd rather be studying."

"Finally, I can go to a wedding with someone. I was starting to believe that would never happen."

"Well, I can go if I get my underwear drawer straightened out. I bought some new boxers..."

"Very funny. Ha! Ha! I've heard that excuse before, and it doesn't work. You might really enjoy going to a wedding. Maybe you will want to get married earlier than what you have planned in that grand scheme of yours."

"I don't know, Emmy, Nikki has her heart set on a..."

"I thought you weren't going to marry her."

"Who should I marry, Emmy? I thought you liked Nikki."

"I thought you might want to marry me," Emmy teased him.

"Oh, you thought I would want to marry you, huh? Well, maybe I'll think about it." He laughed. "By the way, next Saturday is our last home game of the year. We don't have a game tomorrow. Are you still working on Saturdays?"

"Yeah, sorry, but I need the money."

"That's okay. I understand."

Kristen called Emmy's cell phone around noon the next day.

"I'm not doing anything special unless you call doing my laundry along with Diane's special. Why?" Emmy asked as she sorted her dirty clothes.

"I'm bored, and I need to talk to you about something. Can I pop over?" Kristen asked. "And before you even say anything I am not helping with your laundry."

"Heaven forbid the princess stoop to such menial chores," Emmy said. "Come on over. I'll fix lunch in between my other household chores."

"You are too kind. I should hire you as my lady-in-waiting," Kristen said in a haughty voice.

Kristen arrived thirty minutes later, walked in the back door and hollered for Emmy. Emmy ran up the basement stairs and almost bumped into Kristen.

69

"Your back door was open. Don't you ever lock your doors?" Kristen asked.

"I do at night. Are you hungry? I'm making some chicken soup."

"You mean you opened a can, right?" Kristen asked as she walked over to the stove.

"No, I'm making it from scratch."

"It smells good. One of these days I have to learn how to boil water," Kristen said.

"You'll have to learn how to turn on the stove first," Emmy said and then giggled. "This has to simmer for fifteen minutes. Let's sit in the TV room and talk."

Kristen followed Emmy and they sat on the couch.

"Where's Diane?"

Emmy waved a hand. "She's working. She's been working so many hours. I almost never see her. What's new at school?"

"Nothing much. Tess and I have been going out, but not with anyone special."

"Tess Easterly. Is that your roommate's name?" Emmy asked.

Kristen nodded.

"Are you still sharing your clothes with her?"

"We are the same size, so we share." Kristen looked at Emmy's worn jeans and stretched out sweatshirt.

"Whatever," Emmy said as she caught Kristen's frown.

"How's Kenny? When is he coming home?" Kristen asked.

Emmy sighed and let her shoulders slump as she grabbed a throw pillow and held it to her chest. "He won't be home until Christmas Eve."

"Have you talked to him this week?"

Emmy didn't respond.

"Em, did you hear me?"

"I heard you."

Kristen stared at Emmy for a moment. "What's going on?"

Emmy told Kristen about the last time she saw Kenny.

"Becky, huh?"

Emmy nodded.

70

"That sounds like a name for an airhead," Kristen said hoping it would make Emmy feel better.

"Her name is actually Rebecca."

"Oh, that sounds better."

Emmy frowned at Kristen.

"Sorry," Kristen said. "Did you guys do anything before he left?"

Emmy kept frowning and threw her pillow at Kristen.

"I didn't mean that! Did you go anywhere? You know like real couples do. They call it going on a date. You should try it sometime."

"We didn't go anywhere other than the carriage house," Emmy said.

"Look on the bright side, Em."

"And what might that be?" Emmy leaned back against the arm of the couch.

"As long as he's in Europe, Becky can't see him either."

Emmy kicked Kristen's leg just as the timer for the soup went off. "I hate you. Let's eat."

Emmy was disappointed that Tony couldn't be home for Thanksgiving, but he had a good reason. Their last game of the regular season was two days after Thanksgiving against Southern Cal in Los Angeles, and the team had to stay at school. Emmy hoped to spend Thanksgiving with the Colwells and maybe make a quick visit to see her parents. She called Mrs. Colwell on the Sunday before Thanksgiving.

"Hello, Emmy, how are you?"

"Okay, I was wondering if I could come over on Thanksgiving and eat with you guys? I want to see my parents, but I'm not going to eat there. Mom said they're going to Larry's Uptown Grill because he offers free meals to senior citizens."

"You are always welcome—you know that, but we're going to eat at my brother Jim's house. You could come with us. Tom and Sherry will be there."

"Oh, I don't know..."

"You don't need to be shy. Jim and Nora would love to see

71

you again. They haven't seen you for several years."

Emmy nervously wrapped her hair around her finger. "I think I remember meeting them when I was a little girl."

"You know Tom and Sherry. I think her parents are going to be there."

"Thanks, but I would feel out of place."

"I won't force you to come with us, but if you change your mind, just call me. Even if it's that morning."

"I'll think about it. Thanks, Mrs. Colwell."

Emmy sat on the couch and tried to study, but couldn't concentrate. *This is a total waste of time. I can't remember what I read on the last page.* She finally called Mama.

"Would you mind if I come over to eat with you on Thanksgiving? Kenny's parents aren't going to be home, and my parents are going to Larry's."

"You're more than welcome, sweetie, but this year everyone is meeting at Karla and Daniel's place."

"Oh," Emmy said.

"You are welcome to join us."

"I don't know."

"Enough of that," Mama commanded. "You can pick me up."

"All right."

Emmy picked Mama up to take her to the Keaslings' just before noon on Thanksgiving.

"Will you help me carry some of this out to your car, please?"

As Emmy carried a box of food, she bit her lip. "Mama, I'm kinda nervous because your brothers will be there."

"Emmy, you've met them before. Why would you be nervous about seeing them again?"

"I don't know for sure, but I am. What if I forget the names of their wives?"

"Then you call them Mrs. Lombardi. You don't have to call them Aunt Sharon or Aunt Donna."

"Sharon is married to Carmen, right? And Donna is

Vincent's wife."

"See, you know. I'm not sure if Bobby or Brian will be there. I doubt it, but you've met them. I know Vincent's kids won't be there. Grandpa and Grandma Keasling will be there. I'll introduce you to them. They're sweethearts. You'll like them."

Emmy kept quiet at the Keasling house. She let Mama introduce her to everyone, but then she stayed upstairs with Kristen and Derrick. She sat next to Mama while they ate.

Grandma Keasling stared at Emmy long enough to make Emmy uncomfortable before asking, "What year of high school are you, dear? I haven't heard a peep out of you the whole meal."

Emmy felt herself blushing as the whole family turned to stare at her. "I'm not in high school. I'm taking classes at Paul Frank, the junior college in town."

"Oh, I thought you and Tony were dating. Do you get to see him very often?"

"Not as often as I would like," Emmy replied softly as she looked at Kristen for help.

"Why aren't you going to Notre Dame then?"

"Grandma!" Kristen exclaimed. "Notre Dame is very expensive. Tony wouldn't be going there if he didn't have a scholarship."

"Is it more expensive than North Park or Arizona?" Grandma asked.

Daniel Keasling said, "You know it is, Mother. Would someone pass the mashed potatoes, please?"

Emmy realized that everyone at the table had grown up in families where money had always been plentiful. Even Mama lived comfortably while she raised her kids. She never had to leave the house to get a job. Emmy felt a little out of her element even though she and Kristen were best friends. After dinner, Emmy disappeared upstairs with Kristen.

Kristen realized Emmy felt downcast and tried to lift her spirits. "Grandma sometimes speaks her mind without thinking about the consequences. She didn't mean any harm."

Emmy lay on Kristen's bed waving a tennis racquet. "I know, but she made a valid point. Maybe I should try to get in to a

73

different college."

"North Park does offer some financial aid packages. Is that Derrick's?"

"Yeah, I grabbed it from downstairs." She sat up and moved to the edge of the bed. "I know. I checked. It's not that easy though. They don't offer as much as other places. Kenny wants me to go to North Park full-time."

"Did he offer to pay for it?" Kristen knew he probably had.

"You know he offered, and you know my answer, so don't go there."

"You are the most stubborn person I have ever met."

"Thank you. I'll take that as a compliment. Let's play tennis."

"It is November, Em. It might be just a tad cool."

"That sucks!"

"Tony told me that you guys are going to a wedding together. Anyone I know?" Kristen took the tennis racquet away from Emmy. "You're going to break something if you keep swinging that around."

Emmy explained about the wedding.

"Did you tell Kenny?"

"Not yet, but I will. Sometime. He told me to see other people."

"So you asked Tony?"

Emmy plopped back onto her back on Kristen's bed. "I feel safe with him."

Tony and Heather came home on the morning of Sean's wedding. He dropped off Heather, said a quick hello to Mama, and then flew out the door.

"I'm making lunch so you bring Emmy right over," Mama hollered out the door.

"I will."

A few minutes later he arrived at Emmy's house. He bounded up the front steps and knocked.

"Emmy! Tony's here," Diane yelled as she opened the door. "She'll be down in a minute. How's everything going at school?"

74

He explained about finals as he sat on the couch. A couple of minutes later they heard Emmy as she galloped down the stairs.

"I'm ready to go."

"Geez, Em, you sounded like a herd of elephants coming down the stairs," Tony teased.

"I know you're not telling me that I'm fat." She tossed a small overnight bag at him. "Will you throw this in the car?"

He stood up. "Sure."

"Emmy! Where is your dress? You can't wear jeans and a sweatshirt to the wedding," Diane said.

"Ooops! I almost forgot it." She stomped up the stairs making as much noise as possible. She grabbed her dress and silently came back downstairs. "Was that better?"

"Get out of here." Diane shook her head. "Have fun. I'll see you... whenever."

"I'm coming home tonight," Emmy said.

Diane smiled. "We'll see."

For once Tony opened the car door for Emmy. She smiled at him as she slid in. She reached into the back seat and hung up her dress as Tony got into the car and pulled away.

"I like that dress. Is it new?"

"It's fairly new. You probably haven't ever seen it." She fiddled with the radio until she tuned in WSHO, the local SoHam rock station. "Just so you know I'm not still mad at you for... tickling... me that night, but that doesn't mean you can tickle me again."

"I understand. I won't touch you unless we're dancing. By the way, Mama is making lunch, and she wants to make sure you eat enough," Tony mentioned as he drove back home.

"She's always after me to eat more."

"That's just her way, Em. You know she loves you and means well."

After lunch, Emmy got ready for the wedding. She came downstairs and walked into the living room where Mama and Heather were reading.

"You look very pretty in that dress, Emmy. Is it new?" Heather asked.

"Yes, I found it on sale at Penney's."

"It looks very nice, but it's a little short. You need to be careful." Mama pointed her finger at Emmy's legs.

Tony smiled as he admired her legs. "I don't think it's too short."

"You would think that." Heather frowned at Tony.

"I will, Mama. That's why I'm wearing pantyhose. I usually hate to wear them. But I figured I should today."

"Well, you have a good time at the ceremony and reception. Make sure you dance with Tony a lot. He's a good dancer, you know."

"I know, Mama. You made sure of that."

At the wedding Emmy spoke briefly to Sean's brothers, Ronan and his wife and Patrick and his fiancee.

Mrs. O'Brien gave Emmy a big hug when she saw her. "Emmy, it's so good to see you, child. How have you been?"

"I've been fine. This is Tony Bertucci, Mrs. O'Brien."

"Nice to meet you, young man."

"It's nice to meet you, too, Mrs. O'Brien. Emmy has told me how much she enjoyed living in your apartment."

"I wish all tenants were as pleasant as Emmy. We miss you."

Emmy looked around and saw Scott Simmons with a woman. He saw Emmy and walked over to talk to her.

"Hello, Emmy. This is Naomi Nieds. Naomi, this is my friend, Emmy Colasanti." The two ladies exchanged pleasantries and then Naomi left to powder her nose.

"I hope you didn't mind that I gave Sean your address."

"I didn't mind. I've moved around so much. A lot of friends have lost track of me."

"Are you on the lamb? Runnin' from the law? Trying to remain off the grid again, huh?" Scott teased.

"Not exactly," she answered. "Did you meet Naomi at church?"

"Yes, I did, and we have been dating, but nothing more, if you know what I mean."

"Good for you."

Emmy danced with different guys at the reception when Tony needed to take a break. Several of the guys wanted to dance with her, but Tony intimidated them, so only the bravest actually asked her to dance. During one song, Emmy danced with Patrick O'Brien while Tony danced with other girls. Patrick held her very close. When his hands started to slip down her hips, she pushed them back up to where they belonged. After the song faded out, she pulled him into the hallway ready to put him in his place.

"Patrick, what were you doing? You're here with your fiancee yet you're dancing with me like I was your girlfriend."

"Sorry, Emmy, I'm just happy to see you again."

"Well, I'm not that happy to see you. It was all I could do to keep from slugging you."

Sean had seen Patrick with Emmy and brought Patrick's girlfriend with him. His fiancee grabbed Patrick's tie and used it as a leash to pull him along. He followed his girlfriend back inside with his tail between his legs, and he didn't bother Emmy anymore. Sean stayed in the hallway with Emmy.

"I'm sorry about that, Emmy," Sean said. "Patrick can be a handful sometimes. How have you been? It's really good to see you again. Tony's a really nice guy—maybe a little intimidating because of his size, though."

"He is, Sean. He's a good friend."

"Are you saying he's just a friend now?"

"Yeah, I don't think I have a boyfriend at the moment."

Sean knew there had to more to the story, but he didn't pry. They started talking and catching up on less personal things. Sean explained how he injured his shoulder and received a medical discharge. Leah, Sean's new wife, joined them.

"Leah, this is Emmy Colasanti. She used to live in the apartment at my folks' place."

"It's nice to meet you, Leah. Your dress is gorgeous. Sean is very lucky to have met you."

"Thank you, Emmy. I'm sorry, but I need to drag Sean away to meet my aunt and uncle before they leave. Will you excuse us?"

"Certainly," Emmy said.

Before the party broke up, Sean asked Emmy to dance, it

just happened to be a slow song.

"I remember the night we were together before you went into the army, Sean. I remember that you tried to kiss me, but I didn't let you."

"I remember how disappointed I was, but we did have a lot of fun together, didn't we?"

"I remember I said a prayer each night for a few days after you left. I never told you that before, did I?"

"No, you never mentioned that in your letters. Thank you for writing me, Emmy. I'm sorry I wasn't better at returning letters."

When the song finished Sean gave her a hug. "It was really good to see you again, Emmy."

"You, too, Sean. Let's stay in touch." She doubted it would happen because he had not returned her letters after he met Leah.

Tony found her, and they spent the remaining few minutes of the reception dancing together. In spite of the difference in their size, they danced well together.

On the way to the car after the reception, Tony asked, "Should I take you straight home?"

"Do you think Mama would mind if I crashed at your house? I want to talk to Heather before you guys leave."

"Mama won't mind. She put clean sheets on the bed in Marco's room."

Mama didn't mind letting Emmy crash, but she pointed to the phone. "You should call your sister and let her know you're staying here."

"I think she already knows, Mama."

"You call her, anyway. Just to make sure."

"Yes, Mama." Emmy clenched her jaw, but did as instructed.

Diane answered the phone with, "I told you so."

"I'm only staying so I can talk to Heather in the morning."

"And you couldn't do that over the phone?" Diane asked sarcastically.

"Good night. I'll talk to you when I get back." Emmy hung up abruptly.

Mama smiled and hugged Emmy. "That wasn't so hard, was it?"

Emmy forced a smile. *If Diane gets on my case about staying here, I'm going to slug her.*

Emmy had a chance to talk to Heather in the morning. Heather kept very busy working on her doctorate in internal medicine and didn't get home very often, but she had this weekend off, so she came home. Emmy asked a bunch of questions about medicine and Heather's job at the hospital.

"Have you always wanted to be a doctor?" Emmy asked.

Heather answered, "When I started high school I wanted to be a nurse. By the time I graduated, I knew I wanted to be a doctor."

Emmy asked, "Why aren't there any pictures of Marco downstairs except as a kid? There are pictures of everybody else as an adult, but not Marco."

"There used to be pictures of Marco, but one day he and Mama had an argument. Marco moved out and took all the pictures of him just to be mean."

"I don't mean to pry, but why doesn't Marco ever come home?"

"Marco has always been, well, almost an outsider in his own family. He and Tony have never really gotten along since they were teenagers. Not because Tony hasn't tried, but Marco refused to get along with Tony. They used to fight all the time."

"Is Marco the same size as Tony?"

"No, although Tony is younger, he was always bigger and stronger, and Marco resented that. Marco always tried to prove he was tougher or stronger than Tony. It got really bad after Marco got hurt in an accident. He might have died if not for Tony."

"What happened?" Emmy's eyes grew big.

"Tony prevented Marco from bleeding to death until the ambulance got here, but for some reason instead of becoming closer, this drove them farther away from each other."

"That's so sad," Emmy replied. "Tony has never said a word about that to me."

79

"He doesn't like to talk about it. Marco missed so much school that year that he had to repeat one semester. Tony had football to focus on, but Marco just seemed lost. He got into trouble at school, which was totally out of character for him, and hung out with rather some wild kids for awhile. I don't remember all of them, but I think one of them might have been named Delaney."

Emmy's eyes opened wide.

"Yes, I think it was Delaney. Todd Delaney, perhaps," Heather said.

Emmy shuddered involuntarily as she thought about Todd Delaney. *Is it possible that Marco was one of the guys that bullied me?*

Chapter Nine

This holiday season Fridays At Five played concerts up through December twenty-third. Playing so close to Christmas upset Emmy so she emailed Andy Walker.

"Mr. Walker, as the de-facto president of the Fridays At Five International and Interplanetary Fan Club, I must strongly object to the fact you are making the guys play right up to Christmas Eve. I suggest in the future you take measures to remedy this situation.

Sincerely,
Emily Olivia Colasanti, President.

He emailed her back.
"Valued FAF Fan,
Thank you for your letter and your interest in Fridays At Five. The guys in the band appreciate your loyal support. I have enclosed a free bumper sticker and an autographed photo of myself.

With deepest respect,
Andrew Walker, president of Walker Management, Inc.
P.S.
Emmy, you know that the Prater-Saylor Agency handles the booking so please direct your wrath toward them. I'm sorry he has been on the road so much, sweetie. I know how much you miss him, and I promise it won't happen again.

Love,
Cousin Andy

Emmy giggled as she read Andy's reply. She could picture him laughing as he wrote it.

Tony could only spend a couple of days at home during the holidays. Notre Dame suffered only two defeats during the football season and would play Oregon State in the Fiesta Bowl on January first. Coach Theismann rewarded the players for their hard work during the season by giving them a few days off. Tony took advantage of the free time and headed home for Christmas, which pleased Mama and also Emmy. Tony finished practice on Saturday morning and drove home as soon as he could get away. He didn't have to be back at school until Tuesday evening. The weather forecast predicted snow, so Tony wondered how bad the roads would be. The weathermen were wrong, as usual, and Tony made it home without incident. An hour later the snow started falling in SoHam. Emmy happened to be sitting in the living room with Mama when he arrived.

"Hello. Anybody here?"

"We're in here, son," Mama answered.

Emmy ran to the kitchen and jumped into his arms. She wrapped her arms around his neck and hung on tightly without saying a word.

"Does this mean you are happy to see me, Em?"

"Not at all. I saw a mouse run across the floor, and I didn't want it to get me."

She jumped down as Mama walked in the kitchen and smiled at them.

"I'm happy to see you made it home safely. I need a hug."

Tony gave his mother a hug and lifted her off her feet.

"Put me down. You will hurt yourself."

Tony turned to Emmy and asked, "Will you help me bring things in from the car. I've got more than I can handle."

Emmy grabbed her coat, went outside with Tony and helped unload the car. "What's all this stuff?" Emmy asked as she looked in the trunk.

"John gave me all these old records. They belonged to his parents. I thought maybe Kenny would like to see them. There might be something valuable in here."

"Who's John?" Emmy asked, as she pulled out a record.

"My roommate," Tony said as he unloaded his suitcases.

"Oh, right. The guy you tried to set me up with." She held out the record to Tony. "Hank Williams. Are you serious?"

"Hey, I didn't say they belonged to John." Tony took the record from Emmy and glanced at it. "Mama might like this one."

"Give me a break. She hates country music." She pulled another album from the box. "Show her this one. She likes Tony Bennett."

Tony took the album from Emmy.

"Does he have a girlfriend yet?"

"Who?"

"John, you dork! Who do you think I meant?" She shook her head.

"He dates pretty regularly, but he's not real serious about any one girl. Are you interested now? Did you break up with Kenny?" Tony closed the trunk, then picked up Emmy and set her down on the trunk lid.

"I'm not interested in dating a guy three hours away."

"And...?"

Emmy leaned back and used her hands to balance herself. "We didn't exactly break up, but if you have to know, we kinda put our relationship on hold for the time being. I was going to tell you at Sean's wedding, but I didn't have a chance. Neither one of us is ready to get married or anything."

"You are kinda young to get married."

"My mother got married at seventeen," Emmy said.

"Mama was nineteen when she married my father." Tony put a foot on the bumper. "What would you say if he asked you to marry him right now?"

"That's not gonna happen, so I don't even think about it." Emmy scooted forward as she tried to get down. Tony blocked her way. "Let me down," she said sternly.

"Are you mad at me now?"

"No, but I don't want to talk about Kenny."

Tony raised his arms in surrender. "Fine. Be that way."

Emmy hung around for awhile, and then headed home.

Emmy woke up early on Christmas Eve and drove over to the Colwell home. She parked in the driveway instead of putting the car in the garage. She decided to go in the house first and see Mr. and Mrs. Colwell.

"Merry Christmas, almost."

"Merry Christmas, Emmy. It's good to see you." Mrs. Colwell hugged her.

"Is he home yet?"

"He's out in the carriage house. Probably sleeping. I heard him arrive around five. You can go see him. I'm sure he'd rather see you than sleep all day. Do you have your key?"

"Yeah, I've got my key. I'll run out there and wake him up." Emmy turned to leave.

"Elly, aren't you forgetting to tell Emmy something?" Mr. Colwell asked his wife.

Emmy stopped and turned around. She looked at Mr. Colwell, and then at Mrs. Colwell. She had an idea what he meant.

Mrs. Colwell lifted her eyes toward the second floor. "Becky is upstairs in a guest room."

Emmy bit her lip as she looked up. "Oh, I wasn't sure he would bring her, but I did think it was a possibility. Is she nice?"

"We only saw her briefly, Em," Mrs. Colwell said as she put her hands on Emmy's shoulders.

"I'll go see him for a moment and come back in the house."

"Be careful on the sidewalk. It's a little slick." Mr. Colwell cautioned Emmy by moving his hand in a sliding motion.

Emmy laughed as she slipped and slid her way to the carriage house. She opened the service door and tiptoed up the stairs. She quietly opened the door to the apartment. She could see Kenny on the futon still dressed but sound asleep. She slipped off her coat and her shoes and walked over to the futon. She lay down beside him with her back to him and moved his arm over her.

Kenny yawned then said, "Merry Christmas, Em."

"How did you know it was me and not Becky?"

"A couple of ways. Becky is a little bigger than you, and she's never been in bed with me before."

"That's good to know." Emmy turned on her other side to face him. "Is it all right that I'm here?"

"Yes, I'm happy to see you. What time is it?"

"It's about eight thirty. You can go back to sleep. I just wanted to see you for a little bit."

"Are you going to stay?"

"I need to get home. I don't want to bother you since Becky is here." She moved her foot onto his leg.

"Don't you want to meet her?"

"Maybe later. What are your plans for tomorrow?" She moved her foot up his leg.

Kenny knew what she wanted. "Don't, Em." He grabbed her foot and moved it off of his leg. "I know Mom wants to go see Grandma, but other than that, nothing." He brushed her hair off of her face, then put a fingertip on the end of her nose. "I'm so happy to be home."

"I'm happy you're home, too." She grinned as she touched his whiskers. "I need to see my parents in the morning. They know Tony is home and want to see him. I might drag him over there."

"Maybe we can stop over there for a little bit."

"Okay, I'll go talk to your Mom, but then I'm heading home. Will you tell Becky I jumped in bed with you?"

"It's not like we were really in bed."

Emmy leaned over and kissed him. "You can tell her that I kissed you, and we made love for an hour." Emmy giggled as she got off the futon.

Kenny raised up on his elbow and shook his head as he watched her leave. "I do still care for you, Em," he whispered, but she couldn't hear him.

Emmy ran back toward the house and slid for twenty feet on the ice. She talked to Mrs. Colwell for a few minutes before heading home. She finished wrapping her gifts, and started cleaning the house. *As long as I keep busy, I won't have time to think about Kenny and Becky.* She planned to have dinner with Kristen at her house.

Later that evening, Tony and Mama arrived at the Keasling home at the same time as Emmy. Tony noticed the purple ribbon holding her hair in a ponytail and tugged on it.

"Stop that! You better behave."

"I like that bow, Em."

Emmy brought in her gifts, set them in the family room and removed her coat. "Merry Christmas, Mrs. Keasling. Where's Kristen? I need to talk to her."

85

"She's in her room, Emmy. Go on up." Mrs. Keasling took Emmy's coat. "That sweater looks very nice. Is it new?"

"Thanks, but it's not new." Emmy flew up the stairs, ran into Kristen's room and jumped onto her bed. "Kenny's home, and he brought Becky. I went over to see him and got in bed with him."

"Emmy! You did what?" Kristen stopped brushing her long, blonde curls. "What do you mean?"

"Oh, not like that. He was in his apartment on the futon and I cuddled with him. We were both dressed."

"Was Becky with him?"

"No, thank God. She was sleeping in the house in one of the guest rooms, so I didn't meet her."

"Duh! I didn't think you would cuddle with Kenny if she was on the futon, too. Are they coming over here tonight? Did you invite them?"

"No, but they might come over to my parents' house tomorrow. I don't know how I will react to meeting her."

"I know she's pretty because Kenny would never date any girl who wasn't—except you, of course," Kristen teased.

"Very funny, Kristen. What's Derrick doing? Is he in his room?"

"I think he's studying. He left strict orders that I not disturb him under any circumstances." Kristen grinned as she added, "Of course, he didn't say anything about you."

"Let's go disturb him," Emmy suggested.

They hurried down the hall to his room and walked right in. They saw Derrick on the couch reading.

"I told you not to..."

"You didn't say anything about me disturbing you, just Kristen," Emmy said as she sat on the couch.

Kristen stood behind the couch and looked over his shoulder. "What are you reading?"

"The most boring textbook ever written. I give up. I need a break." Derrick closed the book, grabbed Emmy's arm and pulled her closer to him. "Merry Christmas, Em. Can I have a kiss?"

"No way. Kissing you is like kissing my brother, if I had one." Emmy squirmed to get away.

"I guess I will have to kiss Kristen then."

"Over your dead body." Kristen backed away. "You should have brought a girlfriend home with you like Kenny did if you want to be kissed."

Derrick and Emmy looked at Kristen, and she realized what she said. "I didn't mean it like that, Em. I'm sorry."

"Did Kenny bring someone with him?" Derrick asked.

"Yes, and her name is Becky. I'll probably meet her tomorrow." Emmy glared at Kristen.

After dinner, Emmy talked to Tony alone. She bounced on her toes and looked at the floor. "I'm sorry if I was rude to you the other day."

"That's all right. I didn't take it personally." He tenderly placed his hands on her shoulders.

She raised her head and bit her lip. "What are you doing in the morning? Could you go with me to visit my parents? They've been asking about you. They seem to like you for some reason. I certainly don't." She allowed a grin to slowly form.

"I'm not doing anything, so I guess I could go with you." He squeezed her shoulders. "What time?"

"Probably around ten. I can pick you up if you want."

"All right, but I'll drive."

"That's okay. I need to put gas in Kenny's car."

"You will owe me."

She poked him in the stomach and said, "Yeah, okay, I know what a pleasure it is to see my parents."

On Christmas morning Emmy brought Tony over to see her parents. Diane arrived a moment later without Craig. It only took five minutes to open the gifts, and after that, everyone sat quietly in the living room. Emmy asked her mother and sister questions to start a conversation, but received simple answers followed by icy silence. Tony tried to help, but with no better success. The thick tension between Diane and her parents permeated the room. Emmy shrugged her shoulders and gave up. Then the doorbell rang.

"I'll get it," Diane said as she got up to answer the door. "Kenny Colwell. How are you? Come on in."

"Merry Christmas, Diane," Kenny said and then walked into the house as Becky followed.

Emmy looked up at Tony. The dreaded moment had arrived. She got up and moved toward Kenny. "Merry Christmas, Kenny. I'm so glad to see you." Emmy hugged Kenny and then she saw Becky.

"Emmy, I want you to meet Becky Morrison. Becky, this is Emmy."

Becky shook hands with Emmy. "I've heard so much about you, Emmy. I'm glad I finally get to meet you."

Emmy tried to be happy for Kenny when he first told her about Becky, but really her heart had shattered. She wasn't sure what to do now. She bit her lip, then looked at Becky and thought, *You look like Julia Roberts. No wonder Kenny likes you.*

Becky looked at Emmy for a few seconds before shifting her gaze to Kenny. *You really do look young like Kenny said.*

Emmy decided that she liked Becky, so she gave her a big hug. "Becky. I'm so glad you're here. Come and sit by me. Oh, this is my friend, Tony Bertucci."

Tony stood up and shook Becky's hand. He gave Kenny a high-five. "I've got some records out in the car that my roommate gave me. I thought you might like to take a look at them."

"Sure. I like going through old records," Kenny answered.

"I'll bring them over to the house before we leave. Is it okay if I leave them out in the carriage house?"

"Of course. Do you need any help?" Kenny asked.

"Nah, I can handle it."

"I'll leave the door open for you. Thanks, Tony."

"No need to leave the door unlocked I've got my key." Emmy didn't think how that might sound to Becky.

Emmy and Becky sat beside each other on the couch. Tony grabbed a couple of chairs from the dining room for him and Kenny to use. Mom and Dad remained in their recliners drinking their eggnog and rum, and Diane sat with Emmy and Becky.

"Kenny told me that you've been friends for a long time."

"Yes, I was seven when we met. Were you born in California?" Emmy asked.

"Yes, I'm actually a native. I've always lived in Los Angeles. Studio City, actually."

Soon Emmy and Becky were chatting away like they'd known each other forever. Emmy told Becky how she first met Kenny and other stories from their childhood.

After thirty minutes Kenny mentioned, "We need to get going. I promised Mom we would go with them to see Grandma."

Kenny and Becky got up to leave. Emmy hugged Becky again and walked them to the door. She looked at Kenny, and he hugged her tightly.

He whispered in Emmy's ear, "Just because I'm with Becky right now doesn't mean I don't love you anymore, Emmy."

Emmy smiled, and Kenny held her close.

"We will always love each other in our way, Kenny."

After Kenny and Becky left, Diane ran out the back door as if the house was on fire. As far as she was concerned, she had done her daughterly duty. Tony and Emmy stayed for another hour, but then needed to get to Mama's. Tony pulled into the alley, and he carried the records into the carriage house and upstairs. Emmy helped with one box. Emmy looked over to the wall at the old couch. She had never told Tony why Kenny kept the old couch. She smiled and Tony noticed.

"What are you smiling about?" he asked.

"Nothing. I'm just happy because it's Christmas, and Kenny is home."

"You still mean a lot to him, Emmy. I can tell. You don't need to be jealous of Becky."

"I'm not. I have Kristen for my friend, then there's you." She looked at Tony and stuck out her tongue.

"I should hang you from the ceiling in here and leave you." He smiled as he threatened her.

"You better not!" Emmy squealed as she bolted down the stairs. "Make sure the door is locked," she hollered from the bottom of the stairs.

They drove to Tony's house. Mama had prepared a ton of food to take to the Keaslings. Emmy and Tony got back in time to help load the car with the food and presents. Heather made it home, but a snowstorm stranded Marco in Baltimore.

"Do you mind if I drive Emmy over to Uncle Daniel's?" Tony asked his mother.

"Heather can drive me. That way you and Emmy can leave whenever you want."

When they got to the Keasling's home, Emmy ran upstairs to see Kristen without saying hello to anyone. She ran into her room, jumped on the bed, again, and nearly landed on Kristen, who was talking on the phone.

"I gotta go. Emmy is here, and I can tell she has some important news to share. Merry Christmas, Christopher." Kristen hung up. "Okay, what are you so anxious to tell me? As if I don't already know."

"I met Becky today."

"How did that go? Do you like her? Does she seem nice?"

"She is really nice, Kristen. She reminds me of Julia Roberts except she's better built."

"You're such a goof, Em."

Emmy plopped onto her back. "I tried hard not to like her at first, but she is so nice, and Kenny loves her."

"Really? How can you tell?" Kristen moved closer and looked down at Emmy.

"I just can." Emmy bit her lip, as she looked up at Kristen.

"Are you disappointed that Kenny has a girlfriend?"

"I would be lying if I said I wasn't a little disappointed, but I'm happy for them. After all I have you and Tony. You are the best friends ever."

Kristen held out her arms and Emmy sat up. "It's all right, Em. You can cry if you need to."

So she did.

Chapter Ten

Emmy watched everyone as they dashed back and forth through the house. *Christmas Day at the Keaslings is busier than Kohl's on Christmas Eve.*

The decorated, artificial tree reached to the ten-foot-high ceiling in the family room with presents piled all around it. Christmas tunes played on the intercom system throughout the house. Karla and Mama kept busy in the kitchen making sure all the food stayed warm. Kristen and Emmy carried the food into the dining room. Eventually, everything was ready and Mama called everyone to the table. Eight people sat around the table. Daniel and Karla sat at the ends. Mama sat on one side with Kristen and Heather. Emmy was across from Mama between Derrick and Tony.

As Emmy passed Derrick the sweet potatoes she asked, "How much longer are you gonna be in Arizona?"

"I've got one more semester to go, and then it's off to law school. I've been accepted at the James E. Rogers College of Law. I won't even have to move out of my apartment."

"Is that a good school?" Tony asked.

"It's not Notre Dame, but it's not North Park College, either." Derrick took a swipe at Kristen's school.

"Hey! There's nothing wrong with North Park."

"They let you in, so how prestigious can it be?"

Kristen tried to kick Derrick under the table but nailed Emmy instead.

"Ow! Kristen, did you just kick me?"

"Oh, Emmy, I'm so sorry. I was trying to get Derrick. Are you all right?"

"I think you broke my ankle," Emmy said.

Mama looked at them sternly. "Are you going to behave like adults, or do I have to make you eat in the kitchen?"

Emmy and Kristen giggled. "We will behave... for now."

After everyone ate their fill, cleared the table, put away the leftovers and placed the dishes in the dishwasher, Mr. Keasling announced, "I think it must be time to open the gifts. Santa Claus took a long time to deliver everything you wanted, Kristen."

"Oh, Daddy. You say that every year. You do realize I don't believe in Santa Claus anymore, right?"

"Sssh, Krissy, how can you say that in front of Emmy? She still believes in... you know who," Derrick teased, as he put an arm around Emmy's shoulders.

Emmy poked him in his side. "I do not."

"Since when?"

"Since two years ago," Emmy said and then giggled.

Everyone made their way into the family room and found a place to sit. Kristen made sure there were even gifts for Emmy under the tree. Derrick and Kristen tossed wrapping paper at each other and teased each other constantly.

Mama patted Emmy's leg as they sat together on the couch. "They still act the same as when they were kids."

"I think it's special that they're so close. I wish Diane and I had a better relationship."

Once the gifts were all opened, everyone gathered around the dining room table again to play games. They chose to play Trivial Pursuit and decided on the teams. Heather, Mama, Daniel and Karla made up the *older* team leaving the younger people to form the opposition.

Mama said, "I won't be any help to our team, Heather. It will be up to you to beat these young college kids."

Mama surprised everyone by answering more questions than she expected.

After playing games for two hours, Tony and Derrick got up from the table.

"Aunt Karla, is there anything left to eat?"

"Not much, Tony. You and Derrick ate almost everything."

Tony's jaw dropped, and he looked so disappointed.

"I'm kidding, Tony. God, you're so gullible at times. You know your mother brought enough food to last all week. It's in the fridge, and there's more in the garage. You can help yourselves. Maria and I are finished for the day. We are going to take a nap. Save some for the girls, okay."

Tony and Derrick started emptying out the fridge. Heather, Kristen and Emmy watched as the guys filled up their plates again.

92

"Are you going to leave any for us?" Heather asked.

"There's enough left, as long as Emmy doesn't eat it all like she usually does," Tony said as he loaded more mashed potatoes onto his plate.

"I don't eat that much." Emmy smacked his arm.

Tony bent down and kissed her right on the mouth. She bit her lip because she wasn't sure she should let him kiss her like that.

"Sorry, Em," Tony whispered.

"It's all right. No one saw it."

Eventually, Emmy needed to head home. Tony pulled into the driveway, and they both jumped out. He walked her to the front door.

"Are you mad at me for kissing you? I kinda did it without thinking."

She stood on the first step and faced him. "I'm not mad. It's not like it's the first time we ever kissed, but I was surprised."

"I won't do it again unless you tell me I can." He heard the door open and saw Diane watching. "Are we gonna do anything tomorrow? I'll be here most of the day."

"We'll figure out something to do. I'll call you later." Emmy saw Diane as she turned and climbed the steps. She watched as Tony got in his car and drove away.

"Are you gonna stand out there, or are you coming inside?" Diane opened the storm door.

Emmy stepped inside. "I suppose you want to know how everything went today, huh?"

"I'm just wondering how you and Tony are getting along. I'm not trying to be nosy."

"We had fun... "

"Did he kiss you?"

"Wouldn't you like to know." Emmy grinned and gave away the answer.

The day after Christmas, Kenny and Becky picked Emmy up, and they headed over to the Bertucci home. Mama wanted to see Kenny and meet Becky. Tony didn't have to get back to school until the evening, so he still had a few hours to be at home. Derrick and Kristen arrived a few minutes earlier while Mama was busy in the kitchen making breakfast for everyone.

"Mama, this is Becky Morrison," Emmy said because Kenny stuck his nose over the stove smelling the delicious food.

"It's a pleasure to meet you, Becky."

"I'm thrilled to meet you... Mama... I almost said Mrs. Bertucci, but I've been instructed to call you Mama."

"Everyone does."

Becky smiled. "I've heard so much about you that I feel as if I already know you."

Tony moseyed into the kitchen and checked out the food.

"Morning, Kenny. Do you think this will be enough for breakfast?"

"I suppose," Kenny answered, "but what will everyone one else eat?"

Mama walked up behind them. "I know you two have large appetites, but you have to share."

Tony turned around and looked at the girls. Kristen, Becky and Emmy had their heads together and were giggling about something. He caught Emmy's eye and smiled at her. *I know I surprised you when I kissed you yesterday. I wonder if you're gonna let me kiss you again today.*

Emmy smiled shyly as she saw Tony looking at her. She bit her lip as she remembered the kiss from yesterday. *I hope you don't try to kiss me again today.* Then she turned her back to him and listened to Kristen and Becky talk about their brothers.

"What do you kids have planned for today?" Mama asked a few minutes later as everyone sat at the table eating.

"I need to study for four hours sometime today," Heather mentioned between bites. "I will do that this morning, but if you guys are around this afternoon I would be up for something."

Tony raised his eyebrows as he stared at Heather because it was out of character for her to socialize with his friends. "Anybody want to go over to Windsor Park for awhile?" Tony asked knowing Emmy would like that.

"That sounds like fun," Kenny said.

Everyone, except for Mama and Heather, decided to go to

94

Windsor Park. Tony and Derrick got two plastic sleds from the garage and an old plastic disc big enough for two people. They piled in the van, which Derrick had the foresight to drive. The foot of snow on the hill made for perfect sledding and they had fun climbing the hill and chasing each other down the slope.

Emmy thought about the first time Tony brought her to this park. It was their second date, and the day she fell in love with him. She watched Kenny and Becky. *You guys look like a perfect Hollywood couple.* He acted more maturely with Becky around. She listened as Derrick and Kristen teased each other and threw snowballs at everyone within range.

"What are you thinking about, Em?" Tony snapped her out of her daydream.

"I'm watching and listening to everyone." She wondered if he happened to be thinking about the first time he brought her here.

Tony gazed at the other people, and then turned to Emmy. "It's a little different compared to the first time we came here."

Now she knew his thoughts. "It's still fun to go sledding with you as long as you don't smash me."

They paused for a moment. She gazed into his eyes. Tony put his hands on her shoulders. She bit her lip. He leaned closer. She closed her eyes. His lips brushed hers. She backed away.

"No, Tony. Please don't kiss me in front of everyone." She turned to look at Kenny and Becky.

"I'm sorry, Em. I won't try it again."

After nearly an hour, Derrick complained to Tony, "This is no fun. I have to share a sled with Kristen."

Tony suggested they switch. "I'll share the sled with Kristen. I don't mind."

Tony and Kristen shared a sled and Derrick made a couple runs down the hill with Emmy.

Becky put her hands on her knees and looked up at Kenny. "I need to take a break."

"That's all right." Kenny asked, "Would you mind if Emmy and I have some fun together?"

"Go ahead. I just want to rest for awhile and watch you guys. I'm not used to the cold yet." Becky sat on a bench to watch.

Derrick used the disc while Kenny and Emmy shared the other sled. After a couple of runs down the hill, Derrick stopped and sat next to Becky. Kenny and Emmy used the disc and slid down the hill with reckless abandon. They crashed several times and ended up on top of each other in the snow. Becky laughed as she watched them. She knew that Kenny and Emmy shared a love for each other, and wasn't jealous at all.

Derrick mentioned to Becky as they looked up the hill. "Tony and Kristen are as close as could be. They have always been that way ever since I can remember. Does it seem strange to you?"

"Not at all. I have two brothers, and we have always been close." She smiled at Derrick as she studied his handsome face. *You and Kenny are both handsome but there is a difference. You look movie star handsome, and Kenny is rock star handsome.*

Derrick and Becky turned to look up the hill when they heard Emmy scream as she and Kenny started down the hill again.

Becky laughed. "I think Kenny loves Emmy so much because he never had a brother or sister, and she is the closest he has to a sibling. He has told me so many stories about her."

Derrick didn't say anything to Becky, but he knew that Kenny didn't think of Emmy as a sibling.

Just then Emmy and Kenny crashed into Tony and Kristen, and they all ended up in the snow together. They laughed and threw snowballs at each other.

Becky pointed at them as she laughed. "Look at them, Derrick. They're acting like little kids."

"I don't think Tony and Emmy will ever grow up. I hope they don't anyway," Derrick answered as he watched them throwing snowballs at each other. Tony ran after Emmy. Caught her and carried her over his shoulder as she giggled. They joined everyone else.

"Are you gonna behave now, Em?" Tony asked as he set her down.

She picked up some snow, formed it into a ball and threw it at Tony. He stepped out of the way and it hit Becky.

"Oh, Becky, I'm so sorry. I was trying to hit Tony," Emmy said as she covered her mouth.

Becky smiled and made her own snowball. She threw it at Emmy and hit her in the chest.

Emmy walked over and hugged Becky. "I guess we're even now."

Even little kids eventually get tired, so they piled into the van and headed back to Mama's.

"Is there anything to eat, Mama? We're all hungry. Especially Emmy," Tony hollered as he walked in the back door.

Mama had food ready for them and Emmy helped Mama get everything on the table. They sat at the kitchen table and Mama asked, "Did you have a good time at the park?"

They all tried to tell Mama about their day at the same time. Heather came downstairs to see what the racket was all about. Finally, they quieted down enough, and Derrick told Mama about the fun at Windsor Park. Kenny and Becky sat together and held hands while Derrick explained everything to Mama. Emmy saw them holding hands and caught Tony watching them, too. Tony looked at her and his expression suggested he wanted to hold her hand. Emmy moved her hands behind her back. *You can't hold hands with me in front of everyone.* She frowned at him.

Becky watched Emmy and Tony and whispered to Kenny, "She is even prettier than you told me she would be. I can see the love in her eyes every time she looks at Tony." Becky then added, "And she looks at you the same way, Kenny. Maybe not the same kind of love, but she loves you just the same."

"I know, and I love her, too." Kenny stole a glance at Emmy. *Are you and Tony going to try again? Maybe you should find someone new.*

The afternoon passed quickly, and Tony had to get back to school. Emmy helped him pack, then sat on his bed.

"You know if you guys wouldn't win so many games you wouldn't have to go back to school. You could stay here with me."

Tony looked at Emmy to see if she was kidding. She kept a straight face.

"Em, you know..."

"Gotcha! I know you want to win every game. I was teasing you, and you fell for it."

97

"You're gonna get it, Emmy."

Tony quickly moved over to his bed and pushed Emmy onto her back. She looked up at him as her feet dangled over the edge of the bed. He leaned over and kissed her. She wrapped her arms around him and kissed him back.

"Ahem."

Emmy let go of Tony. They looked toward the doorway and saw Mama standing there. Tony released his hold on her, and she fell onto the bed.

"What do you think you are doing?" Mama asked in a rather stern tone with her hands on her hips.

"Nothing, I wanted to make sure he packed everything." Emmy pushed his hand away as she scrambled to sit up.

"Well, don't take too long to pack. He needs to get going soon." Mama closed the door and smiled as she left.

Kristen called Emmy the next evening, "What are you gonna do this week?"

"I have to work. Why?"

"Well, my parents took Mama up to the cabin in Wisconsin. They'll be there all week. We're gonna have a party on Sunday. Will you be all right if I invite Kenny and Becky?"

"Sure. They're actually taking me out for dinner tonight. I like Becky, and I hope we can be friends after she goes home."

Emmy went to the New Year's Eve party, but Tony was in Arizona for his Fiesta Bowl game. Kristen invited Tess Easterly and Jenna Rowe over and they brought friends. Kristen also invited Christopher Braun—they had dated a few times. Christopher brought his brother Randy. Derrick invited Clarissa Morgan and her boyfriend to come over. Kenny and Becky arrived shortly after Emmy. Soon the house was filled with the laughter and conversations of college-age kids.

Emmy stood next to Kristen watching the scene as they sipped on their punch. "Have you been watching how your college friends are fawning over Kenny?"

"Some of them have never met him. You do realize that he's

a famous rock star, don't you?" Kristen chuckled.

"I suppose so, but he can be such a dork at times," Emmy smiled as she heard him do his lame Groucho Marx impression.

They played some music so they could dance. Randy Braun checked the liquor cabinet, but, to his dismay, found it locked. Derrick did have two bottles of champagne ready to celebrate with later. Some of the girls dressed up in fancy dresses. Kristen wore a dress, but Emmy and Becky wore jeans.

"Were you a tomboy growing up?" Emmy asked Becky.

"Most definitely. I've got two older brothers, and I tried to do everything they did. Kenny told me you were just the same, except you didn't have any brothers."

"I still like jeans and shorts better than fancy dresses."

"It doesn't matter, Emmy. You are still so pretty even in your comfortable jeans."

"Why, thank you, Becky, and you look pretty good yourself, if I may say."

Emmy and Becky hung out together at the party while the guys danced with all the other girls.

Derrick opened the champagne just before midnight. They counted down the new year, and then toasted each other. Emmy stood next to Kenny and Becky as the countdown started. Kenny and Becky kissed at the start of the new year. Then Kenny turned to Emmy and kissed her.

"Happy New Year, Emmy. I know you'd rather be kissing Tony, but since he's not here, I thought I would take his place."

"You know I like kissing you, Kenny, but did you have to use your tongue with Becky standing right here?" Emmy teased.

Kenny turned to Becky, who was laughing.

"I wasn't using any tongue, Becky."

"I know how you rock stars are." Becky poked his chest. "You think you can get away with everything."

Emmy saw Christopher Braun looking at her. They smiled at each other. Emmy bit her lip as he walked toward her. She left her friends to meet him. *What are you going to do, Christopher?* She thought about the time Kristen set her up on a blind date with his friend, Dean Rogen. *I wonder if you remember that night. I hope you don't remember that I was more attracted to you than your friend. I can't even think of his name now.*

"Hi, Emmy. Are you having a good time?" Christopher asked as he smiled. *I wonder how she would react if I kissed her. It is New Year's after all.*

"It's a great party."

"Are you here by yourself? I see that Kenny is with someone, and I haven't seen Tony."

"He's in Arizona for the game," she said then turned to look at Kenny. "That's Becky Morrison with Kenny. They met in LA."

Instead of kissing her, he gave her a friendly hug. He whispered, "I won't embarrass you by kissing you in front of everyone, but if we were alone, it would be a different story."

"Call me sometime," Emmy whispered back as she looked at his blonde hair and then into his gray eyes. *Oh God! Why did I say that? He just might go ahead and do it. I should ask Kristen if he's still involved with Victoria.*

Randy came over, smiled, and then hugged her. "Have a happy new year, Emmy."

"You too, Randy."

She sipped on a Dr Pepper and watched as Christopher mingled with the other guests. *His hair isn't as long as when I first met him. I bet he would never treat his date like one of the guys.*

Kristen walked over and touched Emmy's shoulder. "Who are you looking at, Em?"

Emmy jumped. "Geez! You startled me."

"So, who were you staring at? You were in your own little world." Kristen glanced around. "Oh, Christopher."

"I was not!" Emmy said indignantly.

"He's in a relationship, Em," Kristen said, but then realized. *Regardless, he would probably like to take you on a date.* Kristen hugged Emmy and kissed her on the cheek. "You should talk to him. He is charming and intelligent."

"I don't want to break up his relationship," Emmy said.

The party continued for another couple of hours before everyone left. Kenny and Becky were the last to leave. Emmy planned to spend the night at the house.

100

"Becky, I need to talk to Emmy before we leave," Kenny said.

"You want to talk to her in private, huh?" Becky asked. "Go ahead. I'll talk to Kristen."

"Thanks, I just need to say goodbye. I won't be long."

"I'll be waiting," Becky said.

Kenny grabbed her elbow and guided Emmy into the kitchen.

She leaned against the countertop, looked into his eyes and then bit her lip. "This isn't going to be good news, is it, Kenny?"

Kenny looked into her eyes for a few seconds. He hated to tell her his news. "We have to leave in the morning, Emmy. I won't get to see you again for some time."

"Why? I thought you were off for a month."

"The band is, but I'm going to go out to LA. Becky has two weeks off before school starts, and we want to spend some time together." Kenny felt hot all of a sudden.

Emmy stared at him for a moment and then forced a smile. "I understand. It's okay, Kenny."

"I'm sorry, Em. I feel as though I've betrayed you."

"Don't feel that way." Emmy shook her head. "We both knew we were going to see other people. I hope things work out for you and Becky. You know I still love you, though, and we'll always be there for each other."

"I don't deserve you. You are the most amazing person I know."

Kenny hugged Emmy and kissed her on the cheek as they parted.

"You better stay in touch, Kenny. It only takes a minute to send an email."

"You know I will, Emmy."

Chapter Eleven

Two weeks later, Emmy adjusted her purple stocking cap as she gazed at the latest fashions while walking slowly past the mall display windows of Teens Forever. She stopped when she heard someone calling her name.

"Emmy! Emmy! Wait up. Hang on a second."

Emmy looked around and saw someone she thought she knew, but couldn't remember her name.

"Hi, Emmy. Remember me? I'm Shannon Stephenson."

"I'm sorry..."

"We live in the same neighborhood. We played football once with LaRon Robinson and some other kids."

Emmy remembered her now. "Right. Hi, how are you?" Emmy only saw her the day they played football over a year ago.

"I'm doin' great. I'm working part-time at Sainsbury's and getting about twenty-five hours a week." Shannon suddenly grabbed Emmy's elbow. "Look at that outfit! Doesn't it look fabulous. I gotta have that."

Emmy did a double take. "You like that, huh?"

"It's so me!"

Emmy glanced at the outfit again and then checked out the orange streaks in Shannon's hair. "It is you." *That's the most hideous color I've ever seen. It's enough to make me sick to my stomach. I bet it even glows in the dark.*

"Emmy! They have it in lime green, too. I bet that would look fantastic on you. We should buy them. We would be like twins!" Shannon squealed.

I wouldn't wear that for a million dollars. Emmy shook her head and wandered away as Shannon window shopped.

"Hey! Wait up! I'll come back later and buy it if it goes on sale."

Shannon followed as Emmy looked in Marshall Field's for a pair of Tommy Hilfiger jeans.

"Check these out." Shannon held up a pair of white jeans. "I always buy my jeans a size or two small. The guys like 'em when they're outrageously tight."

102

"I'm looking for a pair of Ocean Wash boot cut jeans. Medium blue," Emmy said as she walked away.

Shannon followed and rambled on about her life even though Emmy wasn't really listening.

"Shane Nolan and I are sharing an apartment. He's working full-time for a construction company. I think it's called Cartouchi and Beasland, or something like that. I don't know. Shane is an apprentice electrician and making righteous dough." Shannon picked up a top. "This is outrageous! I'd never pay fifty bucks. Oh, I think it's Barrouchi and Keasland."

Who are you talking about, and it's Bertucci and Keasling Construction, and I'm not telling you that I know both families. Why don't you go away? Emmy didn't remember Shane Nolan and asked, "Do you and LaRon still see each other?"

"No, we only went out once or twice. I haven't seen him for a long time. I had another steady boyfriend for a few months, but we just broke up recently. I guess I'm not too lucky with boys. Haven't found the right one yet, but I'll keep trying. I love trying out new guys. It's simply outrageous what they will do if I smile and flirt with them."

Yeah, I bet you're good at getting what you want. Emmy remembered LaRon was going away to college.

"These shoes are outrageous! I wonder if they have my size."

Oh, God. I'm going to gag if you call another thing outrageous. Emmy headed toward the exit.

"What are you doing for the rest of the day?" Shannon asked.

"I don't have any plans, I guess. Why?" As soon as she said this, Emmy regretted it. *Shoot! I should have told her I had a lot of housework to do.*

"Do you wanna do something? Maybe I could come over to your place."

"I don't think so, Shannon. Anyway, I moved, and I don't live in Crest Ridge anymore."

"That's all right. I'd like to see where you live now." Shannon practically invited herself over.

103

Emmy didn't want to let Shannon know where she lived, but for some reason agreed to let her come over.

"All right, but I've got a lot of housework to do tonight."

"That's okay, I won't stay too long. Maybe we can order a pizza. I'll follow you home. Is it far from here?"

"No, it's not too far away," Emmy said. *Diane is going to kill me.*

Diane happened to be home and met Shannon. Shannon rambled on about her life, and Diane kept looking at Emmy.

"Who in the world is she? Why is she here? Did you invite her over?" Diane asked as Shannon used the bathroom.

"She kinda invited herself and followed me home. I don't really know her."

"Why on earth did you let her follow you home?" Diane made sure Shannon couldn't hear. "She's high on something. Did you know that?"

"No. How can you tell?"

"I can tell. You shouldn't have let her come over."

"I'm sorry. I didn't want to be mean and tell her no."

"You are too nice sometimes. You have to learn to be mean... and ruthless."

Shannon rejoined Emmy and Diane and began rambling about an event in her past. "It was like midnight and still over ninety degrees outside and humid. You know the kind of outrageous night where you sweat just because you're breathing. I had been drinking a few beers, not too many, maybe five or six, and I decided to go outside and have another one." Shannon waved her hands as she talked.

Emmy stared at Shannon. *Please shut up and go away.*

Diane frowned at Emmy. *This is your fault. Get rid of her.*

"Anyway, Shane and some friend of his saw me outside and came over with more beer. We sat on the table in the back and talked until four in the morning. I think we finished off a case of Miller."

"Quite a night, huh? Boy that sure sounds like fun, Shannon." Diane didn't mind having something to drink, but this girl got on her nerves. Diane thought about a way to get rid of

Shannon. "Oh, Emmy, look at the time. We're supposed to be over at the church for that special program? I almost forgot. We need to get going. Shannon would you like to come with us?"

Emmy looked at Diane quizzically. *Oh, I get it. Good one, Diane.*

"You're kidding, right? Do you really mean you're going to church?" Shannon asked.

"Yes, you'd be welcome to join us, but we need to leave right away." Diane grabbed her coat.

"Well, I should get home so I can see Shane. I'll see you around."

Shannon took off as if the devil was chasing her.

Emmy high-fived Diane. "Way to go. I'm so sorry I let her follow me home."

"It's all right. I doubt we will ever hear from her again," Diane said. "But in the future, you have to learn to say no."

"Yes, I can see that now. I think I've learned my lesson."

The cold winter months lasted forever, and a month later Diane suffered from a severe case of cabin fever.

"This cold weather is driving me nuts," Diane said as she stared out a window. "It's Saturday night. I've got to get out of here, Em. Do you want to go out and get a drink?" Diane asked.

"I can't. I'm not twenty-one yet."

"I think I'll call Fernando and see if he's busy."

Diane called Fernando, and he agreed to go out for a drink. He came over to their house and teased Emmy while he waited for Diane to do her face.

He looked at the book Emmy held in her hand. "I didn't know *One Of The Guys* was required reading for high school kids now. Have you read many books by that author?"

"I've read all his books, and I happen to like them. Would you like to read one?"

"No, thanks. I don't have time to read teen romance stories. I'm a mature adult."

"You mean you're an old fart." Emmy teased him back.

Diane walked into the room. "I'm ready to go. We might be

out late, Em. Don't wait up."

"Don't keep Fernando out too late. He might fall asleep."

Diane and Fernando stopped at Sally's Bar and Grille. They found a table and ordered drinks. A few minutes later, Shannon Stephenson waltzed past with an older man and recognized Diane. She didn't remember her name, but knew she looked familiar.

"I know you." Shannon pointed. "You're Emmy's roommate. Do you mind if we join you?"

Before Diane could object, Shannon and the man with her sat down.

"This is Gavin Rogers. He's married, but I don't care. He's outrageous!"

Gavin looked at Diane and smiled. Fernando introduced himself. Gavin ordered a round of drinks. An hour later, Diane and Shannon acted like they had been best friends forever. Fernando needed to leave, but Shannon and Gavin wanted to party some more.

Diane suggested to Shannon, "Why don't you follow us to my house, and we can party there?"

Gavin followed Fernando and pulled his Cadillac into the driveway behind Fernando's BMW.

Emmy sat in her recliner enjoying a quiet night at home reading her book and sipping some hot chocolate. The two cars pulling into the driveway broke her concentration. She heard several voices and looked out the window to see who might be with Diane and Fernando.

Oh, no! Not that girl. Diane, have you lost your mind? What have you done?

Diane and Shannon were talking loudly, and, from what Emmy could hear, she guessed they were both drunk. Diane opened the back door, and they staggered inside to the kitchen.

Diane asked Shannon, "Just how many have you had?"

"Eight or nine, I think. I can't remember for sure. Maybe even more. How about you?"

"Just three. No, wait. It's four now."

"Oh, come on. It's gotta be more than four, Diane."

"No, just four, Shannon."

"What are you talking about, Diane?" Emmy asked as she walked into the kitchen. "Are you talking about the number of drinks you've had tonight?" *You should know better, Diane.* Emmy glared.

Shannon laughed. "Drinks? We're talking about lovers. How many guys have you been with?"

The question first shocked, and then embarrassed Emmy. "I'm not talking about that to you."

"Em, you don't have anything to talk about. You're still a virgin." Diane slurred her words.

Emmy glared at Shannon and then Gavin. *Do I even know you?* "I think you should leave so I can get Diane to bed before she passes out. Fernando, will you stay and help me, please?"

"Sure, Emmy," he answered, more than a little embarrassed by Diane's condition.

"Whoa, Missy, I am not even close to passing out, and, if anybody needs to go to bed, it's you. You need to get laid," Diane said as she sat down clumsily at the kitchen table.

Emmy stood still and mute as if she has been turned to stone.

"Come on, Emmy. I'm sure Diane didn't mean what she said. It's just the alcohol talking."

Emmy frowned at Fernando. "How could you let her drink so much? I'm just as mad at you as I am her."

"I'm sorry. I didn't realize how many Long Island Iced Teas she drank." Fernando took Emmy by the hand and led her to the living room where they sat on the couch. Fernando put an arm around her shoulder. "She seemed all right until her last drink."

Gavin glanced around the kitchen and then looked at his watch and swore. "Gotta run. I enjoyed spending time with you, Diane."

Diane waved at Gavin as he headed out the door. "Call me soon. We can get together again."

"Hang on a minute, Gavin," Shannon called out to him. "You have to take me home."

Gavin put his arm around Shannon's waist, and then moved it down and playfully swatted her bottom. "Sure, Come on. I'll give you a lift."

Diane staggered into the living room and landed on the couch beside Emmy.

Fernando pointed a finger at Diane. "You need to apologize to your sister. That was a horrible thing to say to her, especially in front of everybody. Even if you don't realize it, you drank way too much tonight, and I am very disappointed by your behavior, Diane."

"Oh, screw you, Fernando. You're just a hypocrite. You've been after me since I first moved here. All you men are pigs and want nothing from us but sex."

"Are you finished, Diane? You're right. I have been attracted to you from the first time I met you, but I never hid that from you. I've been honest about my feelings and intentions. Maybe my intentions weren't totally honorable, but we are both single adults and able to make our own decisions. I apologized to Emmy and you should, too."

Diane shrugged her shoulders, closed her eyes and leaned back against the couch.

Fernando turned to Emmy. "I want to apologize again for my behavior tonight. I feel responsible for letting Diane drink too much. I should have stopped her before she became so intoxicated and said what she did to you. I hope you will forgive me."

Emmy looked at Fernando and shook her head. "Just shut up."

Fernando stood up. "Will you be all right, Emmy? I'm gonna head home now."

"I'll be okay, Fernando, thanks."

Fernando left, and Emmy shook her head as she looked at Diane. *You can sleep there all night for all I care, Diane.* Emmy headed upstairs to her bedroom. An hour later, she called Kristen to talk about Shannon and Diane. "I don't know what to do. I worry about Diane because she has been drinking too much, and she's acting so different. Tonight she and Fernando went to this bar, and she got plastered. Totally plastered! They must have run into that Shannon girl because she and this older guy followed Fernando and Diane to the house. Diane and Shannon were talking about

108

sex. I asked the guys to leave so Diane could go to bed and she yelled at me."

"What did she say, Emmy?" Kristen asked.

"She accused me of being a virgin like it was a disease or something, and then told me I needed to get laid," Emmy said and then started to cry.

"Emmy, don't cry. I'm sure Diane didn't mean what she said. She was probably just too drunk to realize what she was saying. You should try and get some sleep."

"I've been trying, but I'm just too wound up."

"Do you want me to come over and stay with you?"

"No, you don't have to. I feel better just to have been able to talk to you. I'll talk to you later."

"Good night, Em. I'm here if you need me."

Emmy fell asleep and worried about her sister. Diane woke up in the middle of the night, still on the couch. She tried to stand up, but fell back on the couch. She passed out again. In the morning Diane didn't remember the horrible things she said to Emmy.

Chapter Twelve

Emmy looked at the calendar at work. *It's already March second. I haven't seen Kenny or Tony since early January.*

She hadn't talked on the phone to either of them for over two weeks. Even her emails to them were down to about once a week. Kenny was more involved with Becky now. Though Emmy kept busy at work and with her night classes, boredom approached rapidly. She called Kristen to vent her frustrations. "I need to get out of the house, or I'm gonna go nuts. I'm sitting in the TV room eating some leftover Chinese staring at some show, and I don't have a clue what it is. The show, I mean. Diane is driving me insane with her complaining about her job and Craig. They try to get together and just end up fighting. Help me before I scream."

"Okay, tomorrow I'll pick you up, and we'll start by going to the basketball game," Kristen said.

"Who's playing?"

"North Park is playing Columbus University. After that we'll hang out at my dorm. After dinner we'll go to a party at Randy Braun's house. There will be music so you can dance with all the different guys you want."

"Will there be beer?"

"I'm sure there will be. Are you planning to get plastered?"

"No. I thought that if they planned to have beer, I might not want to go. You know I don't drink much, and I don't really like to be around kids who are drinking just to get wasted."

"We don't have to stay long, but it will do you good to get out and unwind."

"If they try to force me to drink, I'm outta there."

"No one is going to force 'you' to do anything, Em." Kristen laughed.

Kristen picked Emmy up at noon on Saturday. They went to the basketball game and watched the North Park Redbirds defeat the Columbus Voyagers by twenty points. Emmy and Kristen were chatting with some other students after the game when Kristen saw Annie O'Dell and Matt Sullivan.

"Hi, Annie, some game, huh?"

"Hi, Kristen." Then Annie noticed Emmy. "Emmy! How are you? I haven't seen you in ages."

"I'm doing fine." Emmy looked up at Matt, and he smiled.

"What have you been up to?" Annie asked.

"I'm working for Robertson Industries now in Melrose Grove and still taking classes at Paul Frank. You're going to graduate this year, right?"

"Yeah, it's gone by so fast. It seems like only yesterday that we started together at Roosevelt."

"You graduated a whole year early, and I graduated after the first semester of my senior year." Emmy looked at Matt and asked, "How are you doing? Are you graduating, too?"

"I am." He laughed. "I didn't think it would be possible after my first year. That was a rough year, but I'm actually graduating with a degree in accounting."

"Good for you." Emmy smiled at Matt. *You were kinda wild in high school, but you changed after you started dating Annie. She must be a good influence on you.*

Matt thought about Emmy and Annie. *I remember the rumors that flew around school about you girls fooling around with lots of guys. I doubt if any of them were true.*

They started moving toward the exit as the crowd thinned out.

Emmy remembered that Annie and Mace Franklin were friends. "Do you know how any points Mace scored today?"

"Nineteen points with eleven assists. He's only got three games left and just one here. He's close to becoming North Park's all-time leading scorer, and he's already the career leader for assists."

"He is really good," Emmy said. " Does he think he might play in the NBA?"

"He always said he wasn't going to try, but secretly I think he hopes he at least gets invited to a training camp for some team. If he was taller than six-two, he might have a better chance. He applied for a teaching and coaching position at Roosevelt for next year."

Kristen asked Annie as they made it outside, "Are you going back to the dorm?"

"Just for a little while. I have to read some chapters for my Diagnostic Reading Instruction class. Matty has to be at work at five, and I was going to have dinner at the Lion later with him."

"I'm bringing Emmy over to Howe Hall to hang out until dinner."

Matt suggested, "Why don't you guys come to the Lion tonight and have dinner with Annie?"

"Yeah, that would be fun," Annie said. "The food at the Lion is so much better than at Jordan Dining Hall."

"And the price is right," Matt added.

"Why do you say that?" Emmy asked.

"Matt's father owns The Hungry Lion, so he never charges me to eat there," Annie answered.

Emmy looked at Matt. "I didn't know that. Your father really owns The Hungry Lion?"

"Yeah, that and a couple other places in SoHam," Matt answered modestly. Annie stood in front of Matt and he put his hands on her shoulders. He leaned down and could smell the strawberry-scented shampoo in her hair.

"He owns more than a couple places. Have you ever been to the Lion?" Annie asked.

"Yeah, Tony took me there on our second date."

"Are you still going out with Tony Bertucci? I thought you and Kenny Colwell were like... engaged, or close to it?" Annie asked.

"Actually right now I guess I'm not going out with anyone."

"Why don't you and Kristen join me for dinner at the Lion? My treat." Annie glanced over her shoulder at Matt.

"Yeah, Dad will let you have dinner with your friends, Annie." Matt laughed.

"Emmy and I are going to a party at Randy Braun's later tonight. Would you be interested in going, Annie?" Kristen asked.

"Maybe." Annie looked at Matt.

"You don't have to ask me for permission."

"I know, but I like to pretend I do sometimes," Annie teased. "Yeah, I'll go. What time?"

"Probably around eight or nine, depends."

"I'll see if Erin is busy. She and Mace might have other plans."

Annie's roommate, Erin Bezick, grew up in Kearney, Nebraska and just happened to be engaged to Mace Franklin.

After hanging out in Kristen's dorm room for a time, Emmy and Kristen joined Annie at The Hungry Lion for dinner, and then drove back to Howe Hall to kill some more time before heading to the party.

"Has Annie always lived in this dorm? Why didn't she commute since she lives in town?" Emmy asked Kristen as she sprawled out on Kristen's bed.

"I think she wanted to experience life in a dorm. You do know her father has raised her by himself since she was like five, right?"

"Yeah, I know that, and I know she and Mace Franklin have been friends about as long as Kenny and I."

Tess Easterly walked into the room and tossed her books on her bed. "Hey, Kristen, are you going to Randy Braun's party? Hi, Emmy."

"Yeah, we're going. You wanna join us?"

"Yeah, Erin wants to go and some of the other girls from the first floor are coming. It should be fun. They always have plenty of beer."

Emmy's shoulders sagged as she sighed.

"It will be all right, Em. No one will force you to drink," Kristen assured her.

Randy Braun, a senior at North Park, and his older brother, Christopher, lived a few blocks from the campus. Christopher graduated with a degree in business and now worked for Liberty Manufacturing in SoHam. He and Victoria Madison were engaged and planning a June wedding. Kristen had dated Christopher a few times in the past—starting in high school.

"Are we ready to go have some fun?" Tess asked the other

113

girls as they gathered in the lobby.

"Promise me you won't drink too much, okay?" Kristen asked her roommate.

"I won't get drunk, but I want to have fun."

Emmy asked Annie, "Do you like to drink?"

"I'll have a beer once in a while at home, but not at a party like this. They serve the beer in plastic cups, and you never know what might have been added. It's best to stick to bottled water if you want something to drink."

Emmy agreed with Annie.

They could hear the loud music blasting inside the two-story house as they walked up the sidewalk a few minutes after eight thirty. The living room was packed with kids dancing. Randy kept busy filling cups of beer from the keg in the kitchen. Bowls of chips were scattered around the house. The girls migrated to the dining room because it was the least crowded room downstairs.

Tess grinned at a couple of guys. "Are we gonna stay in here, or are we gonna party?"

"I wanna dance," Emmy said.

Tess and Emmy wedged their way into the living room.

"We can dance together until some guys get brave enough to ask us." Tess knew some of the guys took their time before choosing a dance partner. "Be careful, Emmy, because some of the guys might think you're in high school and easy prey. Don't go upstairs with anyone."

Soon some guys joined them and asked them to dance. They began dancing as a group. Emmy enjoyed dancing and found it took her mind off of Kenny and Tony. She ended up dancing with several guys she didn't even know. They offered to get her some beer, but she declined. Tess didn't share her reluctance and always had a cup of beer in her hand.

After a couple of hours the crowd started to thin out. Many of the kids were just switching locations—they would party throughout the night. Emmy walked into the kitchen looking for a bottle of water. She opened the fridge but didn't see any.

Randy walked into the kitchen and asked, "Do you want some more beer, Emmy? I can pour you a cup."

114

to church with Kenny Colwell and sing songs for the teens? I heard that you write songs about God and stuff."

She stared at him. *Where did you hear that?* "I don't always go to that church, but I have, and I like it. Kenny talked me into singing with him, and we have written some songs together."

"I used to go to church every Sunday as a kid. All the way through high school, I guess."

"Why did you quit?" Emmy asked.

He held up his cup of beer. "Because of this. I discovered that I like beer better than church."

Emmy asked a loaded question because her was pretty much an alcoholic. "Do you think it's wrong to drink beer or wine?"

Randy pondered the question for a moment before he answered honestly, "I think it's wrong to drink the way I do."

"Why don't you stop?"

"I'm not sure I can."

"I remember a Bible verse that the youth pastor at Kenny's church told the teens one night. I think it was Phillipians 4:13 if I remember correctly. 'I can do all this through him who gives me strength.' I think it means that we need God's help to do just about everything."

Randy looked at Emmy with wide eyes. "Are you a believer in Jesus?"

Emmy thought for a moment. "I know I believe in God, and that we need to pray. I've never actually made a 'commitment' like they talk about at Faith Bible Church. I suppose I should, but I never think I understand enough."

Randy shook his head. "No one understands enough, Emmy. It's a faith thing."

"I was raised in the Catholic church, but we stopped going to mass after the priest accused Daddy of being a drunk. I remember what I learned at St. John's, and then I think about what they talk about at Faith Bible Church. I know the priests tell us we have to go to confession and all that. At Faith Bible they teach everyone that you can just pray to Jesus and talk to him about anything."

116

"I will if you want to go. I'll introduce you to Pastor Ronnie."

Randy leaned closer to Emmy. "I'm glad you didn't want a beer, Emmy."

"Are you still thinking about kissing me?" Emmy teased but then bit her lip. *I'll let you.*

"I won't kiss you, but I would give you a hug."

Emmy held out her hands, leaned forward and Randy hugged her.

"This is my number." She waited while he punched the number into his phone. "Call me, and I'll meet you at the church in the morning."

"All right, I will." He put his hands on her waist and she jumped down.

Emmy left the kitchen to find Kristen and Annie. She saw Christopher Braun talking to Kristen, so she wandered over to join them.

"Hi, Emmy." Christopher smiled and Emmy returned it. "Are you having fun? Would you like to dance?"

"Sure," Emmy said.

They danced for a few songs, and then he yelled into her ear, "Would you like to go somewhere quieter so we can talk?"

"Okay." *Are you going to kiss me? I would probably let you.*

He took her hand and led her upstairs. Kristen happened to see them leave together.

"Is this your room, Christopher?" Emmy asked as he closed the door.

"Yes, you're not afraid to be in here with me, are you?"

She grinned as she looked at the Farrah Fawcett poster on the wall. "No, why? Should I be?" *I've always thought you were kinda hot, but Kristen liked you, so I never said anything.*

"You can sit on the bed if you want, Emmy. I'll sit in the chair. How have you been? Are you still going out with Tony, or Kenny?"

She sat on the edge of the large bed. "Not really. I guess I'm available right now."

118

Christopher raised his eyebrows.

She giggled and then said, "That didn't sound right."

"It's okay. I know you're not like Diane, and I'm engaged."

Too bad! Now that I'm available, you're not.

Emmy relaxed as they talked.

Ten minutes later, she heard a knock on the door, and then it opened suddenly. Kristen entered and Annie O'Dell stood in the hallway. Christopher jumped to his feet.

"Sorry to disturb you guys, but I was looking for Emmy. We're ready to go. Are you coming with us?" Kristen glared at Christopher.

"Already?" Emmy asked.

"Yes! We're leaving, and you need to come with us." Kristen pulled Emmy off of the bed.

"We were just talking, Krissy. Nothing more than that."

"Good. Let's keep it that way." Kristen nudged Emmy out the door with Annie, and then turned to face Christopher.

"Chill, Kristen. I never laid a hand on her. We were talking. That's it." He raised his hands in a gesture of innocence.

"Did she tell you that Kenny has a new girlfriend?"

"Yes, she told me she was 'available', but I know she didn't mean it like that."

"She's still kinda naïve about guys. I just wanted to be sure she was all right." Kristen looked over her shoulder, but Emmy and Annie were gone. "I should have known you would be a gentleman. You always were with me."

"She is... adorable, but I wouldn't take advantage of her. It's too bad she and Kenny broke up."

"I'll see you. Say hi to Victoria for me."

Christopher sat back down. *Shoot! I've always thought Emmy was so pretty and sexy in an innocent kind of way. Oh well! I'm engaged to Victoria and I plan to make that relationship work. Unless she cheats again.*

Kristen went downstairs and found Emmy talking to Randy.

"Come on, Em. We're leaving."

"Call me." Emmy put an imaginary phone to her ear.

119

Kristen jerked her away from Randy. "What are you doing?"

"I invited Randy to church. He's tired of letting beer control his life."

"Oh, sorry, Em. Now I feel like a jerk."

"I think it's sweet that you came to my rescue. I like Christopher. I've always thought he was handsome and charming, but he's never even kissed me."

"Maybe you should keep it that way for now." *He's kissed me before and he is difficult to resist. I'm not sure you're ready to handle him.*

Randy called Emmy in the morning, and she met him before Sunday School at Faith Bible Church. She introduced him to Ronnie Rojas, and then walked away so they could have some privacy. During the worship service Emmy sat with Mr. and Mrs. Colwell. She glanced around the sanctuary for Randy but didn't see him.

"Are you looking for someone, dear?" Mrs. Colwell asked.

"I met a friend here earlier, but I don't see him now." She stood up but still couldn't find Randy.

After the service, Randy sought out Emmy. He approached her with a smile. "You were right about that guy. He's got an amazing testimony about how Jesus can change your life."

"I've heard it before." Emmy bit her lip. "What happened? I looked for you, but I didn't see you. Where were you sitting? You could have sat with me and Kenny's parents."

"I sat in the back." He pointed. "I gave my life back to Jesus this morning. Pastor Rojas and I talked, and he explained a lot to me. He really knows his stuff."

"I'm so happy for you, Randy." Emmy wrapped her arms around Randy and rested her head on his chest. "He's an amazing guy, but he would never claim to be anything but a simple servant of God."

I think you're pretty amazing, too. Randy hesitated but then put his hands on her shoulders.

120

Chapter Thirteen

"Hello," Diane answered the phone even though she didn't recognize the number. She paused and heard the sound of kids fussing in the background. She started to hang up when she heard a man's voice.

"Diane, this is Gavin Rogers. We met at Sally's Bar."

"I remember you. What's on your mind?"

"Would you like to get together for drinks later? I've got some free time and thought you and I could get to know each other better."

Diane looked over her shoulder to make sure that neither Emmy nor Kristen could hear the conversation. "I can go out for a while, but I can't stay out real late. Can you pick me up at the house around seven. Do you remember how to get here?"

"Sure, I'll see you then."

Diane knew what Gavin's intentions were and knew what might happen later, so she went upstairs and picked out a sexy dress. She showered and took her time getting ready.

Kristen drank a glass of wine as she watched Emmy preparing dinner. "I can never get my pasta right. I either over cook it or under cook it."

Emmy stirred the pasta. "It just takes experience. When I first made it, I had the same problem." Emmy noticed Diane come downstairs and grab her coat. "Diane, aren't you going to eat with us? I made enough for you."

"Thanks, Emmy, but I can't stay."

"Where are you going?"

"I'm going to go out for a while with Gavin. We're going to grab something to eat and maybe have a few drinks."

Kristen nearly spilled her wine. "Diane, he's married. You shouldn't..."

"Stay out of this, Kristen." Diane pointed a finger at her. "It's my business who I have dinner with, not yours or Emmy's."

"Dressed like that, I'd say you were planning on more than dinner and drinks," Kristen said.

Diane turned to leave as she heard a car pull into the

driveway. Diane gave Kristen a one-finger salute as she walked out the back door. "Don't wait up for me."

"Did you see that?" Kristen actually spilled her wine this time.

Emmy shook her head and frowned. "I'm so worried about Diane. What can I do? She doesn't ever listen to me. She calls me 'Mom' and gives me dirty looks. I'm not trying to run her life, like Mom does to me, am I?"

"I don't know what you can do, Emmy. Diane is an adult, though she doesn't always make adult decisions, and you can't stop her from doing whatever she wants. You can tell her that you love her and worry about her, but it's up to Diane to make the right choices."

"It's just hard to sit back and not do anything, Kristen."

"I know. You should ask Mama. She will know what to do."

Gavin smiled as he opened the door for Diane.

"Where are we going for dinner?" Diane asked as she settled into the black leather seat.

"Your choice," he answered.

Diane chose Wyatt's Table and Gavin agreed. They sat at a table in the corner and flirted as they ate.

An hour later he asked, "Would you like to go somewhere else for drinks, or is this place all right?"

Diane glanced around then said, "Take me to a bar."

They left and he drove to a favorite drinking spot. They stood at the jam-packed bar and ordered drinks.

"This place is too loud and crowded," Diane shouted over the noise of the bar as another couple bumped into her.

Gavin swallowed half of his beer. "Do you want to leave? We could go back to your house."

"I don't want to go home. Emmy and Kristen are there, and they won't give us a moment of peace if I show up with you. Let's just leave and try to find another place."

"We could go to a hotel and get a room." He put a hand on her waist and guided her away from the bar where it was quieter.

"Not a chance. Your wife would find out and divorce you in

a second, and I'll be arrested for being an accomplice and end up in jail."

"You don't get arrested for having an affair, and my wife wouldn't find out because I have my own credit card that she doesn't know about. I've done it before."

"You are a devious SOB, aren't you?"

Gavin smiled at Diane as she thought about his offer.

"No, Gavin, I won't go to a hotel with you. Just take me back to the house. Maybe Kristen and Emmy will be gone, or in the TV room and won't even notice I'm back."

Gavin took Diane home, and they parked in the darkest part of the driveway alongside the house. Emmy and Kristen sat on the couch in the TV room watching a movie and didn't hear the car pull into the driveway.

"How long has it been since you made out in the back seat of a car, Diane?" Gavin asked after kissing her.

"I can't remember for sure," Diane replied as she peered into the back seat.

"It's pretty big."

Diane and Gavin moved to the rear seat of his Cadillac DeVille and began making out like a couple of love-starved teenagers.

"Do you want some more water, Kristen? I'm going to have a Coke," Emmy asked as the TV show went to a commercial.

"Yeah, thanks, Emmy."

Emmy grabbed a Coke and a bottle of water from the fridge. She grabbed a glass out of the cabinet by the sink and looked out the window. "Krissy, come here right now!" Emmy yelled.

Kristen jumped up and came running into the kitchen. "What's wrong, Emmy?"

Emmy pointed out the window. "Isn't that Gavin's car?"

"I don't know, but it could be. What kind of car does he have?"

"I don't know what kind it is. All I know is that it's black and really big. I'm going out there to see if that's him."

"No, Emmy, don't do that." Kristen held onto Emmy's arm.

123

"If it is his car and Diane is with him... please don't."

"I have to!" Emmy broke away and rushed out the door.

Diane and Gavin didn't hear her when Emmy came storming out the back door and saw them in the back seat.

I can't believe it! You should know better, Diane. Emmy raced back into the house, furious at her sister.

"Was it him?" Kristen asked.

"I'm going to kill Gavin. I swear it, Kristen. They are in the back seat and I think they are... you know... making out."

"Are you sure?"

Emmy gave Kristen a dirty look. "Well, no, I didn't go up to the car and ask them, but they are doing something. What should I do, Kristen?"

Kristen put her hands on Emmy's shoulders and tried to calm her down, but couldn't. Emmy started shaking with anger, and Kristen held her until she stopped.

She asked Kristen again. "What should I do?"

"Diane is responsible for her own actions. There's nothing you can do. If you go back out there and make a scene, Diane will hate you for it."

Emmy knew that but needed to do something more.

"Come on. Let's watch TV." Kristen pulled Emmy into the TV room.

A few minutes later, Diane and Gavin got out of the car and came into the house via the front door. They sat at the dining room table to talk.

"Do you want a beer?" Diane asked him.

"Sure."

Diane walked in the kitchen to grab a beer for Gavin and a wine cooler for herself.

Emmy heard the fridge door close and jumped up.

"Where are you going, Em?" Kristen followed her into the kitchen.

Emmy grabbed Diane's arm and angrily spun her around. "Did you have to park in the driveway to make out? I saw you kissing him. The neighbors probably saw you guys."

Diane told Kristen and Emmy, "It's none of your business,

and you should understand my feelings better and stay out of my life. I'm going to talk to him in the dining room. I would appreciate some privacy."

"No! We're going to talk to him, too." Emmy frowned at Diane.

"Kristen, will you talk some sense into her?" Diane pushed Emmy. "Don't make me hurt you, little sister."

Kristen held onto Emmy from behind as Emmy yelled at Diane. "I was thinking we should talk some sense into you. He's a married man."

"She's right, you know," Kristen said as she struggled to hang onto Emmy.

"Shut up, Kristen." Diane turned and left the kitchen.

Emmy and Kristen followed Diane into the dining room and sat on the opposite side of the table. They stared at Diane and Gavin. Emmy's face turned red, and she balled her hands into fists. She pounded the table hard enough to knock over the candles in the middle. "I think you're a jerk for taking Diane out on a date. How could you fool around in the back seat?"

"Look, I didn't plan it that way. It just happened." Gavin smirked as he raised his hands to claim innocence in the matter.

"That is the biggest load of crap I've ever heard in my life. You are a bastard for cheating on your wife and being with my sister. Why don't you keep it in your pants from now on?"

Kristen looked at Emmy in amazement. She walked back into the kitchen and grabbed a bottle of water before returning.

"Will you go away and let us have some privacy?" Diane glared at Emmy.

"No! We're staying right here, and you can't make me leave." Emmy crossed her arms over her chest and scowled.

"Fine! Be that way. You're just proving what an immature brat you are," Diane said. She turned to Gavin. "Just ignore her. She'll get tired of sitting there and go away."

Gavin glanced at Emmy. *I'm not sure about that. She looks like she's really pissed off.*

Diane and Gavin drank their beverages while talking and getting to know each other better. Emmy and Kristen listened to

125

them talking—growing more disgusted with each passing minute. Emmy sat across the table from Gavin—still shooting daggers at him with her eyes. Kristen sat next to Emmy trying to keep her calm but found herself getting just as angry with Diane as Emmy.

Kristen tugged on Emmy's arm. "Come on, Em. Let's go back to the TV room. Diane is going to do whatever she pleases."

"No! I'm staying here." Emmy shook off Kristen's hand. "I'm afraid he will try something else."

Emmy became more and more upset as she listened to Gavin and Diane until she couldn't stomach anymore and finally exploded. She sat up on her knees and leaned on her hands to get in his face. "How many times have you cheated on your wife?"

Kristen thought the chair would break.

Gavin, startled by the blunt question, answered, "Four. Not that it's any of your business, but four times."

"Four!" Emmy screamed. "Your wife should get rid of you because you try to screw every woman you meet."

Kristen held Emmy around her waist to keep her from attacking Gavin and managed to get her to sit down again.

Gavin smirked at Emmy and said, "You didn't complain when I came on to you before."

Diane gave Emmy a dirty look. "Is there something between you and Gavin that I don't know about? Did you and Gavin have sex? Is that why you've been so mean to me lately? You want Gavin for yourself, don't you?" *I know you don't know him, but this should get you mad enough to leave.*

Gavin nodded his head at Diane. "There is some history between us."

This outright lie flabbergasted Emmy and left her speechless for a moment before she slowly told Diane, "That is an absolute lie, and you know it. I didn't even meet him until that night you brought him and Shannon home."

Kristen almost tackled Emmy as she fought to get at him again.

Emmy screamed at Gavin, "Go screw yourself!"

She continued to let Gavin have it using language that would shock a hardcore longshoreman. Kristen's jaw dropped to hear such language from her. Diane started to laugh as her sweet, innocent little sister blasted Gavin with everything in her arsenal including some unique combinations of words that didn't make much sense. Kristen started blasting away at Gavin as well. Emmy and Kristen looked at each other and didn't know whether to cry or laugh at the language they used.

Gavin looked at Diane and hung his head. "I really am a jerk for cheating on my wife."

Kristen harrumphed, "Damn right you are. You... bastard."

"My wife hasn't been interested in sex since having our second child. She only lets me make love to her about once a month, and even then she doesn't seem interested." He hoped this might earn some sympathy.

"No! No! No!" Kristen shook a finger at him. "That still doesn't give you the right to cheat."

Diane told Gavin, "I can't meet you like this anymore. I'm not going to get involved in your marital problems. I've never met your wife, but you need to fix things with her somehow."

"I'll try," Gavin promised.

"Hah! That sounded about as sincere as a politician running for office. You are such a liar as well as a cheating bastard." Emmy screamed at Gavin, and then she ran into the kitchen.

"You don't have a gun in the house, do you, Diane?" Gavin was ready to bolt.

"We don't have a gun, but there are some knives in the kitchen," Diane said just to watch him squirm.

Emmy grabbed another bottle of water for her and Kristen to share and another wine cooler for Diane. She came back out to the dining room and sat down.

"Nothing for me?" Gavin asked as his heart raced.

"No!" all three girls shouted at once.

Gavin shut up while the girls talked. He listened mutely until he decided to leave. Diane walked him back to his car, and Emmy and Kristen followed to make sure Diane didn't leave with Gavin. He told Diane goodbye and waved to Emmy and Kristen as he got in his car. Kristen gave Gavin a special salute with both hands as he left.

"That'll teach him, Krissy." Emmy saluted him, too. She kicked the front step as her anger erupted again. "Ow! That hurt!"

"The steps are harder than your toes, you goof." Kristen laughed.

Kristen put her arm around Emmy as they walked back into the house. Diane came back into the house a moment later, and they all sat in the living room.

Diane told Emmy in an attempt to be humorous, "I'm sorry for being such a slut, but at least now Gavin will never bother you again."

"I never met him before," Emmy proclaimed again. "You have to believe me. I would never do anything with him."

"I know that, Em. I know he lied about it." Diane began to cry, and then confessed, "It's not all Gavin's fault. I could have said no to his advances if I wanted. The fact is... Craig's been having an affair with a lady from work, and that is why I've been seeing other men. I'm trying to get back at Craig for hurting me. This isn't the first time he's cheated, either."

"I'm sorry, Diane," Emmy said. "Do you still love Craig?"

"I think so, but I'm not sure."

Kristen sat watching Emmy and Diane as they held onto each other. "Sometimes I wish I had a sister," Kristen whispered as she began to cry.

Emmy hugged her. "Kristen, I love you, and I'll be your sister whenever you need me."

She held Kristen and they cried together. Diane slowly regained her composure. "We need to stop crying because we are stronger than guys like Gavin and Craig and other jerks like them. All men are creeps and are only interested in using us for sex."

Emmy whispered, "Kenny wasn't like that. He never tried to force me to make love to him, and he would never cheat on me—not even with Becky. Tony would never cheat, either."

"But he's with Becky now," Kristen said. "How can it be cheating if you guys aren't together anymore?"

Emmy bit her lip for a moment. "He still loves me. He said so."

Kristen laughed and told Diane, "That's right. Emmy is the

128

only one of us who has found the perfect man to love. She actually has two fantastic men who love her. You are so lucky, Em."

Diane gathered up the empty bottles from the dining room table and took them to the recycling bin in the pantry. Emmy and Kristen sat on the couch. Kristen put her arm around Emmy and held her close. Diane returned, looked at them and smiled.

"Are you cold, Emmy? You look like you're shivering."

"I can't get what Gavin said out of my mind." Emmy jumped up and bounced on her toes. "You *have* to believe me. I really didn't know him before that night."

"I know. Oh, Em, I'm sorry we ever met him."

Kristen put a finger to her mouth and then jumped up. "I have an idea. Maybe we should call his wife. Do you have his number, Diane?"

"It should be on the caller ID. That would serve him right."

"No! Don't do that. Just don't see him or talk to him ever again. Maybe he will change and fix things with his wife."

Diane and Kristen shook their heads. "Not a chance."

"It could happen," Emmy whispered.

Diane looked at Emmy and smiled. "Oh, baby, you see the good in everyone."

Kristen and Diane hugged her. Then Diane told Emmy for the first time in many years, "I love you, Emmy."

Chapter Fourteen

In mid-March Fernando Ramos received a dinner invitation from Alejandro Santiago; a friend of his who lived in Newcastle, an exclusive suburb not far from SoHam. That evening Fernando walked over to the house with the party invitation to talk to Diane. Fernando hoped Diane would be willing to go to the dinner party with him, but his confidence needed a boost. She hadn't talked to him since the night they went out for drinks the previous week. He tentatively knocked on the front door and waited.

"Hello, Fernando." Diane stood in the doorway with her arms crossed over her chest.

"How have you been, Diane?"

"All right. What do you want?" she asked coldly.

"Could I come in for a few minutes? I need to ask you something."

Diane took a few seconds to decide. "Okay, but you can't stay long."

She moved aside to let him enter. She could smell his Old Spice cologne as he passed.

"I've been thinking about you. I've missed seeing your smile." He smiled again, and Diane's icy attitude melted a bit. "Could I have a cup of coffee, please?"

"Sure. I'm sorry for acting so rude." She led him to the kitchen. "I'm sorta embarrassed about what happened the last time we saw each other. I'm not usually like that."

"Let's forget about that night, okay?"

"That's easy for me since I don't remember parts of it," Diane said.

Diane and Fernando sat in the dining room drinking coffee while he explained the invitation.

"The party is April first, which is a Sunday. I can bring three guests besides myself to the party. There will be a formal dinner with dancing afterward, or just mingling and socializing. The Santiago home is huge. He collects art, and it is displayed all over the house."

"How do you know this guy, Fernando?"

130

"We knew each other as kids. His parents and mine are friends, so we used to see each other occasionally. We have kept in contact over the years, and we get together once or twice a year."

"How many people do you think will be at the party, and is it really on April first?" Diane asked. "If you're playing a joke on me, I will absolutely hate you."

"Normally, there are around twenty people for the dinner and sometimes up to fifty or more for the after-party. It's the only time he opens the house to let people see the art collection. He usually has this party on April first every couple of years."

Diane stared at him as she waited for the punch line. When he didn't say anything else she asked, "How formal is the party? Do I have to wear a gown or something like that?"

"Oh, no, I meant the dinner is formal. You know fancy courses and things. Not like a pizza buffet or something tacky. The guests don't have to dress formally. Most people dress-up, you know, no jeans or t-shirts, but no tuxes, either. It would be a perfect chance to get away and meet some interesting people."

"Who else are you gonna ask besides me?"

"I usually ask Ethan and he brings a date."

Diane thought about his invitation momentarily. "If Ethan agrees to go, then I will, too."

"I'll call him right now." Fernando immediately called Ethan, and he agreed to go.

Fernando asked Diane as he opened the fridge. "What have you got to drink around here?"

"I've got some wine. Let's see. I've got a Cabernet Sauvignon and a Merlot. Which would you prefer?"

"Let's start with the Merlot, and, if we finish that, we can open the other bottle."

Fernando opened the Merlot. They finished the bottle of wine as they sat and talked at the dinner table. Emmy came home from work, and Diane didn't hear her walk into the room. She saw Diane sitting and talking to Fernando.

At least you're not with that jerk Gavin, Emmy thought. *I like Fernando. I'd rather see you get together with him even if he's a lot older.*

131

Diane jumped as her sister touched her on the shoulder.

"Geez! Emmy, you scared the crap out of me. Don't sneak up on me like that."

"Sorry, Diane, I thought you heard me come in. What are you guys up to?"

"We were having some wine and conversation. Do you want a glass?"

"Not right now." Emmy saw the empty bottle of wine on the table and took it to the recycling bin. She returned and sat next to Diane.

"Fernando has invited me to a party. Fancy dinner, dancing, formal kinda event and it's in Newcastle. You know that ritzy suburb up north."

"Sounds too fancy for me. Are all the guests old guys like you, Fernando?" Emmy asked. "Or will there be some younger people who can still get around without walkers or canes?"

"Isn't it past your bedtime, little girl?" Fernando asked. "This is pretty late for someone your age to be up, isn't it?"

They moved into the living room to talk. Diane and Fernando sat on the couch and Emmy plopped down in her big old comfortable recliner. After some talking, Diane kissed Fernando and he kissed her back, reminding her of his prowess as a kisser.

"Ohhhh, you guys. Do you have to do that in front of me?"

"If it bothers you, leave." Diane pointed toward the hall.

Emmy told Diane, "I'm going to my room. Don't stay up too late. Tomorrow is a work day remember."

"Yes, Mom," Diane replied using Emmy's familiar retort.

Emmy told Fernando, "You should get home before you get too tired to walk that far."

"Good night, Emmy!" Diane and Fernando yelled emphatically.

"All right. I can tell when I'm not wanted. Good night." She grinned at Fernando as she walked past.

Emmy went upstairs and changed clothes. She put on her favorite old jeans and lay on her bed to read a new book she picked up *Scout and Treat—The Tails Of Two Kitties*.

Meanwhile, Diane and Fernando practiced kissing on the

132

couch.

"Why don't you come down to my place? You haven't seen the upstairs yet, and I could show you a thing or two."

Diane laughed at the crude pick-up line. "I know what you want to *show* me, Fernando. Maybe another time."

He realized how she took his offer and chuckled. "I meant my antiques."

"Antiques, huh?" Diane laughed. "You should go home. The party is in two weeks. Maybe you can show me your place that night. You have to be patient."

"I'm trying to be patient, but you don't make it easy."

"I'll take that as a compliment." Diane stood up.

As Fernando was leaving, he kissed her once more.

Emmy came back downstairs a few minutes later. Diane wore a jacket as she stood by the front door.

"Where are you going?" Emmy asked. *You better not be sneaking out to see Gavin.*

"I simply love the smell of the air after a rain. It smells so fresh and clean. Do you want to take a walk down to the park?" Diane asked.

"Okay. Let me grab a jacket, and I'll go with you." Emmy put on a jacket, and they headed to the park. Emmy walked along side Diane but didn't say anything. At the park Emmy sat down on a plastic bench by the basketball court.

Emmy looked up at Diane, "Do you want to explain what you were doing with Fernando?"

"I don't have to explain anything to you, Emmy. Fernando and I enjoy each other's company. We shared some wine and conversation like adults. Something you will understand when you grow up." Diane paused, laughed, and then added, "You do realize that you're sitting on a wet bench, right?"

Emmy jumped up and touched the back of her jeans.

"Yeah, I knew it was wet. I just wanted to wash the seat of my jeans," Emmy said and then giggled.

"You are a goof sometimes." Diane shook her head as she continued to laugh.

"I suppose you were having a conversation on the couch

when he crammed his tongue down your throat. Is that a new way to converse with each other?"

"Emmy, I am older than you, and I do not need to be grilled about my life. I can see whoever I want, and do whatever I want. You are not my mother."

"What about Craig? Does he feel the same way as you?"

"I'm not going to discuss my relationship with Craig with you. I never should have told you anything about what happened."

"Are you going to go to the party with Fernando?"

"I'm thinking about it, but right now I'm not sure. It sounds like it could be fun, but then again it could be boring as hell, too. I don't like being around people who are super serious about current events and stuff. I told Fernando that I would let him know one way or the other tomorrow."

"Craig would be upset with you for going out with other guys, and you need to be careful."

"Craig doesn't give a rat's ass about who I see." Diane brushed the hair from Emmy's face and told her, "Oh, honey, you are so pretty and so innocent and guileless sometimes."

Emmy hugged Diane and told her, "I love you, Diane, and I don't want to see you get hurt."

"I know. I appreciate your concern. Come on, let's go home." Diane looked at Emmy, and then up at the stars as she thought, *It seems to me that although we're only two and a half years apart, I'm getting older and you're staying the same. Sometimes I feel like I'm ten years older than you and getting older every week. I'll be your mother soon at this rate.*

Emmy tried to leap over a puddle in the sidewalk, but didn't quite make it. She landed at the edge of the puddle and nearly fell on her butt. Diane shook her head as she walked around the puddle.

On the way home, Diane told Emmy, "You are working too many hours. You need to chill out and have some fun. Can you even remember the last time you went on a date?"

"I enjoy my new job, and we need the extra money."

"You need to find someone, Em. You might not end up with Kenny or Tony."

"You might be right, but I'm not ready to give up yet." Emmy grinned and said, "I'm stubborn, remember?"

The next morning, Diane wanted to ask Ethan about the party, so she called and asked him to come over earlier than normal. Ten minutes later, she met him at the back door, while still in her pajamas and robe.

"Thanks for coming early. Would you like some coffee?"

"Sure."

He came in, sat at the table and Diane poured him a cup.

"Ethan, have you been to one of these parties before?" she asked as she sat across the table.

"I've been to a couple of them. I think you would like it. The people are interesting, but not, you know, like stuck up or high-brow intellectuals that merely like to hear themselves talk. They're normal people like you or me."

Diane grinned. *From what I hear from Emmy, you are kinda like a rocket scientist. I wouldn't call that normal.* She drank more coffee as she thought about the offer. "All right. I'll go, but only if you're going."

"You'll enjoy it, Diane."

"Emmy should be ready soon."

Ethan checked his watch. "We've got plenty of time to get to work."

Diane headed upstairs to get ready for work. Emmy finished getting ready and came downstairs.

"Ethan, how long have you been here? I could have been ready sooner."

"Diane asked me to come over early. She wanted to talk about the party. I think she will have an interesting time."

"Who are you taking? Do you know any nice old ladies from the nursing home over on Exchange?" Emmy asked with a straight face.

"FYI, I have been dating a lady who works in our building for another company. Before you even ask, yes, she can walk without aid, she has her own teeth, and she isn't blind, deaf or dumb. Any other questions, little girl?"

135

Emmy smiled at Ethan. "Nope, I guess that about covers it."

Ethan wondered as he drove to work, *Will Emmy get upset if I ask a bunch of questions about Diane? She might think I'm being nosy. What the heck? I'm going to ask her.* As they waited at a red light, he asked, "Does Diane have a steady man in her life?"

Emmy chuckled as she answered. "No, she doesn't have a steady man, she has Craig."

"What do you mean by that?" He accelerated slowly through the intersection.

You drive like my grandmother, Ethan. "I'm dissing Craig because he is a jerk sometimes. Diane has been dating him for six or seven years, but they always fight and argue. They break up, then get back together. Right now he and Diane are separated."

"Separated?" He turned his head to look at Emmy. "Like they're married and now separated or what?"

"Keep your eyes on the road. I don't want to crash." Emmy pointed out the windshield.

"She doesn't wear a wedding ring. Does Fernando know she's married?" He glanced over at Emmy.

"They're not married. They shared an apartment. But obviously right now they're separated, since she is living with me, duh." Emmy put her hands on the dash as Ethan hit the brakes for a red light. "Diane doesn't like to talk about what happened, so please don't mention it. She would get real pissed if she knew I said anything."

Emmy and Ethan talked about Diane and Craig all the way to work. Ethan would have shown more interest in Diane, but he backed off from pursuing her because of Fernando's interest—and Camille Dempsey, his new lady friend from the office building.

Chapter Fifteen

"Ethan, I stopped at the store and picked up some steaks. Since it's so unseasonably warm for the end of March, I thought we should fire up your gas grill. I'll call Diane and see if she's busy." Fernando felt comfortable inviting himself over for dinner at Ethan's.

"All right. We can do that. Should we invite Emmy, too?" Ethan asked.

"I suppose you could if you wanted, but I thought you would rather invite Camille."

"I would, but I talked to her earlier. She's going to be busy tonight. Something about working late."

Fernando laughed. "I've got four steaks. I suppose it won't hurt to invite the brat over."

"You tease her too much. She's really a very intelligent young lady." Ethan defended Emmy.

"I realize she is very intelligent, but she still looks like a high school kid."

Later that evening, Diane and Emmy joined the guys for a cookout. Ethan pulled out a large platter to put the steaks on after they were done. The phone rang, and Ethan answered after checking the caller ID.

"Hi, Camille, how are you? Have you finished early?"

"Ethan, hi, I have some bad news for you. I just got a call from my sister in Canton. They took my mother to the hospital with chest pains. I've got to leave now because she suffered a heart attack once before, and I'm very concerned. I know this leaves you in a bad situation, since the party is in two days, but I hope you understand."

"Of course, I understand. Your family is more important than a dinner party. Do you want me to go with you?"

"You don't need to. You have your work," Camille said.

"I know we have only known each other for a short time, but if you need help with the driving, I can take the time off."

"That's sweet of you to volunteer, but my brother lives in Autumn Terrace, and I'm going to drive over with him. I'll call you when I get back home."

"Have a safe trip, Camille. I'll be thinking about your family."

When Ethan came outside, Fernando saw the concern on his friend's face.

"Ethan, you okay? Everything all right?"

"Camille just called. She can't go to the dinner party because her mother was just rushed to the hospital. She needs to go to Canton, Ohio, to be with her."

Emmy patted Ethan's arm. "I hope she'll be all right."

Fernando turned his attention back to the grill. "These steaks are done. Will you hold the platter for me, Emmy?"

"Whatever you need, Grandpa," Emmy teased.

They took the steaks back inside, and sat at the antique table in the dining room. Emmy glanced up at the ten-foot-high ceiling. *I wonder if that crown molding is original?*

"Would you like for me to cut your steak into smaller pieces, little girl?" Fernando asked.

"Yes, please! Mommy doesn't let me use a sharp knife. She's afraid I will cut myself."

Diane shook her head. *Oh, grow up, Emmy. That child routine crap is getting old.*

The conversation eventually turned to the dinner party.

"Do you know anyone else to take?" Diane asked Ethan.

"Anyone else? Are you kidding?" Fernando wiped his mouth with a napkin as he waved his other hand. "He hadn't been on a date in three years before he met Camille. How is he going to find another date in two days?" Fernando teased, but felt bad for his friend.

"I suppose I could just go alone. Fernando is right." He shrugged. "I don't even know anyone else to ask. I admit it. I'm a social hermit."

Ethan sounded despondent. The mood around the table turned bleak and somber. The only sounds were the munching of salad and the cutting of steaks with knives.

Emmy broke the silence. "I know someone who could go with Ethan."

138

"Who?" Diane asked as she poured some steak sauce on her plate. "These steaks are delicious. What kind are they?"

"Cow!" Emmy frowned at her sister. *Will you let me finish, Diane?* "Me! I could go. I'm not doing anything that night."

"Emmy, I think Ethan would rather go with a lady more his age, but that's sweet of you to offer," Diane said.

"Diane, you are going with Fernando, and he and Ethan are the same age. You keep forgetting that I am only two and a half years younger than you, big sister. I'm not a child even though you and Mom keep treating me like one."

Diane thought about the puddle of water. "I wouldn't treat you like a child if you acted more like an adult."

Fernando looked at Ethan. "Well, how about it, buddy? Would you consider taking Emmy as your companion? I won't say date because it would be like taking your daughter to the prom."

"Very funny, Grandpa." Emmy frowned at Fernando.

"Well, what do you think, Ethan? Would you like to take Emmy? If she doesn't put her hair in a ponytail, or wear her normal clothes, she could pass for eighteen... maybe," Diane said.

Ethan thought about it for a moment and made up his mind. "Emmy, would you like to go to the dinner party with me? I would enjoy your company, and it would be a pleasure to have such a beautiful and refined young lady as my companion for the evening."

"Ethan, I accept your most gracious and kind offer. I would be elated to accompany you to the ball." Emmy smiled graciously at Ethan and stuck her tongue out at Fernando and Diane.

Fernando rolled his eyes as he threw his hands in the air. "Ethan, have you lost your mind? You're taking a child to the ball. What will everyone think?"

Fernando picked everyone up in his BMW at six thirty on the night of the dinner party. The guys looked handsome in their suits. Fernando wore a tailored, three-piece black Armani suit while Ethan wore a gray suit he had picked up on sale at The Men's Wearhouse the year before. Diane wore a very fashionable sleeveless dress, but Emmy really stunned them. Kristen fixed her hair in a more mature style, and she wore a lavender print dress with a scooped neckline, cap sleeves and a wide, pleated skirt that combined sophistication, sexiness and a touch of edginess. When she made her entrance downstairs, the guys and Diane stared silently for a moment.

"Emmy, is that really you? You look great," Ethan said.

"Yeah, Emmy, you look fantastic. You even look like you are older than fifteen, maybe even eighteen," Fernando teased.

"I'm not going to respond to your puerile and annoying badgering tonight, Fernando. Frankly, I find your taunting to be unsophisticated and juvenile." Emmy lifted her nose haughtily at them.

"I see somebody has been using the dictionary," Fernando responded.

"Not the dictionary. Kristen and I used a thesaurus, so there." She stuck her tongue out at Fernando and made a face.

"There's the Emmy we all know and love. See, you can take the child out of the woman, but you can't take the woman out of the child."

"What is that supposed to mean?" Diane asked Fernando.

"Just paraphrasing a song I heard on the radio today."

"Well, it doesn't make any sense," Diane said.

"I want Kristen to take a picture of us before we go. Come on. Let's go in the living room." Emmy hustled everyone into the living room where Kristen took several pictures for her.

They arrived at the party and met their hosts, Alejandro and Liliana Santiago. Alejandro and Fernando hugged and slapped each other on the back. Fernando kissed Liliana's hand in a formal fashion. Alejandro introduced them to some of the other people in the room. Ethan stayed to mingle while Fernando showed Diane and Emmy around the house.

"I see what you mean about the artwork." Emmy pointed to a Picasso. "This looks pretty real."

"It is real, Emmy," Fernando said. "Don't try to steal it. The house is wired with security everywhere."

"Get out!" Emmy poked him in the side.

They returned to discover Ethan talking to a woman Emmy

140

thought might be from the office building. She looked familiar to her at least.

"How long before we eat?" Emmy asked Fernando. "I'm starving and my belly is growling."

"Probably an hour or so." Fernando grabbed a small plate and some appetizers. "Eat this. It will hold you."

"What is it?" Emmy asked as she took a bite.

"Beluga caviar on a cracker," Fernando said.

Emmy made a face. "I don't like it. It's too salty."

Fernando rolled his eyes and handed her a napkin. "Turn around and spit it out."

"I'm sorry, Fernando. I can wait until dinner."

He handed her a cucumber sandwich. "Just stay with me, and we will mingle with the other guests. I think Ethan might be busy for awhile. I meant it before when I told you that you looked great. You really look very charming and grown up."

She ate the small sandwich and rubbed her stomach. "Thank you, Fernando. I appreciate it."

Ethan finished talking to the lady he met and rejoined Emmy. They were mingling with the other guests when all at once Emmy grabbed Ethan's arm. "Oh, my God! Ethan, is that who I think it is?" Emmy pointed to a man who entered the other end of the large room.

Ethan looked to see who she meant. "Relax, Emmy, Mr. Robertson is a very down to earth guy for someone with a large fortune in the bank. Have you ever met him?"

"No, but I've seen him in the building."

Ethan took her hand. "Come with me then."

"Ethan, I'm afraid. Don't make me do this." Emmy dug in her heels, but it didn't matter as Ethan pulled her along.

"Good evening, Mr. Robertson. My name is Ethan Hanks."

"Ethan, how good to see you again. Are you here with Fernando Ramos tonight?" Mr. Robertson asked while shaking Ethan's hand.

"Yes, he's here somewhere. May I introduce you to Miss Emily Colasanti. She works in the office suite with me and is my lovely companion for the evening. She graciously offered to fill in

141

at the last moment when Camille had a family emergency."

Mr. Robertson shook hands with Emmy. He smiled at her and said, "It's very nice to see you again, Miss Colasanti."

"Yes, sir, it's nice to meet you," Emmy said while looking down at the floor.

Mr. Robertson watched as Emmy hurried away with Ethan. He thought back to a time many years ago and smiled. He saw Alejandro and approached him. "Would you grant me a special request?"

"Certainly, Mr. Robertson. What can I do for you?" They talked quietly for a moment. "I will see to it immediately. I will be glad to accommodate you."

Soon a man Emmy thought looked like an English butler walked stiffly into the room and announced solemnly, "Dinner is served."

The guests gathered around the large polished mahogany table searching for their places. Ethan and Emmy found their seats and sat down. Emmy nearly fainted when Mr. Robertson sat next to her.

"Miss Colasanti, I see I am to have the pleasure of sitting next to you. How fortunate for me."

Emmy gulped, but managed to answer, "Yes, sir, Mr. Robertson."

"You don't need to be so formal with me. My name is Bill."

"Yes, sir. People call me Emmy."

He smiled. "I remember. You look very beautiful tonight, Emmy."

By the end of dinner, Emmy relaxed enough to talk to Mr. Robertson, but, though he assured her he didn't mind, she could not bring herself to call him Bill.

After dinner, the guests meandered into the large ballroom for dancing.

"Holy cow! Look over there." Emmy pointed to the other end of the large ballroom.

"Yes, Emmy, that's what we call an orchestra. They play music so we can dance," Fernando said.

"Please remind me to punch you later, Grandpa."

142

Emmy and Diane traded dances with Ethan and Fernando.

When they took a break, Diane asked Emmy, "Who was that older man that sat next to you during dinner? He looked kinda familiar."

Emmy grinned. "That was Mr. Robertson. You know, the owner of the company."

"Holy crap! Were you nervous sitting by him?"

Emmy nodded. "You could say that. I almost fainted when he sat down."

Later, Mr. Robertson approached Emmy.

Oh no! What am I gonna do? Emmy looked for place to hide.

"Miss Colasanti, might I have the pleasure of a dance?"

"Yes, sir," she stammered, bit her lip and looked at Diane for help.

"Shoo! Go dance, Em." Diane waved her away with both hands.

Mr. Robertson thought about how grown up she looked now and remembered her as a little girl. He remembered her sparkling blue eyes and her smile. *You're older now, Emmy, but you haven't changed much. Diane looks much older than the last time I saw her though. You've retained your charm and innocence but Diane is more cynical now. I remember holding you on my chest while you took a nap. My late wife and I treated you like a grandchild.* After the song ended, Mr. Robertson told Emmy a story. "In my younger days I worked for a man who I respected very much. One day, after I had started a small business of my own, I came to him with a request. I developed an idea for starting a new business and wanted this man's advice. He advised me and even gave me some start up capital. To make a long story short, I owe this man more than I could ever repay. He remains the single biggest reason I am a successful businessman today."

Emmy looked up at him. *I don't know why you're telling me all of this, but you are the founder of the company and chairman of the board. Everyone pays close attention to you.*

He told her more about this man but didn't tell her his name.

"This is my card, Emmy. It has my direct office line and my cell phone number. I want you to feel free to call me at any time if you need anything. Okay, Emmy? Anything at all."

"Thank you, Mr. Robertson," Emmy replied. *Why are you being so kind to me?*

"Thank you for making me feel young for a night, Emmy. I thoroughly enjoyed seeing you again. I would love to stay longer, but I'm afraid I have to leave."

She grinned, and he shook her hand.

As he walked away, Mr. Robertson spoke softly so no one else could hear. "Good night, Little Emmy." He raised his eyes to the ceiling, as if looking into heaven. *I can make good on my promise to you now, Mr. C.*

Ethan took Emmy on a more thorough tour of the house and grounds. An hour later, Emmy wanted to find Diane and go home. She and Ethan went back into the main house and found Diane and Fernando in the library. Emmy and Diane thanked Alejandro and Liliana for an interesting night, and Diane kissed him good night as they left. Fernando hugged his old friend and kissed Liliana again. This time on her cheek.

In the car on the way home, Fernando couldn't stop talking about the party and the different women he met.

When Fernando paused, Ethan casually mentioned, "I met this interesting lady who actually works for the company in another building. I even asked her out on a date."

"For real? Way to go, Ethan. You really asked a 'grown' woman for a date."

"I heard that, Grandpa," Emmy said.

"Did she agree to go?" Fernando asked.

"She actually did. Just imagine, two women have agreed to go out with me in the space of a few weeks."

Emmy sat with Diane in the back seat listening to them talk about the women they met. She got upset with the guys. "Hey! What about me? I agreed to go on a date with you, too. So, that's three women, not two."

"Sorry, Emmy, I guess Ethan is not considering you to be a woman," Diane said.

Emmy glared at Diane. "Do I look like a man in this dress? I know I usually wear jeans and shirts, but I wear a dress once in a while."

"I'm sorry. I forgot about you, Emmy. You are the third lady and the prettiest one," Ethan said.

"Yeah, too little, too late. I never want to speak to you again." Emmy sat back in the plush leather seat and pouted.

Diane rolled her eyes. *Grow up, Emily. You want to be treated like an adult, but you throw fits and pout like a child.*

Fernando talked about two women he met at the party.

Emmy remained upset and reminded him, "What about Diane? Did you forget that she went to the party with you?"

As they waited at a stoplight, Fernando turned around to look at Emmy. "I haven't forgotten about Diane, and we certainly enjoyed ourselves, but we both met other people at the party. We weren't attached at the hip, you know."

Emmy smacked them both and continued to pout.

Ethan asked, "Why did you hit me? I was with you, not Diane."

"You left me to talk to that other woman, remember. And what about Camille? Because she couldn't be here, you picked up another woman. If Mr. Robertson hadn't been so kind to me, I wouldn't have had any fun."

"I'm sorry, Emmy."

"Oh, it's all right. I'll get over it."

Emmy didn't talk to them the rest of the way home. She smiled as she looked out the window and remembered how graciously Mr. Robertson treated her. *Somehow I get the feeling that he knew me before. Is that even possible? Does that mean he knows Diane, too? He did say something about seeing me again. Why did she think he looked familiar? I should ask Daddy about it.*

Emmy didn't realize the man in Mr. Robertson's story was Joseph Colasanti, her grandfather.

Chapter Sixteen

Normally, Emmy selected her work clothes before she went to bed, but this night after the dinner party, she was too tired. She changed clothes and fell asleep within five minutes. In the morning she smacked the snooze button too many times and overslept. Then, jumping out of bed, she grabbed some clothes and quickly dressed.

Shoot! I don't have any clean pantyhose. She searched through her drawer. "These socks will have to do."

She usually put her hair up so she looked older and more responsible, but today she just put it in a ponytail. Emmy looked in the downstairs bathroom mirror just as she heard a knock at the back door.

This ponytail makes me look like a twelve-year-old, but I don't have time to change it.

Ethan gave her a ride to work. "Did I mention I have to fly to Phoenix this morning, and I'll be gone for a couple days?"

"No, you haven't mentioned that. It wasn't on your schedule, or else I would have seen it."

"I'm sorry, Emmy. It's kind of a last minute trip. With all the excitement of the dinner party and everything, it slipped my mind."

"It's all right. It's kinda funny because you're like a genius about some things, but in other ways you are as forgetful as an absent-minded college professor."

"I need to leave my car at the airport, but I talked to a couple of guys and one of them will see that you get home tonight. Are you still upset with me because I left you alone at the party last night?"

"Yes, but I'll get over it. I won't be mad at you for too long."

"When you grow up, Emmy, you will be a beautiful woman," Ethan said.

Emmy stared out the window of Ethan's Accord. *How much more grown up do I need to be. I have a good job and live on my own. I almost support Diane, who wastes the little money she*

146

earns. She arrived at the office and saw her reflection in the windows overlooking the parking lot. A ponytail, white socks, and a polo dress all combined to project an image of youth that she generally tried to avoid. She bit her lip and hoped nobody would notice.

The morning passed quickly, and Ethan left for his flight. The rest of the staff sat around an oval conference table and worked on the final details of a project that had to be finished the next day. Emmy knew that her job entailed much more than making sure they had their "morning coffee and donuts." The maintenance of the files and all the copying required for their projects fell on her. She kept track of all the meetings the guys needed to attend. Some of the meetings were in other parts of the country and occasionally overseas.

"Emily, could you hand me that file beside you. We need the Anderson-Irving Report."

"Yes, Mr. Oliver."

"Thank you."

Emmy reached for the file. "Oh, sorry, I grabbed the wrong one. It must be on my desk. I'll be right back."

She searched on her desk for the correct file. She opened the Anderson-Irving folder.

It was here this morning, she looked at each page.

She opened another folder. *It's not here, either.* Her heart raced. *I know I had it.* She was about to open the top drawer when she saw her shredder in her peripheral vision. *Oh, no! I must have shredded the wrong file.* She held her breath as she turned to look at the guys. *He's gonna be so pissed at me.*

She returned to Mr. Oliver. Her lip quivered and her voice trembled as she explained, "I shredded some files earlier, and I must have mistakenly shredded the file needed for today."

Mr. Oliver frowned. "You will have to find the original document in the archives downstairs so we can finish the project. I will have to go with you because of the security level of the file. Just give me a couple of minutes."

"Yes, sir." Emmy ran to the bathroom before the guys could see her crying. "Of all days to dress like an immature teenager,"

147

she wailed as the tears flowed. Five Kleenexes later, she summoned the courage to face Mr. Oliver. "I am so, so sorry. I should have paid more attention, but I was..."

"This is the first mistake you have ever made, Miss Colasanti, and I guess it just proves that you are human after all." Mr. Oliver tried to reassure Emmy. "Everyone makes mistakes, and, though serious, this can be fixed."

She tried to smile at him but felt like a child on her way to the principal's office.

"Emily, would you be able to stay late today to finish the project, if needed?" Stephen Butler, one of her coworkers, asked on the way back from lunch.

"Yes, I can stay. I don't have any plans for tonight," she answered. *I'll do anything to make up for my mistake this morning.*

Emmy stayed late with Mr. Butler. She retrieved files, brought him reference books and even double checked some math. They worked on the report for two hours, and Mr. Butler realized they still had a couple of hours of work left.

"How would you feel about getting this thing done tonight?" He asked while encrypting an email. "Our other option is coming in two hours early in the morning."

"If it's all the same to you, I would just as soon we finish tonight. The thought of coming in that early in the morning doesn't appeal to me at all."

"Let's do it then. We should be able to knock this out in a couple of hours. Oh, I forgot to mention," he said as he slapped his forehead. "Ethan asked me if I would make sure you got home today. I'm sorry I forgot to tell you earlier. You've probably been worried about how you were getting home."

"I was getting concerned. Thanks for putting my mind at ease, Mr. Butler." *You guys are all the same. You might be geniuses in your field, but you can't remember simple things.*

"Are you hungry?" he asked. "I am."

"We could order a pizza and have it delivered. That way we can keep working until it arrives," Emmy suggested.

"Brilliant! I knew there was a brain in that pretty head."

148

Emmy stared at him.

"No! No! No! That didn't come out right. I didn't mean to be condescending. I apologize."

"It's all right, Mr. Butler. Today I feel like an airhead."

"I assure you that you are most certainly not an airhead."

The pizza arrived, and they took a break. Emmy thought Mr. Butler looked really handsome for an older man. She boldly asked, "How old are you, Mr. Butler?"

"I'm thirty-nine."

"You look pretty good for your age, Mr. Butler." She grinned. *Fernando and Ethan claim to be thirty-nine, too. I wonder if you've stopped counting like them.*

He thought Emmy looked about the same as his sixteen-year-old daughter.

They finished the report, and, as they stood next to each other, Mr. Butler started to give her a hug, but then he stopped. He wasn't sure how Emmy would respond and didn't want to create a conflict. He took her home and said, "I know you usually carpool with Ethan, but I live reasonably close. It wouldn't be too far out of the way to pick you up. Let me know if you ever need a ride."

"Thank you, Mr. Butler, I appreciate the offer. I'm going to drive myself to the office until Ethan returns."

Emmy was humming a Fridays At Five tune and sorting through the mail the next morning when Mr. Oliver stopped by her desk.

"Emily, I am going to need your help this afternoon with a report that is due soon. We can start on it right after lunch and should be finished before the end of the day."

"Yes, sir."

Later, as Emmy helped Mr. Oliver with the report, he received a call from Ethan. He listened for a couple of minutes.

"Are you sure she can handle it? Wouldn't you rather I send one of the more experienced ladies from the office next door?" He listened to Ethan's answer. "Okay, it's your project, Ethan, and I will let you make the decision."

Mr. Oliver hung up, looked at Emmy and reached a

149

decision. "I have a big favor to ask of you. Ethan requires an assistant to help finish the project in Phoenix. Would you be willing to fly out there tomorrow morning and help him? I realize it is very short notice, but this just came up, and it is important. I would really appreciate it if you could help the team. If you feel that you're not up to this, I will understand."

"Of course I will, Mr. Oliver!" Her eyes sparkled with excitement. "What time do I need to leave?"

"Call Mrs. Walters at extension... let me see... 1458. She will take care of everything. She will arrange for your plane ticket and a taxi or limo to pick you up and take you to the airport. Ethan will make sure you have a room in the same hotel where he is staying. If you need to leave early today to pack, go right ahead. We are just about finished, and I can handle the rest."

"I don't need to leave early, Mr. Oliver. It won't take me long to pack. Oh, how many days will I be gone?"

"Two at the most. Possibly only overnight if everything goes well."

Emmy stood up and looked at Mr. Oliver. "Thank you for the vote of confidence, sir. I promise that I won't let you down."

"I know you won't, Emmy," he answered quietly and paternally.

Emmy woke up early even after tossing and turning in bed most of the night. She couldn't get the trip to Phoenix out of her mind. She needed to prove to Ethan and Mr. Oliver that she could handle the pressure. She got ready and waited anxiously for her ride to the airport. She had to convince the driver she was the person he needed to take to the airport.

Later, Ethan met her at Phoenix Sky Harbor International Airport. "Did your flight go all right, Emmy? Did Mrs. Walters take care of all your travel arrangements?"

"She took care of everything for me. I thought I might be able to sleep on the plane, but I couldn't. Too nervous, I suppose. The food tasted good, though."

"You liked the airline food? That's the first time I can remember anyone complimenting the airline for their rubber eggs and cold toast."

Ethan took her to the hotel, and Emmy dropped her bag off in her room. It only took her a few minutes to freshen up. They attended the meetings at the corporate office of the Culliver Aerospace Group, and Emmy helped Ethan with the presentation and installation of the new procedures. She felt mentally exhausted when the stressful ten-hour work day ended. She returned to her hotel room and lay on the bed to relax for a few minutes. The phone rang and Emmy answered.

"Emmy, it's Ethan. I'm hungry. Would you care to join me for dinner in the restaurant downstairs?"

"Sure. That would be great. I'm starvin'."

They went to dinner and Ethan wanted to celebrate the success of the new project he has been developing. Ethan ordered a bottle of wine for dinner and the waiter asked her what she would like to drink.

"I'll take a Coke, please." She realized that in a couple months she would be twenty-one and able to drink legally. She looked forward to being carded and able to prove she was old enough to have a glass of wine, or even a beer.

Ethan offered a toast. "I want to thank you for your help today. You made everything go so smoothly. I couldn't have done it without you."

"Thank you, Ethan. I felt so nervous before we started, but once we got going, I relaxed and concentrated on the job. I didn't have time to be nervous after that."

They finished dinner and went back upstairs to their rooms. Emmy changed out of her dress, and put on a pair of shorts and a stretched-out Fridays At Five sweatshirt with the sleeves cut off. She wore white socks but no shoes. She put her hair in a ponytail and plopped down on the bed to watch TV, but the television in her room didn't work.

"Oh, great. Now what am I gonna do?" she muttered under her breath. She grew bored and didn't know what to do with herself.

Ethan changed out of his suit and into casual clothes. He carefully placed his suit in his garment bag. He plopped down in the recliner near the window. He could see traffic moving on the highway, but not a sound reached the fifth floor of the hotel. He realized he needed to unwind. He jumped up, grabbed his wallet and room key. *I hate these credit card keys. Why can't they use real keys?* He left the room and passed Emmy's room on his way to the elevator. He stopped and turned around. He paused for a few seconds trying to decide whether to take his chances on meeting someone to talk to in the bar, or spending more time with Emmy. He chuckled. *Who am I kidding? The chances of me picking up a woman in a bar are unrealistic.* Ethan knocked on her door.

Emmy put the Gideon Bible back in the drawer and walked over to the door. She opened it without checking to see who was on the other side.

"Hey, Ethan, what's up?"

"I'm going down to the bar for a drink. Would you care to accompany me, Miss Colasanti?"

"I don't think I should, Ethan. I am underage, remember. You can go ahead, and I'll just stay here... Oh, Ethan the TV doesn't work in this room. It's broke. The sound came on but no picture. I wanted to watch something." She pointed to the TV, and Ethan followed her into the room.

Ethan tried to fix the TV in the only way he knew how—he smacked it with his hand. "Hmmm, that always worked for Fonzie," he said with a straight face.

Emmy stared at him with a blank expression.

"Before your time, I guess. Would you rather I order something from room service, and we could watch a movie in my room since your TV is broken?"

"Oh, I don't know. Maybe I shouldn't."

"Emmy, I promise I will behave if that's what you are worried about."

"I'm not worried about that, but what would Mr. Oliver think."

"I understand, Emmy," Ethan replied.

Emmy thought about it. "I don't know what else I could do except go to bed, and I'm not sleepy at all."

Ethan wrinkled his forehead and squinted his eyes.

152

Emmy thought he looked funny, and then blushed as she realized why. "Oh, Ethan, I didn't realize how that sounded. I didn't mean it..."

"It's okay. I know you well enough to realize what you meant, or actually didn't mean. The offer for a movie still stands."

"Okay, but can I have some popcorn and a Coke. I don't want wine or anything alcoholic to drink."

"Of course. The fridge is full of beverages. You can have whatever you want. I'll check on the popcorn."

Emmy grabbed her room key, stuck it in her pocket and giggled. "This will be so much fun, Grandpa."

Ethan shook his head, but then laughed.

They walked over to his room. He tried his room key, but the door didn't open. "I hate these things. I can never get it to work right."

Emmy laughed. "You can create new technology for the aerospace industry, but you can't figure out how to open your hotel room. That is so rich. Let me show you." She took his key and inserted it in the slot. "Now when this light turns green you pull out the card, and voila. Your door is open."

Ethan rolled his eyes. He called the concierge desk, and they promised to send up two packets of microwave popcorn. Emmy opened the fridge and saw an assortment of pop, beer and wine. She chose a Coke, sat down on the king-size bed and bounced a couple of times.

"This is nice and firm, just like mine at home. What are the movie choices? I'd like to watch a love story if they have one, as long as it's not R rated."

"The list is on the dresser. I'll let you choose."

She picked one that she thought would be interesting as Ethan answered a knock at the door. He casually tossed a packet of popcorn to her.

"There's one more if you want."

She put the popcorn in the microwave and sat on the edge of the bed while it popped and the movie started. The microwave timer dinged, and she grabbed the steaming bag of buttery popcorn.

Ethan stood at the opened fridge trying to decide whether to have wine or beer. He decided to settle for the beer. He sat in the recliner in the corner of the room with his feet up. He looked at Emmy as she lay on her stomach, eating her popcorn and drinking a Coke. To Ethan she looked like a teenager without a care in the world. He drank his beer, got up and opened a bottle of wine.

"Would you like some wine, Emmy? I know you drink it at home, and this one is rather good."

"No thanks, Ethan," she answered without taking her eyes off of the TV. "I'll stick to pop or water."

Ethan began to unwind after the two stressful days and the success of his project. He didn't realize how much the beer and wine made him drowsy. Emmy lay in the middle of the bed with her feet up by the headboard. She had a pillow under her chest and her feet up in the air moving back and forth. Ethan looked at Emmy and noticed how happy and contented she looked. The movie continued, and Ethan drifted off to sleep. Emmy didn't realize he had fallen asleep until she heard him snoring.

A few minutes later, Emmy glanced over at Ethan as he jerked his head. The snoring continued, so Emmy turned her attention back to the movie.

Suddenly, Ethan woke up with a start as he felt a hand on his knee. He jerked his head, opened his eyes wide and nearly kicked Emmy, who stood in front of him.

"Ethan, the movie's over, and I'm going back to my room."

He shrugged his shoulders to loosen his stiff muscles and twisted his neck until it popped. He looked at Emmy. "I fell asleep, huh?"

She nodded and grinned.

"I was snoring, wasn't I?"

"You were."

"Was it loud?"

She put a finger to her mouth and tilted her head back and forth a couple of time. "Well, it might have been louder than a train, but not quite as loud as a jet airliner."

"I'm sorry," Ethan said as he got up.

"It's all right," Emmy said and then giggled. "My parents

154

both snore like freight trains. I got used to it."

Emmy talked about Kenny and Tony, and how much she missed them for a while. Ethan started feeling the effects of the alcohol and yawned. Emmy took that as her cue to return to her room.

"Thanks for the popcorn and movie, Ethan," Emmy said as she opened the door to leave.

"It wasn't much of a reward for your help today, Emmy. You made everything run smoothly."

They flew home the next morning and returned to the office. Emmy helped Ethan finish his report about the trip to Phoenix, and they headed home. She made it home from work just after six on Thursday. She sat at the kitchen table and collected her thoughts. *I'm tired because of the trip, but pleased that I proved to Ethan and Mr. Oliver that I can handle anything they ask me to do. That should compensate for screwing up the other day.*

Fernando knocked on the back door a few minutes later.

"Hi, Fernando. Come on in. What's up?"

"Hey, Emmy, I'm sorry for treating you the way I did the night of the party. Sometimes I get carried away with my teasing. You really did look very elegant that night."

"It's all right, Fernando. I'm not upset anymore. I wasn't really mad at you guys."

"Is Diane home?"

"She should be home soon. Can I get you something to eat or drink?"

"Some coffee would be fine if you have any." He sat down in a kitchen chair and looked right at home.

"Sure, won't take but a few minutes. Would you like cream and sugar?"

"Black is all right. How did your trip to Phoenix go? I talked to Ethan earlier, and he told me you were a big help to him. He told me about falling asleep and snoring."

Emmy laughed. "It was kinda funny to hear him snoring. It was loud enough that I had to turn up the TV."

Diane got home and saw Fernando, "Hi, Fernando, what's

155

up? Were you waiting for me?"

"Yes. I wanted to talk to you and see if I could interest you in dinner tonight."

"You might convince me to have dinner with you."

"Would you like to go outside and sit on the deck?" Fernando asked. "It's still in the seventies. Not bad for April."

Emmy checked the calendar on the fridge. "Shoot! It's the fifth. Grandma's birthday. I should call her."

"I'll join you outside, but I want to change clothes first. Emmy will keep you company for now," Diane said.

Diane ran upstairs to her room to change while Fernando and Emmy sat on the deck drinking coffee. Diane returned in a few minutes.

"I'll let you two have your privacy now. I have some work to do in the house."

"I told you I would do the laundry, Em. You don't need to do everything yourself."

"I'll get it started, and you can finish after Fernando leaves. I'm going to call Grandma. I'll tell her happy birthday for you, too."

Fernando and Diane left the deck and walked into the backyard. He wanted to kiss her again.

"Did you enjoy our time at the dinner party? I certainly did." Fernando placed a hand on the small of her back.

"Yes, I enjoyed it very much."

Fernando kissed Diane once, and she backed away.

"We shouldn't be kissing out here, Fernando. You might not be satisfied to just kiss me."

"I won't try anything more, Diane. I just want to kiss you in the fresh air."

"Maybe we should go inside. I think I just felt a raindrop."

Fernando and Diane went back in the house and made arrangements for dinner later that evening.

"I'll pick you up at seven thirty. Is that enough time for you to get ready?"

"It will have to suffice," Diane said.

He left and walked home without kissing her again. Diane

156

noticed Emmy sitting at the dining room table and joined her.

"Grandma said to say hi. Do you realize she's ninety-one now?"

"I know she's getting old. She does all right for someone that ancient."

Emmy looked across the table at Diane. "Are you and Fernando getting serious about each other?"

Diane pondered Emmy's question. "Fernando is very handsome. He is sophisticated and certainly charming, but I'm not falling in love with him or anything. We have a good time whenever we're together, but that's all. Would you like to have dinner with us tonight?"

"No thanks." Emmy shook her head. "I know Fernando doesn't want me along."

"Would Kenny mind if you went to dinner with someone?" Diane got up, walked around the table and stood behind Emmy.

"You mean another man?" Emmy looked over her shoulder at Diane.

"You could ask Kristen to go with us."

"Thanks, but I'll stay home."

"Okay. I know you brought some work home from the office. Are Mr. Oliver and Mr. Robertson working you too hard?"

"No, I just wanted to finish some reports since I won't be at the office next week. The guys are going to be out of town. I guess I won't be needed, so Mr. Oliver gave me the week off."

"With pay?" Diane asked.

"Yes." Emmy pumped her fist.

"The man who owns your company must be very rich. He sure treats his employees a lot better than my boss." Diane poked Emmy in the back. "And he sure treats you well."

Emmy thought about Mr. Robertson and wondered if he would remember her. Little did Emmy know that Mr. Robertson had big plans for her down the road.

157

Chapter Seventeen

With the guys from the office in Denver for an important conference, Emmy enjoyed the freedom of an unexpected week off with pay. She did need to run up to Melrose Grove to stop at the office to drop off the files she worked on over the weekend. Diane had Monday off, so she arranged to meet Craig at Chili's for lunch.

Emmy dropped Diane off at the front door. "Try not to get in a fight, Diane."

"Ya think." Diane slammed the car door shut.

Diane and Craig spent an hour together before Craig needed to go to work.

Diane called Emmy's office. "Are you finished, yet?"

"Yes, I'll be out of here in a minute."

"I'll wait by the front door. Please hurry."

Emmy picked up Diane outside the restaurant.

"Did you guys make up?" Emmy asked as Diane got in.

"We didn't fight. That's an improvement, but we aren't back together yet. I don't know if we will ever reconcile our differences. He can be a total jerk at times."

"Are you sure you want to?" Emmy pulled out into traffic.

Diane laughed. "Well, the sex is good."

"Please tell me you didn't..."

"We were in a public restaurant, Emmy," Diane said.

"Right," Emmy said and then giggled. "There has to be more to a relationship than that."

"It's been enough for Mom and Dad through the years."

"Oh, gross. I don't even want to think about that. Do you think they still... you know?"

"They're old, Emmy, not dead."

On the way home Emmy drove past the Robertson Industries corporate headquarters. She glanced at the glass and steel building and thought about Mr. Robertson. "I want to stop and see if Mr. Robertson can see us." She decided impulsively.

"You can't be serious, Em. You can't just drop in on a man like him. He's probably not even there anyway," Diane said.

"He told me I could stop by and see him if I ever needed, or wanted to. I think he really meant it." Emmy turned around at the next traffic light.

"Emmy, are you sure you want to do this? He's probably too busy to see you. You might get fired for bothering him."

"I know, but I want to find out. Something he said at the dinner party made me think he used to know us or something. I meant to ask Dad, but I forgot. Anyway, we're here, and we might as well try. What have we got to lose? It's not like we're busy."

"I got a bad feeling about this, Em," Diane said with trepidation.

They parked in the visitor's lot and entered the modern building. After being cleared by security, Emmy and Diane took an elevator up to the fifth floor. They walked into Mr. Robertson's office and Emmy approached a lady behind a rounded, modern-looking white desk. Emmy bit her lip as she noticed a bowl of oranges and apples on the desk. Diane followed cautiously.

"Good afternoon, ladies. You must be the Colasanti sisters. I'm Mona. I received a call from downstairs that you were here."

"I'm Emmy and this is Diane. We're sorry to just show up like this, but we... I... was hoping to see Mr. Robertson. Diane told me he would be too busy, so it's not her fault we're here. I take all the blame for that. I understand if we can't see him. I'm sure he's too busy to see people who show up without appointments." Emmy talked too fast and shifted her weight from one foot to the other as she wrung her hands together.

"Please wait right here, and I'll talk to him."

Mona had a smile on her face that made Emmy and Diane feel right at home. Emmy looked at Diane as if to say, "I told you so." Mona had already alerted Mr. Robertson to their presence in the building, and he wanted to see them. She called him on the intercom.

"Mr. Robertson, I have Miss Emily and Miss Diane Colasanti hoping to see you for a few minutes."

"Send them right in, please. Could you see if you can push back the three o'clock meeting to three thirty?"

"I've already done that for you, sir." She stood up. "Let me take you right in, ladies."

Emmy and Diane went in to visit Mr. Robertson. He rose from behind his large wooden desk and came around to greet them. "Emmy, Diane, it's good to see you both. Come and have a seat."

"I'm sorry we barged in like this, Mr. Robertson. We were driving past, and I made Diane stop so it's my fault. If you're busy we can leave." Again Emmy talked much too fast.

Mr. Robertson smiled. "Nonsense, Emmy, I'm not doing anything important, and actually I was just going to have some lunch. Would you care to join me?"

"We'd love some lunch," both girls answered even though Diane had just eaten.

They went downstairs to the building cafeteria and waited in line with the other employees. Much to Diane's amazement, Mr. Robertson knew everyone's name and greeted them with a smile.

They found a table, ate a light lunch of a green salad with strips of chicken breasts, then he asked them, "Would you like a quick tour of the building?"

"Sure," Emmy replied.

Diane frowned at her and whispered, "We shouldn't take up anymore of his time, Em."

"It's quite all right, I assure you," he answered. "Sometimes I feel as though the company doesn't need me anymore, and I get bored."

They entered an elevator but instead of going up, the elevator dropped down to a lower floor. The door opened, and they followed Mr. Robertson.

"This is a health club, and we have memberships for executives, stockholders and their guests. If you would like to work out, or go swimming sometime, I think I can get you in."

"That would be fun." Emmy looked around the room and noticed all the empty machines.

"I use the pool for an hour every day I possibly can. It helps me keep in shape."

Emmy mentioned, "Maybe we could come back another day and take you up on your offer."

Diane pinched Emmy's arm. "Emmy! Don't be so forward. I'm sure Mr. Robertson is just being polite."

Emmy bumped Diane's hip. "That hurt."

"That would be fine. You are both welcome to use the pool and other facilities."

"Thank you, Mr. Robertson," Emmy said.

Fifteen minutes later the tour was over, and they returned to his office on the fifth floor. Diane sat on the edge of her large leather chair while Emmy sat back in hers and looked around. *I would have thought his office would have been fancier. The furniture is nice and the carpet's way better than normal. He's got family photos on the wall.* She turned to look at the opposite wall. *He must like cars because he's got several photos of them.*

"What is your job situation, Diane? Are you satisfied with your current position?" Mr. Robertson sat behind his desk with his hands together and his fingers intertwined as if he was about to pray.

"I have been looking for something different, to be honest with you," Diane mentioned nervously.

Mr. Robertson took a pen and wrote quickly on a pad of paper. "This is the number of the personnel department. We might be able to help you." He stood up, walked around from behind his desk and handed it to Diane.

"Again, thank you for your help, Mr. Robertson." Diane stood up and shook his hand.

"No trouble at all. Stop by anytime, ladies."

Emmy wanted to hug him but didn't know if it would be appropriate. Though somehow she felt it would be. "Goodbye, Mr. Robertson, and thanks for offering to help Diane."

"It's the least I can do, Emmy. I mean it, stop by anytime. If I am here, I will make time to see you."

After they left, Mr. Robertson called the personnel department and talked to Thomas Hawkins. "...Yes, Colasanti, Diane Colasanti, if she puts in an application please find a suitable position for her, or let me know if there is a problem. Thanks, Tom. I appreciate it."

"Certainly, Mr. Robertson. I will take care of it personally."

Two days later, on Wednesday, Emmy and Diane found

themselves back in Mr. Robertson's office after receiving a call from his secretary. Diane had an appointment with Thomas Hawkins, the head of personnel for the company. He 'discovered' an opening in the South Hampshire office he thought would be perfect for Diane.

"I'm glad you could make it today, Diane. I think Mr. Hawkins will be able to help you," Mona said as she smiled.

Diane held out a piece of paper. "I brought a copy of my resume."

"Good. That will be helpful."

Mona escorted Diane to Mr. Hawkins office. "When the interview is over you should come back to Mr. Robertson's office. He might need to talk to you."

Emmy came along at Mr. Robertson's request. He knew she was on vacation this week and thought he might have the opportunity to tell her about her grandfather's request.

"Are you ready to see the gym," he asked.

"I wouldn't mind checking out the gym, if that's all right. Diane told me I couldn't go swimming with you. She said I would be bothering you too much." *Actually, she thought it would be weird because you're almost as old as Daddy.*

"I could show you the gym."

He thought back to a day when Emmy visited him at his home with her grandparents. She wanted to go swimming, and he remembered how quickly she learned. He stood up and started to walk around his desk when his phone rang. He answered and listened for a moment. "I'll be right there." He hung up and sighed. "Emmy, I must apologize to you. Unfortunately, I need to be upstairs for a meeting." He looked at his watch. "I will have one of my assistants accompany you and keep you company. After my meeting I will meet you for a light lunch, if you have time, of course."

"Yes, we have time," Emmy said as she spoke for Diane, still being interviewed.

"Ah, here is Miss Bell now. I will see you in about thirty minutes."

Mr. Robertson had a word with Miss Bell and she nodded.

162

"Hi, I'm Carly Bell. Mr. Robertson told me you are interested in seeing the gym."

"Yes, if it's not too much trouble."

"It's no trouble at all, Miss Colasanti."

"Please, call me Emmy."

"All right, Emmy. I'm Carly. Mr. Robertson told me about you and Diane and your family."

Emmy looked surprised but didn't say anything. Miss Bell took Emmy to see the gym and explained how some of the machines worked.

When they finished touring the health club, Carly asked, "Are you and your sister coming to the next stockholder meeting?"

"What do you mean?" Emmy asked.

"Next week. When all the stockholders have their annual meeting. Your name is Colasanti, isn't it?"

"Yes, but we're not stockholders."

"My mistake. I must have been thinking of someone else." Miss Bell realized her mistake. *The girls must not know about the stock they hold, or else they would be aware of the meeting. I hope I didn't screw something up.*

They finished the tour of the gym, and Miss Bell took Emmy back up to Mr. Robertson's office. Diane sat in a chair waiting for Emmy.

"Mr. Robertson will be here shortly. It was nice to meet you both. I hope we see each other again real soon."

"Thanks, Miss Bell," Emmy answered as Miss Bell left.

"It sure must be nice to be the boss, Diane. Can you imagine being able to swim or use the gym or sauna and stuff anytime you want?"

"I'm sure Mr. Robertson has worked very hard to be successful."

Miss Bell saw Mr. Robertson in the hall on his way back to his office and approached him. "Excuse me, sir."

"Yes, Carly, what is it?"

She took a deep breath. "Mr. Robertson, I think I may have committed an error and made an awkward social blunder. I asked Emmy if she and her sister would be attending the stockholder

163

meeting, and they seem to be unaware they have stock in the company. I hope I didn't cause a problem."

"Don't worry, Miss Bell. Their grandfather put their stock in a trust until they turn twenty-five. It is highly probable that neither the girls, nor their parents, even know of the stock. I don't think it will be a problem, but thanks for letting me know."

"Yes, sir." Miss Bell smiled as she watched Mr. Robertson walk toward his office. *I'm beginning to understand why everyone thinks so highly of you.*

As they waited for Mr. Robertson, Emmy stood in front of Diane. "How was the interview? Did you get hired?"

"I did. I got a new job, and I start in two weeks. It's right in town, too. It's just a small office that handles travel, and I will be working with another lady."

"I'm so happy for you." Emmy grabbed Diane's hands and pulled her out of the chair.

Emmy and Diane were hugging each other as Mr. Robertson returned.

Diane broke off the hug and smiled at Mr. Robertson. "Thank you so much, Mr. Robertson."

"I take it that you accepted our offer."

"How could I refuse?"

"Do you have time for lunch, or do you have to get home?" he asked.

Emmy grinned. "We can stay for lunch if you don't mind."

"I will be in the cafeteria, Mrs. Moneywell." He took their arms and escorted them to the elevator. "I would be thrilled to have two beautiful young ladies as my lunch companions."

As they ate their lunch, Emmy asked, "How old are you, Mr. Robertson?"

Diane coughed as she nearly choked on her sandwich. "Emily Olivia! How could you ask such a personal question?" Diane scolded Emmy for being so bold and nosy. "You can fire her if you want, Mr. Robertson." *I'm glad you had the guts to ask. I wanted to know.*

Mr. Robertson laughed. "That's all right. I don't mind telling you that I am fifty-seven. Old enough to be your

164

grandfather."

Diane told him, "You look very good for your age, Mr. Robertson." She noticed he had some gray hair at his temples. *You look very dignified.*

He winked at Emmy as he responded, "You look very good for your age, too, Diane."

Emmy laughed at his comeback, and Diane gave her a dirty look.

They were about finished when Emmy and Diane saw someone approaching the table. He wore a black suit, gray dress shirt with a bright red tie and carried a black leather briefcase. Emmy thought he could be someone very important because the other employees all called him 'sir.' He sat down at their table.

"Ladies, this is my son, Brady. He is the senior vice-president of the company. Actually, he is the guy who runs the day-to-day business which gives me the freedom to have lunch with people like you. He's also an excellent amateur photographer. I take that back, he's not an amateur photographer anymore. He's a pro now. Brady, please meet Diane and Emily Colasanti."

Ah! The Colasanti sisters. I've heard stories about you all my life. "Hello, nice to meet you." He smiled at Diane, and then turned to Emmy. "Emmy, right? Dad has told me about you and your..."

Mr. Robertson cleared his throat and interrupted. "I'm sorry girls, but I need to rush off. Business never sleeps, I'm told. My son will keep you company if you can stay." He excused himself to leave for another important meeting. "I need a word with you before I go, son." Mr. Robertson whispered something to his son without letting Diane or Emmy hear.

Brady nodded his head. "I understand. Thanks for the heads-up, Dad. I forgot about the trust."

Brady sat back at the table with Emmy and Diane. His attention turned to Diane immediately. "I hear congratulations are in order, Ms. Colasanti. I hear you are a new employee."

"Yes, I am. Thank you for the warm welcome. Your father said you were a photographer. What kind of work do you do?" Diane's eyes shone as she gazed at Brady.

165

He explained about his hobby, and then added. "I have a small gallery where I exhibit some of my favorite photos if you would care to see some examples of my work."

"I'd love to see some of your photographs," Diane gushed. *Either you are totally sincere, or that was the worst pickup line I've ever heard.*

"Excellent," Brady said. He focused his complete attention on Diane.

"I've always had an interest in photography." Diane flipped her hair back in a practiced way.

Since when? Emmy stifled a laugh.

One of the cafeteria workers brought over a tray with Brady's regular lunch of a house salad with blue cheese dressing on the side, a tuna salad sandwich on white bread and a Diet Coke.

"Thank you very much, Melissa." Brady tucked a cloth napkin into his shirt over his tie. "Would you think about letting me photograph you sometime?" He asked Diane as he spread the aromatic dressing on his salad.

Yuck! That stuff smells. Emmy crinkled her nose.

"I would love that," Diane said.

You aren't ever going to take pictures of me. Emmy vowed.

Diane and Emmy stayed with Brady for a time and agreed to meet him the next day at his gallery. He gave them directions. Diane knew the exact location. "You're right next to the Spoonful of Noodles restaurant. Remember, Emmy, we ate lunch there with Kristen a few weeks ago."

"I remember. I had the special and..."

Chapter Eighteen

"There's the restaurant and the parking lot is on the side of his gallery. There, Emmy!" Diane pointed animatedly. "Turn here."

"I can see, Diane. Chill already! You've been so wound up all morning."

"I have not." Diane pointed. "There's an empty space."

Emmy pulled into a different space and they got out.

"What was wrong with that other spot? It was closer." Diane walked quickly toward the front of the gallery.

"Nothing," Emmy said as she giggled.

Brady was waiting inside the front door. "Good morning, Diane. I'm glad you made it." He caught a whiff of her perfume as she walked past while he held the door open. He closed his eyes. *I love whatever kind of perfume you're wearing.*

"Good morning, Brady," she said as she smiled.

He smiled back and let go of the door.

Emmy snuck in as the door was closing. "Hi, Mr. Robertson." She glanced around. "Cool place."

"I'm sorry, Emmy. I didn't see you." He turned his attention back to Diane. "Would you allow me to show you around?" He took Diane's arm.

They walked down the first aisle and Diane admired his photos.

Emmy trailed along behind. *Wow! This is like being in a museum. I figured your photos would be as dorky as you. Maybe I will let you photograph me. That is if you ever stop gawking at Diane.*

"These are very good," Diane said as she looked at a photo of a sunset with so many amazing colors.

"Thank you. I try very hard, and, of course, only the best photos are exhibited here. I have so many thousands more that aren't very good." He explained to them, "I would like to go to this park nearby and use the different light conditions to photograph both of you, and, after we finish, I'll buy lunch. We can go to Spoonful of Noodles if you like, Emmy."

"Sure," Emmy said. *I actually get to have lunch with you. I thought I was invisible.*

"We didn't bring any other clothes to wear. What we have on is all we've got." Diane wore her best, and most expensive, *casual* outfit.

"What you are wearing will be fine for the photos I would like to take," Brady said.

They walked to the park at the end of the block where Brady had taken photos before. Diane posed for some informal photos as they walked around the park. He took pictures of Diane's face from every angle.

He took enough pictures of Diane, and then smiled at Emmy. "Will you let me take some shots of you? I can tell you're kinda shy, but I think you might be surprised at how well you photograph."

Emmy thought about it. "Okay, but I'm not as pretty as Diane." She nearly added, *And I didn't spent over an hour trying to decide what to wear.*

Emmy felt shy and awkward as he took pictures of her in casual poses. She wore a pair of faded jeans and a blue Fridays At Five sweatshirt over a t-shirt with her hair in her usual ponytail. Brady took pictures of her for a while, but then paused. He took his cell phone from his pocket.

"Would you excuse me for a moment? I need to return a couple of calls." He smiled at Diane. "Maybe you could take some shots of Emmy?"

Diane looked into Brady's eyes. "I'm not sure how to use the camera. I don't want to break it."

"I'll set everything to automatic. All you have to do is press this button." He handed the camera to Diane and felt the warmth of her hand. "I won't be long." His hand lingered on hers.

Since Diane was now taking the pictures, Emmy relaxed and started having fun on the swings and slides in the park. Emmy didn't even notice when Diane stopped taking pictures. The camera ran out of memory space, so Diane took the camera over to Brady. She waited while he talked on his phone. *God, I'm starting to freeze. Maybe I should have worn something warmer like Em instead of this Ralph Lauren outfit.*

He finished the call. "I'm sorry, Diane, my secretary needed some info. Did you finish taking pictures?"

"I think I filled up the memory card."

"I have another in the camera bag. Let me grab it for you. Your sister is a natural for the camera. She is so lovely and unassuming."

Diane turned to look at Emmy. *You could add immature.* Diane shook her head as she spotted Emmy hanging upside down from the gym-set.

"I need to make some calls before we can go to lunch. If you want to keep taking some pictures, go ahead. Try taking some of the scenery and see how those turn out."

He smiled at Diane and changed the memory card for her. Diane headed toward Emmy. "Get down from there before you break your neck!" Diane hollered. *You better not ruin this day somehow.*

Emmy dismounted. "I wasn't going to fall."

"Just sit in the swing and let me take some more photos."

Diane took some more shots of Emmy, and then tried her luck with the scenery. Brady took care of his business calls and rejoined them.

"Emmy, you have a very natural beauty about you and it comes across on the camera extremely well. I would like to take some close ups of you if you will let me."

Emmy felt flattered and shyly let him take the close ups he wanted. Diane joined her and let him take pictures of both of them together. Diane gave her a big hug and held her tight while Brady took some shots.

"He likes you, Diane," Emmy whispered.

"Shush. He might hear you." Diane poked Emmy in the side. "Don't you dare say something to embarrass me."

Brady finished taking pictures and smiled at Diane. "I would like to do another session with you sometime if you would be willing?"

"That would be fun." Emmy bounced on her toes. "I felt nervous at first, but I just decided to relax and have some fun. If the pictures don't turn out to be any good, it doesn't matter. I'm not

169

a model or anything."

Diane frowned. *I think he was talking to me, little sister.*

"Would Sunday morning work for you, Diane? I have some time that day but after that I will be rather busy for some time."

Diane realized that Brady was discreetly asking her for a date. "Sunday morning would work for me. I'm not sure about Emmy. She might be busy."

"I'm not busy, Diane. I'd love to let Mr. Robertson take more photos of us."

Diane forced a smile as she stood next to Emmy and pinched her. "That's great, Emily. Sunday will be fine as long as it's not too early in the morning. Would ten be all right?"

"Ten o'clock works for me. I might bring my assistant because I want to use my old camera. Her name is Jill Greenberg, and she's the person who actually runs the gallery for me. She's also my cousin." He added so Diane didn't get the wrong idea.

Brady took them to lunch, and they talked some more about the photos. Diane gave him directions to the house and also her cell phone number.

Emmy and Diane woke up before seven on Sunday morning. They were both excited about the upcoming photo session with Brady, but Diane had another reason to be excited. They ate breakfast, showered and got ready to go.

"Hurry up, Diane. He will be here soon."

"Don't rush me, Emmy! I'm doing my makeup. Not all of us can wake up looking gorgeous."

Diane chose to wear a red dress that buttoned down the front. Then she helped Emmy pick out something.

"This peasant dress will look just perfect on you, Em."

Emmy tried it on and let Diane see. "Does it show too much?" Emmy asked about the close-fitting white top portion as she looked in the mirror.

"No, you look okay. Just don't lean over too much."

Emmy put her hair in a ponytail and looked very young and innocent.

Brady arrived at the house alone with his old fashioned

170

camera. He explained, "Jill woke up feeling a bit under the weather so she stayed home."

"I hope she feels better soon." Diane didn't mind that Jill couldn't make it. "Did you have any trouble finding the house?"

"Not a bit. Your directions were perfect."

"I'm glad. I kinda worried you would get lost and be driving all around SoHam looking for us. What do you plan to do with the photos? Will you exhibit them in your gallery?"

"If you give me permission, we could pick out a few to exhibit. But only if you agree. Otherwise, I will download them onto a CD for you and Emmy and print some of your favorites."

Brady wanted to take pictures of them around the house. He began by taking pictures of Diane. She sat on the couch in the living room while he took the shots. He smiled as he took some full length shots of her but most of the shots were close ups of her face. Brady had Emmy sit on the same couch and repeated the process. After finishing with Emmy, they drank coffee at the dining room table.

"What should we do now?" Diane asked.

"We could walk over to the park since it's such a nice day," Emmy suggested.

"Would that interest you, Diane?" Brady asked.

"Yes, I would like to learn more about your hobby."

"I could spend all day talking to you."

"That sounds like fun."

Emmy listened to Brady and Diane as they flirted with each other. *Oh, Diane, I hope you don't blow it. Even Mom would approve of Brady.*

Brady carried his camera and took pictures as they walked along. The wind caught Emmy's dress and whipped it around as she stopped to pet the neighbor's dog. When they got to the park, Emmy saw eight guys playing basketball.

"No, Emmy, you can't play basketball with those guys," Diane said.

"How did you know what I was thinking?"

"Because I know you. It doesn't take a psychic to know how your mind operates."

171

"I guess I should have worn shorts instead of a dress, huh?" Emmy sounded disappointed.

Emmy and Diane watched the guys play basketball for awhile as Brady took some shots. When the men took a break, Emmy started shooting baskets at one end of the court. Three of the guys came over to talk to her. The guys wanted to play some real basketball, so Brady snapped some photos while the guys played ball. Then he started taking pictures of Emmy and Diane hanging out around the court. He took several of Emmy sitting in the grass Indian-style with her dress tucked between her legs. She sat behind some wildflowers and picked some to smell as she thought about Kenny.

"Put a flower in your hair, Emmy, and get rid of the ponytail," Brady suggested.

She did and Brady captured Emmy looking so happy and innocent. The breeze blew her hair as the sun highlighted her face.

I think this might be an excellent shot to exhibit in the gallery, Brady thought.

He took a whole roll of pictures of Emmy and the flowers before they headed back to the house.

"Where do you guys want to go to lunch?" Brady asked. "My treat."

Diane stared at Emmy.

Emmy caught the look. "Mr. Robertson, would you mind if I didn't go to lunch? I have to finish a paper for my night class."

"That's too bad, Emmy." He sounded thrilled to have an opportunity to spend some time alone with Diane. "Where would you like to go, Diane?"

"You could go to Darby's," Emmy said.

Diane shook her head. "That's too far away. We need to pick someplace closer."

"How about Burger Bob's? There's one over on Thornton." Emmy offered an alternative. "That's close."

"Have you ever been to a Burger Bob's?" Diane asked Brady. She thought he might not enjoy eating at a fast-food chain.

"Many times. I like their bacon cheeseburgers. They might be a heart attack waiting to happen, but they're so good."

172

They decided to go to Burger Bob's. Emmy happily stayed home. She sincerely felt pleased that Diane had met someone as successful as Brady Robertson.

While Brady ate his bacon cheeseburger, Diane asked, "How did you get started in photography?"

"When I turned fourteen, Dad gave me an inexpensive camera as a present. He told me if I learned how to use the 'cheap' camera and became serious about photography, he would buy me a better one. Well, I learned how to use the camera, develop my own film, use different lenses and filters and eventually, I got a really good camera for my next birthday. I just kept buying cameras and lenses and got better equipment."

"How long have you owned your gallery?"

"I bought that building for next to nothing about three years ago. It hadn't been occupied for some time, so the owner was anxious to get rid of it. I spent some money fixing it up, and now I use it to exhibit my work and others artists that I think are talented. I don't really make any money from the place, but it provides an opportunity for some talented people to have their work seen."

Diane listened and thought as she stared into his green eyes. *I like how you exude charm and self confidence without any cockiness or self indulgence. You may not be the most handsome man I have ever dated, but you aren't ugly.*

Brady looked into Diane's brown eyes. *You are absolutely gorgeous. I love your outgoing personality and casual manner. I could stare into these eyes forever.*

Diane chuckled as she noticed some ketchup on Brady's chin. She wiped it off with a napkin.

"Would you like to have dinner sometime, Diane? You aren't married, are you?"

"No, I'm not married and not with anyone at the moment. I would love to have dinner sometime."

"I'll call you and we can arrange for a time that fits our schedules."

Diane smiled at Brady. "I would love that."

173

Chapter Nineteen

"I sat right next to Mr. Robertson, the owner of the company, for dinner. He treated me like he knew me. After dinner most of the guests went into this large ballroom. I danced with Fernando and Ethan most of the time, but I also danced with Mr. Robertson, and..."

Emmy called Kristen after work on Monday to tell her what she had been doing lately. She lay on her bed in a pair of shorts and a t-shirt as she watched the ceiling fan wobble as it spun around slowly.

"Were there any guests our age at the party? I still have a difficult time believing you even went to the party, but you did look amazing that night." Kristen opened her closet door and entered. She looked to her right at the row of dresses.

"I owe that to you." Emmy moved her eyes to follow the ceiling fan. *I hope you don't fall on me in my sleep.*

Emmy told Kristen about Diane's new job and the health club and the swimming pool.

"They even have steambaths and saunas the members can use whenever they want."

Kristen grabbed a dress and held it up as she looked in the full-length mirror. "I've never been in a steambath."

"Well, anyway, I didn't use the steambath. Carly showed me around the health club."

"Who's Carly?" Kristen hung the dress back up.

"Carly Bell. She's one of Mr. Robertson's assistants. She's probably in her late twenties and must make a ton of money judging by the clothes she wore."

"Could you tell what brand she wore?"

"No, but you probably could. They looked real sophisticated." Emmy waved her hand in the air.

Kristen laughed as she searched through her dresses, "You think a new pair of jeans is sophisticated."

Emmy stuck out her tongue at the phone. "Mr. Robertson has been very nice to Diane and me, and I'm not sure why."

"He's not trying to..."

"If you're thinking he's like a dirty old man, forget it. He's a perfect gentleman. He treats me like a father, or maybe a grandfather." Emmy paused as she thought about her late grandfather Colasanti.

"Are you still there, Em?"

"I'm here. I was thinking about Grandpa for some reason. His son even asked Diane for a date."

"You're kidding. Are they gonna go out?"

"Yeah. I'm not sure when, but Diane's excited about it."

"How old is the son?" Kristen picked out another dress.

"I don't know exactly, but I would guess he's in his mid-thirties. It would be fantastic if he and Diane fell in love. He's like the second-in-command of the company."

Kristen held the dress up and glanced in the mirror. "Oooh, what's his name?"

"He's too old for you, Kristen." Emmy rolled over onto her stomach. "His name's Brady."

Kristen didn't say anything for a few seconds, but then blurted out, "I met a guy named Brandon Kelly at school. He is a senior, really handsome and intelligent and sensitive, and I really like him." Kristen rambled on about Brandon more than she had ever talked about any boy before. "He's got blonde hair and these gorgeous blue eyes that just make me feel all giddy. He's about the same size as Derrick—probably six feet tall and a hundred and seventy pounds."

"Did you meet him in a doctor's office and weigh him?" Emmy joked as she sat up on the bed.

"No, I'm just guessing, you goof."

"Bring him over to the house sometime, so I can meet him and make sure he is good enough for you. I will grill him like Mama would."

"Oh, yeah, I can totally see Mama sitting on the couch with Brandon and interrogating him like a vice squad detective with a pimp."

"I can totally see that, too. Mama would make the perfect torturer. She could make Helen Keller confess." Emmy laughed as she imagined Mama and Helen Keller together.

"You are such a goof, Emmy. Do you know anything about Helen Keller?"

"Yeah, I read the book," Emmy said. "Kristen, can I ask you something personal?"

"Depends. Will you let me ask you a personal question, too?"

"I'm serious, *Krissy.*" Emmy stretched out her name.

"I'm kidding, Em. You can ask me anything." *Geez, you get so uptight at times.*

Emmy lay back down and narrowly missed bumping her head on the headboard. "Do you ever get really horny and want to have sex again because you and Ryan did it?" Emmy asked as fast as she could get out the words.

Kristen shifted the phone to her other hand. "Emmy! I'm surprised at you. Are you weakening in your desire to remain a virgin until you get married? You are still a virgin, right?"

Emmy closed her eyes. She started to say something, but stopped.

"Emmy! Talk to me." *Why would I think you're a virgin after thinking you were pregnant?*

"Sometimes I think about sex. Sometimes I think about it a lot—a lot more than I should."

"And just who are you thinking about when you have these thoughts? Kenny? Tony? Or is there someone else that I don't know about?" Kristen asked, as she tossed the dress on her bed. "And don't say Christopher."

"I still love Kenny, but he's with Becky now, and I think they are in love." Emmy flipped over onto her stomach. "So I guess I've been thinking about Tony."

Yes! Kristen pumped her fist in the air. "I don't feel a need to do it again just because I did it with Ryan. I wanted to experience it, and I'm not sorry I did, I guess. But I'm not gonna do it again unless I'm in love and so far that hasn't happened."

"I'm sorry if I embarrassed you, Kristen, but I just wanted to know. I couldn't ask anybody else. You won't tell the guys, will you?"

"I might. What's it worth for keeping your secret?"

176

"Please, don't tell Tony what I said," Emmy pleaded. "I would be so embarrassed if he knew."

"I won't tell him, Em, but I think he already knows. You guys did fight about sex, remember?"

"That was a long time ago."

"Right. What two years ago, or three?"

"Just don't tell him, and bring Brandon over real soon."

Kristen promised to come over soon with Brandon, but before Emmy could even meet him, Kristen broke up with him.

The next day while window shopping at the mall, Emmy asked, "What happened, Krissy? Yesterday you seemed so excited about him. Now you tell me you broke up. I don't get it."

"I know. Hey, did you hear about the lunar eclipse?"

"What?" Emmy turned to face Kristen. "You don't care about space stuff. Tell me what went wrong between you and Brandon."

"All right. Tess found out Brandon was dating another girl in addition to me. I'm sure glad I never slept with him."

"Not again! What's with these guys? Why can't they be faithful? Don't they know how to treat a princess?"

"I'm swearing off men forever," Kristen said as she spotted an outfit in the window of Teens Forever.

"I've heard that before," Emmy said as she followed Kristen into the store.

One morning while Emmy sat at her desk at the office with her elbow on the desk and her chin cupped in her hand, she started daydreaming about how much she missed Tony. After a few minutes, she started to think about Kenny. She got all teary-eyed because she couldn't make up her mind about who she loved more. She sat there absentmindedly, chin in hand, tapping the desk with a pen, when her boss stopped by and startled her.

"What are you thinking about, Emily?"

She dropped the pen, raised her head and nearly jumped out of her seat as Mr. Oliver brought her back to reality.

"You really don't want to know, Mr. Oliver." *You'd think I was crazy if I told you. I probably am nuts.*

"Tony's coming home soon, isn't he?"

"Yes, thankfully, he's coming home for the weekend, so I'll see him for a couple days. I can't wait until this semester is finished."

"What about your other... friend?"

This is different. You don't usually ask such personal questions, but I don't mind that you did. "I'm not sure when Kenny will be home. He might go to LA and stay out there. I'm afraid he might move out there for good."

Mr. Oliver tilted his head. "Why would he do that? Doesn't his family has roots in the area?"

"Yeah, they live in this old brick house at the end of the block. I grew up three houses away." She giggled then said, "We used to play in his yard all the time."

"So you have been good friends for most of your life, correct?"

"I feel like I've known him forever," she said, but then she sighed. *But right now I don't think I know him at all.*

"I will be back in about an hour. I have to meet with the finance committee."

"I will take messages for you, Mr. Oliver."

She couldn't concentrate on work, so she tried to think of something else, but every few minutes her mind wandered back to Kenny and Tony.

Emmy spent the rest of the morning in a state of anticipation as she thought about Tony coming home soon. Finally, she couldn't take it anymore. She walked into the restroom, wrapped her arms around her chest and pretended to be kissing Tony as she looked in the mirror. She felt silly after a moment.

Come on. You have to snap out of this and get back to work.

She used a wet paper towel on her face. She stepped out of the restroom and returned to her desk just as one of the company's mailroom guys opened the office door and walked over. The handsome, slightly older guy who delivered the office mail handed her a stack of envelopes. Emmy faced him and still felt that her

178

face was flushed and red. She looked into his eyes. "Can you keep a secret?"

He answered with an upraised hand. "Yes, I am the soul of discretion."

Emmy grinned at his flair with a word. She checked him out and thought, *You're kinda short and you look really skinny. Kinda the opposite of Tony.*

She quickly sorted through the mail. "I don't know why I'm telling you this. I've been in the restroom looking in the mirror pretending to be kissing my ex-boyfriend. Silly, huh? He goes to college, and I haven't seen him for a while."

"I won't tell a soul. Your secret is safe with me," he said and then smiled. *That is the weirdest thing I've heard around here for a while. Have I told you how your eyes sparkle?*

Emmy smiled and gave him the outgoing mail. *Why did I tell him about that? He must think I'm the biggest airhead in the world. He probably thinks I'm an immature high school kid filling in for a real assistant. I know Tony would tease me for acting so silly.*

After dinner that night, Emmy went upstairs to her room, closed the door and locked it. She lay on her bed and called Tony.

"Are you going to answer that?" John Randolph asked as the phone kept ringing.

Tony stared at the phone. "I don't know if I should. It's Emmy."

John picked it up and handed it to Tony.

Tony frowned. "Thanks."

"Hi, Tony. It's me. Are you busy? I want to talk to you."

"I just finished studying for the night. Are you all right? Is everything okay at home?" Tony closed his textbook, stood up from his desk chair and moved to the edge of his bed.

"Everyone is all right. Have you been seeing anyone?"

Tony hesitated before answering, "No one important. I took a girl from my study group out, but it's not serious. Why? Are you calling just to check how many dates I've been on?"

John heard this and turned around in his desk chair.

Emmy bit her lip. "What would you say if I asked you for

179

another chance?"

"You mean another chance for us? Do you want to try it again, Em?"

"Yes, I miss you, and I don't care if you are three hours away. Is there any way you could make it home for a weekend soon?"

"I'm coming home on the twentieth and planned to spend the weekend. I'd have to go back Sunday night, but I'll be home for a couple of days."

"Would you be willing to go out to dinner with me?" She twisted her hair around her finger.

"Sure, Em. We can do that."

"Great. Call me when you get home, or before that if you want. See ya later."

"Bye, Em," Tony said slowly. He looked at John, who had heard most of the conversation, sighed and shrugged his shoulders.

"What are you gonna do now?" John asked, as he leaned back in his chair. "You will have to choose between the two. Although it might be fun to have a girlfriend in both places."

"Ha! Ha! You're a laugh a minute."

"Nah! You'd feel guilty, but not all guys are as principled as you." John turned back to his desk and slammed boring textbook closed.

"Yeah, I know. I can't help being like that. Emmy is really sweet..."

"But she lives three hours away. Kinda hard to reach out and kiss her. Brenda is on campus. You can actually see her every day." He stood up and grabbed his jacket. "I gotta go see this girl I met at lunch. See ya later."

"I don't know what to do." Tony stared at the picture on his desk of Brenda Rollins. "I really don't know."

180

Chapter Twenty

"I'm not a big fan of rock music, but I am a huge Notre Dame supporter. I've got season tickets, and I'm pretty sure I have even met Tony. Tony Bertucci, right?" Mr. Robertson asked.

Emmy sipped her Coke, nodded her head and looked around. *I wonder what people are thinking. I'm just a new administrative assistant, and I'm having lunch with Mr. Robertson.* Since first meeting Mr. Robertson at the Santiago dinner party, Emmy talked with him several times. She told him about Kenny and Tony. She mentioned that she and Tony may give their relationship another chance.

"I did meet him after one of the games in the media room." Mr. Robertson added while cutting a slice of tomato in two. "He is a very personable young man with a good head on his shoulders."

"I like to think so," Emmy said with obvious pride in her voice.

"Of course. Why else would you be interested in him." Mr. Robertson chuckled. "I met the Colwell family years ago. My wife and I met them at some kind of charitable function."

"Mrs. Colwell is involved with several different charities. She's on the board of a couple of them."

They finished their lunch and Mr. Robertson excused himself.

"Thank you for lunch, Mr. Robertson," Emmy said as she took their trays back.

"You're most welcome, Emmy." He patted her back. "Roscoe will run you back to your building."

Later that afternoon, Brady talked to his father about a recent business trip as they walked down the hall toward their offices. They paused and Brady asked, "Dad, would you care to join me on Saturday night. I'm taking Diane Colasanti and her little sister out to dinner. Tony Bertucci is joining us. We would like to have you join us if you're not busy."

"Really? You want your father along on a date?" *No wonder some people think you're kinda strange.*

"It's not a real serious date. I just want to get to know her better. I thought she might be more comfortable with other people along."

"Saturday night, huh? I'm pretty sure I am free that night." *I really need to tell Diane and Emmy more about my relationship with their grandfather.* "That would work for me. I need to talk to both girls, and I would get another chance to talk football with Tony Bertucci. I'll make the arrangements, and we can go to Avanti's in Brook View. It's one of my favorite places, my treat."

"I will assume Diane and Emmy like Italian and won't mind going to a fancy Italian restaurant."

Saturday night Brady drove his Mercedes-Benz E430 into SoHam to pick up Diane and Emmy. Tony waited at the house, also. Diane introduced Brady and Tony.

"It's nice to meet you, Mr. Robertson."

"Oh, that won't do. Please call me Brady," he said as he and Tony shook hands. "It's good to meet you as well, Tony. Dad has told me about your skill on the football field."

They talked for a few minutes before they needed to leave. Tony explained where he lived when not at school. "I thought I would save you a trip, and I get to see Emmy longer this way. Are you sure we shouldn't take my car, too?" Tony asked Brady.

"No need. I'll bring you and Emmy home after dinner."

He convinced Tony to leave his car at Emmy's.

Brady drove back to the house to pick up his father, and they headed to Brook View. Mr. Robertson sat in the back with Tony and Emmy.

"Tony, it's good to see you again. How is school going?"

"It's nice to see you again, sir. Classes are tough, but I enjoy the challenge. It's nice to be able to get home for a weekend though. Finals are coming up, and I will be busy for the next two weeks."

Tony smiled at Emmy as he held her hand.

At the restaurant, Emmy sank into the plush leather seat and reached out to touch the white linen tablecloth. She glanced at the fireplace, and then looked up at the dark wooden beams. The rich ambiance of the restaurant nearly overwhelmed her. She had never eaten in a place so fancy and sophisticated.

Mr. Robertson noticed her discomfort and put her at ease. "Leave it to me, Emmy. I will order for you if you tell me what you like."

Emmy grinned. "I like spaghetti and mostaccioli... and... uh... lasagna. Pretty much any kind of pasta. I like marinara sauce better than Alfredo sauce."

He smiled and said, "I think I know just what would be perfect for you."

"Can I have a Coke to drink, Mr. Robertson?" Emmy asked much like a child would ask a parent.

"Of course you can."

Emmy smiled and felt more at ease now. She listened quietly to Mr. Robertson and Tony talk about football and watched Diane and Brady. Already a chemistry existed between them.

An hour later Emmy patted her stomach and pushed back from the table. "I am so stuffed. I won't be able to eat for a week."

"Emmy, you're taking half of your entree home with you. Didn't you like it?" Mr. Robertson asked.

"I loved it. I've never eaten ravioli stuffed with salmon before. I just can't eat as much as you guys."

Mr. Robertson turned to Tony and smiled. "You managed to eat that whole chocolate death dessert thing by yourself. I'm impressed."

"Emmy ate a couple bites, too."

Mr. Robertson tried to tell Emmy about her grandfather, but never managed to find an appropriate time.

Tony watched as Diane and Brady laughed at something. *Those guys are having a blast. I wonder how much Brady knows about Diane.*

"I'll carry the doggie bags." Emmy picked them up.

"You want to carry them so you can eat the rest of the garlic bread, that's why you are being so willing," Tony teased.

"I did love the garlic bread, but I still can't eat anything else. Can you tell I had garlic bread for dinner, Tony?" She blew her breath at him.

"You better believe it, Emmy. I can smell the garlic bread

183

from here." Tony wrinkled his nose.

"Then I guess I won't kiss you if my breath is so bad."

"I didn't say you smelled bad, Emmy. I had garlic bread, too, so my breath is just like yours."

"Wow. Doesn't the moon look great tonight?" Mr. Robertson changed the subject. *The things kids talk about today.*

As they left the restaurant, Brady whispered in Diane's ear, "Do we have time to stop at the house? I would love to show you more of where I used to live."

Diane nodded her head. She appeared very eager to go. Tony and Emmy were relying on Brady for a way home. When they got to the house, Brady pulled the car into the garage.

Emmy got out and looked around. *Holy crap! This is even bigger than the carriage house at Kenny's house.*

Tony walked toward some antique cars.

"That's a 1937 Cord," Mr. Robertson explained as he flipped on the overhead lights. "Collecting old cars is a hobby of mine."

Tony walked over to another car.

Emmy looked down at the floor. *I've never seen a garage floor that shined like this. It actually looks wet, and it's got sprinkles in it.*

"That's a 1958 Chrysler Imperial. It actually belonged to my father. He gave it to me when I turned eighteen. I've kept it ever since."

While everyone else checked out the cars, Brady and Diane slipped into the house. He gave Diane a tour of the place. Emmy and Tony checked out the last car, a 1948 Packard convertible, and then Mr. Robertson led them into the house. They walked down a wide hallway and ended up in the den.

"I was watching football earlier today. Would you like to see it?" Mr. Robertson asked.

"Sure! I like football," Emmy said.

"I think he was asking me, Em."

She poked Tony in the side. "I like to watch football, too."

They sat on the couch facing the TV as Mr. Robertson played a tape of a Notre Dame game.

That's the biggest TV I've ever seen, Emmy realized.

Tony and Mr. Robertson were soon deep in conversation about the game.

"We were in a two deep zone coverage on this play. I have responsibility over the middle for the back coming out of the backfield."

Tony explained in detail all the intricacies and responsibilities of the different play calls. Mr. Robertson was very knowledgeable and asked some very interesting questions. Emmy sat next to Tony, holding onto his arm but getting rather drowsy.

Brady and Diane joined them for a moment after the tour, but then Diane wanted to hear some music. Diane and Brady disappeared into another room. Brady turned on some dance music for her and soon he and Diane were dancing away. After dancing Diane wanted to play pool.

"Diane, you sure have a lot of energy tonight," Brady said with a smile.

"I'm so wound up. I feel I could stay up all night long."

They headed downstairs to use the pool table that Brady showed her earlier on the tour. When Diane and Brady finished playing pool, he kissed her. Diane didn't mind. She welcomed the kiss.

"Would you like some wine, Diane?"

"I probably shouldn't. I drank a couple glasses at the restaurant."

"It might mellow you out some. Take the edge off the pills you have been using."

"What are you talking about? I haven't taken anything," Diane insisted. *Crap! Did I just blow it? I never should have tried those pills.*

"Diane, I saw you take them."

Diane looked at him. "Okay, I took some pills because I have been feeling so rundown. I wanted to have enough energy to have fun tonight. I've never used them before, so I didn't realize how much they would affect me. You won't tell anyone, will you?"

"I won't tell."

Brady opened a bottle of wine, and they relaxed on the

couch downstairs. He turned on some music, and they sat back to drink the wine.

"I would like to get to know you better, Diane. Tell me a little about yourself, or else I will start asking questions."

"What would you like to know?"

"Where did you go to college?"

"I'm taking courses at the junior college in SoHam when I can. I have a fantastic new job for a great company. How about you? Where did you go to college?"

"I got my bachelor's from Purdue University and my masters from the University of Chicago. I am working on a PHD in computer science, but that might take a few years. The company is taking more of my time than before."

"Wow. I feel under-educated now. Is that a real word?"

"I believe it might be. At least you are taking classes. You might want to check with personnel about reimbursement for your courses."

"Thanks, I'll check into that." *Oh, God! He's going to think I'm an uneducated bimbo. Oh, well, I guess that I am compared to his education.*

"I'll tell you something else that not very many people know. I want to endow a scholarship at Purdue for underprivileged kids. Now you know a secret about me."

"Can I tell you a secret about me, too?" Diane grinned at Brady as she put a hand on his hip.

"What secret is that?"

"The secret is that I want to spend the night with you." *Now you know for sure what kind of woman I am.*

"I would like that very much, but perhaps tonight is not the right time."

"You're right. Maybe if Emmy and Tony weren't here. You could take me to your house."

"That would make a difference."

Diane kissed him, and they held each other close.

"More wine?" he asked.

Upstairs in the den Emmy excused herself to use the bathroom.

"The closest one is to the right." Mr. Robertson pointed. "The first door on the right." He asked Tony, "Do you get home very often to see your mother and Emmy? I know you keep very busy at school."

"I don't get home as often as I would like, but I'm trying to graduate in three years."

"I suppose your dream is to play in the NFL."

"Yes, I think I have a chance as long as I remain healthy."

"I think you have an excellent chance."

Emmy returned, sat next to Tony and whispered in his ear, "I think that bathroom has real marble floors and the faucet looked like gold or something."

"You didn't snoop around, did you?"

She poked him in his side harder than before. "No! You're a creep."

Mr. Robertson chuckled because he overheard Emmy. *Are you boyfriend and girlfriend, or are you brother and sister?* "How is work going for you, Emmy?"

"Work is great. I really enjoy the team I work with. They are interesting men and the projects they work on are so amazing. It's unbelievable how smart they are."

Emmy kept talking about school and Tony and Diane. Mr. Robertson didn't have any daughters, and it warmed his heart to know that Emmy trusted him enough to tell him things about her life. She continued to talk about Tony and Mama and Heather. Then she became quiet as Tony and Mr. Robertson talked. Eventually, Tony and Mr. Robertson noticed Emmy.

"I'm sorry for yawning so much. I'm kinda tired. I'm not yawning because I'm bored," she said and then yawned again.

"Why don't we go into the kitchen?" Mr. Robertson stood up and looked at Emmy. "I'll see if I can rustle up some coffee or something." *You look tired. I know you work very hard during the week and put in many extra hours.*

He thought of her grandfather and his generosity even when he didn't have much for himself. He vowed to keep his promise to her grandfather to do whatever he could to make her life free from any financial worries.

187

Diane and Brady came back to the den. Tony noticed them holding hands.

"We were just heading to the kitchen. I thought I would make some coffee."

Everyone followed Mr. Robertson into the huge kitchen.

"Have a seat." He waved in the direction of the barstools and started the coffee. "Would you like something to eat or drink? I think I will have some ice cream. Care for some? I've got several flavors."

Emmy grinned as she hopped up onto a barstool. "I'd love some ice cream,"

So much for not being hungry ever again. Tony smiled at her as he sat down at the black granite-topped island. "Sure. Any flavor is fine with me, except coffee flavor. I never could get used to ice cream flavored like coffee, but my mom likes it."

Tony looked around at the rich mahogany cabinets. Mr. Robertson opened a door that looked just like the cabinets. Tony realized the fridge blended in with the cabinets.

Diane and Brady sat on the opposite side of the island as they drank their coffee. They finished their coffee and left the room. Tony, Emmy and Mr. Robertson sat at the large island as they ate their ice cream.

"I feel better now," Emmy said. "I don't know why I was getting so sleepy before."

Tony put his arm around her waist. "You work a lot of hours, Em."

"Yeah, I guess so. Sometimes the men in the office are like absent-minded professors. They forget to do stuff, and I have to get after them." She slapped her forehead. "I'm sorry, Mr. Robertson. That wasn't very nice of me."

"No need to apologize, Emmy. I know how hard you work and you are going to college in addition to your job. I hope you aren't trying to do too much."

"I'm young and I like to keep busy."

"Say! I have an idea. What would you think if I kept you at your present salary, but cut your schedule down to four days a week? You could maybe take another class at school. Or better yet, we have scholarships and low-cost student loans. You could work during the summer until you receive your degree. Would that interest you?"

"That is too generous an offer, Mr. Robertson. I really appreciate it, but I want to pay my own way through college."

"Emmy, I think you should at least consider Mr. Robertson's offer. I know that your goal is to finish college debt free, but maybe that's not realistic," Tony said as he tightened his grip around her waist.

"You certainly don't need to make any decisions tonight, Emmy. Take as much time as you need to think it through."

"Okay, I will consider it." She moved Tony's hand and frowned at him.

Brady and Diane returned to the kitchen. "I gave Diane a tour of the upstairs. I showed her my old room," Brady explained.

"Would you like to see the rest of the place?" Mr. Robertson asked Tony and Emmy.

"Sure," Emmy said.

Mr. Robertson showed Emmy, Diane and Tony the rest of the main floor including his enormous bedroom suite. Tony and Emmy gaped at it in awe.

"My wife designed the bedroom suite. I instructed the architect to leave an empty shell in the plans and she designed everything you see."

"Where is she now, if you don't mind my asking?" Emmy asked as she noticed several photographs on the wall. "She's lovely, and is this another son?"

"She passed away five years ago."

Emmy covered her mouth with her hands. "Oh, Mr. Robertson, I'm so sorry. I didn't know."

"It's all right, Emmy. She had cancer, but she passed quickly and didn't suffer as long as some people."

"I'm sorry. I'm sorry." She bit her lip as she remembered how Grandpa Sandusky had suffered from lung cancer. *Talk about making a fool of myself. I should have known better.*

"The other young man in that photo is Bennett. He's two years younger than Brady, and I believe that was taken during their

189

high school years."

"Does Bennett work for the company, too?" Tony asked.

Mr. Robertson shook his head. "He and his family live in Ghana. He and Marissa are educators."

Tony glanced at an antique clock. "We should be heading home. Thank you for a wonderful evening, Mr. Robertson."

"It's been my pleasure, Tony. I'm pleased I got to see you again. Would you mind if I tagged along for the ride? That way I can keep Brady company on the way back."

Mr. Robertson rode along to Emmy's house despite their protests that it wasn't necessary. He made a note of her address. On the way home he called his attorney with some specific instructions. Emmy didn't realize it, but Mr. Robertson planned to buy the house for her and Diane if at all possible. Then he would give it to them free and clear.

"Please don't say anything, Brady. You understand why I'm doing this right?"

"Yes, I understand, and I think if I were in your position, I would do the same. You have told me the story before about Mr. Colasanti. I will keep your secret. I don't think Diane knows about her stock. She's never mentioned it."

"I believe that's the way old Joe Colasanti wanted it. He wanted to make sure they were mature enough. They won't know until they turn twenty-five," Mr. Robertson explained. "It appears to me that you and Diane got along well."

"Yes, she's a rather charming lady."

"Do you think you might see her again? I hope you don't mind me asking."

"I don't mind a bit, and I asked her for another date. She agreed."

Mr. Robertson thought about his wife for a few moments. "Lily used to say she wished she had grandkids who didn't live on the other side of the world."

Brady laughed. "Mom used to complain about how long it took to fly to Ghana. Do you think Bennett and Marissa will ever move back to the states?"

"No, I think their life is running the university in Ghana."

190

Brady chuckled. "So, it will be up to me to provide grandchildren who live in the States."

"I would not be opposed to having some local grandchildren. Spencer and Abigail are growing up so fast."

Diane went up to bed while Tony and Emmy stayed downstairs in the TV room. She turned on the TV, but they weren't paying it any attention.

"I had a good time tonight, Tony. I'm sorry I was a bit abrupt about the college thing."

"It felt good to have you next to me."

Emmy looked at Tony and moved closer to him. "I know we had trouble before because I wanted you to be more aggressive, but right now we need to take it slow. Like we are just getting to know each other."

"I would like that, Em. I'll let you call the shots. Whenever you are ready, just let me know. I'll do whatever you want me to." *That sounded so lame. She is going to think I'm such a dork.*

Tony stayed for close to an hour and they talked without any physical contact. As he drove home, he thought about Brenda and Emmy. *What's wrong with me? I had a chance to kiss Emmy and stuff, but I didn't. I didn't have the desire the way I did in the past. I need to choose one or the other.* He slapped the steering wheel as he made his choice. "I think this will be for the best." He reached into his pocket for his phone and dialed a number. He smiled as she answered.

Chapter Twenty-One

Emmy had called Tony at least twice a week since they agreed to give their relationship another go. At first he acted excited about getting back together with Emmy, but since the double date with Brady and Diane, something was different. He asked her not to call during finals week, but she called him on Wednesday, anyway. He talked to her for ten minutes, but then needed to get back to his studying. He would be coming home on Saturday, and Emmy couldn't wait to see him.

On Saturday Emmy got caught up on all her normal household chores and did her grocery shopping. She made it to the Bertucci house just after one.

"He's not here yet, honey. Come on in and tell me how you've been." Mama led Emmy to the kitchen. "Are you hungry? I was just gonna have some lunch."

Emmy ate lunch with Mama as they waited for Tony. The afternoon dragged by. Emmy kept looking out the window for him.

"I know you want to see him, but you have to be patient. Why don't you read for a while?"

Emmy sat on the couch and tried to read, but she couldn't concentrate.

An hour later Emmy stood up. "Maybe I should call him. What if he's had an accident or something?"

"I'm sure he's just running late, dear."

Emmy plopped back down on the couch. "Waiting like this really sucks." *Maybe I should find someone other than Tony or Kenny. I'll spend half my life waiting for those two to come home.*

"I'm home," Tony announced as he walked in the back door shortly before six Saturday evening.

Emmy ran into the kitchen. "It's about time. I thought you would get here around noon. I've been waiting all this time." She poked him in the chest, and then waited for a hug.

"Sorry, Em, but some last minute stuff required my attention." He set a duffel bag on the table.

"Well, at least you're home now, and we have a month to be

192

together before summer school starts."

Mama entered the kitchen, and Tony gave her a hug.

"Did I tell you that I'm going to be working for Uncle Daniel while I'm home?" he asked as he kept his eyes on Mama.

"No, you didn't mention anything about that. When did you decide this?" Emmy put her hands on her hips.

"I talked to him a couple of weeks ago. He's got lots of jobs, and I can work twelve hours a day if I want."

Mama turned on the oven, opened the fridge and pulled out a pan of lasagna.

"That won't leave much time for us. Are you really gonna work all those hours?" Emmy complained.

"Yes. It will help me stay in shape. I'm going to work for Uncle Daniel during the week, and, on weekends, I'm going to work for a landscaping company. I want to learn the landscaping business while I can."

Emmy bit her lip as she listened to Tony. "I won't get to see you much at all."

"I'm sorry, Em."

Mama studied the expression on Tony's face. *You are holding something back, son.*

Emmy came over to see Tony on Sunday, but despite her attempts to draw him into a conversation, he remained reticent.

"Can we go somewhere and do something?" she asked as she followed Tony around the yard as he trimmed some bushes.

He paused for a second and wiped the sweat off of his forehead. "I really need to get this done, Em."

"Well, can I at least help? That way I can *see* you even if you won't talk to me." She spat out the words.

"You can stay, but I need to mow the yard..."

"Be that way. I'm going inside to help with dinner. You do whatever you want." Emmy turned and stomped away. She turned as she stood on the front steps. "At least Mama will talk to me."

After work on Monday, Emmy rushed home to change clothes. Then she drove over to wait for Tony to arrive home from work. He walked in the back door shortly after eight. Emmy was in the kitchen with Mama.

"How was your day? Are you hungry?" Emmy asked as she stood in front of him. She was hoping for a kiss even though his face was covered in dirt, but Tony didn't make any move to kiss her.

"It was kinda rough. Hi, Mama, what's for dinner?" Tony asked as he moved around Emmy. He put his arm around his mother.

"I made some spaghetti, and I can heat up a vegetable if you want one."

"That would be all right. Is there any bread?"

"Yes, I'll put it in the oven. You should shower while it's heating up."

"I'll be back," he said as he walked out of the kitchen.

Emmy stood with her hands on her hips. She watched him walk away, and then looked at Mama.

"He's probably just tired," Mama said.

That's no excuse. I'm not letting you avoid me tonight. Emmy followed Tony upstairs. "Hey, are you gonna talk to me?" Emmy asked as she stood just inside the door to his room.

Tony sat on the bed as he removed his heavy work boots. He stood up and took off his sweat-stained work shirt. "Yeah, but I need to shower first."

"Should I help you?" Emmy grinned.

"No, you should go back downstairs, Em." Tony didn't appear to be in a mood to listen to her teasing. "Maybe I'll feel better after I get cleaned up."

"Can I at least have a kiss?" Emmy moved closer and reached out to touch his arm.

"Not now."

Emmy sat on the edge of the bed. Tony turned and stared at her.

"What? Why are you looking at me like that?" she asked.

"Are you gonna sit there while I get undressed?"

"Oh, for heaven's sake!" Emmy jumped up, walked to the door and turned to face him. "Are you afraid to let me see you

194

undress?"

Tony opened a dresser drawer and pulled out some clean underwear. "I'm going take a shower. You can wait here if you want or go back downstairs. I don't care which you do."

He walked toward the door, but she blocked his way.

"Can I get by, please?"

She looked sternly up at him but didn't move.

"Come on, Em. I'm really not in the mood for anything right now."

Without saying a word Emmy turned and headed downstairs. By the time Tony made it downstairs, dinner was on the kitchen table. He took a seat and Mama passed him the food. He ate in silence as Emmy and Mama talked.

"I'll help you clean up, Mama." Emmy put the dirty plates in the sink.

Tony walked out to the living room and sat heavily on the couch. By the time Emmy and Mama finished the dishes, he was almost asleep.

Emmy sat next to him and touched his arm. "Are you totally wiped out?"

He opened his eyes. "It was harder than I expected."

"What did Uncle Daniel make you do?"

"Just the usual stuff." Tony didn't elaborate.

"What kind of *usual* stuff?"

He didn't answer.

Emmy gave up trying to get him to talk after a few minutes.

"If you are too tired to talk to me, I'm going home." Emmy stood up, but Tony didn't budge. She shook her head, and then looked at Mama. "I can't come over tomorrow, but I'll come over on Wednesday."

Mama stood up and walked Emmy out to the kitchen. "I'm not sure why he's acting like this, dear. Maybe by Wednesday he will be back to normal."

Emmy came back to see Tony on Wednesday and Friday but nothing changed. He treated her politely but didn't show any interest in talking to her. She kissed him once, but he didn't kiss her back. She tried to be supportive and understand that Tony was trying to learn how to run a business, but he almost seemed to be driving her away.

She called Kenny to talk about the situation on Saturday.

"I know you probably don't want to hear about my trouble with Tony, but I have to talk to someone."

Kenny waited a moment before replying, "You can still talk to me about anything, Em."

"Thanks. I would talk to Kristen, but she doesn't understand. She wants to see Tony and me together no matter what."

"Are you sure something didn't happen at school? I mean this doesn't sound at all like the Tony I know."

"He treats me politely and all, but when I ask him about his day, all I get in response are one word answers. It's like he wants me to break up with him even before we have really started seeing each other again."

"I wish I could tell you something that would fix everything, but I don't know what's wrong."

"I'm not going to break up with him."

"You're too stubborn for that, Em." Kenny laughed as he teased her. "What has Kristen said? Other than 'you have to be with Tony' or whatever?"

"Nothing. She's in Arizona now. Derrick graduated, so everyone flew down for the ceremony."

Emmy informed Kenny of Mr. Robertson's offer. "What do you think I should do as far as work goes?"

"You may not like to hear this, but I think you should go to school full-time and work for him during the summer. After you get your degree, you will have a great job with his company."

"I'll think about it. Say hello to Becky for me."

"I will, Em. Let me know how things go with Tony and your job." He paused just a second before adding, "You can always talk to me, Em. No matter where life takes us, we will always be friends."

196

Emmy made an appointment to see Mr. Robertson at his office on Monday. Mrs. Moneywell smiled as Emmy entered the office and told her to go right in. Emmy took a seat in one of the recliners facing his desk.

"It's good to see you, Emmy. How you thought about my offer?"

She nodded. "Mr. Robertson, I've thought about your offer and I've reached a decision."

"What have you decided?" He leaned back in his chair behind his desk.

"I would like to reduce my work schedule if possible, but only if you reduce my salary proportionally. That way I can take an extra class—maybe even two. The team often has to bring in a temp, and if I reduce my schedule the temp would get more hours."

He sat up and placed his hands on his desk. "I'm sorry, Emmy, but that will not work. Now before you protest, hear me out." Mr. Robertson stood up and walked around his desk and leaned against the front edge. "You actually started at a lower salary than some of the other administrative aides, but you have earned a raise because of your performance on the job. So even if you reduce your hours, your salary will remain the same."

"But..."

"I don't want to hear it." He held up his hand. "I've made up my mind."

Emmy accepted his offer. She stood up and broke down in tears as Mr. Robertson hugged her.

"I don't know why you are so kind to Diane and me."

"I have a good reason." *Maybe I will explain someday, when the time is right. For now it needs to remain confidential.*

Emmy started working a shorter week and signed up for two summer classes at Paul Frank.

On Saturday morning Emmy adjusted her work gloves, wiped some dirt off of her thigh, and then pulled the remaining weeds from her flower bed in the front yard. She stopped, stood up and turned around at the sound of a basketball bouncing on the sidewalk. She shielded her eyes and looked into the sun.

"Hello, I'm not sure if you remember me. I'm Eric Lowery, one of the guys playing basketball when you were having your picture taken."

"Hi, Eric, I'm Emmy Colasanti."

Eric looked at her as she retied the bandana around her head. She bent over to pick up her gardening tools, and flipped her ponytail out of her face.

"Maybe I shouldn't bother you since you're busy. I know how chores can be." Eric continued dribbling the ball.

"I'm finished with the flowers. I recognize you now. You weren't wearing a shirt that day."

"It's easier to go skins and shirts with that many guys playing."

"Would you like to see the pictures?" Emmy asked. "We just got them back a couple days ago. I haven't had a chance to look through them."

"Sure. I would love to see them."

Emmy assumed he wanted to see the pictures of the guys playing ball, but Eric was interested in the pictures of Emmy.

"I'll be right back. Just wait here on the steps." Emmy went in the house and brought out the photo album. "This isn't all of them. Just the good ones, I guess. We have a CD of all the photos, but I haven't had time to even pop it in the computer."

They sat on the front steps looking at the photos together.

"Would you like a bottle of water, Eric? You will probably get thirsty playing basketball on such a warm day."

"That would be fine, but I don't really mean to bother you."

"It's no trouble, Eric. I want one for myself anyway. I'll be right back."

Emmy went back in the house to get a couple bottles of water. Eric continued to look at the pictures. He saw the pictures of her at the basketball court. She brought out the bottles of water just as Eric closed the photo album.

"I've got to meet my friends at the park to play some ball. Would you like to shoot some baskets while I'm waiting?" He remembered she enjoyed shooting baskets that day at the park.

I'm not sure, she thought. *Why not? Tony is working all*

198

day. I won't have a chance to see him. "Sure, that sounds like fun, and I need a break from my gardening. Just give me a second to grab a cap and lock the house."

Emmy ran into the house. She removed her bandana and grabbed her keys and a baseball cap to wear. She already wore sneakers, shorts and a t-shirt.

"Are you still in school, Eric?" Emmy asked as she ripped the basketball out of his arms.

"Yeah, I go to North Park and work evenings at the college. I live at home and commute back and forth."

"How old are you, if you don't mind me asking?" She tried to dribble the ball between her legs. *Darn it. I used to be able to do this.*

"Twenty-four. I worked full-time for two years after high school, so I could pay my way through college." He stole the ball away from Emmy.

"I'm paying my way through school, too."

"Really? I thought you were still in high school."

"I get that a lot."

They arrived at the park and started shooting baskets.

After a few minutes, Emmy asked, "How about a game of one-on-one? Think you're up to the challenge of playing a girl half your size?"

"Show me what you got, girl." Eric tossed her the ball.

Eric let her score a few baskets. He realized that she was more athletic than most girls, so he stepped up his game. He put his hand on her hip to guard her. Emmy pushed him and fouled him as she tried to guard him to no avail. Eric's size and strength were too much for her. His friends arrived so Emmy and Eric stopped playing.

"You are pretty good for a girl." He wiped the sweat off of his forehead with the back of his hand.

"You're not too bad for a boy."

"I'm better at football. I played for Lincoln High."

Emmy grinned. "My boyfriend plays football."

"For a high school team?" Eric asked.

"He played at Roosevelt, but now he plays in college."

199

"Where? A school I might have heard of?"

"Ever hear of Notre Dame?" Emmy grinned as she watched Eric's reaction.

"You're kidding, right?"

"No, he plays middle linebacker, and he led the team in tackles this year."

Eric thought for a moment. "Your boyfriend wouldn't happen to be Tony Bertucci?"

"The one and only."

"Wow! My brother Eddie played on the same team. He went to Roosevelt instead of Lincoln because my parents moved. He didn't actually get to play much. He was third-string."

"Eddie Lowery? I remember him. He's the guy who ran back the kickoff in the game against Crest Ridge."

"Yeah. That was Eddie. The coach sent all the subs into the game to run out the clock. He got the kickoff and started running like a mad man. He must have run 200 yards on that play."

"The crowd went nuts. He ran from one side of the field to the other. He ducked under some guys and changed directions. He circled back. It was totally nuts."

"He told me after the game that he just ran for his life. He thought he would get hurt if he got tackled, so he just went crazy."

"Yeah. Kids started calling him Crazy Eddie Lowery."

Emmy sat on a bench to watch the guys play ball for awhile. She felt energized as she watched the guys run up and down the court. She wished she could play, but knew the guys were too big, and she might get hurt. Just then Eric knocked the ball away from one of the players. Two of them came running toward her. Emmy screamed, lifted her knees and covered her head with her arms as they almost crashed into her.

Eric sprinted over to her. "Emmy! Are you okay? You're not hurt or anything?"

"I'm fine. The guys didn't really crash into me. They came close though."

"I'm glad you're all right."

"I need to get home and finish working in the yard. You should go back to your friends and your game. Stop by the house another time if you want to play ball again."

"Thanks. I will. When you talk to Tony again, say hi for me and ask him if he remembers Crazy Eddie."

"I will."

Eric started to walk away, but stopped. "By the way, I'm no expert, but those pictures looked really good. Is your father a professional photographer?"

"No," Emmy answered. *Why would you think that?*

"I can tell where you get your looks. Your Mom is just as pretty as you. You can sure see the resemblance between you and her. I really liked that photo of you and your mom hugging."

Emmy realized that Eric mistook Diane for her mother and Brady for her father. "Thanks, Eric. I'll tell Mom when she gets home. I'm sure she will appreciate the compliment."

Emmy couldn't wait to tease Diane later.

Tony finally took a day off on Sunday, and Emmy intended to spend the day with him. They did some grocery shopping for Mama, and on the drive back to the house, she tried to kiss him. He didn't show any interest and reverted to treating her like a kid sister.

"I talked to Eric Lowery yesterday. You don't know him, but his brother, Eddie, played on the Roosevelt team."

"Do you mean Crazy Eddie? I remember him."

"Yeah, Eric is his older brother, and he played at Lincoln High. He and some friends were playing basketball at the park the day Brady took pictures of Diane and me. He mistook Diane for my mother. I teased her about it last night, and she got kinda mad."

"I can understand that."

"She colored her hair because she found a few gray ones."

"She's kinda young to be getting gray hair, isn't she?"

"Mom was pretty young when her hair turned gray, but she's always colored it. I think the stress of her relationship with Craig has caused Diane to start going gray. Can we go to a movie or something later? I would like to have some time for us to be together."

"We're together now."

"I mean away from the house where we can be alone and maybe... you know... kiss and stuff."

"We can go somewhere, but I don't think it's a good idea for us to make out right now."

I'm not putting up with this much longer. Emmy clenched her jaw. "I want to go to Darby's. Can we do that at least?"

Tony agreed to take Emmy to Darby's for dinner, but wouldn't go to a movie. Emmy drove to Darby's. After they finished eating, Emmy took Tony to Windsor Park.

"I don't think there's enough snow to go sledding today, Em," Tony said.

"Can we go for a walk along the river? It's such a beautiful day."

"Sure, we can do that."

They hiked along the Kinmundy River. Emmy chattered away as they took the Riverwalk all the way to the campus of North Park, but Tony spoke only when he needed to answer a question. Emmy did convince Tony to hold her hand for a time. They headed back to the car, and Tony got in on the passenger side. Emmy slid in, reached over the console, took his face in her hands and kissed him hungrily.

"What are you doing?" Tony asked after the kiss.

"I want to go back to my house. I want you to take me to bed. Maybe that's what's wrong with us. Maybe if we sleep together everything will be all right."

Tony put his hands on her shoulders and held her at bay. "You know better than that, Emmy. You can't use sex to solve our problem." He moved as far away from her as possible in the small Civic.

She raised her voice as she responded, "You won't tell me what the problem is! How can I make everything right if I don't know what's broken?"

"There's nothing you can do to fix anything. Can we just go back to my house? I'm tired."

"I'll take you home if I can *rest* with you."

"No! That's not gonna happen. Just take me home."

She started the car and fought to hold back her tears. "Fine!

202

If that's what you want, then I'll take you home, but I might decide to go out by myself tonight. Better yet, maybe I'll call Christopher Braun and see what he's doing. Or maybe I'll ask Randy to go out."

Tony couldn't look at Emmy as he clenched his jaw and smacked his fist against the dashboard. "I know you're just trying to threaten me or blackmail me or something. I know you really wouldn't go out with either of those guys."

"Ha! How do you know I haven't been going out with them already? Maybe I'm going to meet Christopher later tonight."

"Go ahead." Tony shrugged. "Do whatever you want with them. It doesn't matter to me."

She slammed on the brakes.

"What are you doing?" he yelled. "You're in the middle of the street."

"Get out!" She pushed him toward the door. "Get out of my car! I never want to see you again."

"Fine with me." He got out and slammed the door closed. *Great! Now I have to walk home.* "Emmy, wait. I'm sorry. Give me a ride home and I'll talk to you."

"Too late! You had you're chance." She floored the accelerator and sped away.

"Thanks for nothing." He shook his head as the car disappeared around the corner. *I might as well run home.*

He started jogging. Two blocks down the road a car pulled up beside him. He stopped and looked over.

"Get in, but I'm not talking to you. I'm still madder than hell, but I'll call a truce so you don't have to walk home."

"Thanks, Emmy."

"Seat belt." She pointed and didn't say another word until she dropped him off at home. "Don't expect me to be here after work anymore. If you want to see me, you have to come to my house."

"Okay, Emmy. Thanks for the ride," he said. He walked into the house without looking back.

Chapter Twenty-Two

"Tony, I know something's wrong, but you won't talk to me about it. What's the matter? Did you have a hard time with finals or something?" Emmy asked as she stood by the flowerbed next to the driveway at Tony's house.

"No, it's not that, Emmy. I'm sorry, but I can't talk about it right now."

"That's what you said last week and the week before and the week before that. When are we gonna talk about this... gulf that's come between us."

"I need to go, Em." He looked at her car. "Could you please move, so I can get out of the driveway?"

"Fine! Mr. Oliver asked if I could work forty hours this week. I'm gonna tell him I will since you don't give a damn what I do."

She stomped away, got in her car, and if a Honda Civic could peel rubber, she would have laid a streak of it all the way to the corner.

Mama stood on the porch and shook her head.

Later, Emmy lay on her bed as she talked to Kristen on the phone. "Do you know what's up with your cousin. He's acting like an idiot."

"What did he do now?"

"Nothing."

"Nothing? What do you mean?" Kristen checked her freshly painted fingernails.

"He won't kiss me. He barely talks to me. I could strip naked, and he probably wouldn't even look at me."

"Stop that."

Emmy rolled over onto her stomach as she twirled her hair with her finger. "Has he said anything to you? You're his closest cousin. He always tells you stuff."

"He hasn't said anything to me, Em. In fact, I really haven't seen him, either."

"Has your father said anything? Has he noticed a change?"

"The only thing I've heard Daddy say is that Tony works

harder than five men, and he's quick to learn."

"That doesn't help." Emmy kicked at the covers on her bed.

"I'm sorry, Em. I'll call him tonight..."

"He won't talk on the phone."

"Then I'll have dinner with Mama and wait for him. I'll make him talk." Kristen assured Emmy as she thought, *I'll blackmail him if I have to.*

"Call me back after you've talked to him."

Kristen saw her mother in the kitchen. "I'm going over to Mama's. I have to talk to Tony."

"So you won't be here for dinner?"

"Is that all right?"

"Sure. I'll have your father take me out." Karla noticed a casserole dish on the granite island. "Since you're going, would you take this back to Maria."

"No problem. Make Daddy take you somewhere expensive. See you later."

Mama was in the kitchen when Kristen let herself in the back door.

"Hello, dear. I didn't know you were coming over."

"I should have called." Kristen set the casserole dish on the counter. "Mom sent this back."

Mama laughed. "You know better than that. You don't have to call me first."

"That smells good. Is it almost done?"

"Almost. Tony requested spaghetti. He said something about carbo loading."

"Emmy made me come over here and talk to him. She is desperate to learn what's bothering him."

"I know. He won't tell me anything. It's like he's turned into Heather. She keeps her affairs so private."

"Any suggestions?"

"I've tried everything. Maybe you'll have better luck." Mama stirred the spaghetti. "I feel so bad for Emmy. She stopped over here this morning and he made her mad."

Ten minutes later, Tony walked in the back door. "That smells so good. Thank you for making it, Mama." He hugged her

205

and kissed her cheek.

"You're in a good mood for a change."

"I got a call from someone today, so I'm happy."

"Who called?" Mama asked as she took the bread out of the oven.

"Someone from school. I'll shower real quick." He avoided answering the question.

"Kristen's here," Mama said. "She's missed you."

"Great," he muttered. *I bet Emmy asked her to come over and talk to me. Well, I'm not telling her anything, either.*

They sat at the kitchen table to eat. Tony engaged in the conversation as if nothing was wrong. He teased Kristen and told some funny stories from his day at work.

Kristen stared at him. *Is Emmy imagining everything? He's not acting any different as far as I can tell.*

After he emptied the pot of spaghetti, Tony rubbed his stomach. "That was delish, Mama. To show my appreciation, Kristen and I will do the dishes."

"What?" Kristen nearly choked on a piece of bread. "Did you just volunteer to do dishes?"

"I do the dishes every once in a while."

"You were ten the last time I saw you do dishes."

Mama chuckled then said, "I will take you up on your offer. I'll be in my sewing room if you need help."

Tony washed the dishes and Kristen dried.

"Are you going out with anyone, Kristen? You haven't mentioned any new men in your life."

"I'm not seeing anyone special since I broke up with Brandon. How about you? Anything going on with you and Emmy?"

"Nice try." Tony splashed some water at Kristen.

Kristen put the last pot away as Tony drained the water and wiped off the countertop.

"Okay, we can either do this the easy way and you can talk to me, or else we do it the hard way." Kristen twirled the dish towel in her hand.

"I'm not intimidated by your threats."

"What if I call Uncle Carmen?" Kristen snapped the towel at him, but missed.

"I saw him today. He said to say hi. Anything else?"

Tony left the kitchen, walked down the hallway and headed upstairs.

Kristen followed right behind him. She slipped into his room before he could close the door.

"I'm not leaving until you talk to me." She sat on his bed and folded her arms across her chest.

He walked out of the room and headed down the stairs.

"Where are you going? Get back here."

"It's a beautiful night. I'm going for a walk."

"I'm going with you." Kristen scrambled down the stairs after him.

"It's a free country. I can't stop you." He opened the front door and stepped outside.

Kristen scurried to keep up as Tony walked briskly down the sidewalk.

"There has to be something wrong. Emmy is worried sick." She grabbed his arm, and he stopped. "Please, tell me, Tony."

"Kristen, I love you like a sister, but I can't talk about it."

"You have to talk to her even if it will hurt her. She deserves that much."

"No." Tony didn't say another word as he walked away.

"You can be the most pigheaded person I know!" Kristen stood with her hands on her hips. Then she turned on her heals and walked back to the house.

"Any luck?" Mama asked as she sat in her chair with a book on her lap.

"No, he's about as stubborn as Emmy. I have to call her. She won't like it that I haven't had any better luck."

Emmy made one more attempt on Sunday afternoon to talk to Tony. She tried everything to get Tony to show her more affection but nothing worked. He still acted indifferently toward her as far as romance was concerned. He treated her courteously, and even teased her occasionally, but a problem still existed in their relationship.

I'm gonna go nuts if I can't get to the root of the problem.
She thought as she followed him around the front yard. But her
stubbornness would not allow her to break up with him.

"Well, you're leaving tomorrow so we really need to talk
about it right now. Please, tell me if I did something wrong." She
talked calmly and didn't let her emotions get the best of her for
once.

"I really can't right now." He checked the yard for any signs
of weeds.

Emmy tried to kiss him, but Tony didn't refused.

"Why won't you kiss me? I brushed my teeth... just a
couple days ago." Emmy tried to be funny, but it had no effect.
"Summer classes begin in two days." Emmy grabbed his arm and
pleaded with him. "Please, Tony, tell me what is troubling you. I
need to know. Don't you love me anymore? Just tell me if you
don't. Did I do something wrong? I'm sorry if I did something to
cause you to be upset with me, but I can't take not knowing."

Tony placed his hands on her shoulders and apologized.
"I'm sorry for not spending more time with you, but there's
something troubling me, and I just can't talk to you about it now."
He turned away.

At least you admit there's something wrong. That's a start.
She scooted around in front of him. "Are you upset because I'm
friends with Barry or Derrick? Is it because of my relationship with
Kenny?"

"Emmy, it's nothing you have done." He turned away again,
took a few steps and said over his shoulder, "I don't mind that you
are friends with any of those guys. They are my friends, too."

She ran after him. "Is it because of what I said about
Christopher and Randy?"

"No, of course not." He stopped and faced her.

"Is it because I've kissed other boys?" She grinned trying to
use humor to break through.

"I don't mind that you've kissed other boys. I certainly don't
expect you to become a nun and never look at other boys. None of
that matters anymore." He waved his hands in the air. "I still care

208

about you, Emmy, and I always will, but maybe you should forget about me."

Tears welled up in her eyes and overflowed onto her cheeks. "Tony, I can never forget about you. I love you. You are my whole world. Tell me what's wrong."

"I can't, Emmy." He turned to walk away with hands clenched into fists and tears flowing down his face.

Emmy sat on the ground and wept. She stopped crying and for thirty minutes she absentmindedly worked on Mama's flower beds. Tony went in the house and packed his suitcase. He decided to leave right away for South Bend without saying goodbye to Emmy.

Mama walked into his room. "I've never known you to run away from an issue, but that's what you are doing now. You are taking the easy way out, and she deserves better than that. That girl has tried everything this past month to get you to talk to her. If you leave this way, you may lose more than just her love. You will lose her friendship as well. Is that what you want? I know you have been trying to drive her away, but she's stubborn and won't give up."

Tony looked at his mother. He knew she was right. "I'm sorry, Mama. I feel like a complete jerk, but it's for her own good. I'm going to stay with Heather tonight. I'll talk to you soon."

Mama sighed in resignation. "Goodbye, son. I love you, and I will pray for you and Emmy."

Tony loaded his car, and waved goodbye to Mama as she stood by the back door. He slowly backed down the driveway and saw Emmy walking in the front door. It ripped his heart apart to leave this way, but he convinced himself that she would be better off without him. Emmy didn't even hear him leave.

She walked slowly into the kitchen and plopped down hard on a kitchen chair. "Do you have any idea what's bothering Tony? Any idea at all? I've given up. He still won't tell me anything. Can you make him tell me? I'll go crazy if I don't find out what I did wrong. He said it's not because of Kenny, but maybe it is. Maybe he found out what..." She paused because she didn't want to spill a secret. "Please make him talk to me."

Mama looked at her with the saddest expression Emmy had ever seen. "Tony will have to tell you himself, honey. I can't force him, and I'm sorry to tell you but he has already left for school."

"No! No!" Emmy cried out in anguish. She sprinted up to his room and pushed open the door so hard it smacked into the wall and knocked over a picture on his dresser. "Tony, where are you?" She ran out of the room and flew down the stairs. She threw open the front door as she yelled "Tony" over and over. She jumped over a flower bed and looked in the driveway where his car had been parked. "No!" she moaned, but his car was gone. She trudged back toward the house. Mama met her on the front porch. Mama held her tightly to her chest as Emmy sobbed uncontrollably. The fact that Tony left without saying goodbye scared Emmy to death.

The next few days were nightmarish for Emmy. She couldn't sleep. She lost her appetite and even got sick to her stomach. She couldn't keep anything down except for chicken broth. She stayed with Mama until Wednesday. She missed work and worried about that. She didn't realize it, but she lost weight. Mama hugged her and could tell though.

"You have to try to eat something, sweetie. You are just skin and bones. I'm afraid a stiff breeze will blow you away."

"I can't eat anything but soup right now. Tony won't take my calls, and he hasn't answered my emails. I talked to Kristen, but she doesn't know anything." She pleaded with Mama, "Please tell me what's wrong. Not knowing is making me sick."

"I don't know anything else to tell you, honey. If I knew anything, I would tell you." Mama put her arms around Emmy.

"I know you would, Mama. I just can't understand it. Two months ago we went out for dinner and everything was perfect. We were going to take it slow and then when he came home, everything was totally... messed up."

"I know how much you love him, and it breaks my heart to see you suffer so. All you can do is pray, honey. Say a prayer for Tony every night, and God will answer your prayers."

Chapter Twenty-Three

Every night for the rest of the week Emmy knelt by her bed and prayed for Tony. On Saturday night Emmy tried to remember something her friend Lynette Rosas from the Crest Ridge United Nazarene Church told her.

What was it? I know it was something about Jesus loving us no matter what we did. Maybe I should read the Bible she gave me.

Emmy pulled out the Bible that had been covered by her clothes. She noticed an old bookmark and pulled it out. *This is the one Kenny gave me a long time ago. It's John 3:16. I want to find that in the Bible.* She sat on her bed and flipped through the pages. *I know it's in the New Testament. Where is it?* She flipped back and forth until she located the Gospel of John. She scanned through the pages until she found it.

"For God so loved the world, that he gave his one and only Son, that whoever believes in Him shall not perish, but have eternal life."

Emmy turned the pages and the Bible fell open to I Corinthians 13:4.

"Love is patient, love is kind. It does not envy, it does not boast, it is not proud."

Emmy read about love. She read to the end of the chapter and kept going to the end of chapter fifteen. She fell to her knees beside her bed. She grabbed her pillow and buried her face in it as she sobbed. She lifted her head and looked up. Still sobbing, she talked to Jesus just like she would talk to a friend.

"Forgive me, Jesus, because I am a sinner. I don't understand everything, but I realize that I need you to be in my life and guide me. I want to make the same commitment to you that Kenny did. Show me what to do. Please."

As Emmy uttered this simple plea, a peace came into her heart. She stopped sobbing and knew that something had happened.

"Thank you, Jesus. I'm not sure what I should do now. I suppose I should go back to church even though Kenny isn't home."

She went to bed and slept peacefully for the first time since Tony left to go back to school.

Emmy woke up earlier than normal on Sunday morning. She got out of bed, noticed the open Bible on her dresser and read the same chapters in Corinthians. She finished reading and prayed silently. Then she walked to Diane's room. She knocked on the open door.

"What do you want, Emmy? I'm trying to sleep."

"I'm going to church. Do you want to go with me?"

"You're going where? Is Kenny here?" Diane asked as she sat up in bed. "Are you going to his church?"

"He's not here. I'm going by myself. Unless you want to go with me?"

"No, I just want to sleep, Emmy." Diane lay back down and turned on her side. "I'll see you later."

Emmy got ready and grabbed the old Bible. *I'm going to take this with me. Lots of people at that church in Crest Ridge would carry a Bible with them.* She backed the car out of the driveway. "Shoot! I turned the wrong way. Kenny's church is in the other direction." She glanced down at the Bible on the passenger seat. "Jesus, are you trying to tell me something? I don't know how this stuff works. Maybe I should go back to that church in Crest Ridge. I did like the music there better than at Kenny's church." She waited for a moment. She closed her eyes and sat there in the street with the car running. "Okay, this is kinda weird, but for some reason I feel I need to go back to that other church. I hope you won't mind, Kenny. I hope I remember how to get there." She made her way to Crest Ridge United Nazarene, the church that Lynette Rosas first took her to nearly four years ago, without making a wrong turn. She parked the car, got out and closed the door. *Shoot! I forgot my Bible.* She opened the door, leaned in and grabbed the Bible. *I will have to remember to bring you with me.* She stared at the building and noticed the large, metal cross on top of the roof. *I see you're still there.* She took a deep breath, walked up to the large building and entered the spacious foyer. *I don't remember where to go. I think the classes must have started already. I must be late. Maybe I should go home.*

A young man in a suit approached and greeted her with a friendly smile. "Hello, welcome to Crest Ridge Nazarene. Can I help you with anything?"

"Hi, uh, maybe. I don't know if she still comes to church here, but several years ago a friend of mine brought me to this church a few times. I wondered if maybe she would still be here."

"What is her name?" He held out a hand. "My name is Paul Jefferson and you are?"

"Emmy, Emmy Colasanti. I don't remember her last name, but her first name was Lynette."

Paul's eyes lit up when Emmy mentioned Lynette's name. "I believe I can help you, Emmy. Please, come with me." He smiled. *Lord, you surely do work in mysterious ways.*

Paul led her out of the foyer, down a hallway and down some stairs. She waited outside a classroom as Paul opened the door. Emmy saw children sitting on small multicolored plastic chairs in a circle singing a song while making motions with their hands.

Paul stepped inside the classroom. "I'm sorry to interrupt, Lynette. You're not going to believe this, but there is a friend of yours here to see you. She's just outside in the hall."

Lynette turned to look and immediately recognized Emmy. The children kept singing as Lynette hurried over to see Emmy.

"Emmy, Emmy, is that really you? It's so good to see you. Wow, this is really a surprise, but in a way I'm not surprised at all. I thought about you just last night, and I felt a need to say a prayer for you and now here you are. I see you have met my husband."

"Your husband?" Emmy turned to Paul and smiled. "You didn't tell me Lynette was your wife."

"I am sorry for that bit of deception, but I wanted to surprise both of you. Please forgive me." He grinned like a Cheshire cat. "Lynette, do you want me to see if Aunt Doris can step in and take over the class for you? I think Emmy would like to talk to you privately."

"Thanks, Paul."

213

Lynette and Emmy talked for a moment as they waited for Aunt Doris to take over the class. Aunt Doris entered and took over without missing a beat. Lynette and Emmy found a place to talk privately.

"I don't know how to explain this to you, Lynette, but I'll try. A few days ago my boyfriend Tony broke up with me, I think..."

Emmy explained everything that had happened up until last night.

"So last night after I said a prayer for Tony, I got my old Bible out of my dresser." She held it up to show Lynette. "I haven't read it in years, but it's the one you gave me to read. I opened it and read a couple passages, John 3:16, and then I read two or three chapters in another section that talked about love. Anyway, I knew that I needed to talk to Jesus and ask for forgiveness for being such a lousy person. So I fell to my knees and just started talking to Him. I've said prayers for different things or for people before, but this was different. When I was finished, I felt so... so... calm. I don't know how to explain it, but I felt like all the cares that had been just tearing me apart were gone. I felt a peace in my heart and... I don't understand."

Tears streamed down Lynette's face as she held Emmy in her arms. Emmy cried, too, but her tears were no longer tears of sorrow, but tears of joy.

"Emmy, do you know what has happened to you?"

"I know I made a commitment to follow Jesus. I know he died on the cross for our sins, but I don't understand the peace that I feel. I still have the same problems as before. I knew I should go to church, and I intended to go to Faith Bible. That's where Kenny and his parents always go, but I turned the wrong way, and then I just kinda stopped, and I felt that I needed to come here. I just knew I needed to see you, and you could explain it to me." Emmy paused and took a deep breath.

"Emmy, Jesus has saved you from your sins, and now you are a child of the one true God. You have a new friend who will love you, guide you and be there for you whenever you need him. Not in the physical sense, but in your heart. You can call on him

214

any time, day or night, and talk to him just as you and I are talking now. Sure, you still have the same cares and problems as before, but now you have someone you can call on for guidance."

The words kept coming from Lynette as she explained salvation to Emmy. Emmy began to understand the miracle that had happened to her. She realized that she experienced the same transformation as her friends Scott and Randy and even the two girls at Kenny's church.

"Why don't you come with me to my class, and you can help me with the kids?"

Emmy followed Lynette back to the classroom full of children.

"Aunt Doris, this is my friend Emmy. She is a new believer."

"Hello, Emmy, I'm not really her aunt, but everyone around here calls me Aunt Doris. You can call me that, too, if you want. Would you like a piece of gum, dear?"

Emmy shyly smiled and nodded her head.

After the class finished, Lynette took Emmy to the sanctuary for the worship service. Emmy remembered the auditorium-sized sanctuary and noticed the crowd was a mixture of people of all ages and ethnicity.

"We still have a worship band," Lynette said.

"I think that might be part of why I decided to come here. I remembered the band and how much I liked to sing along."

"You have a beautiful voice. I remember that."

Emmy blushed. "Thanks, Lynette." *Should I mention singing at Kenny's church? It wasn't with a full band like Fridays At Five, but I still kinda liked it even if I was scared out of my mind.*

The worship band began playing and Emmy sang along. Lynette stood beside Emmy and listened. *I should tell Chase about you. You are probably a better singer than anyone on the platform.*

Emmy noticed the man who playing the keyboards and singing the melody to the songs. *He looks familiar. I wonder if he's the same man that was here from before.*

After the service, Lynette brought Emmy over to meet the

215

speaker.

"Dr. Ausland is out of town today, but do you remember Brian Riley?"

"I thought he looked familiar." Emmy glanced to the platform where the keyboard player was talking to some of the other musicians. *You have a good voice and you're about as good on the keyboards as Jeremy from Kenny's band. Actually, the whole band sounded pretty amazing. Especially for a bunch of older guys.*

"Pastor Brian, this is my friend, Emmy Colasanti."

"Emmy, it's good to see you again. I remember Lynette used to bring you to our youth group a few years ago. If there is anything I can do for you, please let me know."

Lynette said, "Emmy accepted Jesus as her Savior last night."

"That is certainly great news, Emmy. Would you allow me to pray with you?"

Pastor Brian began to pray for Emmy as she listened, "Thank you Lord for Emmy and her new birth. Please give us the wisdom to lead her in the path that you would have her follow..."

Emmy could sense the love and realized that she had found some special friends to help her in her new journey. Lynette gave her a small book before she left.

"This is a devotional book Dr. Ausland wrote, and he passes them along to all our new believers. I read my devotional book first thing when I wake up. You can see if that time works for you. You can read a small chapter, and it will help you understand the Bible better. You can call me anytime if you have questions. Dr. Ausland will be back next Sunday. He will be so thrilled to see you again."

"Is he the older man who used to preach when I came here before?"

"Yes, he's been our pastor for fifteen years or so."

"I remember him. Love and compassion just radiated from him." She chuckled. "He could recite the whole Bible from memory, too. I know he must be very smart, but he talked to us in terms we could understand. Thank you, Lynette. I will see you

216

again next Sunday."

That night Emmy called Kenny and told him what happened.

"Oh, Emmy..."

Emmy could tell he was crying. She bit her lip as she waited.

"Are you all right, Kenny?"

"I'm... I'm... Oh, Em."

She brushed away her tears as they ran down her cheek.

"That is the best..."

She heard him blow his nose.

"I didn't mean to make you cry."

"It's okay." After a short time he regained his composure. "That is the best news I could possibly hear. I'm so happy for you, Em."

"Now I know what you experienced."

"I will tell Becky. She will be so pleased."

"Is she a believer?"

"Yes, she is, and she helped me realize that I needed to rededicate my life to God. I have been a believer, but I always held something back. I never let God have total control of my life. Becky made me realize that I needed to surrender everything to Christ."

"Where does she go to church?"

"Her whole family goes to Living Water. It's close to where they live in Studio City. The senior pastor is Dr. Behren, and he's really a super guy. He likes to ride his Harley to church sometimes."

"I'm glad you and Becky are going to church together." Emmy's voice cracked just a bit. "I went to church today."

"Good! Did you tell Mom and Dad what you did?"

"Not really." She bit her lip for a moment.

"Weren't they there?"

"I didn't go to Faith Bible. I went back to that church in Crest Ridge. Crest Ridge United Nazarene Church." She explained her reasons for going there.

"The important thing is you went to church. I understand

217

that my parents' church is not for everyone. It's actually kind of old-fashioned."

"They have a really good worship band at Crest Ridge. I think you'd like to hear them."

"Maybe I will someday," he said. "Oh, Em. I can't wait to see you again."

"Lynette told me that when we confess our sins, God doesn't even remember them anymore."

"That's true. I think it's Psalm 103:12 that says, 'As far as the east is from the west, so far has He removed our transgressions from us.'"

"So that means that whatever we did before doesn't matter now."

"Are you talking about..."

"Yes, I know we didn't plan to go that far... but I'm not sorry we did."

"We were lucky. We could have gone all the way."

"I wouldn't have minded."

"Oh, Em."

"I still love you, Kenny."

"I know, and I still love you, too."

During the week, Emmy read the small devotional book Lynette gave her. She went to church again on Sunday, and Lynette introduced her to a small group of new believers like herself that met before the worship service. Emmy began to learn and grow much like a baby would. So much was new to her, and she absorbed this new knowledge like a sponge absorbed water. After church, Lynette reintroduced Emmy to Pastor Herb Ausland.

"Emmy, it is so good to see you again. I am Pastor Herb. Lynette told me you are a new believer. I want you to know that I am here for you if you have any questions. We want you to feel welcome and loved in this church and hope you will allow me to pray with you."

"Thank you, Pastor Ausland. I don't know what Lynette has told you about me."

"She told me that you were a new believer, and you are

friends."

"We are friends, I guess."

"We are all part of God's family, Emmy," Pastor Ausland said.

"I'll see you next Sunday. I need to get home."

Soon her friends began to see a difference in Emmy. She tried to explain what had happened to her. Diane thought it was only a phase and she would soon return to normal. Kristen understood more than any of her other friends and expressed eagerness to learn more about Emmy's new faith. Emmy tried to explain to Kristen what she learned in her Bible class.

"You could come with me, Kristen. Everyone I have met there is so nice, and they're just like regular people. They're not freaks or dorks or anything. They are happy because of their faith. I wore jeans and a t-shirt to church and no one seemed to care. I saw other people dressed casually, and some were dressed up. There were lots of young people and a bunch of different ethnic groups. They all got along like one big family."

"Maybe I will come with you some Sunday."

"I wish you would. I think you would like it."

"You really seem different, Em."

"I am different, Kristen." She paused. "I'm still me, but different in some ways."

"Are you still a goofy tomboy?" Kristen teased.

Emmy chuckled then said, "I suppose some things won't ever change."

Chapter Twenty-Four

"We're still going out to party, Emmy," Barry Newton told her over the phone. "You only turn twenty-one once. You used to talk about this day. You looked forward to going into a bar and ordering a beer even though you still look sixteen."

"I know. I wanted to surprise the bartender and prove I was legal."

"Don't you still want to do that?"

"Not really. I guess it would be fun to be carded and all, but I'm different now, Barry."

"Doesn't matter," he said. "So, are we going out, or not?"

"Yes. I took tomorrow off. I might as well go. I don't want to ruin the night for everyone else. Kristen invited a ton of people."

"We'll be there in thirty minutes. You don't have to drink, but we are going to party."

Emmy remembered how she used to look forward to this day, July 8, 2001, but now she felt differently because of some new priorities in her life. Barry and Linda picked her up, and she climbed into the back seat.

Barry turned to look at her. "Since you aren't going to drink, you are hereby officially designated the designated driver. I want to drink tonight."

Linda rolled her eyes. "You are such a nerd."

"Fine! Kristen is going to meet us at the bar. Have you guys ever been to this place before?" Emmy asked as she checked out Barry's newest old car.

"Sure. Haven't you ever been to Wyatt's Table?" Barry asked as he looked in the rearview mirror. "It's been around for fifty years."

"Sorry, but I wasn't around when it opened," Emmy teased. "Can you turn on some music?"

"No can do. The radio doesn't work."

"Then why did you buy this old boat?"

"Because it's only got fifty thousand miles on it. It belonged to the mother of a guy from work and she only drove..."

"Yeah, yeah, I've heard the story before. It belonged to

grandma, and she only drove it to church on Sunday and never went faster than thirty miles-an-hour."

"It's got power windows and locks," Barry mentioned.

Emmy put her ear against the window. "Can't hear any tunes on the power windows."

Linda turned in her seat. "I agree with you, Emmy. His other car might have been older, but at least the radio worked."

"Maybe you should buy a new car one of these days, Barry," Emmy said.

"Nope! Too much money. I paid cash for this."

"Did the previous owner give you change back from your twenty?" Emmy asked.

They pulled into the asphalt parking lot, jumped out of the car and Barry held the bar door open for Emmy and Linda.

"Thank you, Barry," Emmy said.

"I'm only doing this because it's your birthday."

"Yeah, he never opens doors for me," Linda complained.

Emmy waited a second, and then followed Barry and Linda down a short hall lined with vintage photographs of SoHam. *I know that building. It used to be the courthouse.* She paused.

"Come on, Em. You can look at those later," Barry said as he motioned for her to hurry.

Emmy scooted past two guys leaving. "I'm coming. It's my birthday so be patient."

Kristen met them at Wyatt's. She arrived with a date.

"Happy birthday, Em. This is Brandon Kelly," Kristen said.

Brandon held out his hand. "Yes, happy birthday, Emmy."

"Thank you. I'm glad to meet you." Emmy stared into his blue eyes. *You do look very handsome. Your blonde hair kinda makes you look like a surfer dude.*

Emmy pulled Kristen aside as Brandon headed to the bar. "I thought you guys broke up? Why are you here with him?"

"Brandon broke up with his other girlfriend, and we are going to try again. This is our first date. We are taking things real slow." Kristen glanced around the bar. "What do you think? Isn't he absolutely gorgeous?"

"He looks like a poster boy from California." Emmy

221

glanced at him again. "He kinda reminds me of Christopher, but a smaller version."

"I know, but I'm still a little leery about him."

Kristen experienced a bad breakup with Harrison Stewart that left her unable to fully trust men.

Emmy bounced on her toes—giddy with happiness. "I am so happy for you, Kristen. I hope you will be as happy with Brandon as I am with Tony."

Kristen snapped her attention back to Emmy. "Are you and Tony back together? If you are, I am so thrilled for you."

"We aren't back together, yet, but I know we will be soon. Please don't tell him, but I'm gonna go see him. I want it to be a surprise."

"Are you sure that's a good idea? Maybe you should let him know before you just show up," Kristen suggested.

"I'll see what happens. I'm not sure when I can get over there, yet, but I want to go as soon as I can. I wrote him a letter and tried to explain what has happened to me."

"Just be careful, Em." Kristen put her hands on Emmy's shoulders. "I know how excited you get. I don't want you to get your feelings hurt anymore."

Diane had called Emmy earlier in the day to wish her a happy birthday. Emmy hadn't seen her since she and Craig moved to Toledo, Ohio, quite unexpectedly. Emmy ended the call, sat at the kitchen table and recalled the night Diane came home from work with Craig along.

"Emmy! Where are you?" Diane hollered from downstairs.

"I'm in my room. What's up?"

Diane bounded up the stairs and into Emmy's room.

"I have some news," Diane said as she watched Emmy changing clothes.

"Are you gonna tell me, or do I have to guess?" Emmy slipped on a t-shirt and got her head stuck in the collar.

"For Pete's sake, Emmy. Buy some new clothes." Diane pulled the t-shirt down and pulled Emmy's long hair out.

Emmy picked up her jeans from the bed. At that moment

they heard the sound of something breaking downstairs.

"What was that? Is there someone here?" Emmy peeked into the hall.

"Sorry," Craig hollered. "I dropped a glass."

Emmy looked at Diane. "Craig is here?"

"Yes, I spent the night with him."

"I knew you didn't come home, but whatever possessed you to spend the night with Craig?"

"Craig met me for dinner, and one thing led to another. It wasn't my fault." Diane shrugged.

"You could have said no!" Emmy shouted. "Oh, that's right. You never learned how to say no to a man."

"Screw you, Emmy! He's moving back to Toledo because he got a better job. He asked me to go with him, and I think I just might. That's where he's from. His family still lives there."

"Why? Do you know what you will be giving up?" Emmy grabbed Diane's shoulders and shook her. "You just got a great job, and you and Brady are getting along so well."

Diane backed away. "I haven't totally made up my mind."

"What's there to think about? Brady is ten times the man Craig will ever be. I can't believe you are even considering this." Emmy raised her voice.

"Is everything all right up there?" Craig asked from the bottom of the stairs. "Should I come upstairs?"

"No!" Emmy yelled.

"I'll be right there, Craig. Stay downstairs because Emmy's getting dressed."

"Did you have to tell him that?" Emmy asked as she struggled into her jeans.

A week later Diane resigned from her new job and ended her budding romance with Brady Robertson. She moved to Toledo with Craig leaving Emmy alone in the large house.

Emmy had requested a personal day weeks before because she assumed she would be drinking on her birthday. In fact, she had planned on getting drunk and maybe doing even more if she

223

found the right guy. Emmy surprised everyone by only drinking bottled water. She joined a group of guys playing darts and accidentally hit Barry's arm with a dart.

"I'm hit, I'm hit. I'm dying. So young and my life is almost over." Barry pretended to be mortally wounded, and Emmy fawned over him while everybody else laughed.

Linda made sure that Barry wasn't seriously injured, and then poked him in the side. "Emmy, will you aim better the next time so I can collect on his life insurance."

"Aw, Linda, you would miss me, wouldn't you?" Barry stood up and kissed his wife.

Emmy giggled then said, "I'll be less careful next time."

She saw two men emerge from the hallway and smiled as they approached.

"I hear there's a party for a birthday girl. Do you know anything about that, Emmy?" Christopher Braun asked.

"I didn't know if you guys were coming. I'm glad to see you."

Christopher kissed her cheek. "So, did the bartender believe that fake ID of yours?"

"It's not a fake. I'm really twenty-one now." Emmy protested in a childlike voice.

"Of course you are, little girl," Randy said.

Christopher headed to the bar and ordered a beer.

"Are you still staying away from alcohol, Randy?" Emmy asked.

"Yes, it's been two months, give or take."

"I'm sticking to bottled water tonight." Emmy touched his arm. "Do you want one?"

"Maybe later," he said. "There's an empty table, Em. I'd like to talk to you."

They sat down and right away Emmy said, "I accepted Jesus into my life. I should have done it a long time ago, but I didn't."

"That's great news, Em."

"Are you still going to church?"

"I'm still going to Faith Bible, but I've been thinking about switching. Crest Ridge Nazarene would be closer."

"That's where I'm going! I think you'd like it. They have an awesome worship band. Not as good as Fridays At Five, but good. The people are friendly, and I love Pastor Herb." Emmy grinned as she took a drink of water. "Oh, I should congratulate you. You are a college graduate. I'm impressed."

"Thanks, Em. Not only do I have my degree, but I've been accepted into the graduate program."

"That's great. Do you know what you want to do after you finish?"

"My goal is to be a professor at North Park. If I have to, I'll settle for another university."

They talked about college and church for a few minutes then Randy asked, "How are things going with Kenny and Tony?"

"You haven't heard, huh?" Emmy sighed.

"I guess not. What happened? Did you break up with Kenny?"

"Yes, he's with Becky." She spend some time telling him the details.

"And Tony?"

"Tony and I were trying to see if we could work things out, but it didn't go so well." She explained what happened.

"Emmy, what would you say if I asked you out for dinner?"

She grinned. "Are you asking, or was that a rhetorical question?"

"I suppose I'm asking. What do you think?"

Emmy bit her lip. "I think you're a great guy, Randy, but..."

"Uh-oh, that doesn't sound good."

"My feelings for you haven't changed just because we're both going to church. I consider you a good friend, but that's all." Emmy glanced at Christopher.

Randy turned his head. "Oh, I get it. You know he and Victoria are married now?"

"I know. I wasn't invited to the wedding, though."

"She didn't want to invite too many of his old girlfriends..."

"I was never his girlfriend." Emmy knocked over her water as she protested.

"Yeah, but you guys did have a thing for each other." Randy righted the bottle of water before too much of it spilled.

Emmy blushed. "Maybe I had a little crush on him, but that was a long time ago."

"Yeah, way back in March," Randy said. "I'd say it was more than just a little crush."

"I'm different now." Emmy poked his arm. "There are a lot of single females at Crest Ridge. You might find one you like."

"Maybe I'll check it out." He grinned, as he wiped up the water. "I would wager there are quite a large number of single males, also."

Before they left, Barry took Emmy aside. "You're different. I've known you forever, but now you seem like a different person in a way."

"I am different, Barry," Emmy said. "I accepted Jesus into my life. Tony and I are struggling, and Kenny has a new girlfriend named Becky." She filled Barry in about the changes in her life.

"I'm happy for you, Em, and I hope everything works out between you and Tony or Kenny or whoever."

"I've left it in God's hands. I'm learning to accept that He knows what is best for me."

Barry put his hand on Emmy's shoulder. "What if you aren't meant to be with Tony or Kenny? How would you feel about that? You've never dated very many guys."

"I know." She glanced at Christopher. "I don't have a lot of experience with men. I guess I've always figured I would be with Kenny, or maybe Tony, after I met him, but maybe I won't."

"Em, there are tons of guys out there who would love to be with you. You are still young..."

"Look who's talking? You're not that much older than me, and you're already married."

"Happily married." Barry smiled at Linda.

Linda scowled at him.

Emmy laughed as she saw Linda's expression. "There are plenty of guys at church. Who knows? Maybe one of them will be Mr. Right."

Chapter Twenty-Five

John saw a letter on Tony's desk. "Is that the letter from the girl back home you were telling me about?"

"Yeah." Tony sat on his bed with his back against the wall as he flipped a football from hand to hand. "It's three pages long and I don't understand it. She went to church and... let me see what it says." He reached over, grabbed the letter, read part of it and waved it at John. "She accepted Jesus as her Savior. She's Catholic like me. I don't know why she's going to this other church." Tony handed the letter to John.

"Are you gonna answer it?" John asked, as he glanced at the first page. Then he handed it back.

"I wouldn't know what to say." Tony tossed the letter on his desk.

"Are you gonna tell her about Brenda?"

"Maybe one of these days."

"She deserves to know." John sat on the edge of his desk and faced Tony.

"Yeah, I know, but if you only knew her." Tony tossed the football to John, who dropped it. "Good hands!"

John picked up the football and threatened to throw it back at Tony. "I wasn't looking."

"Yeah, lame excuse."

John tossed the ball back to Tony.

"This will break her heart. She's such a sweet kid despite having had a pretty tough childhood. I was a complete jerk to her when I was home. I did all I could to drive her away."

"Almost sounds like you should be her big brother."

"That would certainly be easier. She's always accused me of treating her like a little sister."

"Have you ever treated Brenda like a little sister?"

Tony snorted. "She'd kill me if I did."

"I saw Brenda at mass."

"Yeah, she's a good Catholic girl."

Tony didn't write back. He didn't return Emmy's calls or respond to her emails.

227

Emmy drove to South Bend to see Tony on Saturday, July fourteenth. She planned to stay with Heather again and hoped to meet Tony for dinner. Tony reluctantly agreed to have dinner, but only after Heather agreed to join them.

"I'd like water with lemon, please," Emmy told the college-age waitress.

Tony ordered a Coke, and Heather chose a red wine.

What should I say? I need something clever to break the ice. Emmy bit her lip, waited a few seconds and then said, "So this is it, huh?" *Great! That was so lame.*

"What do you mean, Em?" Tony asked.

"This will be your final year, right? You're gonna graduate in the spring."

"That's the plan." Tony buried his nose in the menu.

"As long as you pass all your classes," Heather said. *I'm going to strangle you if you aren't at least civil to Emmy. Get your nose out of the menu and look at her when she talks to you.*

"He'll pass." Emmy patted his hand. "By the way, I happened to read an article about the coming season. One writer touted you as a possible Heisman Trophy winner."

"He's blowing smoke." Tony pulled his hand away. "Middle linebackers don't win the Heisman."

Heather noticed and clenched her jaw. *You are so close to me going nutzo on you.*

"Maybe you could break that tradition," Emmy said.

"A lot of it is PR."

"Notre Dame has had its share of winners," Heather said as she sipped her wine. "I'm not an expert, but I think he will get drafted in the first round. If the team does well, he could be one of the first five chosen." *That is if you change your attitude. Because if you don't, I'm gonna hurt you.*

"It would be so cool if the Bears draft him."

"You're dreaming, Em." Tony continued to scan the menu. *Why did I ever agree to this? I know Heather is ready to flip out.*

"Yeah, but I'm also praying for that to happen."

"Just because you say a prayer doesn't mean it will happen. Everybody prays for stuff. Do you think God is like a genie in a

228

bottle who grants wishes?" Tony's voice contained plenty of sarcasm.

"That's it!" Heather looked at Emmy, who shook her head as if saying, *It's all right.*

"I know, but I'm still gonna pray for it," Emmy replied. *I'm not gonna let your lousy mood spoil our dinner.*

After dinner, Heather needed to go to work, so Tony took Emmy back to Heather's apartment. They sat down on the couch.

"Did you get my letter, Tony?"

"Yes, and I have read it over and over again. Do you really believe everything you wrote?"

"Yes, I do. I feel like a new person since I accepted Jesus, and I pray everyday for you and our relationship."

"Emmy, I have to tell you something, and you will not like it, but if we are to ever have a chance at salvaging our friendship, I have to tell you."

Tony looked at her with a sad expression on his face and an ache deep in his heart. More butterflies filled his stomach now than before a big game. Suddenly, the door opened unexpectedly, and Heather walked in on them.

"Why are you home so early?" Tony asked.

"I have a massive headache and wasn't feeling well so I decided to come home. I'm going to bed." Heather glanced at Emmy before going to her room. *I wouldn't want to be in your shoes shoes right now, Emmy. Or Tony's either, for that matter.*

Tony and Emmy stared at each other for a moment.

"I have a confession to make, Emmy."

Emmy hoped Tony would explain what had been bothering him all summer.

"I went out on a date with another girl. I know I promised you that I would go out with three different girls, and I did. I told them about you, and they never went out with me again."

"What did you tell them about me?"

"It doesn't matter, Em." Tony ran a hand through his hair. "Okay, I might have said something like the only reason I was taking them out was because you made me promise to have a social life."

She laughed. "You need to work on your social skills. Sorry, please go ahead."

"Then I asked another girl out for a date. She was in my study group, so we met at the library every week to study. We got along and, well, I guess she actually asked me out on a date, but that's beside the point."

Emmy sat up next to him.

"There's more."

Emmy looked at him lovingly. "Just let it out, Tony. Don't be afraid to tell me."

"Well, I ended up going out more than once with this girl. In fact, I have been spending a lot of time with her."

Emmy thought that Tony had fallen in love with somebody else, and that was why he had been ignoring her calls and emails. Tears filled her eyes. "Do you love her?"

"I'm not sure. I like her a lot. We get along really well, and we don't fight."

"Like you and I do all the time, huh?" Emmy asked. "Is she prettier than me? Does she have a name?"

"No, Emmy, no."

"She doesn't have a name?"

"Yeah, it's Brenda Rollins. I meant you are just as pretty as her though you don't look anything like each other. Nothing happened between us at first except that she kissed me a few times. I guess I kissed her back a few times. We started spending a lot of time together."

"What do you mean by at first?"

"One night she came over to my room with a six-pack of beer. You know I don't drink much, but this night, I did." He sat back against the couch and closed his eyes for a moment. *I know you're not going to like what I say next, but I have to tell you.* "She spent the night in my dorm room. We studied together, drank the beer. One thing led to another, and we ended up sleeping together."

Emmy's jaw dropped lower and lower as Tony described how it happened. Her whole world shattered. Leaving her in a daze. Tony continued to talk to her, but she didn't hear a word he said.

230

When she finally heard him again, he was saying, "I thought she would sleep in John's bed because he wasn't there the night she stayed over."

I don't have any idea of what to say, but I can't just sit here and say nothing. Should I pretend it's not a big deal? I know guys sometimes fool around. Jesus, what should I do? She opened her eyes. "Does she have a better body than me?" *Oh, that was so lame.*

Tony turned beet red. "She's much bigger than you. Anyway, she got undressed and into bed with me."

"Did you do everything?" *Well, of course, you did. What guy would be able to resist a naked girl?* She glanced up at him.

Tony nodded and hung his head. He expected Emmy to scream and yell at him and tell him that she hated him, but she didn't say anything for nearly a minute.

Say something, Em. Don't just leave me hanging here. He waited for a few more seconds and then asked, "Do you hate me?"

I would, but Jesus wants us to love everybody. Emmy sniffled as she tried to hold back the tears. "No, I don't hate you, but I feel betrayed. All this time I thought you wanted to get back together, but you chose her instead of me. I still love you, and I forgive you because it says we should do that in the Bible, but I don't know if I can forget what you've done."

Heather stood in the doorway to her bedroom and listened. Tony had told her what happened, and that he planned to confess everything. Heather made a half-hearted attempt to convince him otherwise, but she knew that Tony needed to tell her.

"You can hit me if you want, Em. I deserve it for deceiving you."

I want to slug you hard enough to knock you out, but that would be wrong. She smacked Tony on his arm and chest, over and over again, but didn't have the energy to even hit him hard. She just went through the motions, and he looked so sad.

"Emmy, I'm so sorry. I should have told you before, but I was trying to spare your feelings by driving you away. You're just too stubborn, though. Can you ever forgive me?"

"It's my fault for forcing you to date other girls."

That's bull, Emmy! Heather thought. *He made his choice, and now he needs to own it.*

"I felt so lonely. I felt sorry for myself, and she just knew how to make me feel better."

If you're not going to smack him, then I will. Heather clenched her hands into fists.

Emmy frowned at him. "You're a jerk!"

"I don't mean it like that. Yeah, the sex felt good, but I'm talking about how we got along."

Heather came over to the couch and Emmy stood up in front of Tony.

"Just because we yell and scream doesn't mean we don't love each other." She kicked his shin, and then turned toward Heather. She paused, turned back to Tony and kicked him again. "I don't care what Jesus said. I hate you! I wish I never met you!"

Heather took her in her arms and let her cry some more.

Tony didn't rub his leg even though it hurt. "Emmy, I don't blame you if you never want to see me again. I wish we could still be friends, but I will understand if you aren't interested."

Heather gave him a dirty look, and then shook her head. *Just shut up before you totally ruin everything.*

Emmy stopped crying and faced him. "I forgive you because the Bible says I have to, but it will take some time before I can forget what you have done. And I'm sorry for kicking you." She kicked him again, but not as hard. "Not sorry!"

Heather felt like kicking him, too. "Come with me, Emmy. I know how much this hurts."

Heather took Emmy into the spare bedroom. Emmy climbed into bed and hugged the pillow to her chest as she curled up in a ball.

Heather sat on the edge of the bed and rubbed Emmy's back as she cried. "Let it go, Emmy." Heather removed Emmy's sneakers and comforted her as best she could, but she really just needed to let the tears flow. Emmy finally stopped crying, and Heather went back the the living room to see Tony. He sat stiffly with his back against the couch and didn't move. The redness of his eyes made it obvious that he had been crying. Heather sat beside

232

him and put her arm around him. Heather held him for awhile as neither of them said anything.

"Look, I don't know what will happen with you guys down the road, but if you can get through this, it will make you stronger."

"Are you trying to go all Nietzsche on me?"

"I'm only trying to help," Heather whispered.

"Yeah, I know, but I doubt she will ever talk to me again, and I don't blame her for that. I wouldn't talk to her if she had been sleeping around."

"This might sound like I'm preaching, or oversimplifying the situation, but you will be able to overcome this, and your love will be stronger than ever in the future. Not because of what you did, but because you overcame what happened. Time will heal her wounds. You have to be patient."

"Heather, I could have prevented this whole thing, but I didn't. At first I blamed that girl and the beer, but it was my fault, all my fault. I never should have started dating her again, but I thought it was all over between Emmy and myself. When you come right down to it, I chose Brenda over Emmy. Maybe because she was here, but maybe not."

"I'm going to bed. You can crash here if you want, but it might be better if you go back to the dorm." Heather stood up and pointed at the spare room. "And don't go in there to talk to her."

"I won't." He finally reached down and rubbed his leg. "That hurt."

"Serves you right. I tried to tell you that sometimes it's not the wisest choice to share every detail of your life. I never do."

Heather left Tony sitting on the couch by himself. He stayed there all night long. He finally walked back to his dorm in the early morning hours before Heather or Emmy were awake.

Emmy woke up still angry at Tony and didn't know if she could forget what he had done. She left Heather's place without bothering to shower or change clothes. She didn't call Tony. Over the next couple of days he called a few times, but she didn't answer the phone. She erased his messages without listening to them.

Chapter Twenty-Six

As Emmy walked in her back door on Wednesday night, she heard the phone ringing. She grabbed it off the wall just before the answering machine took the call.

"Hey, Emmy. Did I catch you at a bad time?" Diane asked.

"Not really. I just got home from church." She walked into the TV room, kicked off her shoes and settled on the couch with her feet under her.

"You're still going to church, huh? Hey! Wait a minute. It's Wednesday. Why are you going to church in the middle of the week? Where were you really?"

"We have a service and a Bible study on Wednesday," Emmy said.

It surprised Emmy to hear from her sister since she almost never called. They talked for a few minutes about nothing more important than the weather.

Finally, Emmy asked, "Is there some reason you called, Diane? You never call just to make small talk. What's on your mind?"

"Craig and I are getting married soon, and I want you to be my maid of honor. Will you?"

"Of course I will, Diane. When is the wedding? Do you have a date set yet?"

Diane didn't answer.

"Craig's older brother, Dennis, is going to be best man. It's just going to be a small wedding and reception here in Toledo. Craig's family lives here."

"Have you told anyone else?" Emmy asked, but again Diane didn't answer.

"Emmy, will you do me a huge favor?"

"I will if I can. What do you need?"

Diane paused for a moment. "Would you go see Mom and Dad, tell them about the wedding and ask them to come."

"Don't you want to do that yourself? I know you and Mom don't get along, but you really should tell them yourself," Emmy said. "You talked to them at my birthday party last year, and you seemed to get along. You did tell them you moved to Toledo, didn't you?"

"That was over a year ago, and it's the only time I've really talked to them in like three years," Diane said.

"See you can talk to them. Mom would be thrilled to hear from you."

"She would probably keel over from a heart attack if I called." Diane chuckled at the thought. "No, I can't."

"You just won't," Emmy raised her voice. "Give me one good reason why you can't."

"I'm afraid to tell them. Mom will just get mad and... Emmy, could you please just do it for me?" Diane pleaded.

"All right, I will, but you're gonna owe me." Emmy sighed in resignation. "When is the wedding, anyway? You didn't answer me."

"It's soon. September first, okay, if you must know."

"What?"

"You heard me. I gotta go. Please talk to Mom and Dad this week." Diane didn't wait for a response. She simply hung up.

Emmy stared at her phone, and then walked into the kitchen and looked at the calendar. *I bet I know why you are getting married so soon, Diane. You should have been more careful.*

Emmy made a special trip to visit her parents after work the next day. Mom answered the door to let her in, since Emmy didn't have a key.

"I was just thinking about calling you, Emmy. How have you been, honey? Come in and sit down." Mom sat in her recliner.

Emmy patted her father's arm as he sat in his recliner watching TV, and decided to get right to the point.

"Diane and Craig are getting married. They wanted me to come and tell you in person. Diane wants you to be there. Please tell me you will go."

"Married! After all this time, huh? Wait a second! Be there where? Isn't she going to get married here? Where is this wedding going to be? Why isn't Diane telling me this instead of you?" Mom gripped both arms of the recliner and shook her head in disgust. *She must be pregnant if she's getting married.*

Emmy realized this wasn't going to be as easy as she hoped. "Mom, have you talked to Diane at all in the last month?"

"I haven't talked to her since your birthday. Why?"

Emmy took a deep breath. "They are getting married in Toledo where they live. Diane moved out of the house and moved to Ohio. Craig's family lives there, too, so that's why the wedding is going to be there. Diane said it would be a small wedding."

Emmy looked at her father to see his reaction. He didn't give any indication he had even heard what she said.

Mom digested this bit of news and gripped her recliner with more force. "I think she should get married here. Her family is here, not in Toledo. How far away is that? We've never been there."

Emmy hesitated to tell her mom what she really thought. *You and Dad haven't been much of a family for Diane over the last few years.* Emmy sighed, but then she got angry. "Daddy, can you turn off the TV for just a few minutes to listen?"

"I want to watch this show."

"No!" Emmy grabbed the remote and pushed buttons until the TV turned off. "You're going to listen to me for a change."

"I'm your father!" he roared.

"Then act like it for once. We are having a family discussion." Emmy stomped her foot and put her hands on her hips.

"Fine. Let's get this over quick." Her father almost smiled. *I'm surprised, but kinda proud of you for being so forceful.*

"All right. This is what's going on. Diane and Craig are getting married in Toledo." Emmy held out her hands, palms down, and moved them back and forth. "Done deal. No arguing about that." She looked at her parents who didn't argue back. *Good. This feels kinda nice. They are actually listening to me for a change.* "She would like for you to be there. She asked me to be her maid of honor, and I said yes. So I'm going to Toledo."

"Does she have a date set already?" Mom asked.

"Yes, it's September first."

Patricia looked at Raymond and nodded her head. *She's pregnant. That's why she's getting married so quick.*

"We'd need to be there for two nights, unless you would want to drive home right after the wedding," Emmy said.

"What do you think, Ray?" Mom asked. *I know what I'm going to do, but I still want to hear what you have to say.*

"I think we should be there. Now give me back the remote, Emily."

Emmy handed the remote to her father, and he immediately turned on the TV and ignored everyone.

Emmy checked the clock on the wall. "I've got to get to class. I'll talk to you more about the wedding later. Can I have your assurance you guys will be there?"

"Fine. We'll go, but I'm still going to try to talk her into getting married here. We're her parents. And another thing."

"Yes, Mother." Emmy rolled her eyes.

"If you ever get married, the wedding will be in SoHam. I insist on that."

"Whatever, Mom. I gotta run." Emmy ran out the door. *Thanks, Diane. Now I know why you wanted me to do this. You're gonna owe me, and I'm not telling them why you're getting married so quick if it's why I think you are. You're gonna have to do that yourself.*

Emmy thought Diane's wedding was a perfect excuse to call Tony. She called him as soon as she made it home after her night class.

Tony checked the caller ID, but decided to answer anyway. "Hello, Emmy. How are you? Is something wrong?"

"I'm fine. Everyone is all right. I just wanted to tell you that Diane is getting married in Toledo on September first. Will you go with me?"

"I'm not sure that's a good idea." *Brenda will be upset if I do.*

"I still haven't told my family about our break-up. Mom thinks we are back together, and I don't want to spoil Diane's wedding with our problems. Will you go with me just to keep up appearances?"

Tony didn't answer right away.

"Please, Tony. Just this once. I won't bother you anymore after this. You and Brenda can get on with your lives."

"All right, Emmy. I'll go because our first game isn't until the following week. You know you'll have to tell your parents sooner or later."

"I know. I'm just putting off telling anyone, I guess."

"I'm sorry about Brenda, and I don't blame you for not loving me anymore."

"I do love you, but I'm still upset with you. I can't talk long. I just wanted to let you know about the wedding."

"Okay, Em. Just email me the details sometime. That way you won't have to talk to me."

Emmy assumed that Tony didn't want to talk to her, and that's why he requested an email. Tony gave her no indication that Brenda was in the room with him.

"What?" Tony looked at Brenda. "I can tell you're mad at me."

Brenda sat on Tony's bed with her feet on the floor. "I'm not upset. But you better tell her to quit calling. You're mine now. You don't belong to that religious fanatic back home."

The mail clerk dropped the office mail in the in box Friday morning as Emmy talked on the phone. He grabbed the outgoing mail and paused as she held up her finger to signal him to wait. He scoped out the office and waved to one of the guys as he stood in front of her desk.

She rolled her eyes to let him know she was trying to end the call. *You're kinda a runt, but you're actually rather handsome for an older man. One of these days I gotta ask you your name.*

He didn't wear a name tag, and she had been too shy to ask his name. He usually stopped and talked to her for a few minutes before he finished delivering the mail.

She finished the call, smiled and said, "Hi."

"Hi, yourself."

"Do you have any special mail for me?" She smiled and hoped she sounded like she was flirting.

238

"I certainly do. There is a letter from corporate that probably has your huge bonus check and the announcement of your promotion to vice-president."

"Aren't you the funny guy?"

He placed his hands on the desk and looked into her eyes. "I try to make all the pretty young ladies smile. I feel it is my company duty to keep morale high."

"I bet you do a good job of that," Emmy said as he turned to leave. She tapped a pencil against her chin as she watched him leave. *You're probably married or something. You just like to flirt.*

Later, Mr. Oliver stopped by Emmy's desk to remind her that he would be in a meeting. He knew that something troubled her but hadn't said anything to her.

"Is that a new dress, Emmy?"

"It's pretty new. I've only worn it once before."

He straightened his tie. "Well, it looks very nice on you."

"Thanks, Mr. Oliver."

He adjusted his tie again. "I don't mean to pry into your personal life, but I've noticed that you have not been yourself lately. If you ever need to talk about something, I am here. Mr. Robertson asked about you the other day, and I mentioned to him that you appear to be distraught over something. He asked me to tell you to call him anytime if you need to talk. He is really a good man, Emmy, and I know he has a deep regard for you."

"I appreciate the concern, Mr. Oliver, but I won't let my personal problems affect my work. I swear."

"I know you won't. I have total faith in you."

Later that day, Emmy placed the last file in the cabinet behind her desk and locked it. She walked over to Mr. Oliver's office and tapped on the open door. "Everything is put away and locked up."

"Thanks, Emily. I'm going to be here another thirty minutes or so. Am I correct in assuming I'm the only one still here?"

"Yes, sir. Mr. Hanks left a couple minutes ago. He's waiting downstairs for me."

"I'll lock up. You have a nice weekend, and I'll see you on

239

Monday."

Emmy got home from work a few minutes after six. As she checked her mail that evening, she tossed the junk mail, and then noticed a letter from the University of Notre Dame. She didn't know if she should open it or not. Only Mr. Robertson knew about her application for enrollment to the university. She stared at the envelope for a moment, and then dropped it on the dining room table and walked into the kitchen. She opened the fridge and found the leftover spaghetti from the night before. She fixed a plate and put it in the microwave. She walked back into the dining room and picked up the letter again. She bit her lip. *Crap, Tony! Things between us have deteriorated so much in the time since I applied.* She set the letter down, but then immediately picked it up again. She heard the timer on the microwave ding. *Oh, Tony. You wouldn't want to see me on campus. I would just spoil your relationship with other girls somehow.* She decided not to open the letter and dropped it in her waste basket—unopened. She didn't give it another thought. She would never read her acceptance letter for admission to Notre Dame.

Chapter Twenty-Seven

Emmy tossed her pajamas toward the laundry basket and missed. She picked them up and slam dunked them into the white plastic basket. She grabbed the blue basket, set it on top and carried both baskets to the basement. *I am so tired of carrying laundry all the way down here. If not for that, this house would be perfect.* She started her first load of laundry, wearily climbed the stairs to the kitchen, grabbed a banana, her notepad and pen. She turned on her Bose music system and hit the start button. She sang along to "Hero For Hire" the title track of the latest Fridays At Five CD. *I need to check the pantry before I go grocery shopping. The last time I went to Sainsbury's I bought a box of mostaccioli when I already had two.* She sat on the couch in the TV room as she made a list of items she knew were needed. She finished her list, tossed the banana peel in the garbage on her way to the pantry as she sang the chorus to "I Was So Excited." She moved her hips in time with the music as she inventoried the pantry. *Sweet solo, Kenny.* She played air guitar using her pen and notepad.

For the next several hours Emmy caught up on all the housework. She did laundry, paid bills and went grocery shopping. By eight o'clock, she felt totally zonked. She was heading up to bed when the house landline rang.

She grabbed it and answered without looking to check the caller ID.

"Hello."

"Hi, is this Diane?"

"No, sorry. Diane doesn't live here anymore. Can I take a message?" Emmy didn't recognize the voice.

"I'm Shannon Stephenson. Is this Emmy?"

Instead of hanging up, Emmy talked to Shannon and, a few minutes later, she accidentally let it slip about Tony's indiscretion.

"Emmy, you need to listen to me. Forget about Tony and find another man for whatever good it will do. All men are cheaters and are only good for sex whenever they get horny."

"That's not true, Shannon."

"Trust me, girl, it is. I've had more experience than you

241

when it comes to men. I just got through a bad relationship with a guy I picked up in a bar."

Emmy shouldn't have listened to her, but she did.

"I still love Tony, and I forgive him for what happened."

Emmy jerked the phone away from her ear as Shannon yelled, "No! Never forgive him because he will probably do it again. You need to date some other people, then you will find out for yourself that men are never to be trusted. Promise me you will start seeing other men. Just don't become emotionally involved with them. That way you can't get hurt."

"I don't want to see other men."

"Emmy, surely you know someone else that you are interested in getting to know better."

"I haven't thought about other guys since I started dating Tony again." Emmy looked at the phone. *Why am I even talking to you?*

"Well, it's time you start. If you can't find anyone, then I'll find a guy to go out with you."

Emmy remembered when Dawn Matuzak found her a date back in high school. *That was a total disaster. I'm never letting anyone set me up on a blind date.* Emmy thought about the company mail clerk. "I might know someone, Shannon. You don't have to set me up with anyone." *I have to ask him his name the next time I see him. He might be interested in dinner.*

"All right, but let me know if you want me to. I know lots of guys. They might not be good for a long-term relationship, but they can be fun for a night."

Emmy hit the end button and slammed the phone back into its wall-mounted base without replying. *How on earth am I suppose to love someone like that?* Emmy lifted her eyes to heaven.

On Sunday Emmy made her way to church and sought out Lynette. "I need to talk to you alone if you have the time. It's very important, and I don't know what to do about something."

Lynette and Emmy went into a small room off of the sanctuary where they could be alone, and Emmy confessed

242

everything that had happened.

"I know I can forgive, Tony, but I don't know if I can forget."

"It will take time to regain the trust in your relationship, but with prayer and a loving heart it can be done," Lynette said.

"What if it happens again? Should I forgive him again?"

"Let me show you what it says in Matthew. Let me find it, Matthew 18:21-22, I think, yes, here it is."

"Then Peter came to Jesus and asked, 'Lord, how many times shall I forgive my brother or sister who sins against me? Up to seven times?' Jesus answered, 'I tell you, not seven times, but seventy-seven times.'" Lynette read the verses to Emmy.

"I don't understand. Do I have to forgive Tony 490 times?"

"I think it really means an unlimited number of times, Emmy. Just as God would forgive us if we were to repent sincerely."

"I think I understand better now. Thank you, Lynette."

"Anytime, Emmy. That's one of the reasons why we are here as a church. To help each other grow as believers."

Emmy shrugged. "But how can I ever forget what happened?"

"That will be harder to do. We are human and we have memories. God doesn't erase our memories when something bad happens to us, but he can help take the hurt away. Let me give you an example. When you get stung by a bee, it hurts, right? If you remove the stinger, it hurts less and eventually the spot where the bee stung you will heal. Jesus will help you do the same thing. Think of his love as removing the stinger enabling you to eventually forget about the pain the bee caused. You might always remember being stung by the bee, but you will forget how much it hurt. Does that make any sense to you?"

"Yes, I think I understand. Thank you so much for taking the time to talk to me."

Emmy took a half-day off work on Monday for a doctor appointment in the afternoon. After yet another disappointing visit to her doctor, Emmy left the building in tears. *No one is going to want to marry me if I can't have a baby. I know both Kenny and Tony want to have a family. Tony wants to have six kids. I pity Brenda if he marries her.*

She didn't think about adoption as an alternative.

Emmy drove home, walked in the back door and immediately called Kristen. "Can you come over? I need to talk to you as soon as possible."

"I'll be there as soon as I can, Em. I need to finish a load of dishes first, and then I have to vacuum the upstairs. Do you know how to hook up the vacuum thing?"

"Kristen, most people have a vacuum cleaner, but you guys have one of those systems where you hook up the hose."

"Oh, right. Those things on the wall. I'll figure it out."

"Now who's a goof."

"Be quiet. Mom has been after me to become more domesticated. She even made me do a load of *laundry*."

"I can't believe it. What has the world come to? The princess is doing her own laundry." Emmy laughed. "I need to alert the media. This should be on the ten o'clock news."

"Ha! Ha! I can't believe how many settings there are on a washing machine."

Kristen pulled into the driveway later that night, walked in the back door, saw Emmy in the kitchen and pulled her into the TV room. They sat on the couch. "Okay, tell me what's bothering you."

"I left work early today. I went to see my doctor again, Kristen. He told me I would probably never be able to have a baby."

"What? Why?" Kristen shook her head. "What's wrong with you? You seem perfectly healthy to me. Aside from being a goof at times."

Emmy explained the doctor's diagnosis.

"So, it might still be possible just highly unlikely, huh?"

"It would take a miracle," Emmy said. "No man will ever want me if I can't have a baby, I know it. I want to have a baby so much."

"That's not true, Em. Not everyone wants to have a family. And you know doctors aren't always right."

244

Emmy started crying and wouldn't stop. Kristen thought there must be something else going on that Emmy hadn't mentioned. Kristen rubbed Emmy's back and finally got her to calm down.

"Is there anything else you want to talk about, Emmy?"

"Yes, it's about Tony." Emmy looked at Kristen and bit her lip.

"Just take your time, Em, and tell me what happened. Did you guys have another fight?"

Emmy shook her head. "We didn't have a fight, but Tony slept with another girl at school. We were supposed to be a couple, and he slept with someone named Brenda."

"Oh, no." Kristen's eyes opened wide. She didn't know what to say and started crying herself. Kristen broke up with Harrison because he cheated on her with a girl at North Park, but she had never told Emmy.

Later, Kristen stayed in Emmy's room until she fell asleep. Kristen slept in Diane's old room in case Emmy needed her.

Kristen heard Emmy's alarm in the morning and jumped out of bed to see if Emmy was all right. She walked into Emmy's room and sat on the edge of the bed. Emmy looked up at her through red eyes.

"Good morning, sleepyhead. How are you feeling this morning? Maybe you should call in sick. I think you have a fever."

"I can't call in sick, and you can't tell if I have a fever by just looking at me."

"Are you a doctor, young lady?" Kristen scolded facetiously.

"No, but neither are you."

"Do you want some breakfast?"

"I'll just grab a banana, or an apple, to eat on the way." Emmy started to sit up but let herself fall back onto the bed with a thud. "I have to drive myself to work this week."

"Are you ready to talk about what happened?"

"Not really." Emmy bit her lip.

"Em, you need to talk about it, or else you will make

245

yourself sick. Maybe I should tell you the reason 'Harry' and I broke up."

Emmy laughed because she remembered how much Harrison hated to be called Harry. "Do tell me about old Harry."

"One of the reasons I broke up with him was because he cheated with Victoria Madison, a girl at North Park. I don't know if you remember her. Victoria Braun now."

"Duh! She's married to Christopher." *I'll never understand why he married her. He deserves someone with better morals.* "She graduated from Roosevelt a year ahead of us."

"That was the final straw. There were other reasons why we broke up, but sleeping with Victoria really settled it."

"Are you trying to make me feel better or worse?" Emmy asked.

"I'm trying to help, you stinker." Kristen poked Emmy in her side, and then lay next to her in bed. "Is that thing supposed to do that?" Kristen pointed up.

Emmy stared at the wobbly ceiling fan. "Not really. Sometimes I worry that it will fall on me during the night. I should get a new one, huh?"

"They don't cost too much. Daddy could send one of his guys over to install it. I'll ask him to send over a hot stud."

"Don't you dare. I don't want to meet another man. Not ever!"

"You know you don't mean that," Kristen said.

"Maybe not, but I think it will take a long time to get over what happened. It's a serious thing to sleep with someone. I could never be as casual about it as some other people I know."

Kristen frowned. "Do you mean me?"

"Oh, Krissy, I'm sorry. I didn't mean you. I was thinking about Diane and that Shannon girl."

"Apology accepted." Kristen nudged Emmy with her foot. "What about Kenny and Becky? Are they lovers?"

"I'm not sure, but that's different. Kenny and I aren't a couple right now."

"Does that mean that since I slept with Ryan one time, no one will want to go out with me?"

"That's not the same thing, and I said I was sorry."

"You're still friends with me even though I had sex. Why are you being so hard on Tony? Doesn't he deserve a break?"

Emmy turned on her side to face Kristen. "Tony and I were trying to get back together, at least *I* thought we were. Then he slept with another girl. You were going out with Ryan when you slept with him. That makes it different."

"You aren't going to sleep with someone just to get even with Tony, are you?"

Emmy looked at Kristen like she had gone nuts. Then she said, "Yes, I'm going to stop at a bar on my way home tonight and pick up the first man who looks like he would make a good lover."

Kristen knew Emmy was kidding. "Tell me one thing, Em. Since you are... rather inexperienced, how will you know which man will make a good lover? Maybe I should go with you since I have a lot more experience than you."

"Maybe I have more experience that you think," Emmy whispered. "Oh, Krissy. What should I do?"

"As your doctor, I think you should get out of bed, take a shower, get dressed and go to work."

"You're trying to tell me to get on with my life, huh?"

"You are so smart, Emmy."

Chapter Twenty-Eight

By the day before Diane's wedding, Emmy still hadn't told Diane or her parents about what happened with Tony. After picking up her mother and father, Emmy headed to South Bend. She made arrangements to meet Tony outside his dorm. Emmy slowly drove up N. Notre Dame Avenue, and entered the traffic circle between Alumni Hall and the law building. She spotted Tony and pulled to the curb. She popped the trunk without getting out of the car. Tony tossed his duffel bag in the trunk and slid into the front passenger seat next to Emmy.

"Hello, Mr. and Mrs. Colasanti, how are you? It's good to see you again."

"It's good to see you, too, Tony. How is school going?" Mrs. Colasanti asked as she smiled.

"Tough, but I'm not complaining."

Tony treated her parents with respect and courtesy, as always.

After entering Ohio, they made a pit stop, and Emmy and Mom went to the restroom together.

"Emily, what's wrong between you and Tony?" Mom asked as they were washing their hands. "You're both acting so quiet and tense with each other."

"We had a fight, Mom, so we're just upset with each other. Don't say anything to Dad or Tony, please."

Emmy didn't answer when her mom asked, "What are you fighting about?"

She tried to keep her outward appearance calm, but on the inside Emmy seethed with anger at Tony and basically all men because of what Shannon told her. They got back to the car, and she saw Tony standing by the driver's door.

"I can drive if you want, Em."

She tossed him the keys. "Go for it," she said sarcastically.

Hey! You asked me to come. I didn't ask for this. He wanted to say, but kept his mouth shut.

After they reentered the turnpike, Mom touched Emmy's shoulder to get her attention. "Emily, your father and I are getting older, and we would like to have some grandchildren before we get too old to enjoy them."

"Hush, Patricia," Raymond said. *I know you think Diane is pregnant, and you want Emmy to do the same thing.*

"I'm just saying..." Patricia rolled her eyes and didn't say anything more.

Emmy took off her shoes and rubbed her feet. *You might get your wish sooner than you think.* Her eyes filled with tears as she thought about her doctor visit. She felt like crap because this would be another way that she disappointed her parents.

After several minutes of silence, Mom said, "I was thirty-eight and your father over forty when you were born. It was not an easy pregnancy by any means."

Emmy realized that her parents never talked to her as an adult. They always treated her as a child even after she left home.

Silently she prayed, *Jesus, I know that you can heal all wounds and perform miracles. I know that Tony wants to have kids, and so do I. Lynette told me that we need to accept your will for our lives, but it sure would be nice if you would allow me to have babies when I get married, if I ever do. But if we can't have our own babies, I guess we will get by somehow. Thank you for listening.* Emmy had not told anyone except Kristen the results of her doctor visit.

Tony saw the tears in her eyes and tried to hold her hand, but she pulled it away. "Don't touch me!" she spat viciously.

"Geez, sorry for trying to be nice." Tony kept his eyes straight ahead as he thought, *This is going to be a lousy weekend. I should have listened to Brenda. She warned me not to go.*

Emmy turned her head to look out the window.

Mom mentioned, "I'm sorry we haven't been close, Emmy, but..."

Emmy rolled her eyes, *Here we go again. Another lecture on how to live my life.*

Mom continued, "I have always tried to do what I thought best for you and protect you as much as I could because of how we almost lost you."

Emmy turned in her seat to look at her mother and father.

249

"What do you mean 'almost lost me.' I've never been lost. Dad, what is Mom talking about?"

Her father frowned at her mother. "Patricia, it's time you tell her. She should know."

Emmy frowned at her mother. "Mom! What is Dad talking about? What is it that I should know, and why haven't you told me before? What on earth are you guys talking about?"

"All right, I'll tell you." Mom paused to gather her thoughts. "When you were eight months old, you became very sick, and you stayed in the hospital for three weeks. A virus attacked your heart, I don't remember what the doctors called it."

"Myocarditis?" Tony asked.

"Yes, I think that's it. Thank you, Tony," Mom said politely.

Emmy frowned at him. "How do you know?"

"Heather is a doctor, remember?"

Mom continued, "It happened so long ago that I can't remember all the details. Anyway, we thought we might lose you, baby. We prayed everyday for you to get better, and then one day, you were all right. Almost overnight you went from the edge of death to being a normal healthy baby again."

"Is this true, Daddy?"

He nodded his head because he couldn't speak as he remembered what happened.

"Oh, Mom, why didn't you guys ever tell me?" Emmy sobbed.

"We didn't want to frighten you, Emmy. We wanted you to be a normal, healthy child and not worry about what might happen to you because of your heart. You don't have to worry now because the doctors told us a few years later that you were as healthy as could be. We still treated you very cautiously though. That's why we've always been so concerned about you."

Emmy now understood her parents a little better and appreciated the suffering they must have gone through.

Dad asked her, probably just to change the subject, "Can you afford to stay in the house and pay the rent without help from Diane?"

"As long as my mother keeps paying the rent, you mean,"

Mom added sarcastically.

"Yes, Daddy, I can, and one day I intend to pay Grandma back. I'm keeping track, and I'll pay back every cent."

"How?" Mom asked. *What difference does it make? She's over ninety. She won't be around much longer.*

"I'll find a way." Emmy often wondered how she would accomplish that. "Let me tell you what happened. I have a new landlord, and the rent is lower than it used to be. I got a letter from the attorney who represents the new landlord explaining things. I couldn't understand all the legal mumbo jumbo. Something about tax liabilities and assessments and other stuff. Anyway, the rent is very affordable now."

Emmy didn't know that Mr. Robertson, acting as her financial guardian angel, bought the house for her and Diane and put the title in their names. He set up an account to pay the property taxes without their knowledge, and everything that she paid in rent now went into an investment account for her. He often did things without drawing attention to his generosity. Mr. Robertson felt a special affection for her and Diane, but especially Emmy since he and his late wife would occasionally babysit her. Now he felt he could repay her late grandfather's generosity by helping her.

They arrived in Toledo and checked into the motel. Emmy shared a room with her parents, and Tony checked into the room next to them. They met Diane and Craig at the church for the rehearsal.

"Hello, Mom. Hi, Daddy." Diane greeted her parents. Craig didn't bother to acknowledge their presence.

"It's good to see you, Diane." Mom hugged her, but it felt awkward to both of them. Mom managed to smile. *Aha! Just like I thought. You're pregnant.* But Mom didn't say anything about the baby.

After the rehearsal, the wedding party went out to dinner at a cheap pizza place.

"I hope the pizza is good," Tony said as he opened the door for Emmy.

Emmy grinned. "Don't hold your breath. Knowing Craig,

251

he probably found the cheapest place in Toledo."

They were seated in a corner of the restaurant and Craig and his family ordered pitchers of beer. Emmy watched as her parents and Diane's future in-laws emptied three pitchers in less than twenty minutes.

A man tapped Emmy on her shoulder, and she turned in her seat.

"Emmy, it's good to see you again. Do you remember me? I'm Gerry Marker. I used to share the apartment with Craig."

"Hi, Gerry, I remember you. This is my friend Tony Bertucci."

He introduced Emmy to his wife. Emmy hadn't seen Gerry for a few years and didn't care about his wife's name.

Yeah, whatever, Gerry. I've got more important things on my mind. Immediately, she regretted her attitude. *Lord, forgive me,* she silently prayed. "It's nice to meet you, Wilma." Emmy talked to Wilma for a couple of minutes before excusing herself. *I need to remember that everyone has issues and problems. I can't let the junk in my life dictate how I treat others.*

A waitress brought out three pizzas, and Tony managed to grab several slices as Craig's family scrambled to fill their plates.

"This might be all we get, Em. I don't think there will be any left."

She smiled weakly. "It's all right. I'm not very hungry."

Tony took a bite, and then grinned at Emmy.

"Cardboard?" she asked.

He tilted his hand back and forth. "Cardboard with cheap sauce and lousy sausage."

Neither one of them minded that they didn't have a chance to eat any more slices.

"Maybe we can find some better food later. Would you like that?" Tony asked.

Emmy bit her lip. "Maybe. I won't make any promises, and don't you dare think of it as a date. I'm still mad at you."

A few minutes later, Emmy finally cornered Diane in the bathroom. "Are you pregnant? Is that why you are getting married in such a hurry?"

252

"Yes, I'm four months along. Can you tell? Does it show already? My regular clothes are getting real tight in the waist. You won't tell Mom and Dad will you? They won't understand."

"I won't say anything, but don't you think they will figure it out when you have a baby in five months. They might be old, but they can still count to nine."

"By then it won't matter. They will be so happy to have a grandchild, they wouldn't care if the baby has three heads."

"Are you supposed to be drinking beer? Isn't that bad for the baby?" Emmy frowned.

"I only had two glasses." Diane held up two fingers. "Mom drank when she was pregnant with us, and we turned out all right."

Emmy tilted her head. *I wonder if that had anything to do with my heart thing?*

"I'm not going to drink anymore," Diane said.

Emmy thought the timing of Diane's pregnancy for a moment. "You were already pregnant when you started dating Brady."

"Yes, but I didn't know it at the time. Oh, God. How different my life would be if I hadn't spent that night with Craig."

"Are you sure the baby is his?"

Diane raised her voice. "Yes, Emmy. I didn't sleep with Brady."

"Are you sure you want to marry Craig?"

Diane shook her head. "I don't want to, but I have to."

Emmy held Diane in her arms as Diane cried.

The wedding ceremony only lasted for fifteen minutes the next afternoon.

"That was short and sweet," Tony said to Emmy. "Why isn't Diane wearing a wedding dress?

"Sssh! Don't let Diane hear you." Emmy poked him in the side. "That is a wedding dress. It just isn't a white one, and in case you're wondering, Diane told me not to buy a fancy bridesmaid dress. That's why I'm wearing this one."

"That dress looks a lot better than the old suit Craig's wearing," Tony said.

253

Meanwhile, on the other side of the small church, Mom was watching as Craig's brother took a few photos. *You've gained a few pounds, Diane. I hope you're eating healthier than you used to. Are you even gonna mention the baby?*

Mr. Colasanti and Mr. Garrett stood a few feet away. Raymond looked over to where Emmy stood with Tony. *Well, at least Diane finally got married. Maybe Emmy will do better with her choice of a husband.*

Craig's parents knew about the baby, but didn't say anything. Emmy congratulated Diane and Craig for finally tying the knot, but knew that married life would not be easy for them. Hopefully, they were both mature enough now, after so many previous ups and downs in their relationship, to make their marriage work. They had five months to prepare for a baby.

The reception followed immediately after the ceremony in the basement of the church. Craig and Diane couldn't afford a large hall or even a DJ. They played music over a small PA system which belonged to the church. They served finger food, punch and provided a small wedding cake.

Later, Emmy watched as Tony danced with her mom.

"Can you believe it, Diane? I never thought I'd see our mother dancing and in front of other people. How shameful."

Diane and Emmy shared a laugh at their mother's expense. Tony danced with her mom, and then Diane, but not Emmy. Soon he kept busy talking to some of the guys about football. Emmy knew he would be busy for some time, so she went outside to get some fresh air.

She began to pray out loud, "Thank you, Lord, for everything you bless us with. I'm kinda concerned about Diane and Craig. They aren't believers, but they could sure use your help as they adjust to being married and raising a baby."

Dennis, the best man, saw her outside and heard her talking. He walked up behind her. "Who are you talking to?"

Emmy jumped and spun around to face him. "Geez, you scared the crap out of me."

"Sorry, I didn't mean to eavesdrop, but I thought I heard you talking to someone, but I don't see anybody. Are you okay?"

254

"I'm fine. I was praying out loud. I hope that doesn't bother you."

"Oh, I didn't know you were one of those kind of girls."

Emmy raised her hands and made air quotes. "What do you mean 'one of those kind of girls?'"

"You know, a Christian. I was actually going to see if you wanted to have a smoke with me, but I guess that's out of the question."

"I don't smoke, and maybe you shouldn't, either, but it's your life. Not my place to tell you what to do." *Why does anyone ever smoke? Don't they know about the damage it can cause?*

For the first time someone she didn't know called her a Christian. Emmy realized that other people could see a difference between her and other girls. She realized she would be scrutinized for any cracks in her character now. Emmy went back inside, saw her parents and sat at their table. She spent the rest of the party talking to them.

When Diane came over to tell her goodbye, Emmy hugged her and whispered. "Take good care of yourself and the baby."

"I will. Thanks for being here for me, Emmy. Did you tell Mom about..."

"No, I haven't. I think you should do that yourself."

Diane looked at her parents. "I will soon, Emmy. I promise."

"You better do it quick, or else I will tell Mom to call you."

Diane and Craig left the church shortly after five thirty. Craig's mother approached Mrs. Colasanti. "We don't have to worry about cleaning up. There are some volunteers from the church who will do that."

I had no intention of cleaning up. This was my daughter's wedding after all. Mrs. Colasanti thought, but said with a jab, "That's fine. It was a pleasure to finally meet you after all this time."

Mrs. Garrett replied, "We were against Craig moving to Illinois, but he needed a job. He never invited us to come and see him, so we didn't want to intrude. You and your husband would be welcome to come and visit... the kids... whenever you have an opportunity." Mrs. Garrett couldn't bring herself to mention the baby. Craig had warned her that morning to keep her mouth shut.

Emmy watched as her mother and Mrs. Garrett talked. Tony walked up behind her but didn't touch her. Emmy sensed his presence, looked over her shoulder and stood up. "I hope Mom doesn't get into an argument with Craig's mother."

"That wouldn't be cool. I'm hungry, Em. Maybe we can take your parents and find a restaurant somewhere."

"That sounds good to me. I'm actually hungry, too. I'm sorry I blew you off after the rehearsal yesterday. I just wasn't hungry. I went to bed early."

"That's all right. I grabbed some junk food from the vending machine. Did you sleep all right last night?"

"No, they both snore like trains. I wish I had a separate room." Emmy looked at her father as he sat in a chair with his arms crossed over his chest. He had a scowl on his face. "I think Daddy is getting impatient. He probably needs a beer."

"We could go back to that pizza place. They had beer," Tony said.

"I'd rather starve." Emmy stuck a finger down her throat as she leaned back against Tony.

He put his hands on her shoulders. When she didn't move them, he squeezed her shoulders tenderly. *I hope your wedding is better than this, Em. You deserve it.*

Emmy patted his hand. *Weddings are supposed to be the best day of a girl's life. This day is kinda depressing. Lord, if I ever get married, would it be wrong to ask for a more pleasant wedding?*

On the way back to the motel after spending two hours at a restaurant, Emmy's mom asked, "Are you ever going to get married, settle down and have babies?"

Emmy's shoulders slumped as she glanced at Tony. "I hope to one of these days."

Emmy waited outside while her parents got ready for bed. Once in bed, she tossed and turned on the soft, sagging mattress. She kept thinking of a hundred different things as she tried in vain to fall asleep. Of course her parents' snoring didn't help matters.

256

Just after midnight, Emmy gave up. She made sure her parents were asleep, quietly got up, slipped on a sweatshirt and tiptoed outside. She knocked Tony's door.

"Tony, it's me. Are you awake? Can I come in? It's freezing out here." She waited for a few seconds, and then knocked again. "Tony, let me in!"

He opened the door. "What are you doing, Em?"

Emmy pushed past him and stood by the bed. "I can't sleep. I need to talk to you."

"I couldn't sleep, either. I've just been tossing and turning, and my mind won't shut down."

She glanced around the room and said, "You've got two beds in here."

"Yeah, so?"

"My parents are snoring so loud. Especially Daddy. I don't know how Mom can stand it." She sat down on the second bed. "Maybe I should sleep in here."

"Not a chance, Em." Tony shook his head. "Your father would kill me if his baby girl got pregnant. Like her older sister."

"I didn't intend to sleep in the same bed," Emmy said as she frowned. "So you know, huh?"

"I'd have to be blind to not see it. She has a baby bump."

"I don't think my parents realize it. Mom hasn't said anything about the baby."

"They know. Maybe they are waiting for Diane to tell them."

Tony sat down on his bed. Emmy looked into his eyes. She began to cry.

"No, Emmy, please don't cry." Tony didn't know if he should hold her or not, so he didn't move.

"I understand if you tell me that you never want to see me again because you like Brenda more. I will still love you as a friend, but I understand."

"Emmy, I don't know what you're talking about, but I'm too tired to think straight. We need to get some sleep."

"I mean because I have changed. I wanted to talk to you about Jesus. I want you to understand that He loves you, and you

257

can have the same joy and peace that I have."

"Okay, Emmy, but I am too tired. Can we talk about it in the morning?"

"Promise?"

"Yes, Em. I promise."

Emmy lay on her back with her feet on the floor. "Please, can I stay with you tonight? You don't snore like Daddy."

Tony's eyes traveled up her body. *No, I can't even think of you like that.* He stood up, took her hands and pulled her upright. "You should go back to your room. Your mom and dad would not appreciate you spending the night in here with me."

"There are two beds." She sat back down on the bed.

"No, Emmy. You can't stay in here."

"Are you gonna pick me up and toss me outside?" Emmy bounced on the bed. "This bed is better than the one in their room."

"All right. Have it your way." He turned and walked toward the door. "I'll sleep in the car." *How can I do that?* He realized. *I don't have the keys.*

"Fine! I'll leave, but I doubt if I get any sleep at all." Emmy stood up and walked toward the door. "Good night, Tony. See you in the morning. We can talk then."

Emmy went back to her parents' room. She opened the door as quietly as possible and slipped into the room. She didn't even yell as she stubbed her toe on the bed. Mom heard her, but didn't say anything. She assumed Emmy had been with Tony. Mom fell back asleep, and, eventually, Emmy did also.

"That's not what Father Perini taught us in confirmation class." Tony sat on the edge of the bed in the morning and shook his head.

"But it's what is in the Bible, Tony. It says so right here. Please read it again." Emmy paced back and forth in the small motel room.

"Emmy, I've read it three times, and I understand what you think it means, but I just don't believe that way. Please try to understand." He looked up at her. "You were raised the same way I was, Emmy. Why did you change?"

"I changed because I accepted Jesus and you can, too, Tony." She stood in front of him with her hands on his muscular shoulders.

"Maybe we should take some time to let things settle down before we start on this religion thing. I think you are still upset with me because of what happened that night, and now you are just trying to force this new religion on me because of that."

Try as Emmy may, she could not get Tony to totally understand what it meant to be saved, and it frustrated her. She didn't yet understand the concept of allowing the Holy Spirit to prepare a person's heart.

Tony called her two days later. "...I know, Emmy, and I care about you, too, but we need to back off and spend some time away from each other."

"We already do," Emmy said. "I never get to see you or Kenny very often. Did Brenda tell you not to talk to me?"

"She would rather I didn't talk to you very often," Tony admitted. "I know we spend almost all of our time away from each other because of school."

"Ya think!"

"I meant spending time away from our relationship," Tony said. "I can sense a small amount of distrust in you, and I understand that. You need more time to get over what happened and truthfully, Em, so do I."

"How much time? Does Brenda want us to completely sever our relationship?"

"I honestly don't know. I do know that if we don't step back and take a good look at where we are headed, we will end up on different paths and eventually drift too far apart and may never get back on the right track."

"This is all because of that girl, isn't it? You still want to see her. Fine! I won't call you or email you or anything until you talk to me again. I will pray for you, though. You can't stop me from doing that."

Tony sighed. "There are other guys out there, Em. You should date someone other than me or Kenny."

"Yeah, I hear that from everyone."

"Even Kristen thinks you should," Tony said.

"Well, I don't want to cause any problems between you and Brenda," Emmy said making the name sound disgusting. "I won't call you or email you until you tell me I can. Will that be okay with her?"

"I'm sorry, Emmy," Tony said.

The company's mail clerk would usually find Emmy at her desk when he delivered the office mail. Emmy always smiled at him, and he smiled back. He knew her name because of the nameplate on her desk, but she still didn't know his. Then one week a new person started delivering the mail.

"Did you just start this job?" Emmy asked.

"This is my second month here, but I just started delivering the mail. I'm so thrilled to get out of the mailroom in the basement."

"I don't suppose you have any idea where the guy is who used to deliver the mail, do you?" Emmy tapped a pencil on the desk, and then stuck it behind her ear.

"Sorry, but I don't have a clue. I never really knew the guy. Why?"

"No reason." Emmy handed him the outgoing mail. *I should have asked for a name.*

Hundreds of people worked in the fifteen-floor office building. Emmy didn't really know many people outside of her group. Everybody kept busy with their own work leaving little time for much socializing, not that there were many people her age who worked there. She thought about the mail clerk and wondered, *Could I have missed out on something special? He was older and a puny looking guy compared to Tony, but he was charming and funny. Nah, his hair was turning gray. People would think he was my father if I went out with him. I'm sure God will provide the right person for me. Who do I know at church who might be the guy?*

Chapter Twenty-Nine

"Hi, Emmy, it's Mama."

"Mama, I was just thinking about you. I'm sorry I haven't called for a while. How are you? Everything okay?" Emmy looked for a bottle of water in the fridge. *I need to buy another case. Kristen has spoiled me. I never used to drink bottled water.*

"I'm fine. My back hurts a little, but I've probably just been working too hard. Been doing some fall cleaning."

"I'm sorry to hear that. Have you been to your doctor?"

"No, I don't like to go to the doctor's office. It's always full of sick people."

"You are so funny, Mama." Emmy laughed as she plopped onto the couch in the TV room. She lay on her back and put her feet on the back of the old couch.

"The reason I'm calling is that Heather wants me to ask you if you would be willing to be a bridesmaid in her wedding."

"What? Are you kidding me?" Emmy sat up. "Heather's getting married, for real? When? Who to? I didn't even know she was serious about anyone."

"Alex, dear, she's marrying Alex Khryzman, of course." Mama laughed. "You really didn't have any idea, did you?"

"None whatsoever. I just thought they were friends. Kristen never said anything. She's going to be a bridesmaid, right?"

"Yes. Kristen is the only other girl in the family," Mama said. "Heather has been with Alex for quite some time, but she keeps her private life pretty much to herself."

"This is unreal. Tony and I were just in Toledo for Diane's wedding and that creep never said a word about Heather being engaged." Emmy covered her mouth. "Sorry, Mama, I shouldn't call him a creep."

"I know you don't mean it, sweetie."

"I never even suspected they were more than friends, and now they're getting married. Wow! When?"

Mama told Emmy the date and all the other pertinent information.

"November tenth, huh? They sure aren't wasting any time."

Emmy wondered why. *She's a doctor. Surely she knows to take birth control.*

"Actually, honey, Heather asked another friend of hers from school to be a bridesmaid, but she had to cancel. She asked two other friends, but they have to work. That's why this is such a last minute thing. They have been planning the wedding for several months, but have kept it quiet. That's just Heather's way. Heather would be so grateful if you would accept her offer."

"Of course I will." *I don't care if Heather asked fifty other people before she thought of me. At least now I have a legitimate reason to talk to Tony.*

As soon as she got off the phone with Mama, Emmy dialed Tony's cell phone number. She let it ring once, but then hung up and bit her lip. *I can't talk to him. He will think I'm pestering him. He might even be with Brenda.*

An hour later she picked up her phone again. She punched in the first four numbers, but then ended the call. *I'm sure he already knows about the wedding and will get mad if I call him.*

Later that night, Emmy got up the courage to call Tony again. He surprised her by answering.

"Hi, Emmy. What's up?"

"I talked to Mama today. I'm going to be in Heather's wedding. She needs a new bridesmaid. Why didn't you ever tell me she's engaged?" She paced up and down the hallway.

"What are you talking about?"

"Heather is engaged to Alex. Come on. You're teasing me." She walked into the TV room, turned off the TV, plopped back onto the couch and assumed the same position as when she had talked to Mama.

"All right, I know, but Heather made everyone promise to keep it a secret until they sent out the invitations. They only told a few people. She wouldn't even let Mama tell Aunt Karla or my uncles. It's been driving Mama mad that she couldn't say anything."

"If I was engaged, I would tell the whole world. I would put it on TV."

"I know you would. Alex told his brothers and his parents,

but I don't know anyone else from his family. How have you..."

"Do you think they're getting married because Heather is pregnant? You know that's why Diane and Craig got married, don't you?"

"I knew about Diane."

"I still don't think Mom knows."

"She knows, Emmy. She might not admit it, but she knows. I told you that in the motel room, remember?"

"Yeah, the night you wouldn't let me stay in your room," Emmy teased. "I had to listen to Mom and Daddy snoring all night because you wouldn't let me use the other bed."

"Stop it, Em. I don't feel guilty about kicking you out of the room."

" I know you don't, but I wouldn't have felt guilty sharing a room with you." Emmy rubbed a small scar on her knee. "Is Heather pregnant?"

"I don't think so, but I can't ask her that. I think they chose that day because they will be on vacation. Also, we don't have a game that weekend. I'm supposed to be in the wedding party in some capacity. Actually, I'm at Heather's, and Alex is standing next to me. Why don't you talk to him, and you can grill him, if you want."

"No, I can't talk to him."

"Yes, you can." Tony handed the phone to Alex. "It's Emmy. Be prepared for the third degree."

"What do you mean?" Alex asked.

Tony shrugged. "She wants to ask you a few questions."

Emmy could hear Tony and Alex talking.

"Hello, Emmy, thank you for filling in at the last minute. We really appreciate it," Alex said.

Shoot! I might as well ask him. He might just hang up, or tell me to mind my own business. Emmy sat up and asked Alex point blank. "Have you been sleeping with Heather? Is she pregnant? Have you been faithful to her?"

"I confess, officer, I have been sleeping with the victim. But to the best of my knowledge, and I am a doctor, the victim is not expecting a child anytime soon."

Emmy began to laugh as Alex kept up his charade.

"I have been with other women in the past, but I have been faithful to Heather ever since we became a couple, and I promise I will be faithful, till death do us part."

"I guess I shouldn't ask you such personal questions, Alex. I apologize if I offended you."

"Not at all, Emmy. I know you care a great deal for Heather and are looking out for her best interests. Mama asked me some questions, but you were a much tougher interrogator."

"Can you put Tony back on the phone, please?"

Alex handed the phone to Tony, but Tony shook his head and waved his hand.

Alex held the phone to his chest. "Talk to her. You can at least be civil to her even if you don't want to be her friend. You will have to talk to her at the wedding."

Tony reluctantly got back on the phone with Emmy. "I'm back."

"Have you been behaving?" Emmy asked.

"I have been behaving, for the most part," he said. "I haven't looked at another female, except for my Sports Psychology 310 professor and she is, uh, maybe sixty years old."

"You mean other than Brenda, right?" Emmy dragged out the name.

"Yes, I have seen her around," Tony said abruptly. *I'm not going to talk to you about Brenda. I never should have told you anything about her.*

"It's all right if you guys are dating." Emmy tried to convince herself. "How are your classes? You're just about finished. Less than a year to go, right? Are you getting excited, or do you think you will miss college after you graduate?" Emmy asked in rapid fire mode.

"Let me see if I can remember all the questions."

"I'm sorry. Sometimes I have a tendency to talk a bit too fast."

He laughed. "That's all right. I'm sorta used to it. I'll be glad to finish classes. The studying six hours a day is getting old, but I will miss the guys and especially my teammates. How about your

264

classes? Are you keeping busy?" Tony waved goodbye as Alex left Heather's place and headed back to his own apartment.

"The classes this semester have been a little bit easier, but school still takes enough of my time. Mr. Oliver lets me off early on Tuesday and Thursday. That makes it more tolerable."

"That's good." Tony sat on the couch. "How's Kristen doing? Is she dating that same guy? What was his name? I've given up trying to kept track of the guys she dates."

"If you mean Brandon, then, yeah, I guess so. She doesn't seem as excited about him as when they first met."

"Why's that?"

Emmy lay on her back and relaxed. "I don't know for sure. It's just a feeling."

They talked for fifteen minutes without arguing. Emmy ended up with her feet on the wall above the couch in the dark room.

"I gotta let you go." Tony stood up. "Heather is chasing me out of her apartment."

"I'll talk to you later. Or maybe I'll email you. That would be better."

"Probably so. I don't always answer the phone."

After she hung up, she remained in the same position as she thought about what to do with Tony. *I really need you to be a part of my life. I'm not sure if you feel the same way, though.*

Tony said good night to Heather and headed back to his dorm. *I should call Brenda. I haven't talked to her all day.* He checked the time. *I better not. It's pretty late. She's probably already in bed.* He thought about Emmy as he walked. *You sure don't make it easy, Em. You have a way of getting under my skin, and I'm not sure if that's a good thing or not.*

He loved Emmy, but not the same way as before. The intense guilt he felt about his indiscretion was waning as he and Brenda became more involved. He felt he didn't deserve Emmy at times. At a time they really needed to be together, they remained separated by school and work.

265

Chapter Thirty

After another typical busy day at the office, Emmy rushed home, changed clothes, turned on some Fridays At Five music and looked through the fridge for something to eat. She opened one Tupperware container and wrinkled her nose at the smell. *I can't even tell what you used to be, so you're going down the garbage disposal.* She found part of a chicken breast and fixed some mac and cheese. She sat at the dining room table and picked at her food as she studied for tomorrow's class. She finished eating, danced and sang merrily as she looked out the window while doing dishes. She dried the last plate, put it away, tossed the towel on the counter, skipped out of the kitchen and down the hall. She opened the door to the small room between the living room and TV room and flipped on the light. She booted up her computer and plopped down in the fake-leather office chair while she waited for the computer to open. She spun around in a circle while she waited. *I need a faster computer. Maybe Barry can do something to speed this thing up.*

Thirty minutes later, she called Kristen. "Hey, what are you up to tonight?"

"Nothing really. Got to read a few more chapters for English Lit. What's going on?" Kristen kept reading as she sat at her desk and talked to Emmy.

"I just got an email from Kenny." Emmy leaned forward with her elbows on the desk in front of her computer keyboard.

"How's he doing? They're still in Europe, aren't they?"

"Yeah, I'm reading his email right now." Emmy quickly scanned the email. "Oh, crap! Kenny and Becky broke up."

"What? I can't believe it. Are you sure?" Kristen stopped reading.

"I'm pretty sure. No, wait. I'm not certain if they broke up or not. He wrote something about Becky needing someone who would be there every night, and he just can't be that guy. It's so sad because they really love each other. She flew back home from Rome to start school."

"She's been in Europe with him all this time, huh?"

266

"Yeah, and I'm not jealous of her, and I don't think about whether or not they've been sleeping with each other."

"You can't fool me," Kristen said. "You think about that every day."

"Do not!"

Kristen exhaled sharply and then shook her head. "I'm not going to argue with you."

Emmy leaned back in her chair, pushed away from the desk and closed her eyes. "I hope they don't break up."

Neither one said anything for a moment. Then Kristen asked, "You aren't thinking about trying to get back together with Kenny if he and Becky break up, are you?"

Emmy opened her eyes and sat straight up in her chair. "What do you mean back together? I don't have a clue as to what you mean."

Kristen closed her book, stood up and sat on the edge of the bed. "Come on. Don't play dumb with me. You know perfectly well what I mean."

"No," Emmy said. "I'm not thinking about Kenny in that way, Kristen. We're just friends—like Derrick or Barry."

"Don't insult my intelligence, Emmy Colasanti. You have never thought of Kenny Colwell the same way you think of Derrick and certainly not like Barry Newton."

"We were very young back then."

"Maybe so, but you loved him and don't even try to deny it. You are still in love with him even if you won't admit it to anyone."

Emmy thought about Kristen's statement as she stood up and walked into the kitchen.

Kristen asked, "Do you ever wonder what your life would be like if you were actually in the band?"

"I used to think about that, but not so much anymore." Emmy opened the fridge and took out a can of Dr Pepper. She held the phone against her ear with her shoulder as she popped open the can and poured the pop into a glass. She swore to herself as the pop fizzed up and out of the glass.

"You could have made it as a singer, Em. You have a better

voice than a lot of artists who are out there now."

"Even so, Kristen, I don't know if I could deal with the media attention. Do you remember when I sang with Kenny at his church?"

"Sorta."

Emmy wet a dishrag and wiped up the counter. "I remember thinking about singing in churches for teens. I think I would have liked that."

"Just singing in church?"

"Yeah, even though I wasn't a believer back then, I could tell that there was something special about the music. It means something. It's not just a bunch of lovey-dovey music about sex and getting together."

"Why don't you give it another shot, Emmy? You could sing with the guys at church."

"I don't know, Kristen. What if I'm not good enough? I don't want to waste anyone's time."

"Trust me, Emmy." Kristen flipped her long hair over her shoulder. "You are definitely good enough."

Emmy thought about what Kristen said. *Maybe God wants to use me to reach teens through my singing. Maybe Tony and I broke up because I was meant to be with Kenny Colwell. Maybe that's why he and Becky were breaking up.* "I should let you go, Krissy. I need to get to work early. It will probably be another uneventful day at the office. Nothing has been happening lately."

"Talk to you later, Em."

Emmy hung up and looked at the calendar. Today was September 10, 2001.

By the time Emmy and Ethan got to work on Tuesday morning just after nine, the world had changed. The guys sat around the conference table watching the news without saying a word. Mr. Oliver told them they could all go home, but no one left. Ethan sat next to Emmy with his arm around her shoulder. She squeezed his hand as she cried. At 9:59 the South Tower collapsed, and Emmy trembled. Twenty-nine minutes later the North Tower followed. Ethan took Emmy home just after noon.

268

"Will you be all right by yourself?" Ethan asked. "I could stay if you need, or you could come over."

"Thank you, Ethan, but I'll be okay. I'll come over if I need anything." She started to turn away, but noticed a tear in the corner of his eye. "Oh, my God! You know someone who works there, don't you? I remember you talking to him the last time you were in New York. I'm so sorry, Ethan."

He nodded as the tears escaped. "I have a friend from college who works in the North Tower. I'm not sure if he was there today. I can't get through on the phone."

"Do you need some company?"

"I'll probably see if Fernando is home."

"I will be praying for all those people and especially for your friend."

"Thanks, Emmy. I'll call you in the morning if I'm not going to the office."

She hugged him and nestled her head against his chest. She felt a teardrop land in her hair, and then Ethan left.

She turned on the TV and watched like everyone else. Kenny finally got through to her and they talked.

"Em, I've been trying to get through for hours. Are you all right?"

"Yes, are you okay? Is everything all right over there? Where are you exactly?"

"I'm all right. We're in a hotel in Madrid. Andy is with me and he says to say hi. Are you still watching the TV?"

"Yes, are we gonna go to war because of this? I'm scared."

"I don't know, Em. We're okay. We don't have a show tonight so we're all just hanging around the hotel. This is just so unbelievable."

"All I can think about is the poor people in those buildings. The firemen and the police officers who tried to help. I hope we don't end up in a war with someone."

"You can't worry about that, Em. You'll make yourself sick."

They kept talking for a few more minutes. Then Kenny explained his email about Becky. "We have broken off our relationship. She wants to be a teacher, and she needs a partner who will be home every night. Unfortunately, I'm not that man."

"I'm sorry, Kenny. I know how much you loved her."

"I'm glad it happened like this before we got too deeply involved." Kenny meant before they got engaged, but didn't tell Emmy.

"Did she make it home all right?"

"Yes, she called when she got home."

"Do you think you will remain friends?"

Kenny ran a hand through his collar-length hair. "I think we will, but there are circumstances that might make that difficult."

"You mean you guys had sex."

Kenny sucked in his breath. "I'm sorry, Em."

"I understand. If I was the same age as Becky, we would have been doing it, too."

"You don't pull any punches, do you?"

"We know each other too well to bother with doing that."

"We won't see each other too often. Becky and me, I mean."

"That's probably wise." She flipped to another channel, but it was the same story. "Will you make sure you email me every day, so I know you're okay? Who knows what will happen in the next few weeks?"

"I'll stay in touch, Em. You take care of yourself."

"Kenny..." she paused.

"Yeah, Em."

"I love you. I just want to tell you that. I'm really sorry about Becky."

"I love you, too, baby. I pray that Becky will find the right person to share her life. She is a very special lady. I'll talk to you soon."

They hung up, but Emmy held onto the phone. *I wish you were home. I miss you so much.*

270

Chapter Thirty-One

The sprinkles turned into a rain shower as Emmy dashed into church.

"Looks like you made it just in time, Emmy." Paul Jefferson held the door open as several people tried to beat the rain.

"Thanks, Paul. Is Lynette around?"

"She was dropping off the girls. Did you need to talk to her?"

"Yeah, but it's nothing too urgent." Emmy looked around and did a double take. "I'll talk to you later. I see an old friend."

Emmy smiled as she and Randy Braun walked toward each other.

"Good morning, Emmy. I hope you don't mind me showing up like this. I thought I would take your advice and give your church a try."

"I don't mind at all. How have you been?"

They reached out to hug, but stopped. She took his hand for a moment instead. He felt the warmth of her small hand as it disappeared in his much larger one.

"Been keeping busy with my graduate classes. Are you doing all right?" Randy pulled her out of the way of a stampede of young kids.

She grinned. "I know you're asking about my relationship with Tony and Kenny."

"You've always been a bright girl."

Emmy pulled him to the side as more people entered the foyer to escape the rain. "If you walk me to my class, I'll give you a quick update."

"Can I join you for your class?"

"Sure. That's what I meant." They slowly walked to her Sunday School room. "Tony is dating a girl at Notre Dame named Brenda. Did I tell you this at my birthday party?"

"Maybe, but go ahead."

"They're going out, and I saw him two weeks ago at Diane's wedding, but we're giving each other some space now."

271

Whatever that's supposed to mean.

"And Kenny was seeing a girl out in California, right?"

"This is my room." They sat at a corner of the large rectangular conference table. "Becky Morrison. But!" Emmy grinned. "They are breaking off their romance. She needs someone with a more stable career."

"Like a nine-to-five type guy?" Randy glanced at the bookcase in the corner. "Can anyone read these books, Emmy?"

She nodded and smiled as Pastor Paul Jefferson, who taught the class, entered. "Exactly! Anyway, he's still on tour until the holidays, so I won't see him."

"Too bad. I know you miss him." Randy smiled at her as he thought, *I wonder if your feelings for me have changed at all. Should I take a chance and ask you out for lunch? I'll have to see how it goes.*

"Good morning, Emmy," Paul said as he extended a hand to Randy.

"This is Randy Braun, an old friend from high school."

"We sorta met in the foyer before you got here," Paul said.

"Did you talk about me?" Emmy grinned and grabbed Randy's arm.

"Certainly." Randy laughed. "I told him everything I know about you."

"Everything?" Emmy bit her lip. *Even about Christopher?*

"Just the good stuff, Em."

During the worship service Emmy and Randy sat toward the back of the youth group.

"There's over a hundred high school and college kids." Randy surveyed the crowd. "That's a lot more than at Faith Bible."

"I think a lot of them are here because they like the music."

They stood and sang along with the worship band. After the first song, Randy stopped singing so he could listen to Emmy. When the worship band finished, Randy whispered, "The band is good, and the guy leading worship has a good voice, but some of the other singers are... horrible. I hate to say that, but it's true."

"I think they lost some singers. Some of them are away at college, and I heard that one family moved out of state because of

272

his job. The husband played keyboards and his wife sang. She was pretty good."

"Have you ever thought about singing with them? You are a better singer than any of them."

"Shush. You're exaggerating."

"No, I'm not. You like to sing, and I know you and Kenny would sing for the teens at Faith Bible. You even write songs."

"I can't. I would be too afraid." She tapped his knee. "We have to pay attention to Pastor Herb now."

They didn't talk about the worship band anymore.

"Did you like the service, Randy?" Emmy asked later, after she introduced him to more of her friends.

"Yeah, I did. It's more of a contemporary type of worship than Faith Bible."

"Some of us are going out for lunch. Would you like to join us?" Emmy asked.

"Sure." Randy grinned. *That solves that. I don't have to ask her out for lunch.*

"If you like, I can drive and bring you back after we eat."

"Sounds good to me, Em."

The only hitch at lunch occurred when Randy offered to pay for Emmy's burger and fries.

"I'd rather pay for my own, Randy. If you pay it would seem like a date."

Randy's heart sank, but he didn't let it show. "Whatever you choose is all right with me."

Emmy grinned at Randy, but then bit her lip as she thought about his brother Christopher. *I wonder if I would let Christopher buy me lunch? I wouldn't mind thinking of this as a date if I was with him instead of Randy.*

On the way back to the church, Emmy mentioned, "There's a group of people our age who get together once a month to play volleyball. Would something like that interest you?"

"I've never been much of an athlete, but it would be a good way to meet people," he said. *I'll do it if I get to spend time with you.*

"It's this coming Saturday. I haven't been to any of these

273

events, but I'd like to start going. We can ride together if you want."

"Sure, would you let me pick you up?" Randy asked.

"Yeah, why not? It's a group thing, so it's not like a date." She glanced at him.

"You don't need to keep reminding me, Emmy. I do have a college education and some experience with girls."

"Sorry."

"It's all right. I know I'm not Christopher." He tapped her knee as he grinned.

"He's married now," she said. "I'm not thinking about him like that anymore."

"If you say so, and I think you had it right when you said he's married now. I wouldn't be at all surprised if that situation changes within a couple of years."

"Why do you say that?"

"Victoria is pestering him to start a family right away, and he wants to wait a few years."

"Do you think she regrets giving up her first baby for adoption?"

Victoria gave birth before enrolling at North Park College. The father's identity had been the speculation of much gossip before she admitted it was Jason Agresta.

"Probably. She was too young to raise a baby at that time. In fact, I still think she is too immature to be a mother."

Emmy pulled up next to his white 1998 Dodge Neon. "I'll talk to you later in the week. We can arrange the details then."

"Have a good week, Emmy. Thanks for lunch. I had a good time."

"So did I. I'm glad you surprised me at church today."

Randy called Emmy on Friday night. "Hi, Emmy, are you still interested in volleyball tomorrow?"

"Yeah, I've been looking forward to it." She leaned against the kitchen counter in the corner.

"Me, too." Randy couldn't help but think of it as a date. "Should we eat before we head to the church?"

274

She grabbed the wash cloth, which had been draped over the faucet, turned on the hot water and wet it. "I don't think so. They are supposed to have pizza and beverages. We might have to kick in a few dollars."

"I can handle that. What time should I pick you up?"

"It's supposed to start at seven, so you could come over here anytime after six thirty," she said as she scrubbed a spot of dried grape jelly.

"I'll see you then."

The next evening Emmy saw Randy pull his Neon into the driveway. She waited for him to ring the bell before opening the door.

"Come on in."

The first thing Randy noticed was the photo of Fridays At Five on the wall.

"Is that you in the photo? You look so young."

"Yeah, I was fourteen, but almost fifteen."

Randy rubbed a hand along the stained woodwork as his eyes took in the living room.

"I'm going to take some extra clothes in case I want to change after we play volleyball," Emmy said.

"I've got some in the car. I didn't know what to expect." Randy noticed the dining room set. "My parents have one very similar to this."

"This one came with the house. It's not mine. We should get going, but maybe I'll give you a tour of the house when we get back."

There were over thirty people already in the large gym when Randy and Emmy entered.

"Did you expect this many people, Em?" Randy asked as he watched four men setting up two volleyball nets.

"I'm not surprised by the turnout." Emmy looked around the larger of the two gyms at the church. "There's Lynette and Paul. Come on." She tugged on Randy's arm as he waved to a couple he had met the previous Sunday.

"Hey, guys, I'm glad you made it," Lynette said.

Emmy thought Lynette looked different in a sweatsuit. "Why are there two courts?"

Paul explained, "One court is for the serious players, like those guys." He pointed at a group of college-age guys. "The rest of us who are just here for fun use the other court."

After ninety minutes of volleyball, everyone took a break. Many of the serious players left.

"Why are they leaving?" Emmy asked.

"They usually leave early so they don't have to chip in for the pizza. Broke college guys, ya know."

The pizzas were delivered, and Emmy and Randy got in line.

"Where should we sit, Emmy?" Randy wondered if they should join her friends or find a spot for just the two of them.

"We can sit with Lynette and Paul. I need to talk to her."

Emmy spent most of the time talking to Lynette as they ate their pizza. Randy and Paul talked about college.

"Would you like another slice, Em?" Randy got up to grab more pizza.

"If there's any of the cheese pizza left, I'll take one. Thanks, Randy." Emmy smiled, and then turned back to Lynette.

"Randy seems really nice," Lynette said.

"He is. He graduated from Roosevelt a year ahead of me and now he's working on his masters."

Lynette took a drink of pop, before adding, "He likes you."

Emmy bit her lip. "I think you might be right, but I just think of him as a friend."

Randy returned with the pizza.

"This was the last slice of plain cheese. I had to fight to get it for you."

Emmy giggled and then touched his arm. "You're funny."

Fifteen minutes later, Emmy started shooting baskets. Randy watched for a time, and then joined her.

"I've heard that you're a pretty good basketball player for a pipsqueak."

"I never played on the school team because I was too short." She swished a shot from the top of the key. "Wanna play one-on-one? Loser has to buy ice cream later."

"Oh, no. I know when I'm being hustled. I'll play, but I'll buy the ice cream, regardless."

"Deal."

Emmy won—easily.

"I'd like a large chocolate fudge sundae with whipped cream, nuts and a cherry on top," Emmy said as she dribbled the ball between her legs.

"I let her win," Randy told everyone.

Paul Jefferson laughed. "You never had a chance, Randy."

The guys put the equipment away and even cleaned up the pizza as the women talked.

Emmy drank a bottle of water as she watched. "You ladies have got these guys well trained."

"It takes years, Emmy," Lynette said as she laughed.

"Are you ready for your ice cream?" Randy walked up behind Emmy and put a hand on her shoulder.

"I'm always ready for ice cream. Just need to grab my jacket. I'll see you in the morning, Lynette."

Randy pulled in at Culver's. "That was fun, Emmy. Can we do it again next month?"

"Yeah, let's plan on it."

He opened the door for her. "I'll work on my moves and next time you'll be paying for the ice cream."

"You better work hard because I didn't use my A game tonight." Emmy grinned as she held the second door open for Randy.

Randy ordered a burger and fries along with Emmy's sundae.

"Let's sit by the windows," Emmy suggested.

"Is Kenny any good at basketball?" Randy tossed his jacket in the corner of the booth.

"He's better than you," she teased.

"I warned you that I was never much of an athlete."

"The bump on your forehead doesn't look as bad now." Emmy reached over and felt the spot where Randy had been nailed with the volleyball.

"That was embarrassing." He grabbed her hand before she could move it. "You have such little hands, Em."

She pulled her hand away. "I know. It makes it hard to play the piano. I can't stretch my hands enough to make some of the harder chords."

Their food arrived, and they ate quietly. He opened the door for her as they left.

"Would you like to come in for a few minutes?" she asked as he pulled into her driveway.

"You promised me a tour, remember?"

"That's right. I did."

She showed him all the rooms on the first floor and then the basement.

"There's an old cistern like that in my parents' basement." Randy could easily see over the top, but Emmy had to stand on tiptoes.

"I don't spend much time in the basement except when I do my laundry," Emmy said while leading Randy back to the kitchen and then over to the stairs leading to the second floor. She stood on the bottom step and faced him. "The bedrooms are upstairs. There's three of them and a bathroom."

He could read the indecision on her face. "You don't have to show me the bedrooms, Emmy. I should take off. We've got church in the morning."

She walked him to his car. "I'm glad you decided to try out my church. Who knows? You might find the perfect girlfriend."

"I can only hope. See you in the morning."

Over the next few weeks, Emmy and Randy sat together during both Sunday School class and the worship services. They attended several church functions together, and they joined a group of North Park students to watch a football game at SoHam stadium.

One Sunday morning one of the college girls asked Emmy, "Are you and Randy Braun dating? You're always together, but I never see you guys holding hands or anything."

"That's because we're friends. We're not like dating dating."

278

Emmy heard Randy talking to some guys behind her. "We're good friends."

"Have you kissed him?"

Emmy shook her head.

Another girl giggled and then asked, "Has he kissed you?"

Emmy grinned. "Not yet. I'm not sure how I would react."

Randy walked up behind Emmy and overheard the conversation.

"Emmy is a great friend. If not for her, I wouldn't be here today." He touched her shoulder tenderly. "She was the only person who got after me because of my drinking."

"Oh, Randy, I didn't do anything special." She turned, lifted her face to smile at him, grabbed his arm and held on tightly.

Her eyes were sparkling as Randy looked down at her. *Maybe I should kiss you one of these days.*

Chapter Thirty-Two

"Hey, Emmy, it's Randy. Are you busy?" He called shortly after eight on Tuesday.

"Not really. I was reading. What's up?" Emmy closed her book and sat up. She had been reading while laying on her stomach on the living room couch.

"I have an extra ticket to see The French Occupation Of Quincy on Saturday night. Have you ever heard of them?"

"Yeah, Kenny has both of their CDs. Where are they playing?"

"At North Park. In the Barclay Center. The gym. Would you be interested?"

"Sure. What time?"

"The show's supposed to start at eight. I could pick you up around seven thirty."

"If you pick me up around six, we could have dinner, and then go to the concert." Emmy felt more comfortable hanging out with Randy now.

"Are you gonna buy?" Randy laughed.

"We can split it the way friends would."

"That works for me. How's school going?" Randy knew she was struggling with her classes at Paul Frank this semester.

"I've never had to work so hard. I'm afraid I might get a B."

"Heaven forbid!" he teased. "I'm sure that won't happen. If you ever need my help, all you have to do is ask. I don't charge too much for tutoring."

"Wouldn't you do it for free since I'm such a good friend?" she asked.

"I'll think about it. I'll call you Friday. If you need any help before then, just call, Em. I might be of some assistance."

"I appreciate it. Say hi to Christopher if you see him. Are you coming to church tomorrow?"

"I think so."

"See ya then."

Emmy rushed out of work the next day. She drove like a

maniac to get home, changed clothes and made a ham sandwich. She checked the mail as she scarfed down the sandwich.

Just junk mail. She looked at the clock, *Shoot! It's almost six thirty already. I gotta get going.*

She made it to church on time and sat with Lynette. She saw Randy and waved.

"Randy invited me to a concert on Saturday," Emmy said and explained who and where.

Lynette watched as Randy talked to some of the men. *I wish he would find one of the other single girls to date. It's not good for him and Emmy to be spending too much time together.*

Emmy was talking to some friends after the service when Randy walked over.

"Hey, Randy, there's a group going over to Beggar's for pizza. Are we gonna go?"

Lynette heard Emmy ask Randy and thought, *It sounds like you're thinking of the two of you as a couple. What's going on?*

"Sure, but we can't stay too late. I've got an early class." He playfully tugged on her ponytail.

"And I have to work. If you want to take your car home, I'll drive to Beggar's," Emmy offered.

"Are you sure? I don't mind driving."

"I'll follow you. No sense in both of us using our gas."

Emmy followed Randy home. He parked his car and jumped in with Emmy. Beggar's was only a few blocks away. The group grabbed a table for eight and ordered. An hour and a half later Randy walked Emmy out to her car.

"Uh-oh! That doesn't look good, Em." Randy pointed to her rear tire on the passenger side.

Emmy walked around to that side. "Oh, crap! I've never had a flat before."

"It's as flat as could be, Em. Don't worry, I'll change it for you. You do have a spare in the trunk, right?"

"I'm sure there is, but I want to change it myself."

"You don't have to. I'll do it."

Emmy opened the trunk. "I need to learn how. I've watched Daddy change a flat, but I need to do it."

281

Randy knew Emmy well enough to know she could be rather stubborn.

"I'll only help if you run into trouble."

Emmy grabbed the jack and was able to lift the donut out of the trunk. "I'm not sure I can lift a full-size tire, Randy."

She positioned the jack and lifted the car slightly. "I know I have to loosen the things..."

"Lug nuts."

"Right. I have to loosen them before the tire is off the ground." She used the jack handle and tried to loosen the lug nuts. She put all her weight on it. But they didn't budge. "I might need you to get them started, Randy."

"It's all right, Em. Sometimes it takes some strong muscles to get them started. Especially if they've been put on with a torque wrench."

Randy loosened the nuts, but then let Emmy finish. She raised the car, removed the lug nuts, took off the flat tire and all the rest. She even managed to get the flat tire into the trunk.

"I did it, Randy!" She high-fived him.

"Yes, you did, Em. Look at your hands." He pointed to her filthy hands.

She wiped them on the sides of her jeans. "I don't mind getting a little dirty." She giggled as she wiped her finger across his cheek. "Do you mind?"

He laughed, then took her hand and wiped it on her nose. "You have a dirty face, but you're still pretty."

"Thank you, sir." She smiled as she held onto his hand. "I'll stop on the way to work and get the tire fixed. There's a place just down the road."

"I hope you don't have another flat on the way home."

Friday evening Randy called as promised. "Did you get the tire fixed, Em?"

"I had to buy a new one, but I took care of it. What are you doing tonight?" She tapped her pen on the dining room table. "Anything special?"

"Nothing much. I've got a little studying to finish. You?"

"The same." She paused. *Should I even mention this?* She quickly decided. "I talked to Kenny's parents last night."

She scooted the chair back on the carpet, stood up and walked into the kitchen.

"How's he doing?"

"Okay. I wish he was home."

"I know you do, Em."

"You're still taking me to dinner tomorrow, right?" Emmy dropped the phone as she tried to get a glass from the cupboard.

He jerked the phone away from his ear. "What was that? Are you still there?"

"Sorry, I dropped the phone."

"Any place special you want to go?" Randy opened his wallet to check his cash level.

"It doesn't matter. Doesn't need to be anywhere fancy."

"Would Mexican be all right?"

"Sure. There's Taco Casa over here by me."

"That will work. I'll see you at six."

Emmy slept until nine. She slowly opened her eyes as she stretched her arms and legs. Cleaning the house, doing laundry, grocery shopping and talking to Lynette and her mother kept her busy until mid-afternoon.

"Emmy, what are you doing tonight?" Kristen called just after three.

Emmy checked the last three slices of bread in the wicker basket on the counter, saw some green mold and tossed them in the garbage. "Randy invited me to a concert at school."

"Really? I'm going, too." Kristen picked out a top from her closet to wear later that night.

"Who are you going with?"

"Brandon got tickets."

"Has he been behaving?" Emmy asked.

"I suppose. I don't worry about that anymore."

"Why not?" Emmy set the fresh bread in the basket.

"I know when I first met him, I thought he was so special, but I'm kinda over that now. He's all right, and I have fun with him,

283

but it's never going to be a serious relationship."

"You mean you aren't going to sleep with him," Emmy said and then giggled.

"Oh, we do that all the time..."

"What?" Emmy exclaimed. "You better not be having sex."

"I'm kidding. He tried a few times, but he's given up hope."

"Good. We're going to Taco Casa for dinner."

"Don't fill up on the cheap chips." Kristen laughed as she remembered the first time she and Emmy ate there.

"Cheap chips," Emmy repeated a few times.

"It's not funny anymore, Em."

"We were both acting silly that day."

"I gotta go. Maybe we'll see you guys at the show."

Emmy showered later and tried to decide what to wear. She tossed a clean pair of jeans on her bed, then looked in the closet at her dresses. *Maybe I should wear a skirt and top,* she thought as she sang along to the *Hero For Hire* CD playing on her Bose system. *I'm sure glad you bought me this for Christmas, Kenny. I was only sixteen, and it still sounds amazing.* She picked out a navy blue skirt, a white top and a baby blue sweater. She dressed, and then looked in the mirror. *I don't care if this makes me look young. I think Randy will like it.*

At 5:58 the doorbell rang. Emmy wiped the kitchen counter one last time, and then tossed the Handi Wipe in the trash. She smoothed out her skirt as she walked to the front door.

"Come on in, Randy. I'll grab my purse and coat and we can go."

"Wow! You dressed up, Em. I assumed you would wear jeans, so that's what I did."

"Do you like?" She twirled around.

"Very much. You look divine, Ms. Colasanti. I've got the tickets and some cash, so you don't need your purse, unless you need it... never mind."

"I'll bring it just in case. Kristen and Brandon are gonna be at the concert, but she didn't say where their seats are located."

"Did you invite them to dinner?"

"No, I didn't think of it. I thought it would be just us."

"That's fine," he said. He mentally pumped his fist.

Emmy locked the house, and they drove over to Taco Casa. They were seated in a booth near the back. They ordered, and Emmy looked at the basket of warm, fresh tortilla chips.

"Don't let me fill up on these, okay?"

"They are good, but they're just cheap chips."

Emmy laughed so hard she started to cry.

"What is so funny, Em?"

She explained what happened with her and Kristen.

"I guess you had to be there, Em," he said.

She stuck out her tongue at him. "We were acting silly."

They talked about church and school as they ate.

Emmy finished her last bite of rice and rubbed her stomach. "I am stuffed!"

"I'm surprised you could finish everything. You had beans, rice *and* two enchiladas."

"You're teasing me," she said softly.

"I'm sorry. I know you don't eat much.

After a couple of minutes, Emmy asked, "Do you miss the beer?"

"Not so much anymore. Do you miss it?"

"I don't really think about it. If I never have another one, I would survive, but I don't think it's wrong to have a beer."

"I know. It's the abuse of drinking that's a sin." He picked up the check and took a look. "I got this, Em. You could leave a five for the tip."

"You really were lost for a while, Randy. I'm glad you're not letting it control your life." She thought about her father. She bit her lip, and then mentioned, "I know you had a few girlfriends during college."

He stared at her for a moment. "Are you asking about my sex life, Em?"

"Maybe. Is that taboo?"

"I guess not. I did have a few relationships, but they were never serious."

She drank the rest of her Coke. "If you had sex, I would consider that a serious relationship."

"Then I guess they were serious. I'm different now, Em. You know that."

"I know." She stared at her hands in her lap.

"Are you trying to tell me something?" He thought about her infatuation with Christopher. "Have you talked to Christopher lately?"

"I talked to him, but I haven't seen him since my party. We never did anything, Randy. I know I kinda liked him, but nothing ever happened."

"He really likes you, but he knew it would be wrong to get involved. He does have a strong sense of morality. Except when it comes to Victoria."

"Does he ever go to church?"

"No, and he refuses to talk about it."

"We can pray for him."

"My parents do everyday."

They kept talking until it was time to head to the campus.

Emmy looked around the Barclay Center as she and Randy entered. "Can you see Kristen?"

After looking around for a minute, Randy spotted her with Brandon. "They're over there, Em." He pointed to his right.

"I see her." Emmy bounced on her toes and waved. "I want to talk to her for a moment."

"Should I wait here?"

"You can come with me." She held onto his hand. "I just want to ask her about Tony's mother."

"Is she all right?" Randy asked as Emmy pulled him along.

"I don't know. I don't talk to her much since Tony and I aren't talking," Emmy said as she dodged through and around people and apologized when needed as Randy held on.

"Hi, Krissy. We made it," Emmy said.

Emmy talked to Kristen and Brandon for a minute before asking about Mama.

"She's doing all right, but she misses you. You should call her sometime, or better yet, go with me when I see her. She would like that."

"I'll think about it."

Kristen turned to talk to Randy, so Emmy asked Brandon, "Are you guys doing anything later?"

"Probably head over to the dorm. Wanna come over?" Brandon asked.

"Maybe. You're not having a wild party in someone's room, are you?"

He grinned. "We could if you want."

Emmy made a face at him. "I don't think so, Brandon."

"We're gonna hang out in the lounge. There's a TV and a pool table. We're not gonna have a party."

"I thought you were gonna graduate last semester. Krissy said you were a senior last spring."

"This is my last semester."

"What are your plans after that?"

"I'm gonna head back to Michigan. I'm originally from the Kalamazoo area."

Emmy wondered if Kristen knew about his plans.

"We should find our seats, Em." Randy took her hand.

"I'll talk to you after the show, Kristen. Maybe we can hang out for a while."

This time Randy led the way and Emmy held his hand as he headed to section 105.

"How do you like these seats, Em? We're off to the side a bit but close enough to see everything." He stood up, looked at the stage and then the people around them.

"They're great seats, Randy. Thank you for bringing me."

"You're welcome."

Emmy thought about Mama Bertucci and Kenny's parents for a moment. "Randy, can I ask you something?" She tugged on his arm.

He sat down. "Sure, Em. What's up?"

"I've never met your parents. Do you think I should?"

He tilted his head. *Why would you think about that?* "Sure, Mom and Dad would love to meet you. I've told them about you."

"Someday soon," Emmy said as the house lights dimmed.

The band finished their second encore two hours later, and the house lights came on.

287

"Do you want to hang around, Randy?" Emmy asked. "I'd like to."

"We can if you want, but tomorrow is Sunday."

"I'll be able to get up for church. Will you?"

He grinned. "Hey, I'm used to staying up all night. I'm a college student, remember?"

"We don't have to stay real late, but I would like to have some fun."

"Does that mean you haven't had any fun hanging out with me?" Randy pretended to be hurt.

"That's not what I meant." She brushed her hand along his cheek. "We have fun together."

"I know we do. Should I call Christopher and see if he's busy?"

Emmy immediately frowned and withdrew her hand.

"Shoot! I'm sorry. I didn't mean it like that, Em."

"You better not."

They found Kristen and Brandon in the lobby and headed over to Asner Hall—Brandon's dorm.

"Did you guys like the show?" Brandon asked. "I've never seen them before, but I enjoyed it."

Emmy answered before Randy could respond. "I've never seen them live, but I've listened to both of their CDs. I thought they were pretty good."

Kristen reminded her, "You're kinda prejudiced, Emmy. You compare every band to Fridays At Five. They can't all be as good as Kenny."

"I guess I do compare them to Kenny."

Brandon wondered about Emmy's relationship with Kenny, but kept his mouth shut. Brandon and Kristen watched TV while Emmy challenged Randy to a game of fussball.

"First one to seven wins, okay?" Randy was eager to prove to Emmy he could beat her at some sport after getting his butt kicked in basketball.

She didn't know that Randy and Christopher had played fussball from the time they could reach the handles.

"Should we make this interesting?"

288

"Are you suggesting a wager of some sorts, Em?" Randy's eyes gleamed.

"We could play for money, or maybe something else." Emmy bit her lip and wondered if he could tell she was flirting.

"How about this, Em? If you win, I owe you five bucks."

"What about if you win? Though I doubt that's even a possibility. I have seen you play basketball, remember?"

"If I win, I get to kiss you." He hoped Kristen couldn't hear.

Emmy grinned as her heart thumped. "Sounds like I will be five dollars richer pretty soon." She looked over at Kristen to make sure she couldn't hear. "Too bad you won't be collecting on that kiss."

Two minutes later, Emmy stared at Randy as he grinned wickedly. "Best two out of three, Em?"

Five minutes later, Randy had won three games by identical scores of seven-zip.

"I didn't even score," she said in disbelief.

"I'm not bragging, but I've won a few tournaments here. It keeps me in spending money." Randy walked around the table and smiled as he put his hands on her shoulders.

"You aren't going to kiss me in front of everyone, are you?" Emmy looked up at him.

He brushed a couple of stray hairs off of her face. "I'd rather kiss you when we're alone."

"You're really gonna hold me to the bet, huh?"

"A bet is a bet, Emmy. Are you gonna back out?"

"One kiss is all," she said. "And no tongue, either." She poked him in the chest. "I better tell Kristen we're leaving."

"We don't have to leave right away. How about a game of pool?"

"All right, but no more bets. For all I know you might be a Minnesota fat guy.

"Minnesota Fats. Not fat guy."

"Whatever! Like I really care."

A couple of minutes later, Kristen looked around and saw Emmy playing pool. She stood up and walked over to Emmy. "Are you having fun, Em?"

"Yeah, we're both lousy at pool." She didn't mention the fussball results.

Emmy leaned over to take a shot and Kristen glanced at Brandon. He was watching Emmy. Kristen moved to block his line of sight.

"Talk to you later, Em. I have to smack Brandon."

After they finished playing pool, Emmy sat next to Kristen on the couch. "We're gonna go. We have to get up for church."

"I'm gonna head back to my dorm. I'll walk you guys out to your car. Talk to you later, Brandon." Kristen looked at Brandon. He turned his head, but she knew he had been looking at Emmy. Kristen thought, *If this was a game of baseball, you just got called out on strikes, buster.*

"Good night, Brandon." Emmy stood up and walked in front of the couch.

His eyes followed her. "Yeah, good night. See you around."

Randy opened the door for Emmy and Kristen.

"I have to admit. You and Christopher are both gentlemen. Your parents at least taught you some manners," Kristen said as she patted Randy's arm.

"We'll walk you over to Howe," Randy told Kristen.

He and Emmy escorted Kristen over to her dorm.

"Night, Krissy. I'll talk to you later."

"I'll call you. I have to talk about Brandon." Kristen made his name sound like a swear word.

Randy waved good night, and then put an arm around Emmy's shoulder. Kristen watched for a moment from inside the door as Randy and Emmy walked to his car.

Kristen wondered, *Are you becoming more involved with Randy?*

Fifteen minutes later, Randy pulled into Emmy's driveway.

She unhooked her seatbelt. "Do you want to come in for coffee or anything?"

"That would be nice unless you want that kiss in the car."

"I was hoping you would forget," she said.

"I'm like an elephant. I never forget a bet."

290

"I didn't know elephants liked to bet." Emmy jumped out and ran to the back door.

Randy laughed as he followed her.

"Do you really want some coffee, or was that just an excuse to get in the house?"

"I could use a cup of coffee. While it's brewing, maybe I could collect on that little wager." He leaned against the counter as she got the coffee out of the cabinet. He watched patiently as she put the coffee and water in the Mr. Coffee machine.

She turned to Randy and moved closer. "You might be disappointed."

"I doubt it, Em." He leaned down.

She closed her eyes. He kept his open. He kept the kiss brief. For a moment neither one spoke.

"Let's try that again, Randy."

He kissed her again—a bit longer this time.

She backed away.

"Are you thinking the same thing I am?" he asked.

"Maybe. What are you thinking?"

"I think you're the... uh... the... uh..."

"Yeah, me, too. It felt like kissing my brother even though I don't have one."

He laughed. "Em, you're a sexy little thing, but you're also the sweetest and most innocent girl I've ever kissed. I'm not disappointed." He kissed her forehead. "At least now we know, and we can concentrate on being good friends."

"Do you still want that cup of coffee?"

"I'd hate to see it go to waste."

They sat at the kitchen table as they drank the coffee and split a day-old donut.

"I better go, Em. I'll see you in the morning."

"Night, Randy. I did have fun tonight. Dinner and the concert were good, and now I know not to challenge you to a game of fussball."

Chapter Thirty-Three

Emmy pulled into the driveway at the Bertucci house and jumped out of the car. *I can't believe Heather's getting married tomorrow. I wonder if she will kiss Alex in public after that. I've never seen them holding hands.* Emmy walked in the back door and saw Mama in the kitchen. "Hi, Mama. Do you need any help?"

"Hello, dear, could you help me with this cake. It needs to be frosted. Here is the frosting and a spatula. I really need to run upstairs and get changed. Thanks, honey."

As Emmy frosted the cake, Heather walked into the kitchen and gave her a big hug.

"Heather, you look so good. It's nice to see you again. Are you nervous about tomorrow?" Emmy asked.

"Not a bit. You're looking good, Emmy. Try not to get cake and frosting all over your face tonight." Heather teased Emmy by putting some of the frosting on the tip of her nose. "Thank you for filling in at the last minute. I really appreciate it."

"It's okay, Heather. I'm glad I could help. I'm happy that you even thought of me." She wiped off the frosting with a finger and stuck it in her mouth. *Oooh! This is really good.*

Tony left school after his last class on Friday and made it home in just over two hours. He saw Emmy in the kitchen and came over to pick her up and hug her like he always did. Before Tony could hug her, though, she put her hand against his chest and stopped him.

"You can't treat me like you used to. You can't just come up to me and pick me up to hug me. Understand?"

"Okay, Emmy. It's so good to see you again. You look really nice tonight. I always like it when you have a braid or two in your hair. I'll do whatever you want me to." He didn't even try to kiss her.

"Thanks, Tony. We can still talk to each other. I still want to know what's happening in your life. You know, how's school and all that stuff. Not how's Brenda doing." She put some more frosting on the spatula. "How is school? Getting close now, isn't it? I saw a little bit of the game against Southern Cal."

"That was a close game."

"It must be quite disappointing to lose so many games in your final season." *Ooops! I shouldn't have mentioned that.*

"We are struggling, but we still have a chance to win six games and make it to a bowl."

"You're three and four. Doesn't look too good."

"We haven't given up."

Emmy wondered who she would be partnered with for the ceremony and found out later at the rehearsal—Marco Bertucci.

"Tony, why is Marco in the wedding party?" Emmy asked as she and Tony walked around St. Raymond's cathedral.

"Marco and Alex are friends, and Marco first introduced Alex to Heather. Marco was, or maybe still is, in school with Alex's brother, Albert, and that's how he and Alex know each other."

"So, I finally get to meet Marco, huh? He's not just a figment of your imagination."

"He really exists." Tony swatted her bottom, playfully.

"Stop that! We're in a church."

Emmy and Tony were walking into the sanctuary when Marco finally arrived for the rehearsal. Emmy saw him and gasped. "Oh, my God!" She covered her mouth as she thought, *Are you possibly who I think you are?* Emmy recognized him from high school. She compared Marco's short wiry black hair to Tony's longer straight hair. Tony needed to shave his thick beard every day, but Marco opted for a full, bushy beard. Emmy thought he must look like his father because he didn't resemble Tony or Heather at all.

"Tony, I need to talk to you alone for a moment."

"Okay. What is it, Em?"

She grabbed his elbow and dragged Tony away from everybody else. Tony wondered what Emmy could be mad at now.

"Emmy, I don't see that girl much anymore, and Heather is not pregnant."

Emmy looked at Tony and sighed impatiently, "That's not why I need to talk to you."

"Then what's up? I need to introduce you to Marco."

293

"You don't need to introduce us. I already know him."

"You do? How?" Tony tilted his head. "Oh, from school. I didn't think you had ever met him."

"I guess technically, I have never met him, but I know him. I know him all too well. Do you remember Todd Delaney, the stalker kid?"

"Yeah, I remember."

"He had a couple friends who would help him pester me and stuff—not directly though. I never knew their names, but I know one of their names now, I think."

Tony rubbed his jaw. "Emmy, are you telling me that my brother was one of the guys who harassed you?"

"Yes, I'm sure of it. I mean, he's got a beard now, but I think he's one of the guys who spread lies about me and put Todd's nasty letters in my locker." Emmy took another look at Marco, and then faced Tony. "Maybe I'm just imagining it. He does kinda look like the guy I remember, but he looks so much older now, and he's starting to go bald. He's even got some gray hair already."

"I'm so sorry, Em. I never knew, I swear. I knew Marco got mixed up with some troublemakers for a time, but I didn't realize he knew Delaney. Should I ask Heather to switch your partner?"

"No, don't do anything and don't say anything to Marco. He might not even be the guy, or even remember me. I don't want to cause a problem for Heather."

Heather came over to Tony and Emmy and asked, "Are you guys ready to join the rest of us? We need to start the rehearsal, please."

"Be right there, Heather," Tony answered. "Come on, Emmy. Let's get this over with."

Kristen rushed in out of breath. She removed her coat and set it on a pew. "Sorry, I'm late, but I had to finish a paper. Did I miss anything?"

"I'll tell you later," Emmy said.

Alex and Heather introduced all the members of the wedding party to each other. Most of their names were immediately forgotten. Marco looked at Emmy but didn't appear to recognize her. He didn't hear Emmy's last name, or else he might

294

have remembered. Emmy thought he looked about five feet eight, but couldn't hazard a guess at his weight because his belly hung over his belt. All during rehearsal Emmy still had doubts about whether she knew Marco or not. It happened over four years ago and Marco gave no indication of ever meeting her before. Emmy felt nervous, and a little uncomfortable with Marco, but he seemed to be a nice guy—rather quiet, but very intelligent.

After the rehearsal, they went to Caio Bella for dinner. Emmy sat at a table with Tony and Kristen. Marco sat at the other end with a lady next to him.

"Who is that sitting next to your brother?" Emmy asked as she stole a bite of Tony's ravioli.

"That's Marco's wife, Nancy."

"She looks older than him, is she?"

"Yeah, she's at least ten years older than Marco and has some kids from a previous marriage. Three of them, if I remember correctly." He swatted her hand away. "Quit stealing my ravioli."

"I just took a little bite." She grinned. "Now what about her kids?"

"I've never met them. I only met his wife once at a family get together. They got married at the courthouse in Baltimore and didn't have a ceremony or reception or anything. We didn't even find out about it until Mama called his apartment and she answered."

"If you ever get married, you better not keep it a secret. I can't believe Heather and Marco are so secretive."

After the rehearsal dinner, Emmy figured she would head home until Mama called out to her, "Emmy, you are coming over to the house, aren't you?" The way Mama said it was not as a question, but more of an order. "Derrick will be there."

"I can stay for a while, I suppose. My car is there so I need a lift back."

Emmy rode in the back seat to Mama's house while Tony drove. She didn't say a word as she thought about her senior year at Roosevelt. She tried to picture the guy she thought might be Marco. *I just can't remember for sure. I only saw him once or twice and never up close.* Tony pulled into the driveway and

Emmy spotted Derrick's car. She jumped out and ran into the house.

"Kristen, will you help me in the kitchen for a moment?" Emmy dragged Kristen to the kitchen. "You are not going to believe this."

"What?"

"I never realized until tonight, but I think I knew Marco in high school. If I'm right, he hung out with Todd Delaney and was one of the guys who harassed me."

"No! For real?"

Emmy nodded. "I'm not a hundred percent sure, but it's a possibility."

"I didn't see Marco very often. We were never close like I am with Tony. I rarely talked to him after we got to high school."

Emmy pulled Kristen to the far corner of the kitchen.

"Did he recognize you?" Kristen asked.

"If he did, he has not let anyone know. Delaney and his gang spread lies about me—lies about sex. He made me cry so many times. I used to hate him and his friends without really knowing them. But you know what, Kristen, I don't anymore. If Marco was one of those guys, I forgive him for what he did to me. He's not gonna be my best friend or anything, but I forgive him."

"Emmy, you have always been such a sweet and kindhearted person, but now you are even more amazing."

"You know why."

"I know, Emmy. Maybe someday I will believe the way you do."

Mama came in the kitchen. "Oh, here you girls are. I need help setting the table."

"Are we eating again?" Emmy patted her stomach, "I'm still full."

"I made some desserts. You don't have to eat anything if you don't want. I'm sure the chocolate cake will go fast."

"I might be able to eat a small piece. Your cakes are so moist and yummy."

Kristen and Emmy helped Mama, but then kept to themselves while the other guests and family members mingled.

296

Emmy talked to Derrick, but noticed that Marco didn't come over to the house.

Emmy looked at the floor as she walked out of the kitchen. She turned the corner into the hallway and bumped into Tony.

"Oh, sorry, Em. I didn't see you."

"It's not your fault. I wasn't watching where I was going."

Emmy stared at Tony, and he looked back at her with such a sad look in his eyes that it broke her heart. She started to get tears in her eyes and held up her arms for Tony to pick her up. Tony picked her up and held her tightly to his chest until Heather came by.

"Tony, stop! You're hurting her. Put her down before you crush her."

Tony immediately released her, and she landed on her feet.

"Thanks, Heather. I couldn't breathe and couldn't tell Tony to ease up."

"Be more careful or else you will break her in two." Heather shook a finger at Tony.

It never ceased to amaze Emmy that Tony could be so quiet and soft spoken with her and Kristen and other people, but so ferocious on the football field. Emmy felt relieved and kissed his cheek when he picked her up again as she put her arms up to his neck. Tony forgot and squeezed her tightly again.

"Tony, I can't breathe."

Tony set her down, and she looked up at him. "You know I love you, and I forgive you for what you did. But you hurt me so much, and I need time to get over everything."

"I know, Emmy. I don't deserve you after what I've done. I made the wrong choice, and now I regret it."

Does that mean you and Brenda broke up? She wondered.

The next day everything went smoothly, and as planned, at the ceremony. Emmy rode with Kristen to the reception at the Barclay Country Club.

"That was a beautiful ceremony," Emmy said.

"Let me fix your collar." Kristen straightened the collar on Emmy's bridesmaid dress. "That's better. Don't ever buy a yellow

297

dress like this. It isn't a good color for you. It works for me, but not you."

"Thanks for the advice. I didn't want to say anything to Heather, but I think the dresses are hideous."

"How are things going with Tony?" Kristen asked as she and Emmy hung up their coats. "Are you even talking to him?"

"You didn't see it, but last night I stepped out of the kitchen and smacked right into Tony," Emmy whispered as she glanced around. "We just stared at each other for a moment. He looked so sad. I held my arms up and he hugged me," Emmy said and then sighed. "It was so romantic except that I couldn't breathe. I think I would have suffocated if Heather hadn't come along and noticed me turning blue."

"Did he kiss you?"

"No, he just hugged me."

Kristen hugged her and said, "We'll talk later, Em. I want to hear more about this."

Marco sat next to Emmy at the reception dinner and asked, "Where do you go to school, Emmy?"

"I'm taking some classes at Paul Frank Junior College and working full-time. How about you?"

"I'm still at Johns Hopkins. I may be there forever if I can afford it. Where did you go to high school? To be honest, I thought you were still in high school."

"I went to Roosevelt."

"I went there, too. What year did you graduate?"

"Just recently," Emmy answered, hoping he would not want to talk anymore about high school. She changed the subject by asking. "Doesn't Heather look beautiful today?"

"She looks great. By the way, how do you know Heather? It can't be from school, you are so much younger than her."

Emmy bit her lip. "I'm just a family friend. I'm filling in for another girl who had to cancel at the last minute."

Marco danced with Emmy later and shook her hand after the song ended. "Thank you for the dance and the pleasant conversation, Emmy."

"It was my pleasure. I've had a lovely evening."

Emmy watched as Tony danced with Heather. Later on, Emmy danced with Derrick and they talked about law school. She danced once with Tony.

"I watched you and Heather dancing. She's almost as tall as you," Emmy said.

"She's always been tall for her size."

Emmy giggled. "You mean for her age, right?"

"Yeah, what did I say?"

"Never mind. It's not important. Did she have dancing lessons, too? You guys danced so well together."

"I think so, but I can't remember."

Later, Kristen and Emmy were drinking champagne when Heather walked over and said, "Emmy, it always amuses me to see you and Tony dancing together. He is so huge and you are so petite. It's like watching a grown man dance with his young daughter. Do you remember the first time you came over to the house? You and Tony played in the snow, then he carried you in the house."

Emmy nodded at Heather.

"I thought you were one of his little friends from the neighborhood. I even thought you were a boy until your long hair fell out of your stocking cap."

"I remember, Heather. That was the day I fell in love with Tony."

Kristen grinned. *Yes!*

"Oh, Emmy, that is so sweet. I hope everything works out, and you get married to that teddy bear. We will be sisters forever."

Emmy and Mama spent some time talking during the reception. Mama knew what happened between Emmy and Tony, and tried to help her understand why sometimes life didn't always go smoothly.

"Honey, is there something else bothering you? You can tell me, you know. You are like a daughter to me."

"I'm fine, Mama," Emmy insisted.

Mama knew better, but didn't pry. Emmy thought about what the doctor told her, but wasn't ready to tell Mama. She spent more time talking to Tony, but only danced with him the one time.

Tony saw Emmy sitting with his mother. He pulled up a chair next to Emmy. "Where are you staying tonight? At your house, or are you going to the Keaslings with Kristen and Derrick?"

"Kristen is staying at my house with me. Why?"

"No reason. Are you guys leaving soon?" Tony asked.

"Probably. Why?" Emmy asked and then giggled.

Are you trying to make me mad by asking why all the time? He looked at his watch. "Just wondering. It's still early for a Saturday."

"You can't come over if that's what you're getting at." Emmy shot him down.

Tony hung his head. *I had thought about asking, but I guess that settles it.*

Later, Tony offered to walk Emmy and Kristen to their cars. Tony walked along quietly as Emmy and Kristen talked.

"I'll see you at your house, Em. Don't take too long to get there." Kristen winked at Tony.

"I'll be right behind you, Krissy."

Tony and Emmy walked over to her car. Kristen took off after a couple of minutes. Emmy stood beside the door with Tony.

"Heather looked great today. I hope she and Alex have many happy years together."

"You look pretty good yourself, Em." Tony touched her cheek.

"I need to get going before I freeze. Kristen will be waiting for me."

They talked for a couple of minutes, and then Emmy let Tony kiss her good night on the cheek. She wasn't ready to forget about his mistake.

Chapter Thirty-Four

"Emmy, I can tell something is distressing you. Would you like to share?" Lynette asked as they sat down in their Sunday School classroom.

"Oh, I'm just feeling a bit discombobulated."

Lynette chuckled. "I don't mean to laugh at you, but... I've never heard anyone use that word like that before."

"Maybe I should say I'm perplexed, but I'll get over it."

"Is it about Randy? I know he wants to be more than friends."

"No, Randy and I are getting along all right. He's dating someone now. We went to that concert about a month ago, and he came over to the house and kissed me."

"What? You kissed him."

"Not like that. Well, like that, but it was because I lost at fussball."

Lynette shook her head. "You've lost me."

Emmy giggled and then explained, "We had a bet over fussball, and I lost. Randy kissed me in the kitchen and we both agreed that it lacked a certain something. So we decided we are just meant to be good friends.

"Okay, I get it now. Is he dating someone from church?"

"He and Vanessa Ortega are seeing each other. She's in her second year at North Park."

"I think I know her. She's rather tall and wears classes."

Emmy nodded. "She's got red hair."

Lynette asked, "Is it about Tony?"

Emmy sighed, lowered her head to the table and rested her chin on her Bible. "Kenny, too. Is it so obvious?"

"You aren't very good at hiding your emotions. You would make a terrible poker player."

"I know."

Lynette rubbed Emmy's back. "Have you seen any of your friends lately? I guess I'm asking if you've seen Tony, but I don't mean to pry."

"I've been keeping to myself since Heather Bertucci's

wedding. Work and night classes have kept me busy, as usual. I didn't even talk to Kristen this past week."

"You can always talk to me, Emmy. I heard some of our friends commenting about you. They could tell something was troubling you."

"Thanks, Lynette. I hate to bother you with my problems. You must get bombarded by people in the church." Emmy sat up as more people walked into the classroom.

"It's sort of part of being a pastor's wife. Would you rather talk after class?"

"It's nothing really. I need to spend more time in prayer. God will show me what to do," Emmy said.

Lynette patted Emmy's arm. *I understand you don't want to talk about your personal life in front of everyone.*

Emmy spent Thanksgiving morning helping to serve a meal at the SoHam Mission Shelter for the homeless. She didn't tell her friends from church about her plans because she didn't want to make a fuss about it. After she finished at the shelter, she headed home and fixed herself a simple meal of soup and a salad. She turned down Mama's dinner invitation and couldn't bear to face her own mother. Mrs. Colwell invited her to go with them to visit Kenny's grandmother, but Emmy declined the offer. The news from Diane that she was getting "as big as a house" cheered her up a little, but then Emmy became dejected and downcast again. She missed Kenny more than ever. Her new faith in God was put to a severe test. Reading her Bible and support and prayers from her new friends at church strengthened her in this troubling time. She did not receive an email from Kenny Colwell for two whole weeks and worried that something terrible happened to him. She emailed Andy Walker, and he assured her that Kenny had just been a bit under the weather. He promised to get after Kenny for not emailing her.

On Monday, December seventeenth, Emmy was upstairs changing out of her work clothes when the doorbell rang once. *Who can that be? I've only been home for ten minutes. Give me a*

302

break. I'm in my underwear right now.

Twenty seconds later it rang again. This time it sounded like a rapid fire machine gun. She threw on her clothes, scurried downstairs, turned on the porch light and looked out the front door. Two men in long, black trench coats and fedora hats stood with their backs to the door facing the street.

She smiled, and opened the door. "I'm not buying anything. I don't care what it is you're trying to sell, I'm not interested."

The two men turned around and the larger man asked, "Are you gonna let us in, or do I have to keep ringing this doorbell all night? It's freezing out here."

"Oh, I suppose I can let you in even though neither one of you has called me or emailed or anything lately. I'm so mad at you both."

Emmy opened the door and Kenny Colwell and Andy Walker stepped inside. She hugged Andy first, and then turned to Kenny as the tears started streaming down her face. "I'm not really mad at you, but I did wonder why I haven't heard from you. I have missed you so much."

He reached out his arms, and she moved close.

"I have missed you more than ever. I'm sorry we didn't let you know we were coming, but we wanted to surprise you. Did we?" Kenny asked as he hugged Emmy tightly to his chest.

"I knew who it was as soon as Andy started ringing the door. You have told me so many times how he likes to ring the doorbell."

"Is it all right if I kiss you with Andy here?" Kenny asked.

"What kind of a kiss do you mean?" Emmy asked as she grinned.

"Like this." Kenny tossed his hat on the couch, and then kissed her quickly and very briefly.

"Is that the only kind of kiss you have with you?"

"I think I have another kind of kiss, but I only have one."

"Try that one, and, if I like it, we can go to the store and buy more."

Emmy closed her eyes as Kenny held her in his arms and kissed her long, deeply and with great passion.

Finally, Andy intervened. "Enough already. We're taking you out to dinner. Would you rather go to Ciao Bella or Taco Casa?"

"Are those my only choices? What about a special trip to Darby's?"

Kenny poked Andy's arm. "I told you she would rather go to Darby's. Pay up, Andy. You owe me a buck."

Andy reached for his wallet and took out a single. "Fine. Darby's it is, but you're buying."

Emmy asked, "Should I change into something a little nicer?"

Kenny looked at her faded, worn jeans and a Fridays At Five sweatshirt from the Transition tour. A rubber band held her hair in a ponytail and she wore scruffy old tennis shoes.

"If you put on a baseball cap, you will look perfect. Just like you're thirteen again." Kenny smiled, as he grabbed his hat.

Emmy hollered as she ran through the house, "By the way, I really like those coats and the hats. It makes you guys look like gangsters instead of dorky rock stars." She snagged a baseball cap from a hook by the back door, grabbed her coat, house keys and returned to the living room.

"FYI, cuz, he is a dorky rock star." Andy put an arm around Kenny's shoulders. "I'm a suave, urbane, debonair entrepreneur who happens to manage a bunch of dorky rock stars."

When they arrived at Darby's, Mr. Darby greeted them with a smile, and then a scowl as Kenny ordered a beef sandwich with red sauce.

"We don't put 'red sauce' on our beef sandwiches. Do you want peppers, too?"

"Yes, please, with large fires and a large root beer. Plus whatever these two guys want."

Emmy looked at the menu board, giggled and said, "May I have a Colwell Dog with all the trimmings, a large fry and a root beer, please?"

Mr. Darby shook his head and hollered through the opening into the kitchen to his son, "Danny, these gangster-looking rock stars and their little friends think they can order whatever they want, even if it's not on the menu."

"You know I'm not a teenager anymore, Mr. Darby. I'm twenty-one now." Emmy used her most childish voice.

"You still don't look old enough to work here. If not for the fact that I've known you all your life, I would say you're still in junior high." He laughed, and then added, "It's good to see you, Emmy. I don't know about that guy, though." He pointed to Kenny who was examining the pictures on the wall.

Andy stepped up to place his order, and Mr. Darby waved his hand. "Let me guess, a dipped beef with blue cheese, mayo on the side, a large root beer and..." Mr. Darby smiled at Andy, "fully-loaded, blue cheese fries. Am I right?"

Andy stuck his thumbs up. "Awesome! You guys have the best blue cheese in the world."

"If you say so, Andy. Are you keeping an eye on our so-called celebrity? Is he behaving? He's not messing around with those girls who always chase after guys like him, is he?"

"No, and just between you and me, he's the most boring rock star in the world. He reminds me of a Sunday school teacher. He reads his Bible everyday, and he's always praying about something."

"I heard he had a girlfriend out in California. Is that true? I'm only asking because... look at them... they look just they did a few years ago when they were in love." Mr. Darby happened to see Kenny kiss Emmy, and she giggled. "I think the world of that child. I know her father, and her mother, too, and I know she hasn't... well, it's not my place to say anything."

"Kenny did have a special girl in LA, but they broke up and are just friends now. I agree with you about Emmy. She is one of a kind. Have you ever heard her sing?"

"Just when she used to sing along with Kenny here in the store. Do you think she could be a real singer? You would know, right?"

"Oh, she definitely could. She has a unique quality to her voice." Andy looked over at Kenny and Emmy. Kenny held out his hands and she tried to slap them before he could move them, but never succeeded. "Will you stop goofing around and grab a table."

Mr Darby shook his head and said, "She's tried that for years, and she never wins."

"Kenny has the quickest reflexes of anyone I know. Even faster than pro athletes. I think it comes from genetics but also from playing the guitar." Andy smiled as he heard a 'thwack.'

"I got you! I win!" Emmy yelled, threw her hands in the air and danced in a circle. "I won! I won!"

"You didn't win. I let you do that. I didn't even try to move my hands."

"No, you didn't. I won fair and square. Don't give me that excuse. I'm not buying it."

Kenny smiled and kissed her to keep her quiet.

After they finished eating, Kenny dropped Andy off at his new townhouse.

"Do you wanna come in for a few minutes?" Andy asked.

"Yes, I want to see this place." Emmy hopped out of the car. "It's about time you bought a new place in town."

"I guess so. I think it's safe to say now that the band might have some success, and I need a place closer than Albuquerque."

"Did you sell that house?" Emmy asked.

"No way. I still love it there. I spend more time there than any where else, other than on the road. Let me give you a quick tour of this place." Andy showed Emmy around his recently purchased townhouse. Kenny had seen the place, so he made some calls from his cell phone.

"This is really nice, but are you ever going to put anything up on the walls?"

"No. I don't like clutter. I've got a picture of the band in the den, but that's all."

"You should let me decorate it for you. I could hang pictures on this wall, and put knickknacks everywhere."

"I will have to fire you if you do."

"You can't because we're family."

"Distant family, cuz," Andy teased as he embraced her.

After dropping Andy off, Kenny and Emmy headed to her house. He came inside with her, and she kissed him in the kitchen. She bit her lip as she asked, "Will you spend the night with me? I haven't seen you for so long. No one will know if you do."

"Oh, Em, I want to very much." He kissed her again.

She tried to pull him toward the stairs, but he didn't budge. She looked into his eyes. "You aren't going to stay, are you?"

"No, Em, I can't. It wouldn't be right for me to spend the night."

"Is it a sin to do that even if we love each other?"

"I think you know the answer to that. Believe me, it would be so easy to give in."

"But it wouldn't be right, huh?"

Kenny shook his head.

"Can you at least stay for a little while and talk to me. I need you to hold me close."

"Okay, Em, I will stay for a few minutes."

They sat on the couch in the TV room. He held her close as they talked.

"I have to work all week, but then I'll be off until January second. That's a Wednesday."

"I have enough stuff to keep me busy during the day, but I'll come over in the evening," he said.

After thirty minutes, Kenny stood up. "I have to leave now, or else I won't be able to."

She stood up and followed him out to the car. She could see her breath in the cold, crisp air.

"I will call you tomorrow, Em." He kissed her good night and left.

Kristen came over on Friday, and Kenny took them out for dinner at La Cantina.

"What have you guys been doing all week?" Kristen dipped a tortilla chip in the freshly-made salsa and dribbled some on her top. "Darn it. I just bought this top." She wiped off her top with a napkin, and then looked across the booth at Emmy and Kenny. He had her hair pulled back and looked like he was about to nibble on her ear. "Or shouldn't I ask what you've been doing?"

"I've been working all week, but Kenny came over in the evenings. We didn't go anywhere except for Wednesday."

Kristen checked Emmy's eyes. Emmy looked away.

I don't even want to know. Kristen realized.

Kenny took a drink of his Dr Pepper. "On Wednesday evening we went to Faith Bible Church. Emmy sang a couple of songs with me for the teen worship service. Other than that we didn't do much of anything."

"I'm just concerned. I know how much she's missed you."

"Kristen, did I mention I'm on vacation until the second?"

"I think you might have mentioned that a few times, Em. Did I mention that classes don't start until the fifteenth?"

"Sure, rub it in. One of these days you will graduate and join the real world," Emmy said with a bit of envy.

"Not if I can find a rich man to marry." Kristen crunched into another chip.

Emmy brought half of her dinner home with her. She made room for it in the fridge while Kenny and Kristen went into the living room and sat on the couch.

"What are you gonna do tomorrow, Em?" Kristen hollered.

Emmy closed the fridge and walked into the living room. "I have to clean the house and do some grocery shopping." She plopped down on the recliner. "Wanna help me, Kenny?"

"I promised to have breakfast with Mom and Dad, but I can come over after that."

"Krissy, do you want to come over, too?"

"No, thanks. I know you guys want to be alone, and I'm not gonna be a third wheel. You guys can do whatever you want."

Emmy giggled and then said, "We will."

Kristen threw a decorative pillow at her. "I didn't mean that. You have to behave."

"I'm pleased you decided to join us today, Emmy. I know how much you're enjoying going to your new church." Mrs. Colwell hugged Emmy as she walked into the kitchen with Kenny on Sunday morning.

Emmy sat at the breakfast counter next to Kenny on the same stool she had been sitting on for years. "I really like it there. They make me feel like family even though it's such a big church."

"We might have to check it out one of these days."

Emmy leaned against Kenny and said, "I told Pastor Ronnie that I would come to church today. He tried to talk me into singing, but I told him I couldn't."

"You should be singing in church. You have a beautiful voice." Mrs. Colwell poured Mr. Colwell a cup of coffee. "Don't you agree, Carter?"

"Definitely." He waved his coffee cup in the air.

"Carter, you spilled coffee on the counter."

"I'll get it, Mrs. Colwell." Emmy jumped down, grabbed a paper towel and wiped up the spilled coffee.

"Thank you, Emmy. I really meant what I said. You should be singing. You might even be able to make that a career. I know a few people with less talent who've managed to make a living by singing." Mr. Colwell slapped Kenny on the back and managed to spill more coffee.

Mrs. Colwell shook her head as she took his coffee cup away. "Have a muffin instead."

Tom and Sherry Hanna stopped by after church.

"It's good to see you, Aunt Elly." Tom kissed her cheek. "How's Uncle Carter doing?"

"I'm doing all right, Tom. Sherry, you look more beautiful every time I see you," Mr. Colwell said as he sipped his coffee from a covered container.

"Thank you, Uncle Carter. Please keep up the flattery," Sherry said. *Tom takes me for granted at times.*

Kenny and Emmy came downstairs. They had changed clothes after church.

"Well, hello there, Miss Colasanti. It's a pleasure to see you again."

"Are you gonna tease me, Mr. Hanna?" Emmy smiled. "You know I still think of you as my teacher."

Emmy didn't catch the look from Sherry as she and Kenny held hands.

"Maybe one of these days you will get over that."

Andy stopped over and brought a surprise guest—Frankie Hanna—Tom's older brother and the first tech guy Fridays At Five ever hired. In the beginning, he did everything—lights, sound, loading and unloading, everything. Frankie enjoyed the life of a confirmed bachelor, and anyone who knew him realized why. He loved the band first and guitars and amps second. He usually didn't say much of anything, but if he got upset with something, he would start talking to the guitars. If the guys on the crew heard that, they knew to leave him alone. True to form, Frankie didn't speak as he ate lunch. After they finished eating, Emmy volunteered to clean up.

"You don't have to do that, Emmy," Mrs. Colwell said.

"I don't mind. Andy will help me. Right, Andy?" Emmy looked over her shoulder as Andy walked up behind her.

"Whatever you say, princess." Andy squeezed her shoulders.

Kenny took Frankie out to the carriage house to show him his apartment. Frankie looked around with indifference until he saw a guitar case and opened it.

He looked at Kenny and asked, "When did you get this? I didn't know you bought this."

"I just got it a few days ago," Kenny answered.

"You shouldn't leave this out here. It's too valuable. You know this is a 1959 Gibson Sunburst Les Paul, right?" Frankie asked.

"I didn't know exactly. I just liked it."

"How much did you pay for it?" Frankie never shied away from asking Kenny questions like this.

"I paid five grand for it—with the case. Did I get a good deal?"

Frankie looked at Kenny and smiled. "Just keep it in the house locked in a room, all right. It will be worth a fortune someday."

Back in the house, Tom asked, "Aunt Elly, could I talk you guys for a minute?"

"Certainly, what about?" She sat in her recliner facing Tom and Sherry, who sat on the couch.

"Uncle Chester has talked about selling one of the horse farms to us sometime down the road. I've always loved Virginia, so we're considering it."

"Doesn't Chester have a couple of sons?" Carter asked.

"Yeah, Bill and Gary. Bill will inherit the large farm outside of Catawba, and I think Gary wants the one in Unionville. That leaves the smaller one down in Roanoke County. It's only ten acres, but that's big enough for us."

"How soon are you talking?" Elly asked.

"Five to ten years probably. We want to stay close to Mom and Dad for now."

"Would you be able to find teaching positions?" Carter asked.

"I think so," Tom answered. "Roanoke is a pretty big city and there are other large towns in the area. Sherry's parents always had horses, so she kinda misses being able to ride."

Elly sighed then said, "I love parts of Virginia. We try to get back to see Carter's brothers once a year or so, but it's getting more difficult. Kenny will miss you guys if you ever do move back there."

Chapter Thirty-Five

Emmy took Kenny to visit her parents on Christmas Eve morning. Mom let them in, and Emmy saw her father with a beer in his hand as he sat in his recliner. "Isn't it a little early for that, Daddy?"

"Are you gonna get on my case, too? We're out of eggnog, by the way. Your mother forgot to pick it up."

"You have two legs, you know. I shouldn't have to do everything for you," Mom grumbled as she clutched the remote in her hand. "I'm hanging on to this while we have company." She plopped down into her comfy old recliner.

Emmy and Kenny sat on the couch and listened as her parents bickered with each other. Then Mom complained about Diane's wedding. Though the wedding took place nearly four months ago, Mom still griped.

"We are her family, and she should have gotten married here so we wouldn't have to travel. And why didn't she tell me she was expecting? I'm not stupid. I could tell as soon as I saw her that she was pregnant. I didn't say anything, though. I wanted her to tell me."

Emmy rolled her eyes and said, "Mom! Why are you still bellyaching about the wedding? It's over. Just move on."

Kenny chuckled as he glanced in the corner. *No Christmas tree. At least that's become a tradition.*

"Did you know about the baby?" Mom asked.

"I asked Diane at the wedding, and she told me. I didn't know for sure before that." *But I sure suspected it.*

Mom snorted. "I bet they are divorced in another year. Kid or no kid."

"How can you say that?" Emmy shouted.

"Patricia! That's not a very nice thing to say."

"You told me the same thing, Raymond. You don't like Craig, either. You never have." Her mother looked at Emmy, and then Kenny. "You better be careful, or you will end up in the same condition, Emily."

"No, I won't."

"Are you being careful?"

"Mom! Geez! I'm not talking about this in front of Daddy."

Mom carried on and on until Emmy decided to leave.

"I'm sorry, Kenny," Emmy said as they walked out to the car. "They haven't changed. Do you wish they could be like Becky's parents?"

"They are who they are, Em."

"At least your parents don't yell at each other."

"They still have differences of opinion."

"Yeah, they just solve them without screaming and throwing things at each other," Emmy said. "I should stop and get some eggnog for Daddy. He will be a total grump if he doesn't have his eggnog and rum."

"We can stop if you want, Em. I'd like some eggnog, too."

"Do you want some rum to add to it?" Emmy asked sarcastically.

"I like it plain," he said. *Don't take it out on me, Em.*

Emmy saw Kristen on Christmas morning, but stayed only long enough to exchange gifts. Kristen tried her best to get Emmy to go with her to Mama's, but Emmy's stubbornness won out. Emmy headed over to the Colwells and spent the rest of the day with them. She watched old movies on TV with Kenny and his parents. After watching *A Christmas Story*, Emmy looked at Kenny and sighed.

"You're bored, right?" Kenny asked.

"How can you tell? Was it the yawning, or the general indifference to a movie I usually enjoy, or something else?"

"Let's go somewhere," Kenny suggested.

"Where? Everything is closed today. It's Christmas, remember?"

"I don't mean right now, silly girl. I mean tomorrow. Let's go on vacation somewhere warm."

"You mean just the two of us?" Emmy smiled as she asked.

"Yeah. You're on vacation, and so am I. Why shouldn't we go somewhere together?" Kenny shrugged.

Emmy bit her lip. "Well, for one, we're not married."

"So, we can get a room with two beds, or if you are uncomfortable with that, two rooms. Let's go to Florida."

Emmy looked at Kenny. "You're totally serious."

"You bet I am."

"We could stay with Grandma Isabel. She's in Florida now."

"Would she have room for us?"

"Oh yeah. She's got a big house in Ft. Myers. I haven't been there for several years, but it's a nice place. She's got a pool."

"Would she let us stay, since we aren't married?" Kenny teased.

"We could lie and say we're on our honeymoon."

Mrs. Colwell looked at the kids and asked, "You wouldn't really tell Emmy's grandmother that, would you?"

"No, we'll just say we're engaged and are on our pre-honeymoon," Kenny joked, and then pulled Emmy off of the couch. "Dad, can I use your computer for a few minutes?"

"Sure, do you know the password?"

"Is it still *FridaysAt5*, or did you change it?"

"Still the same."

"You need a more secure password," Kenny said.

An hour later Kenny printed out their flight information into Ft. Myers and the confirmation for a rental car.

Emmy called her grandmother. "Merry Christmas, Grandma, it's Emily."

"Merry Christmas, dear. How are you?"

"I'm on vacation, and I'm bored. Would it be all right if I come down there to see you?"

"Of course, child. You are always welcome. When would you be coming?"

"Tomorrow. Is that all right?"

"Certainly."

"Grandma, Kenny is coming with me."

"That's okay. I have lots of space upstairs that never gets used."

"Thanks, Grandma. We'll see you tomorrow."

Emmy and Kenny high-fived each other. "Let's go to your

house so you can pack."

"Yes, and I need to call Kristen to ask if she will watch the house for me. She has a key already, so that's taken care of. I will have to dig out some summer clothes."

"Make sure you pack a bathing suit."

Emmy called Kristen and even called her mother. Kristen agreed to watch the house, check the mail and whatever else needed to be done. Mom made a big deal out of Emmy going on vacation with Kenny. Emmy listened for a moment, and then hung up.

Why did I even bother calling her? You'd think I'd know better by now.

By four thirty the next afternoon, Kenny and Emmy stood outside Grandma Isabel's house.

"Hi, Grandma, we're here." Emmy skipped over to Grandma Isabel, who knelt on her knees as she worked on her flowers.

"It's so good to see you, dear. How are you, Kenny?"

"I'm doing fine, Mrs. Sandusky. Thanks for letting us crash here."

"You're very welcome, but, please, call me Isabel, or Grandma, if you prefer."

"All right, I will."

"Let me show you kids to your room."

Emmy looked at Kenny, and then at Grandma.

Grandma saw the look and asked, "Am I being presumptuous? You can stay in separate rooms if you want. I just thought... well you know how your mother is."

"She probably told you we were sleeping together. Did she call you?"

"Yes, she called this morning. She wants me to find out if you are expecting. I told her to mind her own business. She is my daughter, but she can be a royal pain in the butt. You kids can work out whatever sleeping arrangements you want. There are three empty bedrooms upstairs, and I never go up there. You can do whatever you like. I am much too old to be concerned with your

315

love life."

"If Mom calls again, you can tell her that I'm not pregnant—yet. That will give her something to think about." Emmy laughed as she looked at Kenny. "While we're here, we will help you with whatever you need, Grandma. We don't want to be a burden on you."

"Good gracious, Emily. Do you think I'm a doddering old woman who needs to be taken care of? You kids do whatever you want. I have a woman who comes in and cooks, does the laundry and cleans the house. I have other more important things to do. If there's anything special you want to eat, make a list and put it on the fridge. Oh, the security code for the garage and the front door is 4-5-1-9-1-0."

"That's your birthday." Emmy realized at once.

"It's one thing I can remember. The beach is that-away, but I'm sure you can find it without any trouble. If you don't want to go to the beach there is always the pool out back. You should use it as much as you want. Lord knows I pay that young pool boy enough to take care of it. He's rather good-looking. Oh, I guess you don't need to hear that since you have Kenny here with you."

"We will try to stay out of your hair, Grandma. You do whatever you usually do, and Emmy and I will take care of ourselves." Kenny walked over to the rental car, popped the trunk and pulled out their luggage.

"I'll help you carry it upstairs." Emmy grinned, and then whispered, "We can check out all the bedrooms and see which one has the best bed."

"Ssssh! Em, you have to behave. God knows..."

"I know He does, but we can have a little fun." Her eyes sparkled and danced.

After a light dinner of tuna sandwiches, store-bought potato salad and potato chips, Emmy and Kenny headed back upstairs.

"Did you decide which room you want, Em?" Kenny asked. "Our luggage is still in the one overlooking the backyard."

"There are two beds in there," she said as they walked hand in hand into the bedroom.

He shook his head. "All right. We can keep the luggage in

316

here, but I'm going to sleep in the room next to the bathroom."

Emmy opened her suitcase and dug out her bikini. She held it up and waved it at Kenny. "I'm going to put this on and use the pool." She dropped the top and held the bikini bottoms up to her jeans. "Do you think you will like it?"

"I'm sure I will." He smiled, but then turned around and started to leave.

"Where are you going?" Emmy bit her lip.

"I thought you were going to change."

She opened his suitcase. "Where are your trunks?"

"They're right on top."

"These things?" Emmy held up his large swimming trunks.

"Yeah, why? Is there something wrong with them?"

"Don't you have one of those skimpy little things like I've seen in magazines?" She tossed his trunks toward him.

He caught them. "No, and I'm not going to buy one. I happen to like the trunks I already own."

"You are the dorkiest rock star ever," she teased. "I'll meet you at the pool in ten minutes."

They spent an hour in the pool as Grandma sat in her lounge chair and watched. *If I didn't know better, I would think you were about fifteen, Emily. I hope you kids have fun while you're here.*

The next day Kenny took Emmy shopping for a new bikini.

"You can buy the skimpiest one you can find and wear it at the pool. That way you can work on your tanlines a little."

"I could wear my birthday suit and get rid of all my tanlines," Emmy said as she walked around the store. "Grandma won't care."

"I don't mind that you have some tanlines."

Emmy held up a tiny string bikini and said, "The pool boy might like this one."

"You are not buying that," Kenny said.

"I would never buy something like this." Emmy tossed the bikini aside and soon found one that was more modest. "I wouldn't mind if the pool boy saw me in this one."

317

"What day does he come?" Kenny asked.

"Don't know. We can ask Grandma. Maybe I will do what we did in Colorado and take off my top."

Kenny looked at Emmy. "Are you kidding?"

"Maybe, maybe not."

Kenny bought her two bikinis because she couldn't decide which one she liked better.

After lunch, they made use of the pool.

"Don't forget to use extra sunscreen," Grandma said. "The afternoon sun here can be much stronger than you're used to back home."

"I will be careful, Grandma," Emmy said. "I don't want to get sunburned."

A little while later, they sat under Isabel's patio umbrella and sipped some freshly-squeezed lemonade.

"Did I ever tell you about the afternoon the girls spent the afternoon working on our tans in Colorado?"

Kenny shook his head. "If you did, I don't remember it."

Emmy grinned and told Kenny what happened.

"Did Linda really get burned on her... you know?" he asked.

"She did, but I was more careful. Of course, I have a darker complexion to start with. Poor Barry," she said and then giggled. "Linda wouldn't let him touch her for several days."

After dinner on New Year's Eve, Emmy got back in the pool as Kenny and Grandma sat under the patio umbrella drinking sweet tea. She swam for quite a long time before getting out and walking over to sit down with Grandma and Kenny.

"Did you get burned at all this week, Emily?" Grandma asked.

Emmy shook her head. "I was careful."

"This has been a great vacation, Grandma Isabel," Kenny said.

"Yeah! We got to use the pool everyday and go to the beach. We went out for dinner several times, and best of all, Mom wasn't around to harass us."

"One of these days she will let you live your life as you see fit," Grandma said.

" Do we really have to leave tomorrow?"

"You are supposed to go back to work, Em," Kenny said.

"I could get used to spending the winter in Florida."

Grandma smiled. "Now you see why I spend my winters here. You are always welcome to visit me. You can even bring Kenny."

"We really needed this vacation," Kenny said.

Emmy started to giggle.

"What is so funny, Em?" Kenny asked.

"Grandma, when Mom calls to snoop about us, you should tell her we shared a bedroom."

"Emmy!" Kenny exclaimed.

"Well, we did. Mom won't know there were two beds in the room, and we took naps in there."

Grandma shook her head, but then smiled. "I'm not going to tell Patricia anything. That will bother her more than anything."

The vacation ended too quickly. They needed to fly back on New Year's Day so Emmy could be at work on Wednesday.

"Thank you for letting us stay, Grandma. We really needed this break. I love you."

"You're welcome, child, and don't worry, I won't tell your mother a darn thing about what you kids did down here. It's none of her business."

Kenny gave her a hug. "Thanks, Grandma. Take care of yourself."

Emmy hugged her grandmother and kissed her cheek. They headed to the airport early because they weren't sure how busy it would be. To their amazement, they walked into a nearly deserted airport, but they still needed to go through the increased security measures that had been instituted since 9/11.

The flight attendants didn't mind letting them move to the back of the half-empty plane. Emmy kissed Kenny and smiled.

"Why are you smiling, Em?"

"This has been such a great week. Are you mad that I made

you stay inside that afternoon?"

"No, how long were you... topless... that day?

"Not too long. I didn't want to get a sunburn like Linda did in Colorado. I did lie on my stomach for quite a while though. I don't think there is a tanline on my back anymore."

"There's not. I checked. You did let me work on my tan when you were on your stomach all the other days."

"I didn't mind."

Kenny smiled and rubbed her back. "You have a really nice tan. You look as brown as the pool boy."

"Grandma was right about him. He was gorgeous and so tanned," Emmy said and then giggled.

"He did have a head start, Em."

They landed in Chicago and headed back to SoHam.

"Are you going to stick around, or do you have to head home?" Emmy asked as Kenny carried in her suitcase.

"I can stay for a while, but I can't spend the night."

We'll see about that! Emmy grinned. *You're so funny. We just spend a week sleeping upstairs at Grandma's without doing anything too naughty. Are you afraid to stay here alone with me?*

After unpacking, Emmy called Kristen. She rushed over and took a look at Emmy.

"You are as brown as a... a... bear or something."

"You look as tan as a bear, too, Kristen. A polar bear," Emmy teased.

"Very funny. I can't help it that my skin is lighter, and I burn easier. Em?" Kristen didn't say anything for a moment.

"What? I know you want to ask something. You can ask in front of Kenny."

"Do you still have tanlines or not?" Kristen asked.

"Wouldn't you like to know?" Emmy teased.

"Did you share a bedroom? Or a bed?"

"Not every night," Emmy answered, and then grinned at Kenny.

Kenny shook his head at Kristen. "We didn't," he whispered.

"We did take naps together." Emmy put her arms around

320

Kenny's waist and held him close.

They ate dinner and talked about everything they did that week. Finally, Kenny noticed the time. "I should get going. It's after eleven already."

"You could stay here, Kenny. It is rather late." Emmy tried to persuade him to stay overnight.

"Okay, if you insist." It didn't take much persuasion for Kenny to agree to stay. *We can't make a habit of this, Em.*

Emmy nervously played with her hair. "You can stay, too, Kristen. I have to work in the morning, but Kenny doesn't have to be anywhere."

"No, thanks. You guys can have the house to yourselves. I don't want to be in the way. I'll see you later. Call me." Kristen hugged Emmy and headed home.

"Emmy, why did you tell Kristen what you did about the bedrooms?"

Emmy shrugged. "Are you angry that I did?"

"I suppose not."

"What should we do now?" Emmy asked as she bit her lip.

"So, do you have any tanlines?" Kenny asked as he chased her out of the kitchen into the TV room.

Emmy squealed, "We're not at Grandma's now, so you have to behave."

Tony returned home for the holidays on the twentieth of December because the Fighting Irish finished the season with a losing record—five wins, six losses. The year ended with the December first win at Purdue. Tony spent the semester break at home, but boredom soon set in. Emmy would not talk to him, and she didn't even come over to see Mama at Christmas. Tony acted as stubbornly as Emmy. He wouldn't call, or go over to see her. He spent time with Derrick and Kristen. He got together with some old friends from Roosevelt High, but he realized they didn't have much in common anymore. After putting up with his moping about the house for long enough, Mama finally convinced him to at least call Emmy.

Tony called her the first Sunday in January, "Hey, Emmy.

It's Tony. Just wanted to hear your voice." Tony got the machine and was ready to hang up when Emmy answered.

"Tony... Hi. I couldn't find the phone. Kristen left it in the TV room. I just got in the door. Lynette and I went out for lunch. How are you? I watched the Purdue game. I can't believe it came down to the last play of the game, and you guys pulled it out."

"I'm happy about that game, but really disappointed to end my career with a losing season."

"Have you thought about playing one more year? I know you are going to graduate, but you still have one more year of eligibility." Emmy walked into the TV room and jumped onto the couch. She accidentally bumped her head on the arm. *Ow! That hurts.* She rubbed the back of her head.

"I have given it some thought lately. I'll have to wait and see. You know Mama is very disappointed that you haven't come to see her. Maybe you could come over sometime when I'm not here. There are some cookies for you. I ate some of them, but there's still two nearly full tins."

"I suppose I should. I feel really bad about not coming over for Christmas. I didn't even go to Kristen's New Year's Eve party. Did you go?"

"Yeah, I went. By myself," he added quickly. "I spent most of the night talking to Derrick."

They talked about school and work, and then Emmy inquired, "Is there anything special you wanted to tell me, or ask me?"

"I need to tell you something, Emmy."

"Okay, tell me." She turned over onto her stomach and bit her lip. *I wonder if Kristen told him about Kenny and me going on vacation together? I guess it doesn't matter if he knows.*

"I saw Brenda again on campus and we started talking and..."

"Tony, so help me God, if you slept with her again, I will kill you." She kicked the arm at the other end of the couch in anger.

"No, nothing like that. She asked me if I wanted to go to a Lost Dawgs concert at the Joyce Center. You know how much I like that band, so I went with her."

Emmy let her hot Italian blood get the best of her, and she and Tony argued. Emmy yelled, "I never want to see you again. We are finished. It's over. I don't even want to be your friend." She hit the button to end the call, and then threw it against the wall. *I hate these new phones. You can't even slam them down to let the other person know how mad you are.*

She kicked the couch again and turned over onto her back. Ten minutes later, she had calmed down. *Why do I get so pissed off at him? He didn't do anything except go to a concert with Brenda. He would have every right to be mad at me for spending my vacation with Kenny.*

Kenny came over later. He watched as she muttered under her breath while dusting all the furniture in the living room and dining room. "Are you going to tell me why you're upset, or do I have to guess?"

"Tony called me and told me he's still seeing that Brenda girl. I got mad at him and told him I never wanted to see him again."

"Did you lose your temper again?" Kenny asked as he smiled at her.

"Yes, I don't know why I let him get under my skin so much. I don't let other people bother me."

"You have never been in love with other people. You will always have some feelings for him. It will always be a bit tricky to be friends, but he is a good guy, Em."

"I know, and I'll call him back and apologize sometime but just not now. I want to be mad at him for a while. Mama made cookies for Christmas and even set some aside for me. I should at least go see her and pick up the cookies. Will you go with me?"

"Of course, I will. But I get to eat some of the cookies." *I hope I don't have to break up a fight between you and Tony.*

Tony looked at the calendar above the kitchen table. "What am I gonna do for another week? The dorms don't open until January thirteenth."

Mama continued to mix the batter for chocolate chip

323

cookies. "You could call Derrick and go somewhere, or maybe call Emmy."

"I'm not calling her. She let me know how she feels."

"Nikki Foster is home from college. I talked to her and Dr. Foster at the store. Why don't you call her?"

"Maybe I will, but she's got a boyfriend."

"You can still be friends," Mama reminded him. *Just like you can be friends with Emmy.*

Tony decided to call Nikki, and they got together for dinner on Monday. He took her to Ciao Bella, and then back to her house. Since they stopped dating, they had become friends. Tony talked to Dr. Foster about his remaining year of football eligibility and made his decision about whether to play one more year or not.

Emmy and Kenny stopped by the house to see Mama and brought her a gift.

"Thank you for the chocolates, sweetie. I can't resist them," Mama said. "You know you can always come and see me, Emmy. You are still very dear to me, even if you and Tony are both too stubborn to be friends."

"I'm sorry, Mama. Sometimes I let my temper get the best of me. Then I'm too stubborn to admit I'm wrong. Is he here?"

"No, he took Nikki Foster to dinner." *Why can he be friends with her and not you?* Mama looked at Kenny and asked, "How are you able to deal with this child?"

"I smile at her when she gets mad, and she eventually calms down. It's simply this effect I have on people."

Emmy rolled her eyes as she poked him in the ribs. "You're too dorky to stay mad at."

At church that Wednesday, Emmy talked to Lynette about her fight on the phone with Tony. "I got so angry that he would see that girl again that I blew up. I told him I never wanted to see him again."

"It has to be very difficult for both of you being apart all the time. You will have to decide if your relationship is important enough to fight for and make it work."

324

"We don't have a relationship anymore. We're not friends or anything." Emmy shook her hands. "I'm back with Kenny. I don't care if he's gone for most of the year. I'm going to finish college, and then join his organization. We'll be together. Uh, I can't believe Tony saw that girl again." Emmy stomped her foot. "Oh, he made me so mad. I could scream. He is probably still dating her and afraid to tell me."

Lynette looked at Emmy and asked a simple question. "If you are *through* with Tony, then why do you care so much that he is seeing someone? You should be happy for him. Unless, you still have feelings for him and won't admit it, not even to yourself."

"Do you really think so?"

Lynette nodded.

"I don't know what to think anymore, Lynette. Maybe we need to not talk or see each other for a while and let things cool down. Maybe I should apologize to him. It would be foolish to lose such a good friend over a girl. After all, he's a good-looking guy, and he's bound to find a girlfriend at school."

Chapter Thirty-Six

"Come with me, Emmy, I'd like to introduce you to Pastor Chase Hillman." Lynette Jefferson pulled on Emmy's arm after the Wednesday evening service. "He is our worship pastor, so he's responsible for what you see and hear on the platform before Pastor Ausland takes over." They met at the bottom of the platform. "Chase, this is Emmy Colasanti."

"It's a pleasure to finally meet you, formally, Emmy," Chase said as he offered a hand. "I've seen you before, but we haven't been introduced."

Emmy shook his hand. She looked at him and did what she often did when meeting someone new; she compared his looks and size to Kenny. *You're about as tall as Kenny, but a bit heavier. If you were taller, you would be kinda like Tony.*

Chase said, "Lynette told me you are an excellent singer, but you seem rather shy and quiet."

"I guess I am." Emmy bit her lip. "I really love the way the band sounds."

"Emmy has a beautiful voice, and she has some experience singing with a band. I think she would make a great addition to the worship team," Lynette said.

"In that case we should go back to the music suite and jam on a few tunes. I think my wife is back there somewhere. What do you say?" Chase asked.

"Okay, but I hope you're not disappointed," Emmy answered.

Chase and Emmy walked back to the music suite.

"Lynette mentioned that you have just recently made a commitment for Christ and are rather new to our church."

"I started coming here in June. I came here one summer a few years ago, but then I stopped."

Emmy entered the music suite for the first time.

"This is the main music office, and my office is through that door."

Emmy could see a potted plant in the corner. Yvonne Hillman walked out of Chase's office as she heard his voice.

"Yvonne, this is Emmy Colasanti. We're gonna sing a few tunes."

Yvonne understood he was using code for auditioning her.

"Hello, Emmy. Do you mind if I hang around? I've got to sort through this mail."

"I don't mind." Emmy noticed the large room used for rehearsing. She followed Chase over to the baby grand piano.

"Are you familiar with this song?" He played the intro to "Amazed," which they sang earlier that evening in the service.

Emmy nodded and Chase began singing. She sang the melody with him.

"Can you sing a high harmony to this?"

She picked out a part and nailed it. Five minutes later, Chase had stopped singing as Emmy sang the lead to another, more difficult song. He knew immediately he had found a new lead singer.

"I should get going," Emmy said a few minutes later.

"Thank you for stopping by," Chase said. "The worship team meets on Thursday evenings to rehearse. We would love to have you on the team."

"I will pray about it."

"Rehearsal starts at six thirty, and usually ends by eight thirty," Chase said. He waited until Emmy left, and then smiled at his wife. "Did you hear that voice?"

Yvonne put an arm around her husband's waist. "I had to look twice to make sure that voice was coming from that tiny young lady. She seems rather shy, but she sounded amazing."

"I'll have to talk to Brian and see what he knows about her, but I think we're going to hear more from Emmy Colasanti."

"Hi, Emmy. How are you tonight?" Pastor Brian asked. "Are you here for the rehearsal?"

"I'm fine, Pastor Brian. A little nervous, but I'm okay. I'm sorry I'm a little late, but I had to talk to someone at school about switching a class."

Brian checked the time. "It's only six thirty-five. Come on. I'll introduce you to the guys. You probably know most of them

327

already."

"I've seen them on stage, and I know who they are, but I don't think I've ever talked to any of them. Except Pastor Chase. I talked to him yesterday."

Pastor Brian introduced Emmy to all the worship team members. They didn't waste any time and started rehearsing right away. Chase played keyboards and usually sang lead. Emmy sang a harmony part, and she nailed it. Chase persuaded Emmy to sing lead on a couple of songs. Emmy relaxed as the musicians and other singers made her feel right at home.

"Emmy, you pick everything up so fast. Have you taken lessons or anything?" Chase asked after practice.

"I took piano lessons for a couple years, and I used to sing with my friend Kenny."

Chase dropped his sheet music and looked at her with surprise. *So it's true. You know Kenny Colwell?*

"He sings and plays guitar for this local band." Emmy didn't want to reveal too much about her relationship with Kenny. She wanted to earn a spot on the worship team through her own merits.

"How do you know him?" Hank, the bass player, asked.

"We grew up together. We've been friends forever. I used to sing sometimes with him and the guys."

"That's cool," one of the other guys said.

"You used to sing with Fridays At Five?" Chase whispered as he and Emmy squatted down to pick up the music.

"Yeah," Emmy said modestly. "Please don't tell everyone."

"I'll keep it a secret if you wish."

Emmy impressed Chase with her natural ability to pick up a song so quickly and easily. He asked Emmy a question, "Would you like to join the worship team and sing on Sunday mornings?"

"Sure. I could sing harmonies for you guys. I know almost all the songs by heart."

"No, Emmy. I want you to sing the lead. I'll lead the worship, but I want you to be the featured singer," Chase said.

Emmy's jaw dropped and her eyes opened wide. "I don't know if I could do that, Pastor Chase."

328

He took her aside so none of the other guys could hear.

"Emmy, Lynette told me you sang in front of thousands of people with Kenny Colwell. I think you can handle singing in front of a few hundred at church, and, please, call me Chase."

"I'll have to pray about it first."

"Take all the time you want," he said. Then he patted her hand and grinned. "As long as you are ready for this Sunday."

Emmy and Kenny prayed about this, and she decided to give it a try. She called the church on Saturday and asked to speak to Chase.

"Did you reach a decision, Emmy?" Chase asked. "I hope you have."

"I've decided to try it. Kenny has often told me that God has a plan for my life, and that it's probably as a singer."

"He has certainly blessed you with the talent to do that," Chase said. "Will you be willing to sing lead on the two songs we practiced Thursday? You might as well jump in the deep end."

She bit her lip before answering. "I will. God will give me the strength."

Kenny didn't want to interfere, so he decided to keep going to his own church for now.

On Sunday morning, Emmy sang lead on two songs, and, though she was nervous, she did a great job. After the service, she saw Chase and Yvonne talking to an older couple and a young lady.

"Emmy! Come here, please." Chase waved his hand.

Emmy slowly walked over. *Oh, no. I hope I'm not in trouble. Did I screw up the songs? I hope those people aren't complaining.*

Chase smiled at her. "Emmy, I'd like to introduce you to some important people in the history of the church."

What can I say if they didn't like the way I sang? Oh, maybe it's because I moved around. Emmy bit her lip.

"This is Emmy Colasanti. She is the newest addition to our worship team." Chase stood behind her with his hands on her shoulders.

Emmy glanced at the young lady. She was smiling, but nervously braiding her hair at the same time.

"Emmy, may I introduce Jason and Margaret Lindower."

Mr. Lindower reached out a hand. "Everyone calls me Dick. It's a pleasure to meet you."

Emmy shook his hand.

"Hi, Emmy. I'm Marg, and this is my granddaughter Liz Kimmerle." Mrs. Lindower smiled at Emmy and set her at ease.

Emmy grinned. *You're shorter than me. That's unusual.*

Chase continued, "Mrs. Lindower was the choir director when the church first opened, and Dick was the Controller and Business Manager for North Park College."

"Don't forget St. Mary's," Mr. Lindower added. "I worked there for almost fifteen years before I retired."

"That's right." Chase squeezed Emmy's shoulders.

"I would like to compliment you on the songs you sang. You have a beautiful voice," Mrs. Lindower said as she smiled.

"Thank you. I hope I didn't sound too awful." *Whew! That's a relief. I thought you were going to tell me that I should never sing in front of people again.* Emmy's eyes sparkled.

"Dick and I were in the area showing Liz the campus of Olivet Nazarene University, so we thought we would make a side trip back to SoHam," Mrs. Lindower explained.

Chase let go of Emmy, and she took a step toward Liz.

"Did you like the campus?" Emmy asked.

"I did. I'm pretty sure that I will be attending there when I graduate."

"Would you excuse us, please?" Mr. Lindower said to Emmy. "I see some old friends that we need to greet."

Chase escorted the Lindowers leaving Emmy and Liz together.

"Where are you from?" Emmy asked. "I've lived in SoHam all my life."

"We live in Hillsdale, Michigan. My parents are doctors." Liz told Emmy more about her family.

I don't have any brothers. You're lucky you have two of them and your little sister sounds adorable, Emmy thought as she

330

listened. "My name is actually Emily, but I usually go by Emmy."

"My older brother attends Taylor University in Upland, Indiana," Liz said.

"I've got a friend who attends Notre Dame. He plays football."

"That's so cool. Grandma and Grandpa live in South Bend. He worked at St. Mary's."

"Oh, now I understand. That's the college by Notre Dame."

Emmy and Liz talked as they slowly made their way back to her grandparents.

"Did I mention that I have a boyfriend named Tyler Hammond?" Liz grinned. "He plays tennis for the Hillsdale High Hornets. He lives to play tennis."

"That's cool. My best friend's brother played in high school. He actually got a scholarship to play at the University of Arizona."

Emmy and Liz continued to talk as Liz waited for her grandparents.

Emmy grinned and then whispered, "I have to confess something."

Liz leaned closer.

"When I first saw you guys with Chase, I thought your grandparents were complaining about my singing. Today was the first time I ever sang with the worship team, and I was really nervous."

"I agree with Grandma. You sounded fantastic, and you didn't look nervous. I liked the way you kinda danced around." Liz shuffled her feet in a little dance. "I think singers should express how they feel."

"Thanks, Liz. I should let you go. I have to meet my friend and have lunch with him and his parents."

"It was a pleasure to meet you, Emmy. Maybe we will run into each other again sometime."

Later that afternoon, Emmy sat at the table to eat lunch with Kenny and his parents.

"How did it go, Em?" Kenny asked. "I know you're dying to tell me."

She took a drink of water, and then began, "When I first got to church, I was so scared. I didn't know if I could go through with it. I found a quiet corner and asked God for the strength."

"That's a wise choice." Kenny grinned and stole one of her potato chips.

"Kenny, let her tell the story," Mrs. Colwell said, then grabbed a napkin. "Carter, you're dripping ketchup everywhere."

"I remembered the verse in Philippians 'I can do all this through Him who gives me strength.' I realized that I didn't have to rely on my ability, and that God would help me through everything. During the actual service my stomach felt full of butterflies at the start, but then I surrendered to the spirit."

"I'm so happy for you, baby. Do you remember when we talked about God having a plan for your life?"

"Yeah, I remember."

"I think you are starting to realize what that plan is."

"He wants me to be a singer?" Emmy asked.

"I think so. He has given you a natural gift for that."

"That's what Chase said." Emmy grinned. "And he does music for a career, so he might know what he's talking about."

"You're a real stinker, Em," Kenny said as he kissed her cheek.

Emmy thought about what Mrs. Lindower and Liz had said. *Actually two people told me that I have a good voice today.*

After Emmy headed back home that night, Kenny wanted to talk to his mother. He walked into the living room as she sat in her recliner, reading a book. Dad had already gone upstairs to bed.

"Hey, Mom, got a few minutes?"

"I have all the time in the world for you. What's on your mind?" She smiled as she closed *Melissa's Dream*—her new Denise Bartell book.

Kenny sat down on the couch and looked at his mom. "I have been doing a lot of thinking, and I realize that I want to marry Emmy. I know that I kinda felt the same way about Becky just a short time ago, but I think our relationship ended because I am meant to be with Emmy. I think I was attracted to Becky because she reminded me of Emmy in some ways."

Mom smiled. "There might be a slight resemblance

between Emmy and Becky, but they are as different as could be. Becky is so easy going and *settled* for want of a better word. Emmy is... she's like a powderkeg waiting to explode. She is so passionate, and you always know what she is feeling."

"You do like her, though?"

"I love her to death. I always have. I know she and Tony always fight. You have the ability to calm her down. Your relationship with her is more stable, and I know you love each other. She never stays upset with anyone when you are around. You probably know her better than anyone else—even more than her family. I've always felt so empathetic toward her. She survived through a difficult childhood to say the least."

"Becky's family is certainly more stable and grounded. They are Christians, and Becky grew up in the church."

"Emmy has certainly grown in her faith. She is still so innocent about some parts of life though."

"I wish we could get married before I leave in February."

"Have you talked to Emmy about this at all?"

"No, not really."

"I'm pretty sure she would want to get married in the church, and that takes time to plan."

"I know, but sometimes I feel that I will lose her if we aren't together soon."

"She is very young to take this step. I know some of her friends from high school have already gotten married, but I'm not sure she is ready for marriage. That might sound strange because she lives on her own and has adult responsibilities."

"I know sometimes she still acts like a kid or a tomboy."

Mrs. Colwell chuckled. "That's something different. She will always be that way. Even when she's much older, she will act like a child at times, and she's always going to be athletic, or a tomboy as you call it."

"I'll have to think about this. If I do ask her now, and she says yes..."

"She will say yes if you ask. I have no doubt about that."

"I suppose we could wait to get married until after she graduates."

333

Mom laughed softly. "You know she will not want to wait too long."

Kenny turned a bit red because he knew what his mother was saying between the lines. She noticed his embarrassment, but didn't say anything more.

After the morning service on the twenty-seventh, Emmy wanted to talk to Lynette in private so they used the music office.

"What's on your mind, Emmy? I can tell there is something troubling you."

"It's man trouble, or I guess I should say men trouble. I told you about going on vacation with Kenny, right?"

"Yes, you said you had a great time visiting with your grandmother."

"We always have a good time when we're together because whenever I see him, he's on vacation. I'm not sure how it would be to be on the road with him. Our relationship will never be normal because of the music."

"Plus the fact that he's a celebrity. You will always have to deal with that, Emmy."

"It's funny. If his fans only knew what a regular guy he is when he's not performing, they would never think of him as a celebrity. Sometimes I forget that the world sees him one way while I know him as my... boyfriend."

"You said men before. Are you having more trouble with Tony?"

"I told you he called during the semester break, and I ended up yelling at him. I told him I never wanted to see him ever again."

"Did you mean it?"

"No, I lost my temper because he saw that girl again. I do still like him, and I want him to be a part of my life." Emmy paused and looked at Lynette. "Sometimes I still wonder if I should be with Tony instead of Kenny. I get so mixed up."

"I think you are still young enough that you can wait and see what happens."

"I guess so. I certainly don't want to get married and have kids yet." *Adopt kids, I mean.*

334

"I will remember you in my prayers."

"Thanks, Lynette. I'm glad you're always willing to talk to me about my boy problems."

Emmy hurried home to make sure she got there before Kenny arrived to watch the NFL playoffs. She and Kenny were sitting on the couch in the TV room watching the game when Kenny mentioned, "Emmy, I am blown away by how great you sound. The website has a link to the recording of last Sunday's service. I always knew you possessed a great voice, but you sound even better now."

"Are you trying to flatter me so you can kiss me?"

"Not at all. If I didn't think you sounded great, I wouldn't say you did. You know you can sing. You have a God given talent, Emmy Colasanti, and you need to use it."

Emmy did use her voice—she screamed as the Patriots scored a touchdown on a punt return.

"Now what did you say about using my voice?" Emmy grinned.

Kenny grabbed her and pulled her close. "Just wait until between games, you're going to get it."

"What about at halftime? Am I gonna get it then, too?" Emmy put a finger to her mouth.

Kenny tickled her and she squirmed and giggled until he ended up on top of her. She kissed him.

"Are we going to watch the game, or do I need to go home to watch it?" Kenny asked as if it was all Emmy's fault.

"I swear I will behave," Emmy said and then giggled. "Until between games."

They watched both games and then ordered a pizza. They talked more about Emmy singing with the worship team as they chowed down on the pizzas. After they cleaned up the TV room, Emmy pulled him over to the couch. She sat next to him and kissed him. She pushed him onto his side and lay next to him. After a few minutes of kissing, she sat up.

"You can spend the night if you want. There are two empty bedrooms upstairs." She grinned wickedly. "We can pretend we are at Grandma's house."

He thought about her offer, but then remembered what his mother said between the lines. He knew what would happen if he spent the night. "You know I want to stay, but I really shouldn't."

"You know I've never... kissed... anyone the way I kiss you, right?"

Kenny knew what she meant. "I know, baby. We need to be cautious."

"You could buy some..."

"No, Em. I really need to go." He kissed her again and rubbed her lower back. He thought about how much he would like to stay. *I really need to find a ring because I'm not sure how much longer I can hold out.*

"That feels good, Kenny." She told him as his hand moved lower.

He broke off the kiss and moved his hand. "I really gotta go now, Em."

"Okay, but will you call me after work?"

"Yes, I'll call, but we may not see each other until Wednesday."

As Kenny drove home, he thought about his discussion with his mother. He needed to talk to her again. He parked his car in the carriage house and, instead of going upstairs to the apartment, he walked over to the main house. He found his mother in the living room, sitting in her recliner reading the same book.

"I need to talk to you again."

Mom put down her book and took off her reading glasses. "Is it about what we discussed earlier?"

"Kinda, sorta." He waved his hands. "I know what you meant even though you didn't come right out and say it."

"It's human nature."

"How am I suppose to... When we are on the road, the temptation is always there. There are so many willing women around. It's easy to say no because... well..."

"I understand, son."

"When I get home, and I'm with Emmy, who I love more than anything, it's not so easy to resist. It's not easy for either of us. Sometimes we... we are only human, and we sometimes make

336

mistakes."

"Patience is not always an easy virtue to practice. Especially at your ages," Mom said. "Believe it or not, I do understand what it's like to be a teenager in love."

"Oh, Mom. I know you do." Kenny felt his blood rush to his face.

"Emmy is twenty-one now. Your father and I were already married at that age. We didn't have to deal with some of the 'situations' you and Emmy are facing. I hope and pray that you guys will... you know what I mean. Just remember that God is forgiving when we fall short of perfection," Mom said.

"Are you saying it's all right to... you know?"

His mother picked up her book and smiled. "You know the right thing to do. That often makes life more difficult."

"Maybe I should start looking for a ring," Kenny replied. "Real soon."

While Emmy worked on Tuesday, Kenny checked out three jewelry stores. He realized he didn't know much about diamonds. After listening to three different salespeople, he was more confused than ever. He saw many rings, but none of them jumped out as being the perfect ring for Emmy. He returned home, went upstairs to his apartment and played his guitar.

Kenny and Emmy saw each other on Wednesday evening at Faith Bible Church. She sang for the teen group and shared her story with them. Although still naturally shy, Emmy opened up to the teens. Looking like a teenager herself helped. In fact, most of the kids treated her like a teenager.

Kenny came over to her house after church on Sunday. They ate lunch in the TV room. Between bites of his sandwich, Kenny asked, "How did the service go today, Em? Did you feel more comfortable singing in front of the congregation?"

"I think so. I paused a moment to pray before we started, and I asked God for the strength to lead the service. I even talked to the people today."

"I am so proud of you, baby. I wish I could have seen it."

"Will you come to my church someday to hear me?"

"Yes, I promise."

"Kenny," Emmy said slowly.

"Yes, Em. What is it?"

"If we were married, and I'm just saying if, which church would we attend?"

Emmy's question took Kenny by surprise. He wondered if now would be the time to pop the question, but he didn't. He didn't have a ring. "I've been thinking about that, too. I think it might depend on where we're living. We might not even live in SoHam in twenty years."

"Do you mean I have to wait twenty years for you to marry me? No way."

"Seriously, I think if... you know... right now... I think... we would go to your church."

"Really?" Emmy asked. She felt pleased by his answer.

"Yes, do you think I'm good enough to join the worship band as a guitar player?"

"Oh, I doubt that. The guys we have are professionals. I'm not sure you could pass the audition," Emmy said with a straight face.

Kenny tried to grab her, but she jumped off the couch and ran away. Kenny chased her into the living room and tackled her onto the couch.

"Okay. Maybe you would be good enough to play rhythm guitar and sing some harmony." Emmy giggled as Kenny held her arms and kissed her.

"What time does the Super Bowl start?" Kenny asked.

"Not until five thirty unless you want to watch four hours of pregame shows.

"So we have time to do something without missing any of the game."

"What did you have in mind?" Emmy asked as she grinned.

He wondered if there were any jewelry stores open on Sunday as he kissed her again. "Would you like to work on some songs? That way you can practice your keyboard."

"Do we have to do that all afternoon?" Emmy bit her lip.

"We might have time for something else..."

Emmy talked to Diane almost every day now as her due date grew closer. Emmy arrived home a bit later than usual on Friday after work. She ate dinner and had just set her plate in the sink when the phone rang. She checked the caller ID and squealed.

"Hey, Emmy, it's Craig. We have a son. His name is going to be Carson David."

"That is great news. How is Diane doing? Is the baby all right?"

"They're both fine. Diane told me to tell you he weighed seven pounds and four ounces and he's twenty feet tall..."

Emmy giggled as she imagined a twenty-foot-tall baby. "Did you mean twenty inches tall?"

"Yeah, what did I say?"

"You said twenty feet tall. How long was Diane in labor?"

"About six hours. It seemed a lot longer than that though. I didn't think Carson would ever come out."

Emmy talked to Craig until he told her, "I've got to go, Emmy. I still have to call your parents and my parents. So many people on this list."

"I'm glad everything is all right and thanks for calling, Craig."

Emmy looked at the calendar on the wall. She pulled a red marker from the drawer and circled today's date—February eighth.

Kenny and the rest of the band were scheduled to leave on February tenth. They would be recording their new project—*The Ballad Of Johnny March*—in Los Angeles for a month before returning home to finish the recording process at the new Steward Music Group studios.

"Are you going to see Becky while you are in LA?" Emmy asked as she scooped out some sweet and sour chicken from the container on Saturday evening. She added it to the fried rice already on her plate.

"I think so, but it will probably be something like a Sunday dinner at her parents' house. Will that be okay with you?"

"Of course. I know she's still a friend. She's my friend, too. Just make sure you don't kiss her like this." Emmy showed him what she meant.

"I don't think I've ever kissed her like that, Emmy." He eyed the small portions on her plate. "Is that all you're gonna eat?"

She grinned, and then popped another spoonful of fried rice in her mouth. "Don't worry. I'll be hungry again in no time."

On Sunday morning Emmy went to Faith Bible Church with Kenny, and they ate lunch with his parents after the service. Kenny seemed to have something on his mind. She thought Kenny was going to ask her a very important question. Especially after what nearly happened on Super Bowl Sunday. She knew what her answer would be. But the afternoon passed quickly and nothing monumental happened. At three o'clock Emmy and Kenny said goodbye to each other, yet again. This time Emmy didn't cry. She felt more secure than ever in their relationship. She also realized she was getting too used to his leaving her behind.

Chapter Thirty-Seven

Mr. Oliver, the department head, convinced the guys to chip in for Valentine's Day roses for Emmy. When Emmy made it to the office on Thursday, she walked over to her desk and smelled the flowers. She smiled, crossed her fingers and inwardly hoped they were from Kenny, though she knew differently. She opened the card and read it. The guys watched, and she looked over to where they stood.

"Thanks, guys. I really appreciate the thoughtfulness. I know I've been kinda quiet this week."

"You've been more than just quiet," Mr. Oliver said as he walked over to her desk.

"I suppose so." She hung up her coat, and then faced Mr. Oliver. "I miss Kenny."

"Well, happy Valentine's Day, Emmy. We want you to know how much we appreciate you." He headed to his office. He felt a bit confused by Emmy's on and off relationship with Kenny and Tony. He was never quite sure which guy was her actual boyfriend.

Emmy had been distracted, and a bit sad, since Kenny left for Los Angeles. She thought he might propose to her before he left and felt disappointed when he didn't. Her co-workers tried to get her to smile or laugh by telling her humorous stories. She appreciated their caring, but she also felt a bit guilty for the way she yelled at Tony.

The next day as Emmy was returning from lunch, a man rushed into the elevator as the door began to close. She looked up at him and smiled as she recognized the mail clerk though now he wore a suit.

"Hello, Emily. It's good to see you again. Do you remember me?"

"Yes, I do. You used to deliver the mail. Where have you been?"

"It's a long story," he said as they moved to the back of the elevator.

She grinned and said, "Tell me, I'm all ears."

"How about I tell you over a drink after work tonight?"

Emmy looked at the other people on the elevator. "I appreciate the offer, but I don't think I should."

"Maybe I shouldn't have asked it like that. Would you like to meet me at the coffee shop on the corner? I promise I won't keep you out very long."

"Coffee, huh?" Emmy figured she could order bottled water. "Okay, sure, that would be nice... I mean I will need to check my social calendar, and see if I have any free time coming up. So busy, you know."

"Right. I understand." He thought she was serious at first.

"I'm kidding. I know I am free tonight, but I can only stay for fifteen minutes."

"Great! How about I meet you at your office at five." He checked his watch out of habit.

"Make it five thirty, and it's a deal. Do you remember where my office is?"

"I remember. I'll never forget the location."

Emmy laughed, but then blushed like a schoolgirl.

The elevator stopped again, and the door opened.

"This is my floor," he said.

"I'll see you at five thirty," Emmy told him as he scurried out before the door closed.

Five thirty is going to take forever to get here. Emmy watched the clock all afternoon.

At four thirty Mr. Oliver asked, "Emily, what are you so nervous and anxious about? You keep staring at the clock like it's your last day on the job."

"It's nothing, Mr. Oliver," she insisted with a wave of her hand.

"Emily, I know you better than that."

Finally, she confessed to him, "I'm meeting someone after work tonight."

"Who are you meeting?" Mr. Oliver's bushy eyebrows shot up. *Oh, no. I can't believe I actually said that. I have to remember not to act like her father.*

"Do you remember the man who used to deliver the mail a while back? You probably don't, but I met him in the elevator and... he asked out for a drink so he could tell me where he's been. I told him no, but then he suggested meeting for coffee down at the Beanz 'n' More, so I agreed."

Mr. Oliver grinned. *You are a paradox, Emmy. Most of the time you are so quiet and don't say a word. But then you start talking ninety miles-an-hour, and I have to really concentrate to understand everything.*

She did not think of it as a date, and the only reason she accepted so eagerly was because Kenny was in Los Angeles and Tony was back in South Bend. She hadn't even talked to Tony since their fight on the phone. Soon all the guys in the office knew about her plans.

One of the guys asked, "Who are you going with, Emmy? Kenny and Tony are both gone. What's his name?"

She blushed with embarrassment. "I don't actually know his name. I never asked him, and he never told me. Do any of you remember the mail clerk who used to deliver the mail up until a while back?" She waited for an answer, but no one remembered him. "Well, he's back, and that's who I'm seeing tonight."

"Emmy, you mean to tell us you're having a drink..."

Emmy held up her water bottle. "Just coffee, or more likely bottled water."

"Excuse me. You're having bottled water with a man who's name you don't know, you don't even know if he's married, you don't know anything about him, except he used to deliver our mail. Is that true?"

Emmy bit her lip and nodded.

Mr. Oliver told her sternly, "Young lady, you are not going out with him until we find out more about him. He could be a criminal or something. I realize that I'm not your father, but we all care very much about you and don't want to take a chance on you being hurt again. I'm going to call the personnel department right now."

The guys treated her very protectively, like a daughter, or niece.

"Oh, please don't make this into a big deal. It's not a date, and he's been very polite so far. There's no reason to cause him any trouble," Emmy pleaded, but Mr. Oliver made the call anyway.

"I'll let you talk to Miss Colasanti. She can describe him to you."

Emmy described the mail clerk to personnel. "They want to talk to you again, Mr. Oliver." She handed him the phone.

"Yes, I see. Three days, huh? Are you sure? Really? Hmmmph. That's not good. Well, if that's the way it has to be. Not much we can do about that, is there? Okay, thanks, I appreciate the info." Mr. Oliver looked at Emmy who shifted her weight from one foot to the other as she waited to hear the results. "Emily, I have good news and bad news, which would you like to hear first?"

"The good news, I think. No, wait. Tell me the bad news first. I want to know the worst."

"The bad news is your bonus check will not be ready for three days. An accounting error, I'm afraid. Not much we can do to change that."

"That's the bad news?" Emmy sighed with relief. "I thought you were going to tell me he's married or something. What's the good news?"

"The good news? Oh, yes, the good news. Well, I have a name for you," Mr. Oliver said.

"Please, Mr. Oliver. Tell me."

"It will cost you."

"Anything, Mr. Oliver, I'll do anything. I'll work extra hours and come in early. Please tell me his name." She put her hands together as if she were praying and stood on her tiptoes.

"I'll tell you his name, but you have to promise me one thing."

"What do I have to do?"

"You have to promise to behave on your date and..."

"Yes, Daddy, I promise to behave and be home by ten. And it's not a real date. We're simply getting together so he can tell me where he's been. I wouldn't be going if Kenny was home." Emmy smiled at Mr. Oliver because he was acting exactly like a father giving his daughter instructions before her first date.

344

Mr. Oliver looked at Emmy and pictured her as a young girl. He remembered how he felt when his daughter went on her first date many years ago. He smiled, and then laughed. "All right his name is... Richard Demarco."

At last Emmy had a name to go with the face.

That evening Richard took Emmy to Beanz 'n' More. He persuaded her to order a sandwich along with her bottled water.

"Okay, are you ready for my long story?" he asked as they found a table in the corner.

"Yes, tell me. I want to hear all about it."

"I took a job in Kansas, and that's where I've been for the last few months. Bored out of my mind. So, when I learned of an opening back here, I jumped at the opportunity. I've been back for three days, and I work five floors below you now. My new job has kept me so busy. I tried to run up to your office and see if you still worked here, but I didn't get the chance. I tried calling your office suite, but got voice mail. I didn't want to leave a message because it would have seemed too weird. Besides I didn't think you would remember me anyway." He rambled on and on.

"When did you call?" Emmy asked when Richard paused to catch his breath.

Richard told her the approximate time he called.

"We were in a meeting on another floor at that time. I have something to tell you, I didn't know your name until today. You never wore an ID badge, and I was too shy to ask. I told my boss, and he called personnel. He made me promise to behave and not stay out late tonight before he would tell me your name."

"Is that why you are calling me Richard?"

Emmy felt mortified. "Isn't that your name? Richard Demarco."

He smiled at Emmy. "It is. I'm just teasing you."

"You're a stinker."

The fifteen minute non-date date turned into forty minutes before Richard drove Emmy back to the office to get her car.

"I'm thrilled I got to see you again, Emily. Can I call you sometime? You don't wear a ring, so I'm going out on a limb here, but I assume you are not involved with anyone. Is that true?"

"I'm not involved at the moment."

"That's great!"

She immediately regretted her statement but didn't have a chance to explain that Kenny would be in Los Angeles for a few weeks.

"I will call you at the office on Monday. Good night, Emily. I had a wonderful time."

Richard left without trying to kiss her. Emmy drove home thinking about the wrong impression she gave Richard. *Why didn't I tell him about Kenny being in LA? Now he's gonna think I'm available.* She pounded her hand on the steering wheel. The horn beeped and startled her. *I really need to call Tony and apologize before it's too late and he hates me forever.* Her heart raced as she thought about Kenny. *I wonder if he's seen Becky. It's all right if he does. I'm sure she won't change her mind about his lifestyle.*

By Sunday morning Emmy had almost forgotten about Richard Demarco. She thought about calling Tony on Sunday afternoon, but chickened out. She talked to Kenny for two hours.

"I wish you were home. I miss you so much."

"You could always fly out here on the weekend to see me, Em."

"Would you have time to see me?"

"I might be able to squeeze you in for an hour or so," Kenny teased.

"I might take you up on that. I've always wanted to see California. Would an hour be enough time to see everything?" she teased back.

"It might take two hours."

Emmy seriously considered flying out to Los Angeles the next weekend. She knew if she did, she wouldn't return home until Kenny did. She had never been a quitter, though, and wasn't going to give up her job and quit school to run off to see Kenny.

Richard called her at the office Monday morning and made arrangements to meet her for lunch in the cafeteria. Emmy wasn't

346

sure she should, but Richard was very charming and persuasive. She met him for lunch so she could tell him about Kenny. She didn't have much of an opportunity though because Richard dominated the conversation. He did not know how to listen. For twenty minutes he talked about himself. He revealed his age inadvertently as he rambled. Occasionally he asked Emmy a question, but then started talking about his life again. Emmy, naturally quiet anyway, didn't want to interrupt him.

"After high school, I spent eight years in the army before I went to Purdue. After Purdue I took a couple of jobs I didn't like, but I needed the money because I was married at the time. Then I got the job here in the mail room. I knew I wanted to work for this company, and needed a way to get my foot in the door. I got my promotion and now, here I am. Tell me your life story. We have," he looked at his watch, "three minutes left."

Emmy giggled. She already knew that she liked Richard's sense of humor from his time as her mailman, but not the fact that he talked about himself so much. Emmy squeezed in a brief moment to tell Richard about Kenny, but didn't mention her family or Tony. Richard didn't really understand the importance of her relationship with Kenny. His mind, and eyes, drifted to a woman at another table.

She thought, *He's fourteen years older than me. He's close to forty. That's like ancient. He's almost as old as Fernando and Ethan, but he is rather handsome... for an older man at least.* She waited for him to tell her about his marriage, since he referred to it in the past tense, but he didn't say anything more about it. It also turned out that he lived in SoHam only a few miles away from her house.

"I drive to work everyday by myself. We could carpool sometime if our schedules allow," he said.

"I normally ride with my neighbor Ethan, but sometimes he is out of town for meetings and I drive myself into work."

Richard asked, "Would you like to go out for dinner sometime?"

"Oh, I'm not sure. Why don't we maybe do lunch here at the office, and see how it goes. I'm not ready to date anyone other than Kenny."

"But you said he's in Los Angeles. Does he expect you to sit home and wait for him to return?"

"No, he encourages me to have a life."

"Well then, why don't we have dinner? Are you busy tomorrow night?"

"I have a night class on Tuesdays and Thursdays and church on Wednesdays."

"Church? That's interesting."

"It's actually a Bible study class tomorrow night." Emmy thought maybe Richard would be interested in the Bible study. "Would you be interested in joining me for that? We meet for about an hour, then usually sit around talking and having refreshments."

"I wouldn't want to intrude on your friends. Maybe next week. Are you busy Friday night? Maybe we could have dinner and see a movie?"

"I'll think about it, but I want you know that I'm not interested in anything other than a casual friendship."

"I need to get back to work, Emily. I'll call you Friday morning and we can finalize our plans. See you later."

"See you, Richard, thanks for lunch."

Emmy called Kristen after work and told her about Richard but didn't divulge his age.

"Emmy, you need to be careful about getting involved with another man right now. You may not realize it, but some guys like to take advantage of rebound situations. They prey on vulnerable women and you certainly fit that profile."

"I do not," Emmy insisted.

"Yes, you do. You're lonely because Kenny is gone, and you still care about Tony, too. And what did he mean about being married at the time? Is he divorced, or could he still be married? You need to find out more about this guy, Em."

"I don't think he's like that, Kristen. I told him about Kenny, but I didn't tell him anything about Tony."

"What? You didn't even tell him about Tony? Why not, for Christ's sake?"

"Because there's nothing to tell. He asked me out for dinner

348

on Tuesday, and I told him I had a class. I told him about my Bible study group. He seemed to be interested in that."

"Did he agree to go with you?"

"He said he didn't want to intrude, but he might go next week,."

"You don't even realize how vulnerable you are right now. I am worried about you. Promise me you will be careful with this guy."

"I probably won't see him again. It's a big building, but I promise not to get too deeply involved and be very careful if I do see him again, Mom."

"Don't you take that tone with me, young lady. I am your mother and you will do as I say," Kristen said and Emmy laughed.

Later, Kristen bit her nails as she thought about Emmy. *Em, you need to be very careful.* She worried about this new man Emmy met, so she called home. "Hi, Daddy. How are you?"

"I'm fine, honey. How are you? Is everything okay? You usually don't call this late."

"I'm fine, but I'm concerned about Emmy."

"Has something happened to her?"

Kristen explained everything as her father listened. "Will you talk to Detective O'Dell, and see if you can find out something about this guy for me?"

"I will find out everything about him, Kristen. If he has a speeding ticket, or a late fee at the library, we will soon know about it."

"Thank you, Daddy. I love you."

"I love you, too, sweetheart."

Chapter Thirty-Eight

Emmy overslept and looked at the clock when she finally woke up. "Oh crap! I really need to get a new alarm clock." She jumped out of bed and rushed to get ready for work. Ten minutes later she ran down the stairs to the kitchen. She heard Ethan pull in the driveway. She grabbed an apple and her coat and purse and sprinted out the door.

"Good morning, Emmy. How was your night?"

"Okay, I finished that book. I overslept though. I just got up ten minutes ago."

He scrutinized her appearance. "Well, no one would ever be able to tell. Which book was that again?"

"That romance novel about a girl growing up in a small town." She checked her purse to make sure she had some money for lunch. "You wouldn't be interested in it."

He looked over his shoulder as he backed out of the driveway. "By the way, before I forget, I will be on vacation next week. Just wanted to remind you."

"Thanks, I'll make other arrangements to get to work. Richard offered to carpool if I need a ride. He lives in town somewhere, but I'll probably drive myself."

That morning at work, after a short meeting in the conference room, Mr. Oliver asked, "Since you are not going to tell us on your own, I need to ask something?"

"Yes, Mr. Oliver." *I think I know what you're going to ask. It's so sweet that you guys care about me.*

"How did your date go the other night?" Mr. Oliver asked. "We want a full report."

Emmy immediately felt her face turn red. "First off, it was not a date. We had a sandwich at Beanz."

"Did he explain where he's been?"

"Yes."

Stephen Butler mentioned, "I saw the two of you together at lunch yesterday."

"We did have lunch, but he spent the whole time talking about himself. He did ask me to go out for dinner on Friday." She

350

bit her lip. *I probably shouldn't have mentioned that.*

"Are you going?" Mr. Oliver asked.

She decided to tease the guys. "I haven't made up my mind. What do you guys think I should do?"

Everybody expressed concern, and they told her to be careful because some guys were only after sex.

Emmy replied with a smile, "Don't worry, guys. I've dealt with that, and I assure you there is no chance of that happening tonight, or anytime in the near future."

Later that night, Emmy rushed out of her Tuesday class at North Park. She sprinted through the parking lot to her car. She tossed her backpack in the back seat and broke all the speed limits as she raced over to Lynette's house for the first meeting of a monthly small group Bible study. She joined everyone in the family room and plopped down on the couch—totally out of breath. "Did I miss much?"

"Just ten minutes or so. We waited for a while," Paul said and then quickly explained the important points she missed.

After the Bible study ended, Lynette introduced Emmy to a new member in the group. "Emmy, I would like you to meet Reggie Lennon."

"Hi, Reggie, I'm Emmy Colasanti. It's nice to meet you." She shook hands with him. *Wow! Your eyes are really green. They match your shirt.*

Emmy talked to Reggie and caught Lynette looking at her. Later, she had a chance to talk to Lynette.

"I appreciate what you are doing, but I'm not interested in dating anyone right now. Kenny will be home soon."

"What about that guy from work you told me about?" Lynette asked. "You said he was charming, but a bit older."

"That wasn't a date. Just lunch and coffee."

Lynette grinned. "I bet he thought it was a date."

"Well, it wasn't. Now you're setting me up with Reggie." Emmy placed her hands on her hips. "You do know that I'm in a serious relationship with Kenny now, right?"

"I know. Emmy, you don't have to marry him, just go out to dinner or something. He's a really nice guy. He used to attend our

351

church when he was in high school, but then his family moved to Nebraska. He moved back a few weeks ago and doesn't know many single women, so I thought I would introduce him to you. I'm really not trying to be a matchmaker, Emmy."

"'Yes you are!" Emmy grinned. *You should get together with Kristen. She's just the same.*

Friday morning Richard Demarco called. He waited on hold for five minutes as Emmy took another call.

"I'm sorry for the wait. How can I help you?"

"Emily, would Italian be all right for tonight? Or would you prefer something else?"

"Richard, I never said I would go out tonight for sure," Emmy whispered because Stephen Bishop stood a few feet away.

"You are going to eat dinner tonight, aren't you? You might as well let me pay for it. I would like the company. We don't have to do anything else, and I'll bring you right home after we eat. Unless you want to do something else. I'm always willing to be spontaneous and just see what happens..."

Emmy rolled her eyes. *You talk more than any other man I know.* She interrupted him. "If I go, it's not a date. It's simply two people having dinner."

"Whatever you say is fine with me. How about Italian?"

"All right, I'll have dinner with you, but would you mind if we didn't have Italian. I eat that all the time." Emmy spoke in her natural tone since Mr. Bishop had walked away. "There is a new restaurant over by the oil change place, I can't remember what the name is, but over on Ottawa past the car dealers."

"I think I know where you mean. That's fine with me. It's not connected to the oil change place, is it? They're not like the same business, are they? You know get a fifteen-minute oil change and some fries and a burger to go."

"No, I don't think I would care for that. We might end up with motor oil instead of barbecue sauce on our food," she said

He laughed a bit too much at her weak joke, and Emmy wondered why. *It wasn't that funny. That laugh sounded forced and insincere.*

She gave him directions to her house, and he picked her up at six thirty. As soon as they had ordered their drinks, Richard started to talk about work.

Emmy checked her cell phone. *You've been talking non-stop for almost five minutes.* "Richard, I'm sorry to interrupt, but I have to tell you something that's very important to me."

"Sure, go ahead, Emily. I know I tend to dominate the conversation, so I'll be quiet for a moment. It's a character flaw, but I'm trying to correct it. I think I'm getting better at listening, but it's still a problem. I suppose everyone has problems..." He continued to ramble on.

She stared at him until he stopped talking. "I go to Bible study and church because I am a believer in Jesus, and he is my personal Savior. I am in a relationship with Kenny Colwell, and the only reason I agreed to have dinner is because he's in LA now."

"Okay, I understand."

"Also, I fell in love with a boy when I was seventeen and hoped to spend my life with him, but we broke up a few months ago. I don't know if we will ever get back together as friends, but I wanted you to know about him. His name is Tony, by the way, and he goes to school at Notre Dame."

"Thank you for telling me. I recently broke up with a woman I dated for three years, off and on. I appreciate your faith, too. I grew up going to church with my family. We went to church every Christmas and Easter and sometimes even more often, so I know what you are talking about."

She realized Richard did not understand her deep commitment to Jesus. They finished eating and walked out to the car. Emmy shivered despite wearing her winter coat.

"You look like you're getting chilled."

"I am cold. Could we go somewhere to get coffee?"

"Of course, Emily. Whatever you need."

"Thanks, Richard. There's a Burger Bob's on the way home. We could go through the drive-in."

"We can do that. I might get a couple of their apples pies, too. They're pretty good."

"I would like something else, too."

"What else?" Richard asked. *For Pete's sake! Are you going to be one of those high-maintenance dates that demands everything under the sun? You are pretty and have a nice body, but I don't know if you're worth all that trouble.*

"Everybody calls me Emmy. Only my grandmother and my boss call me Emily. I feel like I'm in trouble if someone calls me that."

"Oh. Sure, Emmy." *I'll call you whatever you want.*

Richard took her to the Burger Bob's. They sat in the car while Emmy drank her coffee and they split a dessert. After they finished, Richard asked, "Should I take you home now?"

"Yes, I'm ready to go."

Emmy waited for him to tell her about his marriage, but he didn't, and she didn't have the courage to bring it up. Emmy kept quiet on the short ride to her house, but Richard didn't notice. He rambled on again about his time in Kansas. He pulled in the driveway, and they got out. He took a look at the house. "This is a nice-looking house. Certainly lots bigger than my apartment."

"Thanks. I used to share it with my sister, but she moved to Ohio and got married." She looked at him. "Would you like another cup of coffee?" She cringed. *Why did I offer him more coffee? I wish I could take that back, and why did I even mention that Diane moved? I need to be more careful about giving out personal information.*

"Sure, I'd love one."

"All right, a cup of coffee, but then you've got to go home."

"One cup, and I'm gone. I promise." He held up his hand in a salute.

Emmy decided not to show Richard around the house. Richard stayed in the kitchen with her as she made the coffee.

"I stopped going to church in high school, I guess."

"You would be welcome to come with me if you like."

They sat at the kitchen table drinking their coffee and Emmy started getting tired and yawned several times.

"Emily, I should go home. You are getting tired, and I don't want to overstay my welcome. Thanks for the coffee and the pleasant evening."

354

"You're welcome, Richard." *I wish I could wipe your memory clean like they did in that old Will Smith movie, so you wouldn't remember where I live. Who knows? You might be an alien from another galaxy.*

Before she went to bed Friday night, Emmy turned off her cell phone and pushed the 'do not disturb' button on her landline. She needed an uninterrupted night of sleep. Instead, she tossed and turned as she thought about three men—Richard, Tony and Kenny. She tried to think of the strengths and weaknesses of each man. She ruled out Richard right away. He would never be more than a casual acquaintance at best. She thought about Tony and once again promised herself to call him to apologize. She wondered about her relationship with Kenny. She knew without a doubt that they loved each other, but like Becky, she wondered if they could ever have a normal relationship with him being gone so much. Eventually she fell asleep, still as confused as ever.

Emmy slept until nine on Saturday, and then started doing her weekend chores. She sorted through her bills and wrote out some checks. She opened her email and deleted all the junk. She replied to a message from Andy Walker.

"I'll be more than happy to watch your townhouse, but it will cost you dearly." She thought about something outrageous to demand. "You will owe me an entire month of no band shows."

She checked the pantry and the fridge and made a list of groceries she needed. Just a typical boring Saturday. The phone rang and she answered without checking the caller ID.

"Emmy, it's Richard. Are you busy this afternoon?"

"I wasn't planning on doing anything except some laundry. Do you have something more fun than laundry in mind?" Emmy joked.

"Would a basketball game interest you? I checked online and the North Park College Redbirds are playing this afternoon. I wanted to see if you would go."

"I don't like basketball as much as football, but more than laundry I suppose."

"Good. Let's go to a game. I'll pick you up."

"I don't know." She hesitated and bit her lip. *Come on. Just tell him no and be done with it.*

"You need to have some fun on the weekend, but I don't think there are any football games this time of year. Basketball is just as entertaining. What do you say?"

"I really need to get my laundry finished..."

"I'll buy you a hot dog," he said.

"Oooh! How can I pass that up?" she said and then giggled. "I'm sorry but I can't."

"I understand. I didn't want to say anything, but my mother called earlier. My father is in the hospital back in Nevada, and I wanted to get out of this apartment. I thought a basketball game would take my mind off of things."

Emmy thought about it for a few seconds. "All right, I'll go to the game, but it's..."

"I know. It's not a date."

Emmy wondered. *Crap! What will Kristen think if she sees me at the game with him?*

A light snow dusted the town as Richard drove over to Emmy's house. Emmy sat outside on the front porch steps bouncing a basketball as she waited for him. She wore faded jeans and a Fridays At Five sweatshirt over her t-shirt. She tucked her ponytail under her heavy winter coat and wore a red stocking cap and sunglasses. Richard parked in the driveway and walked toward her. He didn't recognize her because she looked like a kid.

"Hi. Is Emily home? I'm supposed to pick her up."

"She's not here. Would you like to pick me up instead?" *Shoot! Why did I say that? He might get the wrong impression.* She checked out his knee-length topcoat. *You're wearing dress pants and shoes. If you're wearing a tie, I'm not sitting with you.*

He recognized her voice immediately. "Emily, I didn't even recognize you. I thought maybe it was your brother or your sister. Why are you waiting out here? It's cold."

"I wanted some fresh air, and the house is a mess. I don't have any brothers, and my sister is older than me and she is married and lives in Ohio, remember?"

"Yeah, right, I forgot. Are you ready to watch some

356

basketball?" Richard sounded enthusiastic.

"As long as you are buying the refreshments." She opened the front door and tossed the basketball inside. "How is your father doing?"

"Not too great. He has a problem with his liver."

"I'm sorry. I'll remember to pray for him."

"Thanks," he said. *It's his own fault. He's been an alcoholic all his life. Serves him right to have liver trouble.*

Emmy navigated as Richard drove to North Park College.

"Have you ever been on the campus before?" she asked.

"No, but I did see some pictures online." He started talking about his years at Purdue and rambled on for five minutes.

Emmy closed her eyes for several seconds. *All right, I deserve it for agreeing to come to a game. I have to learn how to say no and mean it.* "Make a right at the next corner."

"Down this street, right?"

"The gym is that building over there." Emmy pointed out the side window. "We can park anywhere in this lot."

Richard pulled into a space. Emmy jumped out of the car and saw a patch of ice. She took a running start and slid for twenty feet. Richard shook his head as he watched. *Dumb kid. You could fall and bust your head.*

As they sauntered into the gym, Emmy looked around to see if she could spot Kristen or any of her friends from Roosevelt. She knew where they usually sat. She saw some people she knew, but not Kristen. She pulled Richard to the other side of the gym. He removed his topcoat, folded it neatly and set it on the empty seat next to him.

Really? She tilted her head. *You're wearing a dress shirt, an ugly sweater and a tie. Good grief! Don't you own a pair of jeans and a sweatshirt?*

They watched the game, and Emmy got a kick out of yelling at the referees. At one point the basketball flew out of bounds and directly toward Emmy. She stood up to catch it, but the guy behind her reached up and took it away.

Emmy turned around. "I almost had it."

The guy looked at Emmy, and then Richard. "I'm sorry. You

357

can have the ball." He handed the basketball to Emmy and told Richard, "I didn't mean to take it away from your daughter. She can have the ball."

Emmy giggled as she grinned at Richard and used her most childish voice. "Look, Daddy! I got a basketball."

Emmy tossed the ball back to the referee, who held out his hands impatiently. Richard smiled outwardly, but inwardly, he didn't appreciate Emmy teasing him.

As they headed out of the gym after the game, Richard asked, "Would you like to come over for dinner? I can cook your favorite dinner as long as it's pasta because that's about all I have in the apartment right now. I need to go grocery shopping sometime."

Emmy replied, "Any kind of pasta is my favorite meal. I would love to let you make me dinner sometime, but not today. I've got stuff to finish at home." *I don't trust you enough to go to your apartment.*

"That's okay, I need to get ready for the coming week. Maybe another time." His steady voice didn't indicate any disappointment. *I can be patient up to a point, Emily, but you're not the only female in the city.* He drew out her name in his mind.

Richard took her home and Emmy mentioned that she was not going to carpool with Ethan the coming week. Richard offered to carpool with her on Monday, at least, and Emmy accepted. He left without even a handshake. Emmy realized that Richard still hadn't told her about his marriage. She sent a long email to Kenny. After going back and forth, she worked up the nerve to call Tony, but he didn't answer the phone.

"Hi, Tony, it's Emmy. Just wondered how you were doing. Talk to you later." She left a short message, but doubted he would return her call.

Richard picked her up for work on Monday, and he barely spoke on the drive to work.

"Are you all right, Richard? You seem rather quiet this morning."

"Sorry, I have something on my mind," he answered.

Whoa, someone got up on the wrong side of the bed. A little

358

grumpy, are we? She thought, but didn't dare say. *I'll drive myself to work for the rest of the week.*

Emmy waited for him to say more, but he didn't. She decided not to pry. When she got to her office, the guys asked about her weekend. They wanted details. They were like a bunch of gossipy, old women. Emmy sighed and pulled a small notebook and a pen out of her purse. She flipped it open and pretended to be reading from it.

"Let's see. I ate dinner on Friday night with Richard. We went to Willie's Surf & Turf. I ordered salmon and a baked sweet potato. He had a steak and fries. The fries looked greasy. I rated it two stars out of five. He brought me home and I made coffee. Maxwell House. He drank his black. I added a little sugar to mine. I was in bed by ten thirty. Alone," she said in a monotone while tapping the notebook with the pen.

"That's good," one of the guys said.

"Saturday morning I did laundry and cleaned the house. I ran out of Lemon Pledge as I dusted. In the afternoon we went to a basketball game. He bought me a hot dog and a Coke. He had onions, mustard and relish on his. I didn't have any onions, and I put some ketchup on mine."

Mike Clancy shook his head. "You're not supposed to put ketchup on a Chicago dog."

"I like ketchup." She stuck out her tongue at Mr. Clancy. "Now, where was I? Oh, yeah. Sunday I went to church in the morning by myself, and then went grocery shopping. There were six bags of groceries, I think, and a gallon of milk—two percent."

The guys were getting impatient waiting for some juicy details about her weekend.

"I made sandwiches for lunch and watched the Redbirds on TV. And FYI nothing happened all weekend. Not even a kiss on the cheek. I'm not grounded, or anything, am I?"

"How was the salmon?" one of the guys asked.

Emmy groaned and rolled her eyes.

359

Chapter Thirty-Nine

Richard hung out by the cafeteria on Tuesday hoping he could accidentally meet Emmy for lunch. He waited for fifteen minutes before he spotted her. *That sucks! She's with some people. Oh, well. I'll see if I can talk to her for a couple of minutes.*

He walked in behind her and joined her in line. "Oh, hi, Emmy. How's your day going?"

"All right, so far. You?" Emmy asked as she picked out a salad for lunch.

"It's been a good morning. Do you have plans for tonight?"

"I'm actually very busy during the week." Emmy paid for her salad and bottled water. "I have classes on Tuesday and Thursday and Wednesday is church."

"That does sound like you keep busy. I'll try to call you later. I should get back upstairs."

She watched him leave. *Thank God he didn't try to have lunch with me again. I'm not interested in whatever game he's playing.*

She didn't think about him for the rest of the day, or at all on Wednesday.

Richard called on Thursday afternoon as Emmy ate a sandwich. She let the answering machine take the call because she needed to get to class and then worship team rehearsal. She listened to his message after she got home around nine.

"Hi, Emmy, would you be interested in another ballgame on Friday? The Redbirds are home this weekend, and, if you want, we could go Friday night to watch the men, and the ladies' team is playing Saturday afternoon. Give me a call sometime. I should be home around midnight."

She checked the time and called him back hoping to leave a short message, but instead he answered.

"Hello."

"Richard, you're home." She frowned at the phone.

"Yeah, change of plans. What's up?"

"Sorry about Friday, but I'm meeting my friends from

church and we're going to a concert. I would ask you to go, but I don't think there are any extra tickets. I think I'll be too busy to do anything Saturday."

"That's all right, Emmy. We could go to the game Saturday afternoon if you change your mind."

"I'll let you know. I need to do some work around the house in the morning, but I should be finished by noon." Emmy realized she needed to end this relationship before it spiraled out of control. "But I might not. I might be busy all afternoon."

"Thanks for calling. Maybe I'll see you Saturday."

Emmy hung up and pounded on the table. "Shannon! Shannon! Shannon! I need to remember the lesson I learned about Shannon and stop being so nice. I have to get rid of Richard for good."

On Friday evening Emmy drove over to the church. She and two dozen other people were going to see Third Day and The Lyricon in concert in Elgin. They were using the church's small bus to carpool. Reggie Lennon, Randy Braun and Vanessa Ortega were part of the group. Emmy was sitting by herself when Reggie saw her.

"Are you alone?" he asked.

"Yes, have a seat unless you're with someone." Emmy looked around to see if he might have a date.

"I'm alone, too." He sat next to her and they chatted on the way to the auditorium.

"Hey, Em, I'm glad to see you again." Randy sat next to her in the auditorium.

"Hi, guys," Emmy smiled at them. "How have you been?"

"Doing good. School is all right." Randy leaned forward and smiled at Reggie, who sat down next to Emmy.

"I bought Cokes and some popcorn, Emmy. I thought we could share the popcorn."

"Thanks, Reggie, have you met Randy?"

"Duh! We're in the same Sunday School class, Em," Randy said.

"Sorry, I forgot."

361

The concert lasted for two and a half hours.

"That was really good," Reggie said as he helped Emmy on with her coat.

"Yes, it was. I really enjoyed it." She grinned. *But I know of a band I like a lot better.*

Emmy sat by Reggie Lennon again on the ride back to the church. Randy and Vanessa sat across the aisle.

"Did you enjoy the bands, Emmy? Have you ever seen them before?" Randy asked as he leaned over.

"I've never seen them, but I have a Lyricon CD. I really like the one I have, and I bought another one tonight. The other guys were good, too, but I liked The Lyricon better. Which group did you like better, Reggie?" She turned to Reggie who sat by the window.

"Third Day is one of my favorite bands. Maybe my all-time favorite. Do you have a favorite band, Emmy?"

She leaned against him as the bus took a corner a bit too fast. "Oh, yeah. Have you ever heard of Fridays At Five?"

"Of course, who hasn't? Is that your favorite band?"

"Always has been and always will be. I grew up with Kenny, the lead singer and guitar player. Actually, I've known all the guys in the band since I was a kid, but I've known Kenny since I was seven."

Reggie took a chance. "Emmy, are you busy tomorrow night? I would really like to get to know you better, and I wondered if you would like to go out for dinner?"

"Reggie, I guess I should have told you this before, but Kenny and I are in a relationship. He's on tour for much of the year, but whenever he's home we are together."

"I understand. I didn't know." He stared at her out of the corner of his eye. *How serious can it be? He's probably on tour most of the time.*

"Reggie, I think you are a really nice guy, but... I don't think we should be more than friends right now. I would go to dinner with a group from church, but..." Emmy saw Lynette, and remembered what she told her about Reggie. She changed her mind. "You know what? I will go out to dinner with you tomorrow, but only if you let me pay my share. That way it won't seem so much like a date. We can be ourselves and relax and have fun. I'm sorry, and I certainly don't want to hurt your feelings, but I want you to know how I feel."

"I understand, Emmy, and I appreciate your honesty. I don't know many people in town anymore, so I thought I'd ask. It's good to know that we can be friends, though. I like talking to you and maybe if you have any single friends... who knows?"

"What time do you want to pick me up?"

"Would seven be too early?"

"That'll work for me. I'll be ready at seven."

She gave him her phone number and address.

Saturday morning Emmy cranked up her Bose system and listened to some tunes as she kept busy cleaning the house. She lost track of time, and before she knew it, it was noon. The doorbell rang, but she ignored it. When it rang two more times, she ran downstairs to answer the door. She swore under her breath. "Crap. I really didn't want to see you today, Richard." But she let him in.

"I didn't know you were coming over," Emmy said, obviously annoyed, but it didn't faze Richard. She wore old jeans, a faded Fridays At Five sweatshirt and hadn't even showered yet.

"I happened to be in the neighborhood, and thought I would drop by."

Emmy clenched her jaw. *That's a load of crap. Why would you be in my neighborhood?*

"Are you interested in the game? I'll buy lunch, too."

"Richard, I'm sorry, but I've been working all morning. I haven't even..." She decided not to share any more information.

"It's just a basketball game, Emmy. I've always liked watching basketball. I'm going to the game even if you aren't interested." He turned to leave.

She exhaled and let her shoulders slump. "All right. If you give me twenty minutes, I can be ready to go."

"Sure, we've got plenty of time to get to the game."

"Make yourself at home, and I'll hurry."

363

"Take your time." Richard looked at the pictures on display in the living room. He saw a picture of Emmy with a really big guy and figured it must be the Tony she mentioned.

She ran upstairs and grabbed some clean clothes. She locked the bathroom door, which she never usually did, and took a quick shower.

He saw a picture of Emmy on stage with a band and another picture of her with one of the guys from the band. He glanced in the dining room, and then sat on the couch to wait. He kept looking at his watch, tapping his foot and rolling his eyes. Emmy came flying down the stairs fifteen minutes later.

"I'm ready to go."

"That was fast. The women I have known would take forever in the bathroom."

Emmy wore comfortable faded jeans and a relatively new sweatshirt from the Fridays At Five Transition Tour. Richard wore his usual attire except for the tie.

"I've heard of that band. Not exactly my kind of music though."

Emmy didn't say anything, but counted it as a strike against him.

Richard drove over to the campus, and they watched the Lady Redbirds play the Lady Huskies from Beloit College. Emmy stood to her feet and yelled at the referees several times during the game. At halftime Emmy scrambled down the bleachers and bumped into one of her teachers.

"Hello, Professor MacBride. Enjoying the game?"

"I am, but there is a young lady sitting a few rows behind me who is constantly yelling at the poor referees."

"Oh, that's terrible." Emmy grinned at the professor, and he smiled back. "I will try to control myself for the second half."

"You don't need to, Miss Colasanti. Those refs are terrible. I think that one is actually legally blind. If I wasn't a dignified old professor, I would have been yelling at them, also. Is that your father with you?"

Emmy realized this was the second time someone thought of Richard as her father, "No, he's a friend of mine who's new in town and likes basketball, so I came with him."

After the game, Richard brought her home. He came in the house even though Emmy didn't invite him in. Emmy looked at the clock. She could talk to Richard for a few minutes. Reggie wouldn't be here for three hours. She and Richard sat in the TV room.

"Do you want to order a pizza for tonight? We could have pizza and watch a movie."

"I'm sorry, Richard, but I made plans for tonight. Maybe we can do that another time."

"Okay, no problem." He looked at his watch and stood up as if he was ready to leave. "Is that Tony in that picture in your living room?"

"Yes, and the other picture is me with Fridays At Five."

"Tell me about Tony. How long were you together?"

"I don't want to talk about Tony right now, Richard."

"Sure, Emmy. I won't ask about him if it makes you uncomfortable."

Emmy stood up, too. *It wouldn't be fair to ask Richard about his marriage now, since I don't want to talk about Tony. Not that I really care anymore about his marriage or anything else.*

They walked into the kitchen. Emmy tried to think of a way to get him to leave. She remembered how Diane got rid of Shannon Stephenson one time. She thought it might work on Richard.

"Are you interested in going to church with me in the morning? If we are to be friends, I would like for you to go to church with me."

He surprised her with his answer. "Okay, Emmy, if you really want me to, I will go with you. What time should I pick you up?"

"I usually leave at nine," she stammered. "I guess I assumed I would meet you there, but if you want to pick me up, I suppose that's all right."

"All right, nine it is. I will pick you up then. Do I need to dress up, or is it casual?"

What do you consider dressing up? A suit or a tux? I've

never seen you in casual clothes. "You can wear something comfortable. I usually wear a dress, or a skirt, but not always."

Richard grinned at her.

Emmy laughed, "I didn't mean to imply that you have to wear a dress."

"That's a relief because all my good dresses are at the cleaners."

She stared at him. *That was so lame.*

She expected him to leave, but then Richard surprised her with a kiss. She backed up so he couldn't kiss her again. "Richard, I'm not ready for this. I don't want to give you the wrong idea, and I don't want to lead you on. I want to be upfront with you. I want to be friends, okay? And I don't allow friends to kiss me like that."

"Okay, Emmy. I understand. I want to let you know that I find you very appealing, though."

"Thank you, but I'm already in a relationship."

Richard said, "My last relationship ended badly, and I'm not ready to become involved in another serious relationship, yet. I hope we can still see each other occasionally."

"We will see each other in the morning, remember?"

"Yes, I will pick you up at nine."

"When you say your relationship, are you talking about your marriage?" Emmy asked. *Shoot! Why did I even ask? Now he might stay for another hour.*

"No, I meant another relationship, not my marriage."

Emmy waited to hear if Richard would tell her about his marriage, but he didn't. He suddenly remembered that he needed to take care of something important. He left without kissing her again. She thanked God for that. She spent more time cleaning up the house, but then needed to get ready for Reggie and their dinner date.

Emmy finished getting ready at six forty-five. Reggie arrived fifteen minutes later. He rang the front doorbell. Emmy gave the room a once over glance, and then let him in. He handed her a bouquet of flowers. "I hope you don't mind me bringing you some flowers, Emmy."

"That's very sweet of you, Reggie. I don't mind at all. Why

366

don't you come into the kitchen with me, and I'll find a vase for them." *You look good in those jeans, and I'm sure glad you didn't wear a tie.*

Emmy wore a different pair of jeans tonight. Reggie noticed as she bent over to retrieve a vase from the bottom cabinet and couldn't help but think. *Wow! You look fantastic in those tight jeans.*

Emmy found a vase, filled it with water, added the flowers and set it on the table.

"I'm ready to go if you are."

"Is there any place special you wanted to go, or should I choose?" He noticed the clean, uncluttered countertop and thought he could smell something lemony.

"What do you have in mind?" she asked.

"Do you like pizza? We could go to this place I like. Kerry Lynn's. It's over on... I know where it is, but I can't remember the name of the street."

"I know it. That's one of my favorite pizza joints."

"Is that all right?" *Ah, you use a lemon-scented cleaner.*

"Sure. You do remember our agreement? I want to pay my share."

"You don't have to do that, but if that's the only way you will go, then I'll go along."

"Let's say for tonight it will be the arrangement." Emmy realized that she might like Reggie a little more than she thought at first. He didn't try to charm her the way Richard did. He seemed to be just as he appeared—a friend with no hidden agenda.

Emmy locked up the house, and they headed over to Kerry Lynn's. Along the way, Emmy told Reggie about Richard.

"He's a guy I know from work, and we've gone to dinner and two basketball games, but just as friends—at least on my part. I get the feeling that he wants more than friendship though, and I'm not interested in that at all."

Reggie understood.

The hostess seated them at a booth, and they looked over the menu. Reggie ordered a pitcher of Dr Pepper. Emmy was glad he didn't order beer.

"What do you like on your pizza, Emmy?"

"I like just about everything... except anchovies. Does anybody ever order anchovies on their pizza?"

"Oh, I always do. I never eat pizza without anchovies," Reggie said with a straight face.

"Okay, I guess I could try them."

"I'm kidding, Emmy." He laughed as he filled their glasses with pop. "I don't even think I've ever tasted anchovies."

They settled for a pizza with pepperoni, mushrooms and green peppers. As they waited for their pizza, they talked about their families and work—just making small talk. Emmy couldn't help but feel drawn to his smile and his sense of humor. He looked younger than Richard, but older than Tony or Kenny. Emmy didn't ask his age at first, but then Reggie volunteered the information.

"I was born at St. Bart's on July 6, 1972."

"You're kidding! I was born there two days later."

"Really? I thought you were much younger," Reggie teased her.

"Oh, I meant I was born on the eighth, but in 1980."

"That's more like what I thought, although I did think you might be even younger."

"I know. Everyone thinks I'm still in high school."

"It's not a bad thing to look so young, Emmy."

Emmy leaned over to smell the pizza when their waitress delivered it to the table. "This is going to be yummy."

"Would you mind if I pray first, Emmy?"

"Not at all. I do that, too. Most of the time. Sometimes I forget." She started to like Reggie Lennon even more because of his genuineness.

They managed to eat the whole pizza and finished the pitcher of pop. When they got the check, Emmy paid her share. Reggie didn't mind, but hoped she would let him pay if they went out again. Reggie pulled into her driveway and left the motor running.

"I had fun tonight, Emmy. Thank you for going with me."

"Me, too." She smiled and, after a few seconds, added, "It's still kinda early. Would you like to come in for a few minutes?"

"I'd love to, but I won't stay too long. You probably have things to do."

Emmy gave him a tour of the house. Something she hadn't done with Richard. She trusted Reggie. She even showed Reggie her messy bedroom. It didn't faze him.

"This is a nice place. Kinda big for one person though."

"My sister used to live with me."

After showing him the house, Emmy turned on some music. They sat on the couch in the living room.

"I asked Richard to come to church with me tomorrow, and he agreed. I hope that's all right with you."

"Of course, Emmy. I think it's great that he's coming to church. Are you meeting him there, or is he picking you up?"

"I wanted to meet him, but he's going to pick me up. That might work better since he probably would need directions."

"I would be untruthful if I said I'm happy he is coming with you. I guess I'd rather you let me bring you to church, but since we've just met..."

"Reggie, I think we can be good friends. With Richard it's different. I met him at work. I don't know enough about him to totally trust him, but I feel that I can count on you already." She bit her lip. *Oh, God! Did I just relegate him to friend status?*

"I'll take that as a compliment, Emmy." He managed a smile. *I've just been classified as a friend. Too bad. I really like her, and she's so sexy in an innocent sorta way.*

"Are you thirsty or hungry?" Emmy asked.

"Not really, but if you're thirsty, I'll have something to drink."

"I could make some tea. I have some herbal tea that doesn't have caffeine."

"Tea would be perfect."

They went into the kitchen, and Emmy started the tea. Reggie sat at the table and noticed the calendar above him again. He wondered why she circled a certain date. He didn't ask in case it might be too personal. Emmy filled two cups with tea and found a jar of honey in the cabinet.

"I like to put honey in my tea."

369

"I don't drink a lot of tea, but I'll try the honey."

She giggled.

Reggie caught on. "You could add a little tea to my honey."

"You're too funny," she said. *Your humor is genuine. I like that. Richard's laugh is insincere most of the time.*

After they finished the tea, Reggie stood up and set his empty cup in the sink. "I should be going, Emmy. We have church in the morning. I'll see you there. I can check out the competition."

"It's not a competition, Reggie."

"I know. I'm teasing you. I've enjoyed the last two nights. Who knows what will happen in the future? I hope to be your friend, and if God wants us to be more than that, then I'll willing to follow His plan." He grinned. "After all, He knows what is best for us."

"You're funny, Reggie. I like your sense of humor. I'll see you in the morning."

Chapter Forty

Emmy looked in her full-length bedroom mirror as she held up a dress. *I like the other one better. But I think I'll wear the skirt.*

She felt better in the skirt even though it was shorter than the dresses. She put on a pair of black leggings since the day promised to be rather cool.

A few minutes later she heard the front doorbell. She looked in the mirror one last time, and then ran downstairs.

"Emmy, you look fantastic, but I couldn't find a decent dress. I hope these slacks and jacket are all right," Richard teased as she let him in. Emmy smiled, but Richard reeked of insincerity.

"I'm ready to go. It won't take too long to get there."

Richard noticed that Emmy carried her Bible with her. He opened the car door for her, and they headed to the church.

"Turn left at the next corner, and it's right there where that blue car turned. We can park anywhere."

"I see the car." Richard parked and asked, "Is this space all right?"

"It's fine. We don't have assigned parking spaces, or anything, if you were wondering about that," she said facetiously.

Emmy took Richard to her Sunday School class and, true to his character, he tried to talk about himself.

Oh, please don't embarrass me, Emmy prayed.

Richard realized he needed to shut up.

After class, Richard shook hands with all the men, and then asked Emmy, "Where do we go now?"

"Follow me, and we'll find seats in the sanctuary."

Emmy saw Reggie and smiled at him. He smiled back, but Emmy didn't introduce Reggie to Richard.

"Are these seats all right?" Emmy asked.

"Sure. It doesn't matter to me."

"Okay, I have to run back to the music room. I'm part of the worship team now, and I have to sing this morning. I'll come and sit with you after our part is finished."

"I'll be all right by myself," he said as he looked around and noticed some attractive women. "I'm looking forward to hearing you sing."

Emmy joined him after the worship band finished.

"You're really talented. The whole band sounded great," he said.

They listened to Dr. Ausland's message, and Emmy introduced Richard to Lynette afterward.

"Lynette, this is Richard Demarco. Richard, this is Lynette Jefferson. Her husband Paul is one of the pastors on staff here."

Lynette smiled at him and extended her hand. He shook it.

"Let me introduce you to Dr. Ausland. He is the senior pastor, and he's such a sweet humble man. He's such a good speaker, too, as you found out today. Everybody here loves him."

After waiting while he talked to another visitor, Emmy introduced Richard to Dr. Ausland.

"It's very nice to meet you, Richard. Thank you for joining us today. I see you are a friend of Emmy's. She has been a pleasant addition to our congregation and a blessing to all of us. If there is anything I can do for you please feel free to contact me."

"Thank you, sir. I will." Richard shook hands with Dr. Ausland. *You remind me of my grandfather. He's a preacher, too.*

Emmy and Richard were ready to leave when Lynette approached. "Emmy, would you and Richard like to join us for dinner? We are having a few people over for a cookout since it's such a nice sunny day."

Emmy looked at Richard.

He forced a smile. "Whatever you want to do is all right by me."

"We would love to come over. Do you want us to bring anything?" Emmy asked.

"No, only your appetites. We have plenty to share."

Emmy directed Richard to the Jefferson home. When they got inside, she saw Reggie Lennon talking to Maria Juneau; one of the single ladies from church.

Later, Reggie helped Paul with the grill while Lynette and the other women prepared the rest of the food. The rest of the men stood in the garage to keep warm. Paul noticed Richard standing alone. He walked over and asked, "So, Richard, how long have you known Emmy?"

"Not very long at all. We work in the same building. I've been working in Kansas until recently, and we reconnected a short time ago. We saw each other a few times before I left for Kansas, but we didn't really know each other then."

"Emmy is a part of our Bible study. Maybe you can join us sometime. We are currently studying Philippians."

"Yeah, sure," Richard answered.

Emmy came out carrying a platter. "Lynette asked me to bring this to you, Paul. Are the burgers about ready?"

"Soon, Emmy, soon."

"I'm hungry enough to eat all those burgers. Aren't you making any for everyone else?" Emmy smiled and headed back in the house. Paul and Richard watched her as she skipped along merrily.

"Emmy is such a precious child," Paul told Richard as he flipped a couple of burgers.

"I don't think of her as a child," Richard said rather casually.

"I was referring to her as a child of God. She is a new believer and is like a child in the church. She is learning and growing much as a child does."

Paul watched as Richard looked at Emmy through different eyes. He saw a desire in Richard's eyes and hoped Emmy realized Richard's intentions toward her.

"Burgers are ready. Let's eat," Paul announced as he and the men joined the rest of the hungry people inside. Paul offered thanks for the dinner, and they dug in.

"Emmy, how can someone so tiny eat so much?" Paul teased her later.

"I only ate two burgers, Paul."

"Have another one. There are three left."

"Oh, I can't. I'm so stuffed I'm going to pop."

"How about you, Richard? Room for one more?"

"No thanks, Paul. Two burgers filled me up, but thanks."

Emmy helped Lynette carry the leftovers into the kitchen. "I would love to be able to make potato salad as good as yours."

"Oh, Emmy, it wasn't any better than what anyone else makes."

"I liked it better. I've tried to make potato salad, and mine never turns out as good."

"I'll email you my recipe if you want it, Emmy."

Emmy and Richard thanked Paul and Lynette and headed back to Emmy's house.

"Would you like to see my apartment, Emmy? It's not too far from here."

Emmy wondered if she should. *Is this where you try to seduce me? It ain't gonna happen, buster.* She looked at Richard, and he smiled in his charming way. She decided it will be all right. "Okay, I want to see if you are a typical messy bachelor."

Richard took her to his apartment and opened the door for her. "This is the living room."

She looked around. "I'm impressed. It's clean. Small, but clean."

"The kitchen is over here. It's small, too." He walked into the galley kitchen.

I could never get used to this tiny kitchen, she thought as she ran a hand along the countertop.

"Would you like to see the rest of it?" He pointed to a closed door.

"No, I've seen enough," Emmy said as she grinned and walked back into the living room. *I'm not interested in seeing the bathroom or the bedroom.*

"What do you want to do with the rest of the day, Emmy?"

"Actually, Richard, I need to get home. I've got laundry to do, and I need to finish cleaning up the house. Plus, I need to go see my folks later. My dad hasn't been feeling well so I want to go see him."

"I could help you if you want, Emmy. I know how to clean, and I've been doing my own laundry for many years. I would like to meet your parents, too."

Emmy thought about it. *No way am I gonna ever let you meet my parents, and I'm certainly not going to let you help with my laundry.* "That's very nice of you to offer, Richard, but I don't

374

think so."

"No problem, Emmy. I'll run you home."

On Wednesday night, Emmy sat next to Reggie Lennon at church. They talked, but Reggie didn't ask for another date. Emmy wondered why and asked Lynette if she knew anything.

"Em, I think he might have asked Maria Juneau to dinner. I hope you don't mind. She's closer to his age," Lynette said.

"It's okay. I saw them talking to each other Sunday, and they seemed to be having fun together."

"What about the man you were with on Sunday?"

Emmy waved her hand. "No way! I know him from work, but I'm not interested in a real relationship with him."

"I don't really know him, but.. well... he didn't make a good first impression. Not like Reggie."

"Reggie and I can still be friends. I like him as a person, and I'm sure we'll see each other at social events. He's funny and really sweet. He brought me flowers the night we went out for pizza." Emmy smiled, but felt a little disappointed. She actually wanted to end her friendship with Richard and only "date" Reggie.

Emmy saw Richard in the cafeteria at lunch on Thursday. She tried to get away before he saw her, but didn't quite manage it.

"Hey, Emmy. I've got a table over there. Wanna join me?"

She bought her lunch, and then followed him to the table.

"Would you like to have dinner on Friday? I found this great place that serves authentic Indian food."

Emmy had a different plan in mind. "I'm sorry, but I really can't."

"Oh, is your boyfriend back in town?"

"Not yet, but he will be soon."

"What kind of plans do you have?" Richard dumped three packets of sugar into his iced tea and noisily stirred it with a spoon as he looked around the cafeteria.

Emmy took a bite of her fresh fruit chunks and chewed it slowly. "I really want to see this band. The Notable Exceptions are playing at a local club. I guess I'll go alone since Kristen can't go."

She thought about asking Reggie to go, but if he liked Maria, she didn't want to intrude.

"Maybe we could grab an early dinner, and then go see the band."

"I'm not interested in Indian food. It's too spicy for me."

"We could eat somewhere else. I'll let you choose."

Emmy waved to a lady from the office suite next to hers, hoping she might join them, but she joined some other friends.

"I'm not going out to eat. I'm going to see the band. They're friends of mine. If you want to join me for that, we can grab a bite to eat at the club. The place will be noisy and crowded. It will be a younger crowd." She hoped that might discourage him.

But it didn't. Richard agreed to go with her, but only after failing to change her mind. He underestimated her stubbornness.

Richard picked Emmy up at eight thirty on Friday. They arrived at the club as the band started their first set. They found a table and ordered drinks. Emmy ordered a Coke—Richard needed a beer. Emmy waved to Paul Joseph and the guys in the band.

"Richard, do you want to dance?" Emmy asked.

"I'm not really into dancing, Emmy. I hope you don't mind if I just listen to the band." He looked at the people in the club and thought. *I've got to the the oldest person in here. These people all look like they're in college.*

"That's all right." Emmy shrugged and bobbed her head in time with the music.

"Emmy! Emmy!"

She looked around. *That sounds like Barry.* She saw him walking toward her. "Barry, what are you doing here?"

"Linda and I are here to hear the band, of course. How are you? We haven't seen you for so long."

"Good, you? I haven't seen you since I hit you with a dart at my birthday party."

"Married life is great. Wanna join us? We've got a table over there against the wall." Barry pointed to where Linda sat, looking at the menu. Emmy waved to Linda.

"Richard, would you mind if we join Barry and Linda?" *Of*

course if you do mind, I'm going over there anyway.

"Not at all," Richard managed to say politely, even though he really didn't want to meet her friends. They joined Linda and exchanged small talk.

"Emmy, do you wanna dance?" Barry asked. "Linda's feet are sore, and she won't dance with me. Come on."

"Do you mind if I dance with Barry?" Emmy asked Richard.

"Go ahead. What do you want to eat? I'll order while you're dancing with Larry."

"How about an order of nachos for now, and his name is Barry, not Larry."

"Sorry, Barry."

Linda frowned at Barry. *Hey! Wait a minute. I'm not sitting here with this old guy. Who in the world is he?* She excused herself to use the restroom.

Barry and Emmy began dancing, and he asked, "Emmy, who is that old guy you're with? Did you and Kenny break up? Or are you dating Tony? I can't keep track of who you're with. What's going on? I even heard that you and Randy Braun were dating."

"Kenny's out in LA." Emmy nodded toward Richard. "His name is Richard, and he works for Robertson Industries—just like me. We actually work in the same building. Do you really think he looks old?"

"Yeah, he looks like forty or something. With that gray hair he looks old enough to be your father, and he's so skinny. Is he a drug addict?"

"You're the third person to mention that, and we're just here as friends."

"Did you break up with Randy?"

"Randy and I are friends. We hung out together, but we weren't really dating." She grinned. "But we kissed."

"You and Randy?" Barry looked surprised.

"Yes, but we both thought it was like kissing a brother or sister."

"I can understand that," Barry said. "If I ever kissed you it would be like kissing my sister."

377

"You're an only child, doofus."

"You know what I mean, Em."

While Emmy and Barry danced, Richard ordered the nachos.

"Could I get another Heineken and another round of whatever the kids are drinking?" He waved a hand over the glasses on the table and smiled at the waitress. As she walked away, Richard leered at her.

Richard watched Emmy dancing and enjoying herself with Barry. He especially admired her trim body and her tight-fitting jeans. He hoped that later tonight she might be more open to his advances. Emmy and Barry returned to the table as Linda and the drinks arrived.

Barry took a swallow of his beer, and then looked at Richard. "Thanks for the drinks."

"My treat," Richard said with a smile that instantly set off Barry's BS detector.

The nachos arrived, and everybody ordered more food. Richard ordered another beer even before he finished his second one. They listened to the band and made small talk when they could without shouting over the sound of the band.

After the second set Richard asked Emmy, "Do you want to get out of here, Emmy? We could go back to your place and watch a movie."

She agreed after listening to a couple minutes of his persuasion.

"We need to see each other more often, you guys." Emmy hugged Linda.

Barry held her close and whispered, "Be careful, Em. I don't trust this guy."

"He's a harmless flirt," Emmy said. "You didn't trust Scott Simmons, either."

Richard drank four beers, but Emmy didn't know and couldn't tell. He drove back to her place without any trouble.

"I'm in the mood for a movie. How about you?" Richard asked. He walked into the TV room before Emmy could answer.

Emmy followed him and pointed. "Those are the movies I

have in the house. Do you want some coffee? Just take a minute."

"Coffee would be fine." He grabbed a DVD without even checking the title.

Emmy started the coffee. *Shannon! Shannon! Shannon!* She kicked at the garbage can next to the fridge. *When am I ever gonna learn?*

She returned to the TV room but sat at the opposite end of the couch from him as the movie started.

"Do you ever drink alcohol, Emmy? I noticed you haven't when we go out."

"I grew up drinking wine for dinner sometimes, and I used to drink beer at parties occasionally, but I don't anymore. I don't miss it, and I don't think about it. I don't think it's wrong to have a glass of wine or a beer sometimes, but I think it is wrong to drink to excess. I noticed you drank a few beers tonight and at the ballgame the other day. Is that normal for you?"

"I like to have a few beers sometimes when I go out, but I might go a month without any sometimes. Tonight I felt like having some."

Richard hadn't gone for more than a day without beer in several years.

"I think the coffee's ready. Black, right?"

"Right, thanks, Emmy."

She fixed the coffee and sat on the couch. *I wish I could fast forward through this.*

They watched the movie for awhile and finished the coffee.

"I'll take these back to the kitchen," he offered politely.

"Thanks, Richard." *I wonder if I have enough time to skip forward in the DVD?*

He took the coffee cups and set them in the sink. When he returned, he sat close to her. "I want to kiss you, Emmy. Is it all right?"

"I'd rather not..."

But Richard kissed her anyway. The phone rang once, but didn't ring again. Emmy wondered who called, but didn't get up.

"Don't do that again, Richard. In fact, I think you should leave unless you promise to behave."

He behaved for five minutes, but then he kissed her again and grabbed her shoulders. "I want you, Emmy. I want to make love to you. I want to make love to you tonight."

Emmy pushed his hands away and stood up. She felt her heart racing, and she had trouble breathing. "No, Richard, I won't do that. I told you that before and you should go home." She pointed toward the door.

"Come on, Emmy, you know you want it. I watched you dancing with that kid, and I could tell you and Larry, or whatever his name is, were lovers by the way you were acting."

Richard attempted to kiss her again, but didn't grab her.

She backed up. "Stop it, Richard. If you come any closer, I will knee you in your balls, and I mean it!"

He backed up. "I'm not going to force you, Emmy, but I think you want me to kiss you again."

"You've had too much to drink if you think that. I am *not* going to make love to you now, or ever and, if this is the way you are going to behave, then I don't want to see you again."

Richard lunged forward and grabbed her around the waist. He tried to kiss her again. She could smell the beer on his hot breath. She turned her head. Just then, the phone rang.

"Stop it, Richard!"

"Oh, come on, Emmy. Don't be a tease."

She twisted out of his hold and kicked his shin. The answering machine took the call, and she heard Mama's voice.

"Shut up, Richard! I need to hear this."

"Come on, Emmy. We would be good together," he said as he rubbed his leg.

"Richard! Shut the hell up!" Emmy screamed.

He shut up.

Emmy stood transfixed to the spot as she heard Mama say, "Tony was in a car accident today, and he's in the hospital. Heather called, and told me I should come to South Bend as soon as I can. I thought I should call you, Emmy. Call me back as soon as you can. Bye, honey."

Emmy stood stunned. Richard took a step toward her.

She held out her hand. "Don't come any closer."

He held up his hands in surrender. "I'm sorry. I thought this was what you wanted."

"No, it's what you wanted. You need to leave RIGHT NOW! Don't bother calling me again, either."

"Oh, come on, Emmy. Don't be that way."

She took a step toward him—ready to smack him senseless, but held her temper in check. "Richard, I want you to leave, and I meant what I said about not calling me again."

"Okay, okay. Just don't hit me." He cowered and covered his face and groin with his hands. He turned and ran as Emmy practically shoved him out of the TV room. Emmy followed him to the back door, and, when he stopped to turn around, she shoved him out the door and locked it. She waited to make sure Richard left, and then she called Mama.

"Mama, what happened? Is Tony all right?"

Mama answered, "Heather called back a couple of minutes ago. She told me Tony's injuries are not life threatening. Thank God. I felt that you needed to know so you could pray for him, honey."

"Do you know how it happened?"

"All I know is that a truck skidded on some ice and hit him."

"Hit him? Was he walking?"

"No, the truck hit his car," Mama explained. "Heather said his car got totaled."

"Do you want me to take you to South Bend right away?"

"We can wait until morning. Heather said we could wait till then. Are you all right, Emmy? You're breathing so hard, and your voice sounds like you are shaking."

"I'm fine now, Mama. I'll see you in the morning, bright and early."

Emmy called Kristen and told her what happened to Tony.

"Emmy, shouldn't we leave right away? How bad was Tony hurt?"

"Mama told me we can wait until morning, so he must not be hurt too bad. I need to talk to you about something else, Kristen. I went out with Richard again tonight and..." Emmy explained what happened.

"I'm calling Detective O'Dell right now!" Kristen shouted.

"You can't! You're talking to me."

"Then I'm hanging up and coming right over. We can both call him."

"Bring your overnight bag, so we can leave early in the morning."

Kristen arrived twenty minutes later. She pulled into the driveway, slammed on the brakes and ran inside.

"Where are you, Em?" Kristen yelled.

"I'm in the living room."

Kristen darted through the dining room and ran smack into Emmy.

"We are always running into each other." Emmy grinned as she recalled how she and Kristen first met.

"It's not funny, Emmy! He could've raped you!"

"No, he couldn't have. I threatened to kick him in the nuts, and he turned into a wimp. I think he just had too much to drink."

"He is a bastard. I knew he would try to take advantage of you. Anyone who's been married and involved with another woman for three years is going to want to have sex. You are too trusting for your own good sometimes."

"He treated me so nice at first, Krissy."

Emmy broke down and sobbed as Kristen held her. "I'm so glad that everything is over between you two. You shouldn't have let it go on this long."

"I tried to break it off, but he was so insistent."

"I hope you've learned your lesson, Em."

Now Kristen wouldn't have to tell Emmy the disturbing information Detective Keith O'Dell discovered about him. He had once been arrested for assaulting his wife. Emmy tossed and turned in bed—still too upset to fall sleep. She eventually managed to sleep for three hours.

Chapter Forty-One

Emmy emailed Kenny in the morning. She informed him about Tony's accident and that she would be taking Mama and Kristen to South Bend, but she didn't mention Richard. She and Kristen picked up Mama and headed to South Bend as fast as they could. Emmy drove like a maniac, at least to Mama.

Mama put her hands on the dashboard. "Slow down, Emmy. We don't want to have an accident ourselves."

"Maybe you should let me drive, Em. You have a lead foot even when you're not upset."

Kristen took over driving, leaving Emmy free to sit and worry about Tony.

"Do you think he's going to be okay?" Emmy wrung her hands together.

"I'm sure he will be all right," Mama said. "Heather would have told me to come last night otherwise."

Heather met them at the hospital.

"Mama, he will be all right. He has a broken arm and lacerations, and the only reason we kept him here overnight was to make sure he didn't have a concussion. It's hard to tell with him since he has no brain activity under normal circumstances."

Everyone felt better since Heather joked about her brother's condition.

"Can I see him, Heather?" Mama asked.

"Of course you can. He is groggy from some pain meds, but I'm sure he will be happy to see all of you."

Mama walked quietly into his room. She looked at his face, and then his bandages and the cast on his arm. She didn't cry only because of great self control. She kissed his forehead gently, and he opened his eyes.

"I'm all right, Mama."

"I was so worried about you, but Heather promised me you were going to be all right," Mama said and then sat down.

Kristen and Emmy entered the room a minute later. Emmy sat on the edge of the bed and kissed his cheek. Kristen sat on the other side of the bed and held his hand as she looked at the cast on his left arm.

He smiled at Emmy and said softly, "I was dreaming about you, Em."

"Was it a good dream?" she asked.

"A very good dream."

Kristen teased him. "You don't look too bad. What does the truck that hit you look like?"

"I heard it didn't have a scratch on it, but my car is totaled."

"Oh, Tony, does it hurt much?" Emmy asked.

"It hurts right here," he pointed to his cheek. "And right here," he pointed to the other cheek. "And it really hurts right here."

Emmy tenderly kissed his bruises. He put his finger on his mouth.

"Emmy, you shouldn't kiss him there because that will hurt too much," Kristen said.

"It's all right. I can take the pain, Emmy."

"Okay, but just one little kiss. I don't want to hurt you."

Emmy kissed him once on the mouth very tenderly. "That's all I'm gonna kiss you."

Mama smiled as she watched them kiss.

"What were you doing? Where were you going?" Emmy asked.

"We're on break this coming week, and I decided I would come home because I wanted to see you."

"You were coming home to see me?" Emmy asked.

"I needed to do some shopping first, but then I was going home."

Kristen sat on the side of the bed, still holding his hand. She looked at the cast and noticed some people had already signed it. Kristen retrieved a pen from her purse, signed the cast and then giggled. "I wrote something naughty. I wrote..."

At that moment Tony's best friend and roommate, John Randolph, walked into the room and Kristen never finished her explanation. When Tony didn't introduce him, John took the initiative.

"Hi, I'm John Randolph, Tony's roommate."

384

"I'm Kristen, and this is Emmy."

"I've seen pictures of you both, but I don't think we've ever met."

Emmy stood up. "We'll let you talk to Tony."

She and Kristen moved close to the door. John stood by the bed. Kristen noticed him stealing glances at her as he talked to Tony and whispered to Emmy, "Have you ever met his roommate before? He certainly is a hunk."

"I've never really met him, but I've seen pictures of him. We saw him play football. I remember that Tony tried to set me up with him."

"I'm glad you didn't take him up on the offer."

Emmy looked at Kristen, and then at John. *Maybe it's my turn to play matchmaker.*

John smiled at both girls, but then his eyes lingered on Kristen again.

Heather walked into the room holding a medical chart. "Tony will be released later this afternoon, and you can take him to my apartment. But don't pamper him or he will become insufferable, and I will have to put him to sleep. I'm allowed to do that in the state of Indiana," Heather said without cracking a smile.

The doctor released Tony two hours later, and Emmy, Kristen and Mama took him to Heather and Alex's place. Heather arrived home later and Mama made dinner for everybody—except for Alex. He was still on duty at the hospital. Tony still had an appetite so Mama knew he would be all right. Emmy and Kristen treated him like an invalid and almost hand-fed him.

Heather rolled her eyes. "Will you two knock it off? Stop treating him like a baby. He's not crippled or anything."

Tony grinned at Heather. "They can treat me any way they like as long as I get to be pampered."

"Enjoy it while they're here, little brother. You will have to deal with me later." Heather shook a finger at him.

Tony needed to get back to his dorm after dinner, so Emmy and Kristen drove him. John sat on a love seat watching TV in the downstairs lounge. Kristen saw him.

"Go talk to him, Krissy. You know you want to." Emmy

pushed her toward John.

"Stop it, Em." Kristen pushed her hands away. "I'll talk to him in a minute."

"Go! Talk! Now!" Emmy insisted and pushed Kristen toward John.

John heard the commotion and turned to look. He smiled as he saw Kristen and stood up.

Kristen started talking to John. "So you play football, too."

"Yes, but I play on offense. He's not smart enough, so he plays defense."

Kristen laughed and said, "Believe me, I know it."

"He's mentioned that you guys are pretty close. I'm not supposed to tell you, but you're his favorite cousin."

"Don't say anything to him, but I feel the same way."

Emmy made Tony sit down in a large chair. She stood next to him as they talked. A few minutes later, some friends stopped by. Emmy thought they must be football players because of their size. Some females came along, also. One of them started to approach Tony until John stopped her. Emmy wondered if this might be Brenda. Emmy looked at Tony. He looked at the girl. The girl smiled at Tony. He shook his head almost imperceptibly. Emmy thwacked the back of his head.

"Ow! What was that for, Em."

"Just making sure you still have a brain in that thick skull of yours."

After visiting with his friends for a time, Tony headed upstairs.

Emmy followed Tony for a step, but then turned to Kristen. "Are you coming upstairs with us?"

"Not yet. I think I'll talk to John for a few minutes."

Emmy grinned, and took off after Tony as he waited by the elevator.

"I have to get ready for bed, Em," Tony said as he let her into the room.

"Do you need any help?" she offered thinking about the cast on his arm.

"Geez, Emmy, I can get ready for bed by myself. I don't

need your help."

"I was just trying to show some concern." Emmy looked at the poster of Dick Butkus and a photo of Walter Payton.

"I appreciate the thought, but I can manage." Tony stood by his bed and glared at Emmy.

"What?"

"Are you gonna watch while I get undressed?"

"Oh, for crying out loud. I know you're gonna sleep in your boxers and t-shirt. I've seen them before."

"I'm not Kenny..."

"Fine, I'll turn around. You're a dork, anyway."

"Why did you say that?"

She turned around as he dropped his jeans, "I'm not stupid. I know that tall girl with the dark eyes and brown hair was Brenda. She came to see you. If I wasn't here, would she be in the room with you?"

"No. She hasn't been up here for..."

"I don't want to know." Emmy pushed him in the chest as tears started to flow down her cheek."

"I'm sorry, Em." He reached out to hold her. He held her in his arms for a moment until she stopped crying. Just then the door opened, and John and Kristen entered the room.

"Oh, did we interrupt something?" Kristen asked and then giggled.

"No, why?" Tony asked.

"Well, it's just that you are holding Emmy and your pants are on the floor."

Emmy suddenly realized how it must have looked. She backed away. "We weren't doing anything. I started crying, and he hugged me. I wasn't going to do anything."

Tony reached down and pulled up his jeans.

"Yeah, if you say so, Em." Kristen grinned.

Emmy stuck out her tongue at Kristen. John laughed because Emmy seemed to be exactly as Tony described her over the years.

"We need to get back, Em. You guys can finish tomorrow," Kristen teased.

387

Emmy mouthed a couple of naughty words to her. Kristen and John laughed.

"Good night, Tony," Emmy said. "I hope you sleep all right. We'll see you in the morning."

Emmy kissed him good night on the cheek, and then she and Kristen left. As they walked out to the car, Emmy nudged Kristen. "Thanks a lot for making it look like I was going to fool around with Tony. John must think I'm a slut."

"He does not. He told me he thinks you are adorable. In a little sister kind of way."

"I hate you with all my heart!" Emmy turned away from Kristen.

Kristen put her arm around Emmy as they approached the car. "I know you love me, and I love you, too."

As she drove back to Heather's, Emmy wouldn't look at Kristen. "I know that girl was Brenda. She came over to see Tony."

"Is that why you were crying?"

"Yes, but I'm over it now."

"You did look funny hugging Tony."

"I don't want to talk about that." Emmy bit her lip.

They drove along in silence. Kristen turned toward Emmy, but then turned back toward the window. Emmy glanced at Kristen. Kristen turned her head away. A few seconds later, Kristen looked at Emmy again. Then Emmy looked at Kristen.

"I know you have something on your mind. Spill it!" Emmy ordered.

"It's nothing, really."

"Kristen," Emmy said slowly. "I know better than that."

"Okay, John is so good looking, and he's funny. I wish we could stay longer to get to know him better."

"Maybe you will have a chance to see him tomorrow."

"I hope so. Don't you think he is handsome?"

"Yeah, I guess so, but he's so tall. He's at least a couple inches taller than Tony."

"Yes, isn't he." Kristen sighed as she wrapped her hair around a finger.

Emmy and Kristen decided to get a hotel room for the

night. They checked in, got ready for bed, and Kristen kept talking about John till they fell asleep.

They came back to Dillon Hall to see Tony early on Sunday morning.

Emmy knocked on the door. "Are you up and dressed?"

Tony opened the door and let them in. He scratched his stomach and then grabbed his jeans. He hopped around as he tried to put them on with one hand.

Emmy giggled, and Kristen rolled her eyes. "Do you need help?" Kristen asked.

"I can do it. I'm not helpless." He tripped, tumbled onto his bed and finally managed to pull his jeans up.

Kristen shook her head. "You're such a dork. Where's John?"

"He went out for breakfast."

Emmy sat down on the edge of Tony's bed and looked around the room. She wanted to see if Tony had a photo of Brenda anywhere.

Kristen stood in front of John's desk. "Does he have a girlfriend? He's not married or gay, is he?" She picked up a photo of John with two other guys. They looked like brothers.

"No, he's not married and certainly not gay. I'm not supposed to say anything, but he asked me a bunch of questions about you."

"What did he say? Please, tell me." She put the photo back, and turned to face Tony.

"He said you were too fat and really ugly."

Kristen smacked Tony on his good arm. "Do you want me to break your right arm? I'll do it if I have to."

Tony relented. "All right. John is attracted to you. Only God knows why, but he is. He asked a lot of questions about you. I tried to think of something nice to say, but all I could think of to tell him is that you are not totally rotten, just partly."

Tony smiled as Kristen kissed him on the cheek. She knew Tony told John nothing but good things about her.

They took Tony over to Heather and Alex's, and Mama
389

fixed breakfast for everybody. Emmy treated him like a baby again.

Heather rolled her eyes and said, "Will you please stop it before I puke?"

Tony whimpered, "But I'm helpless, Heather, and I need to have round the clock nursing."

Heather shook her fist at Tony. "I'll give you round the clock nursing."

Mama looked at the clock on the wall. "We need to be ready to leave at five, promptly at five."

Kristen smiled. *That will give me enough time to see John again.* "Tony, will you call and see if John is busy for lunch, and don't you dare tell him I wanted you to ask him."

Emmy asked, "Tony, would you like to go to church with me this morning? I saw one down the street. I would appreciate it if you would go with me."

"Yes, Emmy, I will go."

"You will?" Emmy's eyes opened wide.

"I'll go, too," Kristen said.

Emmy smiled, turned around and looked up. "Yes! Thank you, Lord."

Tony, Emmy and Kristen met John after church for lunch. Kristen and John hit it off right away, and he asked for her number. He would have been back in Ohio if not for Tony's accident, or if it happened an hour later.

Emmy whispered to Tony, "Something good may come out of this accident after all. I think maybe Kristen has found a new boyfriend."

"Oh, that's too bad. I think John really likes her," Tony teased.

She poked Tony in the side. "You are gonna get it as soon as you are well." Then Emmy remembered what she was doing when she got the call from Mama. Her eyes started to tear up, and she shivered involuntarily.

"Em, are you all right? I wasn't hurt that bad. I'll be okay."

"I'm okay, but don't you ever get hurt like this again."

"I won't, Emmy. I promise. I think maybe we've reached a

390

turning point in our relationship."

"It's too bad you had to break your arm for us to realize it."

"I can live with a broken arm, but I don't think I can live without you, Em," Tony confessed as he looked into her deep blue eyes.

Emmy looked at Tony with surprise. She certainly didn't expect to hear that.

www.ingramcontent.com/pod-product-compliance
Lightning Source LLC
Chambersburg PA
CBHW050903250626
47155CB00001B/78